365

W/D

Quechee Library
P.O. Box 384
Quechee, VT 05059

P9-CLD-009

THE SUMMER GUEST

Also by Justin Cronin

MARY AND O'NEIL

Justin Cronin

THE SUMMER GUEST

THE DIAL PRESS

THE SUMMER GUEST
A Dial Press Book / July 2004

Published by The Dial Press
A Division of Random House, Inc.
New York, New York

This is a work of fiction. Names, characters, places,
and incidents either are the product of the author's imagination
or are used fictitiously. Any resemblance to actual persons,
living or dead, events, or locales is entirely coincidental.

All rights reserved
Copyright © 2004 by Justin Cronin

Book design by Francesca Belanger

No part of this book may be reproduced or
transmitted in any form or by any means, electronic or mechanical,
including photocopying, recording, or by any information
storage and retrieval system, without the written permission
of the publisher, except where permitted by law.

The Dial Press is a registered trademark of Random House, Inc.,
and the colophon is a trademark of Random House, Inc.

Library of Congress Cataloging-in-Publication Data is on file with the publisher.

ISBN 0-385-33581-4

Manufactured in the United States of America
Published simultaneously in Canada

BVG 10 9 8 7 6 5 4 3 2 1

for Leslie
and
for Iris

I'll look for you in old Honolulu,
San Francisco, Ashtabula,
Yer gonna have to leave me now, I know.
But I'll see you in the sky above,
In the tall grass, in the ones I love,
Yer gonna make me lonesome when you go.

—Bob Dylan, "You're Gonna Make Me
Lonesome When You Go"

THE SUMMER
GUEST

Prologue

North of Boston they followed the sea. A day in January, 1947: the carriage of their train was nearly empty. Just the three of them, the man and his wife with the little boy on her lap, and far ahead, a lone man in uniform, his head lolled forward in sleep. From the window they watched the rough-hewn coast slide by: the great slabs of ice, heaved and broken against the shoreline; the frozen, time-stilled marshlands; the rocky promontories fingering a winter sea. At intervals the conductor passed through, idly humming as he announced the names of the towns, his heavy steps sure despite the old rail-bed that made the car sway like a ferry's deck.

While Amy and the baby dozed, Joe rose to stretch his legs. Thirty-one years old: he had been a lawyer, and then a soldier, but now was neither one. He made his way forward through the train, three cars to the engine and back, then paused at the doorway to look down the carriage. The uniformed man sat with his chin propped on one hand, a thatch of brown hair hanging loosely over his forehead as he slept. He was just a kid, Joe saw, eighteen and a day; probably he had enlisted just as the war was ending and had never seen an hour of combat. His other arm was thrown about his duffel bag, which rested on the seat beside him. Had he ever looked like that, Joe wondered, so completely at ease, untouched by life? But then the sleeping soldier turned, extending one leg into the aisle, and Joe realized, with a jolt, that he was mistaken. Between the rows of seats, the boy's left foot rested at a strange and careless angle: a prosthesis. The long hair: he should have known. Joe had grown such hair himself, in the hospital.

He returned to his seat. Amy was still sleeping, her head resting on a folded coat against the window, but the little boy's eyes were open and looking about. Joe lifted him from his wife's lap and placed him on his own. The tang of urine and the thickness of the baby's diaper told him he would soon need changing; before long he would begin to issue the first complaints, the barks and squeaks that burst forth randomly like the notes of an orchestra tuning up, a warning that would quickly gather into a wall of sound that seemed to Joe to communicate nothing less than a permanent cosmic sorrow. In any event, his wife would have to awaken soon. He jostled the little boy on his knee, singing a quiet tune under his breath, notes strung arbitrarily together from a dozen different songs. "You'll like Maine," he whispered into the boy's small, sweet-smelling ear. "There's a forest to play in, and a lake where we can swim and fish. I'll teach you, when you're old enough, all right?"

The train swayed and clacked; Joe watched the landscape as they passed. Miles of open coastline, and then the small towns pressed close to the water, quick glimpses of life as the train skimmed the fences that guarded the houses and yards. They passed through a railroad crossing, gates down and lights flashing; by the roadside, despite the cold, a group of children were waving from the seats of their bicycles. The world from the train window opened and closed like this, like the pages of a book. A simple pleasure, Joe thought, reserved for the living: to sit with his son on his lap, beside his sleeping wife, on a train taking them away, into a new life they could only guess at.

When the baby began to fuss, Amy awoke to change him, and when she was finished they opened up their picnic basket: sandwiches and hard-boiled eggs, a thermos of coffee, cookies from the Italian bakery where they had shopped for years.

"How long did I sleep?" She yawned into her palm. "I didn't know I was so tired."

They had been packing for days, finalizing their arrangements, saying their good-byes. Of course she would be exhausted.

"At least an hour." Joe shelled an egg into a napkin on his knee. "Sleep more if you want. You need your rest. It'll be a long ride yet."

They finished their lunch, and as they were packing it away, the conductor came through the car.

"Portland, Portland is next." The accent of a true Mainer: not "Portland" but "Paht-land." As a boy vacationing with his parents in Bar Harbor, Joe had wondered how anybody in their right mind could talk that way—though his own accent, he knew, was different only by degree. The conductor paused at their seats, his eyes scanning the little pocket for their ticket stubs. "Portland for you folks?"

"Augusta." Joe had taken the stubs with him, when he had gone to look through the other cars. As he handed them to the conductor, he tilted his face, as he had learned to do, so that his good eye lined up with the glass one. The need to do this had troubled him at first, but it had soon become second nature; there was no other way to meet and keep a man's gaze.

"We change there," he explained.

"Augusta's a good ways yet." The conductor considered the tickets without interest and returned them to their holders on the headrests. On Amy's lap the baby gurgled contentedly, and the conductor reached down to tousle his hair with a large hand chapped red by the cold. "He's a quiet one, now. Like the train, do you, little fella?"

"How much longer to Augusta?" Amy asked.

The conductor looked at his watch, a gold disk on a chain that he kept flat against his belly in his vest pocket. "Ninety-three minutes. Could be longer with the snow. Nevah know this time of year."

"The snow?"

He clapped his watch closed. "Coming down north of he-ah, what they're saying."

Past Portland, the first flakes appeared, white streaks that skated by the train window like shooting stars. The houses, the trees, all faded under a fresh coating of white. The train veered inland; to the north and west, mountains rose out of the dense, whirling air. Joe felt the first stirrings of worry; he hadn't planned on snow. Stupid, but he had never once thought it. If they missed their connection, they would have to spend the night somewhere. Or, they might arrive too late in Waterville to drive the final fifty miles.

By the time they reached Augusta, it was after two. Joe waited on the cold train platform for their luggage while Amy took the baby inside. They had brought just a few bags with them; the rest would follow later, by truck: furniture and kitchenware, trunks of clothing and books and linens, even Amy's piano. The day's light seemed to drain away into the falling snow; already three inches had fallen. Joe gave the porter fifty cents to cart their bags into the station, where he found Amy seated on a long bench with the baby on her lap. Heat blazed from a roaring woodstove; the floor was slick with melted snow. Joe went to the ticket window to ask about the weather.

"All trains still running." Behind the counter, the clerk, an older woman in a denim workshirt, was absently stamping paper. A lit cigarette hung from the corner of her mouth; the bright red of her lipstick seemed like the only spot of color in the entire state of Maine.

"Is the train to Waterville on time, please?"

"Everything's late, with the snow." The woman lifted her eyes to look at him. Her stamper paused midair.

"Good God."

It was a relief, he thought, when people were so surprised they could only be honest. And yet he had never learned quite what to say, beyond the simple facts. "I was shot in the war," he explained.

Her gaze was even, unchanged, as was her voice when she spoke the sentence he had somehow known would come.

"My boy was killed."

"Where?"

She gave a small nod, her eyes locked on his face. "Salerno."

"I was near there. In Sicily, with the 142nd." He touched his cheek. "This happened later, though, after Rome."

"Wait here a minute." The woman rose from her stool and disappeared through a door behind the counter. He heard the crank of an old-style telephone, followed by her voice speaking to someone down the line; then she returned.

"Stationmaster in Bosun says thirty minutes."

If the weather held, they would be all right. "Thank you."

She looked past him into the waiting room. "Does your family need anything? While you wait?"

He had grown wary of strangers' generosity, which too often felt like pity. But in this case he saw no reason to turn it away. "A quiet room would be nice," he ventured. "The baby's probably wet again."

She waved him inside. "Come back then, all of you."

She led them into the office—a plain, high-ceilinged room with a huge partner desk and, beneath the snow-frosted windows, a sagging couch with lion claw legs. On the wall was a large chalkboard listing arrivals and departures by their destination or city of origin: the smaller towns up north, and Boston and New York, but also Chicago and even Los Angeles. From this tiny station a person might go anywhere, Joe realized, board a train and vanish down the long corridors of the continent. Amy changed the baby on the sofa, then warmed a bottle for him on the hot plate while Joe rinsed out the dirty diaper in the washroom sink. By the time he returned to the office, the diaper wrapped in newspaper, the woman had made tea. In the wintery light of the room's tall windows her face had taken on a pale glow. She had large, damp eyes and hair the color of dry wood, blond gone not quite gray. She handed him a cup, gingerly, so as not to spill any of it into the saucer. While Joe sipped his tea, from the top drawer of her desk she removed a small framed photo and gave this to him also.

"This is my boy," she said. "Earl junior."

Joe put down his cup and accepted the photo. A young man in an undershirt and jeans, his chest and stomach washboard-thin, with fading stains of acne on his prominent cheekbones: he stood astride a bicycle and was leaning slightly forward, his arms surprisingly muscular where they were draped over the handlebars, his eyes and face squinting in a cockeyed half-smile for the camera. Joe could see something of the boy's mother in his face, the angles of the bones and the slightly too-long distance between his nose and upper lip. His hair, too, was a Nordic blond—the color hers had been, Joe guessed. It was not, on the whole, a degree of likeness that one would notice right off—it was more suggestion than resemblance— though probably people had always said how much he looked like her.

"We called him Skip, so's not to confuse everyone. He never did like that." She shook her head distantly; talking about her son, part of her went someplace else entirely. "I took this in forty-two, the summer before he went into the service."

Joe held the photograph another moment before passing it to Amy, who nodded without expression and returned it to the woman.

"What unit did you say he was with?" Joe asked.

The woman raised her head. Her voice was proud. "Eighty-second Airborne. The 509th."

So, Joe thought, the boy on the bicycle had jumped out of planes. Fantastic, how the war had made such things possible; before those days, Joe himself had never even held, much less fired, a gun. He thought again of the woman's son—how strange it must have been for him, one minute to be diving off the rocks into an ice-cold quarry lake, trying to impress his friends or a girl who sat on a blanket nearby; the next to find himself in the belly of a C-47 with a hundred pounds of gear strapped to his frame, the cabin pitching and rocking in the dense, violent air, ready to hurl himself out the door into a sky lit up by antiaircraft fire, over a country he had read about in social studies but might have gone his whole life without seeing. And yet he had died there: at Salerno, the 509th had dropped behind German defensive positions, straight into a Panzer Division. Or at least that was what Joe remembered hearing. The ones that had made it to the ground had been cut off for days, some without so much as a weapon. There were always stories like this. In the confusion, Joe had found it best to simply believe all of them.

"I knew some Eighty-second guys. Everybody said they were the toughest."

The woman returned the photo to its place in her desk. "Well." She cleared her throat. "I don't know about tough." She sat on the sofa next to Amy and the baby. The little boy's face was watchful and contented, as it always was after he'd been changed. "How old is your son?"

"Seven months," Amy replied.

Amy had undressed the baby to change him; his feet were bare. The woman bent her face toward him and took his feet and placed their soles against her lipsticked mouth. She pursed her lips and hummed a little tune; the baby laughed, his eyes darting around the room, searching for the source of these wonderful sensations.

"You like that?" the woman asked. She blew, hard, into the soles of his feet. The baby found her with his eyes and waved his arms and shrieked with pleasure. She seized his feet and blew again. "You like that? Is that funny? Is that funny?"

They hadn't even learned her name. And yet a feeling of closeness had settled over all of them, a kind of shared knowing. Joe thought he would be happy to stay with her forever in her warm office, drinking tea and watching his little boy laugh while outside the world was slowly erased by falling snow. The moment he recalled this, months later, he would realize how close he'd come to turning back.

"Such sweetness," the woman said. She kissed the baby once, and stood. "I remember those days. Whatever else happens, you know, they're a present you get to keep."

He remembered only small things from his last days of the war: the hard nugget of a stone in his boot as he walked; the taste of cold coffee and powdered eggs; a view of the sky from where he sat to smoke a cigarette under a lemon tree, and the way the smoke from his lungs gathered in a pocket of stillness before the breeze found it. They were pleasant memories; they could have come from another time, another life. His platoon, thirty-six men in his command, was in the Maremma, five klicks south of Magliano, advancing on a cluster of stone buildings hemmed by hills that were now, just a few minutes after dawn, veiled in a ribbony vapor of clouds. Along the left flank at two hundred meters stood an old church, mortared and half-collapsed around its modest steeple, which somehow still stood; and beyond it, curved at the top of a hill, a low stone wall, guarding a grove of gnarled olive trees. It was a Tuesday, a Tuesday in June. Odd, he had thought, how the days of the week had lost all meaning, and yet he knew it was a Tuesday. Rome had been theirs for a week; word was going around that they would be recalled to Anzio in a few days and shipped north to France, where the real war was still on.

He was finishing his cigarette when the platoon sergeant approached him. At thirty-five, Torrey was the oldest man in the unit, a figure of calm authority that Joe, though he was technically in charge, could never hope to match. The joke was that, before the war, Torrey had been a dancing instructor.

"Supporting fire's in position."

Joe tossed the stub of his cigarette on the ground and crushed it under his heel. "All right," he said wearily. "Tell them to hold fire. This is just a clearing op for now. The S2 says nobody's home."

Torrey frowned. "Fuck battalion. I don't like it. There's way too much cover on the left."

"I'll put it in the suggestion box." Joe rose and shouldered his weapon. "You take first squad down the right, I'll take second squad up the middle. Anselmo keeps the third squad in reserve and waits for my signal. And Mike?"

"Yeah?"

"Tell your point man to keep his eyes open. I don't like it either."

They moved in two lines of twelve men across the field, the low morning sun behind them. Below them the village lay dormant, no movement at all, not even the sound of a chicken to say that people lived there. Grasshoppers buzzed in the knee-high grass, leaping ahead of their boots as they advanced. The adrenaline of battle usually brought Joe into a vivid awareness of his surroundings, as if he were viewing events from several angles at once, but not this morning. The flicking grasshoppers, the swishing, dew-drenched grass, the silent town with its old stone buildings and terra-cotta roofs glowing in the morning sun: all combined to give the scene a feeling of dreamy unreality. He had been a soldier at war for 412 days, 342 of these as a platoon leader, not counting today, this Tuesday in June. It was not so strange he knew these numbers; everyone did. But as the days moved by, the meaning of the numbers changed: all they meant was, I'm not dead yet.

They had approached to within fifty meters of the church when it happened.

"Down!"

The point man, Reynolds, dropped to the ground, his figure instantly swallowed by the tall grass. Everybody hit the dirt.

There had been no shot; it all took place in quick silence, twenty-four grown men flinging themselves to the earth. Reynolds had seen something, Joe knew: a glint of light off a rifle scope, movement behind a window, camouflage being lifted off a mortar emplacement or the swinging barrel of an MG42. He eased up slowly on his palms, his eyes reaching just over the tips of the grass, twisted his head right, found Torrey. Their eyes met, and Joe mouthed the word: *What?* Torrey pointed at the steeple.

"Fuck." Joe pressed his face to the ground. The job was his: he would have to move forward and find Reynolds. *Fuck the S2, fuck battalion, fuck fuck fuck.*

Joe had lifted his face a second time to find his point man when the sniper in the belfry—the son of a music professor from Bremen—took him in his sights: the bullet pierced his cheek, blowing fragments of bone and teeth up into his left eye, crossed the damp interior of his mouth, and found the far line of his teeth and sheered them off in a second explosion of bone and silver before blasting through his jawbone. "Lieutenant!" he heard. "Lieutenant!" And then more gunfire, the MGs and then the big German 88s opening up and his own machine guns firing in reply, and the thud of mortars all around, but nobody was asking him for orders; his men had pulled back, thinking him dead, and left him alone. His pain was surprisingly vague; he wondered if this meant the end was near, or had somehow already occurred. The first medic who reached him took his dog tags and hurried away; this man with the ruined face, one eye gone under bloody shadow, how could he still be alive? He lay in the grass through the rest of the day, listening to the distant contest for Magliano, looking through his one eye at the flattened sky, and what he thought of wasn't the war, or the men with whom he'd fought—elsewhere now, pinned down by fire or sleeping on the hard floor of an empty farmhouse or

moving through the trees on the far side of the little town—or the people he had left at home in Boston, Amy and his parents and his sister,
Eileen, who would learn about his death, he guessed, a week from now
or even later. None of these. He closed his one good eye and what he
saw behind it was a lake, and mountains, and a river flowing through
an open field into woods. Was this heaven? But it was a real place his
mind saw; if he lived, he would find it, and claim it as his own.

They traveled north, and by the time they reached Waterville a gray
dusk had fallen. They made their way wearily out of the empty station;
at least the snow had stopped. In the lot he found the truck that had
come with the bargain, a '32 Ford with a rusted tailgate and bits of
straw still in the bed. He searched the cab: no note, but taped to the
steering wheel a map to the camp, and above the visor a heavy ring of
keys. As Amy took the passenger seat, a sudden fear twisted through
him: what if it didn't start? But when he opened the choke and pressed
the starter the old engine sputtered obediently to life.

Amy pulled her coat around the baby, who was still, somehow,
asleep. "How far is it?"

He unfolded the map over the wheel. "A couple of hours. I guess it
depends on the roads." He had only made the drive in summer, when
time did not matter and the weather was good; now he thought only of
getting them to the camp before it got too late to travel safely. The road
north, he knew, had no towns on it at all. It was entirely possible,
where they were going, to lose your way in the dark, to become
stranded and wait for hours, even a day, before somebody came along
to help. The train had pulled away; the lot around them was empty,
devoid even of tracks in the snow. He thought of trying to find a room
for the night, but pushed this idea aside: in for a penny, in for a pound.
He depressed the accelerator and listened as the engine settled
smoothly back on its idle.

"Your new truck," he said optimistically. "How do you like it?"

"You know, I never expected in my whole life even to *own* a truck."
Amy peered out the windows. "All right, where is everybody?"

"Inside, I guess. Keeping warm."

"Maybe they know something we don't."

The roads were clear, and where the plows had not been, the snow was only a few inches deep. The storm had slid south, after all. They drove two hours, arriving at the camp in darkness. Huge drifts lined the long drive, eight miles in from the main road and following the river. The camp had been closed for three years, but the owners had left a caretaker—the same man, Joe supposed, who had plowed the drive and left the truck for them at the station. A dozen cabins sat on the lake, their windows shuttered and boarded up. Beyond them, the main lodge was a dark, uninviting bulk. It was all theirs, and the land besides, two hundred acres along the river and lake; he had purchased it all, virtually sight unseen, for forty thousand dollars.

At the end of the drive Joe parked the truck and turned off the engine. In the sudden silence they sat without speaking, amazed at what they'd done. So many months of planning; now they were here.

He took his wife's hand. "Let's get inside."

The air in the lodge was musty and still, and smelled vaguely of animals. Joe tried the lights but nothing happened. A fuse had blown, or maybe some wires had been nibbled away by mice. The heat was out as well; their breath clouded thickly around them.

"Did something die in here?" Amy whispered.

"I can't see a goddamn thing." Joe stepped forward with his arms held protectively before his face. At once his right knee banged into something solid and sharp: the edge of a table. "Shit, shit, shit!" He tried to back away but his right foot tangled with the table's leg. Something heavy and made of glass thudded to the floor. It rolled away unbroken, but then found a set of steps—steps? he thought; what steps?—and bounced down and away, picking up speed before shattering into pieces somewhere below them.

Behind him, Amy started to laugh.

"It's not funny!"

"Okay," Amy said, still laughing, "it's not."

"There's probably a flashlight or candles in the kitchen," he said. "Stay put."

"Try not to break anything else on the way there," she said.

By now his eyes had grown accustomed to the darkness; at least he could make out the more obvious obstacles. He made his way into the main room, through the dining area, then farther back, through a pair of swinging doors into the kitchen. The smell of animals had grown richer, muskier. Where would the candles be? In the cabinets? In the pantry somewhere? But then he noticed, on the sideboard, a dark shape he recognized as a kerosene lantern. He took the lamp in his hands and shook it: a slosh of fuel. Not much, perhaps an hour's worth, but enough to get them settled for the night.

"Joe? Joe, where are you?"

"Just a minute! I've found something!"

He took his lighter from his pocket and lit the lamp. A small brass wheel adjusted the wick. He turned it down to conserve what little fuel he had, then held the lamp aloft, bathing the kitchen in a flickering glow. Cabinets and shelves, a stove and sink, a wide plank table: all just as he remembered it, from ten years ago. A bag of flour was spilled on the floor, its contents strewn in a wide path that ran to one of the lower cabinets, which stood open. The flour was dotted with animal tracks; pelletlike droppings littered the area around it.

"Joe? It's dark out here, you know!"

He followed Amy's voice back to the lodge's main room—a kind of sitting area, with a sofa and chairs, forming a U around a huge stone hearth. The furniture was draped with white cloths. The check-in desk was positioned by the entrance, and on the wall above it, a calendar, frozen in time: April 1943. By the fireplace, wood lay neatly stacked in a wrought-iron holder.

"We can sleep here tonight," Joe said. "Let's get the baby down. We can figure everything else out in the morning."

They found that the stove was working; at least the propane tanks were full, as promised. The cabinets contained no food at all, but in the pantry Joe found some tins of sardines and, in a tightly sealed jar, cubes of dried boullion. With no running water—the pipes were drained—they melted snow in a battered pot to make the broth, and heated some canned milk for the baby. While Amy laid out the couch cushions on the floor for the night, Joe retrieved their suitcases and got the fire going; soon the room was filled with a dancing light. Tomorrow he would see about the fuses, turn on the furnace, get the water running, chase down whatever it was that had left its droppings all over the kitchen and pantry. For now they needed sleep.

They got under the blankets. Beside them the baby slept soundly, oblivious. At last they were here, and yet Joe lay with his eyes open, his mind swarming with worry. The rigors of travel had kept his misgivings at bay, but now, their long journey accomplished, a flood of doubts seized him. What had he done? What kind of stupid idea was this? He thought of Amy, sleeping beside him. She was a physician's daughter, educated, a woman with friends and connections. Nothing in her life had prepared her for this: the cold, dark house, the wind moaning in the trees, nothing around them for miles, a landscape as empty as an unpainted canvas—no shops or restaurants, or music to dance to, or women like her. What would she do for friends? Whom would she talk to? She was a pianist, with a good ear and long fingers made to play; she might have gone on to a real career, played before audiences, but had chosen to teach instead, reserving the pleasure of the music to herself alone. Where would she find students up here? In such a place, who would be interested in playing the piano?

In the morning he awoke to dazzling sunlight, and cold so intense it seemed to stop time. The fire had burned down to a cone of popping ash. While Amy and the baby slept, Joe heated a pan of water on the stove and took it to the bathroom to shave. His demolished face: he sometimes wished he could shave with his eyes closed. The depression in his cheek was the size of a dime, wrapped by scars that whorled around it like the arms of a galaxy; his jaw was half-collapsed, held together by bars of steel. Only his front teeth were his own: the rest were porcelain, fixed in place on a nexus of wires and hooks. He spread the cream on his cheeks, paused with the razor in his hand, and began to scrape his beard away. Then Amy was standing behind him; their eyes met through the mirror.

"Good morning," he said.

Her face was tired. He wondered if she had been crying. "Joey's not awake yet," she said quietly.

"He will be, soon enough." He finished shaving and dabbed his face dry with a towel. "If you want breakfast, I'll have to get the supplies in from the truck. We'll need more wood, too. I saw a pile out back."

Something was different about her; he turned from the mirror.

"It will be . . ." He paused, searching her eyes. "It'll be all right. You'll see."

"Kiss me," she said.

His body missed her, ached for her. Yet he hesitated: his ruined mouth. Even when they made love, he kept his face away. It was as if this part of him had not come home from the war.

"No," she commanded. She put a finger over his lips. "This is nothing. Kiss me."

He did; they kissed each other. Moments passed; time flowed around them. Then, behind them, they heard the baby's first fussing, followed by a sharp cry as his lungs filled with air.

"How *does* he know?" Amy joked, and pushed away, laughing. "I'm afraid the two of you will have to share."

She picked up the baby to feed him, and Joe dressed in his coat and boots and stepped outside. The cold was stunning; at his first inhalation the metal in his mouth hummed with it, plucked like strings by the icy air. And yet, under the strong morning sunlight, patches of snow on the roof were melting; long icicles hung from the gutters, sharp as knives and gleaming with wetness. He carried the box of supplies in from the truck—just a few days' worth; they would have to get to the store soon—then stepped outside again. In the shed by the woodpile he found a hammer and wedge and set to work. He had dined in good restaurants, read serious books, argued the law before judges; now he lived in the forest and chopped wood, like a character in a fairy tale. It was, he knew, the very reduction he had come to claim: a pure life, a pure world. His sledgehammer rose and fell: one stroke, two strokes, then he was through; the wood was dry and split easily. In the hospital he had learned how to aim with his one good eye, making tiny adjustments to gauge the distance and bring his target into the crosshairs. The first time he tried to smoke he had missed the ashtray by almost a foot. But now such tasks came easily. He paused to remove his coat and hat and hung them on a nail on the door to the shed. His muscles ached, his breath steamed in the air around his head, his frame was damp with sweat. His mind was free, uncluttered, cleansed even of memory. For the rest of his life this moment would rest in his mind like a jewel: this glorious hour splitting wood, the taste of Amy's kiss on his mouth, his new life commencing.

He filled a basket with logs and returned to the house. As he entered, the first thing he noticed was the smell: the dry, dusty scent of old air rising through the floor vents on waves of heat. He found Amy at the kitchen table, Joey nestled on her lap; she was spooning watery cereal into the little boy's mouth.

"How did you . . . ?"

She looked up, her lips pressed in a smile she could not contain; he could tell she was delighted with her surprise. "It wasn't so hard," she said dismissively, and wiped the boy's chin with a rag. "There were instructions on the burner. The oil tank is practically full. And look."

She rose and carried the baby across the room to the cook's desk; on the shelf above it sat an old, cathedral-style radio. The dial was yellowed from years of heat from the radio's tubes. She turned the knob and Joe heard static as the tubes heated up, then, rising behind it like a cloud, a strange and distant music—fiddles, an accordion or hand organ, bells that chimed with a hollow, concussive sound. It was a sort of music he had never heard before. So far north, the station was probably Canadian.

Amy was holding the baby against her chest; she took his tiny hand in hers and, still holding him against her, swayed back and forth, dancing in place.

"What do you think?" she asked the baby. "How about a little dance with your mother?" She looked at Joe, her face pleased. "There was a package of fuses by the box," she explained. "I guessed which one and got it right."

He removed his gloves and sat at the kitchen table, stunned. Already the room was warm enough for shirtsleeves. Holding the baby, Amy took three steps across the room in time to the music, turned with a flourish, and took three steps back.

"Well, that's the way to do it, I guess."

"Don't just sit there with your mouth open," she said, still dancing. "I'm not a child, you know. What's the matter with Daddy?" she said to the little boy. "Does he think Mommy's a baby? Does he? Are you the baby, or is Mommy? Hmm?"

He laughed and shook his head. Gone so long; of course she would have learned to do such things. He recalled how in one of her letters she had mentioned, casually but with unmistakable pride, that she had changed a tire on the car.

"I'm sorry. I know you're not."

"Oh, for goodness' sake, save your apologies." She shooed him out of the kitchen. "Go set us a fire while I make breakfast."

They had powdered eggs and coffee, and Spam fried up with butter on the stove. They were clearing away the dishes when water began to pour in.

"Ice dams on the roof!" He was yanking every pot he could find from the kitchen cabinets and tossing them onto the floor. "We turned on the heat, and now everything behind them is melting and backing up under the shingles. Goddamnit!" They scurried around the lodge doing their best to catch the leaking water, which seemed to come from everywhere—down the window jambs, along the crown molding, even out of the light fixtures. The problem was more than ice dams, he realized. The roof was full of holes.

"So, what do you know about roofing?" he asked her.

"Heating and electricity only," she answered, and passed him a pot: it was all a great adventure, suddenly, a game without consequences. "The rest, I'm sorry to say, is up to you."

He went outside into the snow and found a crowbar and an old wooden ladder in the shed. The snow at the base of the eaves was at least a yard deep; he pushed the base of the ladder into it, then stepped on the lowest exposed rung and ascended, crowbar in hand. Amy watched from the ground with the baby in her arms as he banged away at the ice that had backed up over the gutters. Chips flew everywhere, diamondlike bits that gleamed in the sun. He made his way across the front of the lodge, hammering off the ice in chunks, then took a shovel up to the roof to push off the snow.

"Be careful, Joe."

The roof was steeply pitched, but in the soggy snow he found his footing. Whole areas of shingling had rotted away. Here and there someone had covered the worst of it with a tarp, but even this was nearly gone, frayed and ruined from exposure.

"It's a mess up here," he called down. "The whole thing will probably have to be reshingled."

"Please, just leave it, Joe. You'll break your neck up there."

It was almost funny: after all that had happened, she was worried he'd fall off a roof. He climbed to the apex, where he dared to stand upright, one foot positioned on either side of the roof's crest for balance. The frozen lake stretched away from him like a huge china platter, the sunlight blazing so brightly off its surface he could barely absorb it; on the far shore, dense woods marched up the hillsides and away, into ice and nothingness, the very top of the world. The cloudless sky was the color of cobalt, so blue he felt he could suck the whole thing into his lungs, breathe it in and out and become a part of it.

"Joe, for god's sake. Get down from there."

"It's spectacular!" he cried out. "Unbelievable!"

"Never mind that, just get down."

At last he inched down the roof on his backside and descended the ladder, breathless.

"We'll need to call somebody to fix this. Or at least get the worst of the holes covered." He was so energized he could barely contain the sensation. Of course he would try to reshingle the roof himself. The hammer in his fist, the tool belt at his waist weighed down with nails, the hours of intensely focused labor: each sensation was as precisely drawn in his mind as if it had already happened. Fixing a roof: how hard could it be?

"Amy, you've got to see the view," he said.

"Are you crazy? I'm not going up there."

He thought a moment. "Maybe there's another way." He took the baby from her arms. "Come on."

He led her into the house and upstairs to the staff quarters, which they had not yet explored. Five tiny bedrooms tucked under the eaves: he selected a door on the north side, facing the lake, and opened it. The room was a disaster. Some small animal, a squirrel or chipmunk or even something the size of a raccoon, had gotten in, leaving tufts of fur and debris scattered everywhere. On the bureau sat an empty whiskey bottle, and beside it, an ashtray full of butts. The mattress was bare and stained. It was the same room where Joe had slept the summer before law school, when he had worked at the camp as a dishwasher.

"What a mess," Amy said, and wrinkled her nose. A look of alarm crossed her face and she quickly took the baby from him and backed out the door. "Do you think it's still in here?"

He pointed to the ceiling, where scraps of wood had been nailed over the hole that led, Joe knew, to a crawl space, and above it, the threadbare roof. "I doubt it. Whatever it was, it's long gone."

He stepped inside, ducking his head under the narrow eaves of sagging plaster, and over to the room's only window. Outside was a broad overhang, like a terrace; he had passed countless summer nights there, sitting and smoking, alone or with other employees of the camp, young men like him on a lark between college and whatever came next, talking about girls or their plans for the future or even, as some believed, the coming war. He had even kissed a girl up there once, a waitress at the camp; for a languid hour they had listened to the loons and kissed one another under the stars, like a scene in a movie, but she had a boyfriend in town, and that was as far as things had gone. He had actually convinced himself he was in love with her, and for weeks he had moped about it. But then, in the last days of summer, he had driven with some of the staff down to Blue Hill for a Labor Day dance and spent the night talking at a table with a friend's cousin, a girl from Back Bay with intense gray eyes who was studying piano at the Conservatory. When he returned the next week to Boston he phoned her, and within a year he and Amy were married and living together in student housing across from Harvard Stadium.

The room had a small desk and chair; he pulled the chair over to the window, opened it, and bent his back low to step outside. The overhang, exposed to the sun, was clear of snow. It was almost six feet wide, and yet the urge to keep his weight low was strong; in his knees he felt the gathering softness of his fear, the absurd belief that somehow he would pitch forward into space. He pushed this thought aside and stood upright, filling his chest with air: below and before him he beheld, once more, the lake and woods, and beyond it, unseen but felt, the border across which had issued the morning's strange music. He could still hear it in his head, the way the high notes of the fiddle had seemed to dance over and around the bass line of thumping bells. He turned and reached through the open window to help Amy up.

She frowned, incredulous. "You're kidding."

"Not a bit."

"You think I'm going out there? I am *not*."

"Don't be ridiculous. We used to come out here all the time." The happiness he'd felt all morning was still building within him. It seemed to course through his very veins. He could do anything; anything was possible. "Hand me Joey first. Then I can pull you up with my free hand."

On tiptoes she lifted herself to peer out the window. At last she groaned in surrender and lifted the baby toward him.

"Please, Joe, be careful."

He took the baby from her. Their little boy was wearing a blue snowsuit with silhouetted reindeers dancing across it, and a cap that Amy had pulled down over his ears and forehead so that only his face showed. His hands were bare; clipped mittens dangled from his sleeves. Joe settled his son into the crook of one elbow, then lowered himself again to the window to offer Amy his free hand. But she shook her head and bent her back low, as he had done, gripping the window frame to pull herself through.

"Just don't drop him," she warned. She blew the air from her lungs and rocked her weight back with one foot on the chair. "This is absolutely the stupidest thing we've ever done, bar none."

He wanted to laugh. "You'll see."

She gave herself a pull and at once she was up and outside, beside him. As he watched her, the fear melted from her eyes. In its place he saw the pure radiance of her astonishment.

"For the love of God, Joe."

The first day, he thought. For all their lives, in hours dark and light, this was the day they would always remember. In his arms, in the bright sunlight, his little boy looked at him inquiringly, as if to say; why am I on this roof?

"For this," Joe said, and held him high, to show him what was his.

Quechee Library
P.O. Box 384
Quechee, VT 05059

A Girl Can Talk to Her Dad About Peas

Quechee Library
P.O. Box 384
Quechee, VT 05059

Jordan

Everybody has a story, so here is mine—the story of me and Kate and old Harry Wainwright, and the woods and lake where all of this takes place. My name: Jordan Heronimus Patterson Jr., son of the late Captain Jordan Heronimus Patterson Sr., USN, both of us Virginia born and bred, though now I live here, in the North Woods of Maine, where I make my living as a fishing guide. My father, a Navy pilot, loved the air, as I love what's beneath it—the sun and light and snow and mountains of this remote place, and the big trout under the water. To meet me, you might think I must be simple, or unambitious, or just plain lazy, a grown man who fishes for a living; that is, a man who plays. When I take a party out on the lake, or downriver for the last of the spawning runs when they'll still take a streamer, the man may ask me, or the woman if there is a woman, "What else do you do?" Or, "Do you really stay up here all winter?" A question I don't hold against them, because I'm young, just thirty, and here is far from anywhere, the hardness of winter plain to see even on the sweetest summer afternoon in the twisted way the pines grow; they're asking about movies and restaurants and stores, of course, all the things they love, so it's natural to ask it: What else do I do? So I tell them about taking care of the boats and cabins, and hunting parties in the fall, which I'll do if I have to but don't really care for; and I may throw in a thing or two about college, how I didn't mind going when I was there (University of Maine at Orono, class of 1986, B.S. in economics with a minor in forestry, thank you very much); and the man will nod, or the woman, thinking: Why, here's a man of no account! And for one silent second they're me, and happy because of it, and then they'll ask me where to fish or what pattern to use on the line, and they'll catch something because of what I tell them and go home to Boston or New York or even Los Angeles, and I'll stay here as the snow piles up, something I can't explain to anyone, not even to myself.

And if I sound as if I don't like these people, that isn't at all true. The camp is far north, four hours by car from Portland and tricky to find, and the people who will make such a journey are serious about fishing. They are rich, most of them, a fact they cannot hide; one sees the evidence in their cars, their clothes, the good leather of their luggage and shoes. It's large what's between us, make no mistake, and I know that to such people I am just another body for hire, like the nanny who raises their children, the broker who sells them the stocks that make them more money, the lawyer they retain when they wish to divorce. But because they are rich enough to have these things, they are gracious to me, even respect me, for I know what they do not: where the fish are and what they are likely to take. For this they rent me, body and soul, at two hundred fifty dollars a day, a hundred fifty for the half, as pure a bargain as I know about, and dirt cheap if truth be told.

There are regulars, too, people who come up here every year at the times they like best: early summer for the big mayfly hatches, or else the long dry days of August, after the blackflies have gone, the days are as crisp as a butterfly on pins, and the fish have wised up and aren't especially hungry besides—not the easiest time to catch them, but that's not why these folks are here, and not why I'm here, either. Which brings me to the last summer I saw Harry Wainwright—*the* Harrison P. Wainwright, he of the thirty-odd consecutive summers, the Forbes 500 and the NYSE and all the rest—who came up here at last to die.

We put on the dog for lifers like Harry Wainwright, which up here is really just a state of mind, since there's no way to be fancy. The cabins are identical, rustic and spare, each with a couple of creaky cots, a potbellied stove, and a tippy porch on the water with a view across it to the mountains. What I mean is, we're ready to see him, glad as hell to see him, because lifers like Harry are the bread and butter of a place like ours; we can't afford to advertise, and don't have a mind to anyway, having never bothered to begin with. At the time I'm speaking of, Harry was probably seventy, though until he'd gotten sick he'd aged easily, like the rich man he was. He owned a string of discount drugstores in the South and Midwest (I'd heard it said that if you bought a bottle of aspirin anywhere from Atlanta to Omaha, you probably paid Harry Wainwright for the privilege), and a lot of other things besides, a veritable empire of goods and services in which I had no stake, except for what he paid me as a guide. He hardly needed one; he'd fished this spot since Kennedy was in the White House and knew it as well as any man alive. His tips, always embarrassingly huge, were just another way of expressing his pure happiness to be here.

Did he impress me? Who wouldn't be impressed by Harry Wainwright?

So, the story: In rolls Harry, whom we all knew was dying of cancer, late on an August afternoon in the Year of Our Lord 1994, with his second (i.e., younger) wife, his son and tiny granddaughter, all heaped into a big rented Suburban to haul them up from the airport in Portland with their gear: as beautiful a family as ever I've seen. The day's just tipped toward evening, the best time to arrive, and it's late enough in the season that the birches and striped maples are just beginning to turn in bright crowns of yellow and red, set against the blue, blue sky. Harry is stretched out on the second seat, his back propped against the door with pillows, like old Ramses himself; Harry Jr. (who goes by Hal) is driving; second wife Frances is in the passenger seat; January (named for the month of her birth or the month of her conception, take your pick) is tucked into her comfy car seat in the way back; the car cruises down the long drive. Everybody loves the last eight miles: when you finally arrive, it's like you've already done something, like the fun's already started.

We were expecting him, of course. The night before, we all sat down for a meeting, after Joe had taken the call from Hal, saying Harry wanted to come up, short notice he knew but was there space, and so on. We met in the dining room after supper: me, Joe's wife, Lucy, who ran the kitchen and took care of the books, and their daughter, Kate, who was a junior at Bowdoin and worked in the summers as a guide, and Joe told us what he knew—that Harry had cancer and wanted to fish. The rest, about dying, was in there, but nothing he dared say. The next afternoon Hal called us from a pay phone in town to tell us they were thirty minutes away, so when the car came down the drive, Kate and Joe and I were waiting for them.

Still, when Hal opened the old man's door, it was a shock, and for a moment I thought maybe we'd all missed something and they were bringing his body up for burial—though a man like Harry Wainwright should go to his reward in a pharaoh's robes, not the frayed khakis and tennis shoes and ratty blue sweater, all of it looking pale and loose, that he had on. The sight of a rich man dying is one to shake all your assumptions about a free market economy; here is something—life, health, a fresh set of orders for maniac cells run amok—that can't be bought. As Hal swung the door wide we all held our breaths a little, deciding how to be normal, looking at the sneakers, white as the underbellies of two freshly bagged trout. Hal gave Joe's hand and then my own a solid shake—as I said, he's a good-looking man, his hair gone prematurely silver and tied in a hipster ponytail, the skin around his eyes handsomely crinkled from squinting out over the world's warm waters at all times of year—and then said loudly, to me and everybody else, "Pop? Jordan's here to help us get you out."

Which proved tricky: the cancer, which had started in his lungs, had spread to the bones of his back. The poor guy was stiff as a cracker. Those last eight miles, as bouncy as a carnival ride, must have felt as bad as anything in his life. I scampered around to the rear passenger door; Frances climbed onto the backseat of the Suburban to hold his hands and keep him upright, and I popped open the door and let him sink into my arms. From the other side, Hal and Frances pushed his feet toward me, and as I pulled him out the old guy unfolded like a pocketknife; in a wink he was standing erect, me hugging him from behind, a little unsure if I should let him go or not. He weighed almost nothing, poor bird, although I also believed that if he fell the ground might actually shake, and it would be the worst moment of my life so far.

"Thank you, Jordan."

I looked past his ear and saw that I was supposed to hold him until Frances came around with the walker. Frances was maybe fifty, and I always thought of her as a little mannish, though in a pleasing way: she's a solid woman, her thickness like the thickness of a good book. Fixed to one of the walker's legs was a shiny chrome tank, about the size of a propane canister, with a clear plastic tube that ran to a heart-shaped mask that Frances wedged over Harry's head to ride in the folds of his neck.

"I am, as you see, much reduced, and I thank you."

This was Harry's way of speaking; he liked to use expressions like "much reduced" when he meant sick as a poisoned rat. It's easy to be dumb about the rich, but Harry Wainwright really was different from anyone else I knew. If you've read the articles, you know the story— Harry made sensational copy—a classic all-American bootstraps tale of ingenuity and elbow-grease, the hard lean years and the big idea and then the one-way rocket ride of his amazing life; point being, he was entitled to use any turn of phrase that pleased him. He also cursed a lot, though I could tell it made him happier to do than it makes most people. When Harry Wainwright called a fish "one whomping badass motherfucker," I knew it really was.

"Sure thing, Mr. Wainwright," I said. "It's great to see you again."

Silence, and I was surprised he hadn't corrected me. For eight summers the joke was always the same: I'd call him Mr. Wainwright, he'd say, *for god's sake, Jordan, call me Harry,* though I never, ever did. I wondered if he'd forgotten, and then if maybe he was too sick to re-member who I was. But of course he'd call me Jordan. A dumb idea for certain, but still I thought it: How many Jordans could he know? My own father, who died when I was three, was the only other one I've heard of, and him I barely got to know, before his engines failed one summer night off Newport News and he crashed into the sea. (For a few bad months in college, when I'd fallen into a deep funk over noth-ing obvious, I passed a few hours in the company of the campus psy-chologist, an earnest young woman with a smile like something she had gone to school to learn. She got it in her bean that the fact that my father's body had never been recovered was probably the root of all my woes—not wrong, but not exactly rocket science, either. In any event, one day my bad mood lifted and never returned.)

By this time, little January had been sprung from her car seat and was toddling around the driveway, dragging a stuffed Humpty Dumpty. I should say at this point that Hal's wife, Sally, rarely came to the camp; I'd probably laid eyes on her twice in my life, though she was some sort of Wall Street lawyer and was probably just too busy. It was nice to see a man who would actually bring his eighteen-month-old along on a last-minute jaunt to the North Woods, but I could also tell that Hal was about at the end of his patience. He scooped his little girl up onto his hip and gave us all a weary look that said, *Long day, not my idea, could we please just hustle this along and get the old man indoors?* He lifted an eyebrow at Kate. "Could you?"

Kate stepped up and took January from him, making cooing promises about going down to the lake to see the ducks; Hal, his hands free, moved around the walker and pulled the mask up to Harry's face.

"We've got dinner waiting for you in the dining room, Harry," Joe said. "We can take your things to your cabin for you, so you just go along and get yourself settled."

Harry said nothing; for a moment, we all just stood there, watching him haul in the air like a man with his face in a two-pound rose. It hurt like hell to see him that way; no one should have to think about *breathing,* which by then every one of us was.

Then, from inside the mask: "Jordan?"

"Yes, sir?"

"Goddamnit, it's Harry, Jordan."

And what else could I do? I laughed, relieved as hell. And then Kate laughed, one of my favorite sounds in all this world, and Hal, and everybody else—even little January—all of us glad for the moment to hear a joke, to let the day's minefield of a mood and this god-awful sense of death in our midst evaporate like a morning fog.

Harry looked around like we had lost our minds. "What's so funny I'd like to know?"

Hal put a thick hand on his father's shoulder. "Nobody's laughing at you, Pop."

"Well, you could if you liked." Harry pulled the mask from his face and let it dangle there. His damp gaze drifted up into the pines, then fell back on me, standing there with one hand still on the walker, wondering what to do next.

"Jordan, I'm here to catch a trout before I croak. Can you do it?"

I shot a glance at Joe, who was gathering their bags, then at Kate, keeping January busy with the Humpty Dumpty, and I saw that they were thinking the same thing I was: none of this was anyone's idea but Harry's. Pure harebrained whimsy, no matter how you sliced it: Harry was in a lot of pain, and he belonged in a hospital or at least in bed, not floating around the lake with me and scaring the wits out of absolutely everybody.

But then I thought: a last trout. Not out of the question, and of course that was what he'd want. More to the point, what difference did it make what Harry wanted, so long as he wanted *something*? It could have been a trip to Disney World or a glorious hour with a three-hundred-dollar hooker (though Harry never struck me as the type for either one), as long as it was something still ahead of him.

"Hell yeah, Mr. Wainwright. We can do that for you." I gave him my best you-betcha nod. "Why just the one?"

Harry managed a crafty smile. "On a dry fly, Jordan."

Now, this was a taller order. I saw no chance that Harry could actually wade the river, his best chance to take a fish on top. As for the lake, the summer had been hot and practically rainless, and what trout there were had long since headed for the lake's colder waters, resting above the thermocline like so much unexploded ordnance (or, come to think of it, one very old and barnacle-encrusted F-4 Phantom lying in the drink off Newport News). It was productive if dull fishing if you were willing to take your time and drift a nymph or pull a wooly bugger below the surface; but to take one on top, as Harry wanted to do, would take plenty of raw luck and a first-class presentation besides, to land the fly as light as a baby's kiss right on the nose of some off-chance cruising lunker. All of which, not incidentally, Harry certainly knew.

"On top?" I thought a gentle approach might nudge him around to the idea of a low-stakes outing on the lake with no hopes in particular.

"I have to say we'd do better underneath. It's not really the best time for dry fly."

Harry shook his head. "Time I haven't got, Jordan. Hal's given me just twenty-four hours for this."

Joe, who'd mostly kept silent until now, jingling the change in his pockets and shuffling his feet on the loose gravel of the parking area, slid me a look that said we'd talk later, that there was more to this than I knew.

"I think what Jordan meant," Joe said, "is that it's entirely possible."

"Twenty-four hours, Jordan," Harry said. "Then it's back to the hospital, where they'll hook me up to every machine they've got and shoot me full of so much morphine I won't care that I'm dying." Harry stopped, looking as if he were about to cough—a prospect I dreaded almost physically—pulled the mask back up to his face, and took a pair of long, whistling breaths. Frances moved to his other side, cupping his elbow and watching his face as he pulled the air in. I could tell it had been a long, hard haul for her. It's easy to imagine the worst when a rich man like Harry marries a younger woman late in life, to see it as one more of the world's cold-blooded calculations—in this case, some eleventh-hour deathbed care for a piece of Harry's not inconsiderable drugstore pie. But to watch her watching Harry struggle with every breath to pull the sweet taste of oxygen over his ruined lungs was to know that she truly cared about him, loot or no, and had trucked to hell and back.

"Harry? All right?" Frances looked deep into his face, and Harry gave a faint nod. We waited while, bit by bit, some color flowed back into his cheeks. The sun had dipped below the line of mountains across the lake, and suddenly it was full-on night in the North Woods, the temperature falling like a stone. A shiver uncoiled around my spine, and I wanted to get Harry inside.

At last he drew the mask away, pulling with it a spaghetti strand of spittle. Frances produced a handkerchief to blot it away.

"They mean well, Jordan, and I've got no problems with it. But it's not how I'd do things."

I wasn't sure if he meant the doctors, or Frances and Hal, or maybe all three. In any case, it was clear to me that he was hoping he'd die before he ever got home, and the thing he feared most was that this probably wouldn't happen.

"All right, then," I said. "We'll get the job done."

"Twenty-four hours," Harry said, and began his long creep toward the dining hall, Hal and Frances each taking a side. Kate was still carrying January, who had fooled us all by falling asleep. "One fish, Jordan. My way. That's the deal."

Joe

When Hal telephoned to tell me his father was dying, I couldn't help myself. My first thought was: *Thank God.*

It is possible to hate somebody you also love, as I both loved and hated Harry Wainwright, though it was a lesson I learned not from Harry but my father, the great war hero. He taught me this the day my mother died, when he asked me, a boy of nine, to be brave when I could not; and again three days after Halloween, 1968, when, a man at last or so I thought, I was made to give that manhood back to him and forever be a coward and a criminal.

I asked Hal how long.

"Months. It depends. He's tough, you know?" Hal cleared his throat. "A tough nut. He's got a deal to offer you, Joe. One I think you may like."

Which told me that I would also hate it. "Deals are what he's best at."

"He wants you to fly up to New York. We'd like to send the plane for you. Excuse me one second?" The sudden, deep well of the hold button, long enough for me to wonder if he'd forgotten me. Then he returned. "Joe, I'm sorry, but there are some people here I have to see. Totally urgent stupid stuff, but there you are. Where did we leave this?"

"I think you were . . . sending me a plane?"

"Not showing off here, Joe. Just trying to move things along. You'll like it, I think. Be sweet to the pilot and he may even let you sit up front and play with the wipers." He cleared his throat. "And, because we're friends, and in an effort to be less than totally vague, I will also tell you that you may want to have a lawyer handy."

"Isn't Sally a lawyer?"

Sally was Hal's wife, a real legal sharpshooter from what I'd heard, though I mostly knew her as a pretty woman in a flannel shirt who usually sent her backcast looping into the trees behind her head. The last time I'd seen her, two summers before, the flannel shirt was a big one of Hal's, hanging halfway to the backs of her knees but riding up in front over the big belly of her pregnancy.

"Yes, but in this case Sally would be what you would call the *other* lawyer."

"So we all need lawyers, is what you're saying. For whatever it is you have in mind."

Hal sighed. "This is *Harry,* Joe. He likes drama. I'd tell you more if I could. I've got a cousin just out of law school. Not too bright and his suits are bad, but he means well and he needs the work. I'll put you in touch. Lucy fine?"

"You know Lucy."

"Pleased to hear it. Our love, all right? And to Kate."

"You serve those little whatyacallums on that plane of yours? You know, in the foil packets?"

I could practically hear him nod. "Honey peanuts."

"That's it. Honey peanuts."

"There's more than peanuts in this for you. I'll say it again. Think about it, all right? But think fast. He's dying, Joe. 'Months' is what they say when they mean dying as we sit here talking."

This was back in April, before Harry pulled his big surprise; Lucy and I were still in Big Pine Key, finishing out our third winter in the stolen sunshine. It was a good life shaping up down there for us—I had two boats working, a solid and growing list of clients, and a tan that would have made me nervous if I were one to worry about such things—all of it just profitable enough that it didn't feel like a vacation. Our condo, which I had bought for a song at a sheriff's auction, was, like everything else on Big Pine, made of materials as light and phony as a child's art supplies, but it did the job: two bedrooms, one of which I used as an office for bookings and paperwork, a little kitchenette, and a balcony off the living room with a view of the docks where I kept the boats, and beyond them, on the far side of the bay, the Key Highway, leapfrogging over the water to Marathon. We didn't feel as if we belonged there, but we weren't exactly homesick either, and evenings when we didn't rent a movie or hover by the phone waiting to hear from Kate (who had survived twelve years of, let's be honest, completely so-so public education courtesy of the Greater Sagonick Community School District to hit the dean's list at Bowdoin six semesters running and had MCAT scores through the high heavens), Lucy and I would sit for hours on the balcony, drinking something and maybe talking a bit, but mostly watching the headlights soar like distant angels over the water and feeling amazed that such a place existed.

That night, I sat with Lucy and told her about Hal's call. She cried at the news, as I knew she would, though she also did not want me to watch her: she averted her face and wept without making a sound, and when she turned again to face me I knew the crying was over.

"You should go," she said to me.

"To New York?"

She sighed and wiped her eyes with the tips of her fingers. "He wants to see you, Joe. Or Hal does. Honestly, what harm could it do now?"

"That's what I'm wondering. Hal said I would need a lawyer, for starters."

"That sounds like Hal, not Harry. He won't even let his father go to the head without running it through legal."

"Even so. It's a reason to be cautious, don't you think?"

On the causeway, headlights floated dreamily past; looking the other way, out toward the channel and the open sea, I could make out the twinkling bulk of a cruise ship, its boiler stacks strung with lights, pushing south from Miami like a floating Christmas tree turned sideways. This close in, she was probably headed for Key West, where the fun, I was told, never stopped.

"Luce—"

She stopped me with a hand. "Joe," she said. "Joe. It was all a long time ago. Go see what's on his mind."

As we both knew I would, which is how things are when you've been married twenty years and spent most of this time as isolated as a couple of bears in the Yukon: a lot of what passes for discussion is really just taking in the scenery, and a recap of something you both already know. Hal's cousin called the next morning, right on schedule, but I told him I was tied up and would call him back, having no intention whatsoever of actually doing so. I like lawyers fine—despite the jokes, most are just people with a job—but whatever Hal had to offer, he would have to offer me alone. I had one boat on the water for the day; Tyrell, my sole employee, had taken out the smaller of the two with a group sent over from the big resort on Hawk's Cay. But the second, the Mako, which I used for deep sea, was in for engine maintenance, so I spent the afternoon doing various odds and ends to prep it for a weekend party and keeping an eye peeled for Tyrell's return. My deal with Tyrell was a sweet one; unless somebody asked for me in particular, all the flats-guiding was his to do, with the two of us splitting the take, plus the tip, which he got to pocket free and clear. On any given day I'd have him out on the water for at least four hours, making money for both of us and generally scaring the whiskers off our white-bread clientele with his dreadlocks, Jamaican accent, and twelve-o'clock doobie (he thought I didn't know about this; of course I did), though by Miller time everybody would be happy as a band of Smurfs, full of stories about the huge fish they had caught or not, and a permanent appreciation for Tyrell's mystical ability to tell them where to drop a cast. No doubt most attributed this to some kind of island wisdom, or else the dope, but I knew better. Tyrell was actually from Corpus Christi and had a master's degree in marine bio from Texas A&M. The accent was pure theater, something he had picked up in the Peace Corps.

By two o'clock he hadn't returned, a good omen, since his party had signed on for only half a day but now had obviously sprung for the full ride, so I decided to kill the rest of the afternoon by driving up to have a look at a boat I was hoping to buy. I say "hoping" because there was no way on God's green earth anybody was going to loan me the scratch for it, and with Kate planning on medical school—she had her heart set on either UCLA or Dartmouth Hitchcock—I saw nothing but the worst kind of cash squeeze in my future. But this boat! A 1962 38-foot Chris-Craft Constellation with twin MerCruiser Blue Water 350s, totally restored with glossy teak from bowsprit to transom, more varnished wood in the wheelhouse than in all the pubs in Dublin, all of it completely top-shelf right down to the bait wells with custom circulating pumps and enough electronics on the helm to command the U.S. Seventh Fleet: in all my life, I had never seen a boat like this. It wasn't the best rig for deep sea, or fishing of any kind, as I would spend half my time mopping up the blood and reminding people to use the goddamn coasters. But we want what we want, and I wanted this boat, never mind the price tag, an eye-popping $220,000, about the same as four years of medical school in sunny California or snowy New Hampshire, take your pick. She was docked in Marathon, and the only reason she hadn't sold was that the owner, a former "labor official" from Providence, was now out of the country "indefinitely" and had left the sale to the yard where she was kept. This was a fox-henhouse proposition if ever there was one, as the slip fees and maintenance on a boat like that easily brought in three times the money they would see from a brokerage commission, so the thing had sat through two winters with nary an offer I knew of.

I parked the truck in the yard lot, ducked into the office to fetch the key, and walked down to the slip where she was waiting, in all her forgotten glory. I had met the owner, Frank DeMizio, once before, when I'd first gone to the yard to take a peek—a tough-looking, squarish little man with a face like a piecrust and enough hair on his back to throw a shadow. He was wearing nothing but a Red Sox cap and a pair of aquamarine bikini briefs, and when I introduced myself and told him I was there to see the boat, he didn't offer me his hand to shake but simply grunted and went back to wiping down the bait boxes with a shammy cloth.

"*Felicity,*" I said, reading the name off the transom.

"Means 'pussy' in Latin," he said.

"I think it means 'happiness,' " I said.

He shrugged his big shoulders and wrung his cloth into a bucket. "Same thing, innit?" He rose then and had a hard look at me where I stood on the dock. "You cocksuckers never give up, do you?"

"Excuse me?"

"Fucking IRS. Nothing satisfies you, you parasites."

"I'm not from the IRS. Ask Carl." Carl was the yard owner; he knew my business, who I was.

"That lying rat fuck?" He crossed his beefy arms over his chest. "He's twice as dirty as I ever was. You tell Agent Tortorella to check *his* books, he wants a good laugh."

I fished through my wallet for a business card, which I held out to him over the gunwale. "Listen, I'm really not from the IRS. I run a charter service out of Big Pine."

He rolled his eyes, but then took the card and looked at it. "Joe Crosby." He frowned and lifted his eyes to me. "That you?"

"That's right. I just told you."

His face softened. "Well, fuck it. So you did." He sat down heavily on the bait box and shook his head regretfully. "Sorry about that. You gotta believe me, these guys have been all over my ass. I can't take a dump without some fed reaching out of the bowl to grab the paper from my hand."

"Forget it," I said. "If you don't want me to look at the boat today, I can just come back another time."

"No, the hell with it." He waved me up like we were the best of friends. "Who knows if there'll be a next time, the way this is playing out. Might as well come on board and have a look around."

He gave me the full tour, even started up the engines and took us for a quick spin out to Key Vaca, and by the time we returned, he seemed to have forgotten all about his troubles. We sat on the aft deck and shot the breeze over a couple of cans of Coors; he told me how he had found the boat nine years ago in western Connecticut, falling apart in somebody's barn, and had put it back together piece by piece, hoping someday to retire someplace warm and spend the rest of his life puttering around on it. His marriage was long over, his kids were grown and gone. Except for a crappy little townhouse in Providence and a ten-year-old Cadillac, the boat was what he had. He'd gotten as far as bringing her all the way down from Newport, piloting it himself right down the East River and under the Verrazano Narrows Bridge. But then he had come into his office one day to find the place crawling with police, not just local cops but IRS and FBI, his file cabinets and desk and computer all sealed with yellow tape and making their way on handcarts to a step van parked in the alley.

"I'll tell you one thing," Frank said, lighting up another of the long brown cigarettes he had smoked all afternoon. "You think those cocksucking Kennedys were ever put under investigation? They never did anything I ain't done."

"Can't say I know much about it, Frank. I've heard that, though."

"Well, they sure as hell weren't." He shook his head and smoked. "Irish trash from Southie. They're no better than me, and look at the fix I'm in." He fell silent for a minute, then flicked his cigarette over the transom. "So, you innerested?"

So much time had passed I had almost forgotten the boat was for sale. I felt a little stab of shame that I didn't have the money, or anything close to it. All I was doing was window-shopping.

"Two-twenty's a pretty big nut, Frank. For a guy like me, anyway. She's a beautiful boat, though."

"Beautiful doesn't begin it," he corrected. "Beautiful is something you say to a broad. You're beautiful, sweetie, yes you are." With a bear-like hand he patted the gunwale. "*This,* my fucking friend, is a work of fucking *art.*"

"It's a shame you have to sell," I said. "I'm not sure I'd even feel right taking her from you."

"Yeah, well." He looked dismally out over the water, squinting into the fading light. Nearly four hours had passed since I'd appeared on the dock. "Listen. Do me a favor, will ya?"

I nodded. "Sure thing."

"Be a good guy and get the fuck out of here." He waved his can of beer toward the parking lot, now all but empty, except for my truck.

"Go on. Back to where you came from." He frowned and looked at his hands. "Just leave me the fuck alone."

I did as he asked, leaving him there with his melancholy thoughts, and when I called the yard a month later to order a new propeller for the Mako and asked Carl if *Felicity* was still for sale, he told me that Frank had flown the coop. There were no liens against the boat, IRS or otherwise, as far as he knew; the maintenance bills were being sent to a PO box in Coral Gables and paid by wire from an offshore account— fishy as hell, but probably legal or at least hard to touch. Since then she had sat through summer and another winter, soaking up maintenance fees and pelican poop and bobbing forlornly in the swells. The odd thing was, the one time Carl had talked to Frank, and told him that I still came around the yard from time to time to look at her, Frank had said it was all right with him if I wanted to take her out. According to Carl, Frank had said he was sorry, and that it was a shame for a boat like that not to get any use at all, especially from someone who appreciated her.

That afternoon, with Tyrell still AWOL and nothing else on my plate—except of course for Hal's airplane, and a certain amount of melancholy brooding of my own—I took *Felicity* out to Key Vaca, as Frank and I had done that afternoon a year ago. Despite her bulk she did a comfortable fifteen knots that sliced nicely through the swells, and it was easy to understand, sitting at the helm, the attraction of such a thing—why Frank had wanted it, and maybe done one or two things wrong in his life in order to get it. (Okay, not maybe, and not one or two; but I liked to think he hadn't done anything truly terrible, such as kill someone, up there in dirty little Providence.) It was nearly a quarter of a million dollars' worth of luxury pleasure craft, but in a way it was also a small thing; when you're in a boat on the open sea, that smallness is what you feel, and the memory of this feeling is what calls you back. In his haste to depart, Frank had left an open chart on the table of the main salon: the Caymans, of course, world-class haven for tax cheats. Beside it I found a little pad of paper with course headings and distance calculations written in a small, almost girlish print. *Too fucking far,* Frank had written, underlining the words twice, hard enough to break the tip off his pencil. The thing was, it wasn't too far for a boat like that, not if you knew what you were doing. It was just too far for Frank.

From a pay phone at the dock I called Kate. It was just evening, a little after seven, and I hoped she would be back in her room after dinner. If she didn't answer I was prepared to hang up and head home, but she took it on the third ring, a little out of breath.

"Hey, kiddo."

"Daddy? Hang on a second. I just got in."

"Take your time, Kats."

She held her hand over the receiver to talk to someone, then came back on the line. "Sorry. Here I am."

"There you are."

"Is it, like, eighty degrees down there? Because today it fucking, excuse me, snowed. *Again.* In *April.*" She laughed at someone in the room. "I'm glad you called, actually."

"How's that?"

"Daddy, Daddy, Daddy." She sighed theatrically into the phone. "California. Airline tickets. Re*mem*ber? We were supposed to sort it out by last week."

We had talked about it over her spring vacation; at the end of May we were planning to fly, the two of us, out to LA to visit medical schools: USC, UCLA, UC San Diego. Maybe a jaunt in a rental car up the coast to San Francisco, to see Stanford and UCSF.

"Right you are. Must have slipped my mind. I'll get on it, Kats, I promise."

"I don't mean to nag, but you know. It's important. Like, my whole entire life, to be exact. I also wouldn't mind seeing that Universal Studios Tour. I could use some serious kitsch about now."

"Got it. Serious kitsch. Your whole entire life. Roger wilco."

"Daddy? That's not the reason you called, is it?"

"Sure it was. Planning for California. I'm on the job, Kats."

"Daddy."

"Okay, you've got it out of me. The truth is I just took out somebody's boat for a little spin, and it put me in the mood to hear your voice."

"Not the naked gangster's Chris-Craft?"

"Labor official, Kats. Labor official. Nice fellow, too, once you get past the gruff exterior and the grand jury indictment."

Kate paused for adjustment. "Dad? This isn't one of those your-mother-and-I-have-decided-to-take-some-time-apart calls, is it? Because a lot of that has been going around up here. And if you'll pardon my saying so, you sound a little strange."

"No worries, Kats. Your mom and I are fine, unless you know something I don't. Looks like I'm going to be taking a little trip, though."

"I thought Big Pine was a little trip."

"A trip from my trip, then. A kind of a business thing."

"Hmmm. Very mysterious."

"I'd tell you more, but it's top secret, I'm afraid. At least for now."

"Daddy, I know you. You don't *do* top secret. Top secret is not your thing."

"Don't be so sure. I might surprise you, Kats."

"Speaking of which. You know, there's a girl in my dorm who thinks her dad works for the CIA." Kate lowered her voice, having fun. "Supposedly he's an accountant for the State Department. But then he up and disappears for weeks at a time. She also thought she saw him on CNN, in the background of a shot taken in, like, Turkey or someplace. He was wearing sunglasses and a turban."

"Sounds pretty fishy."

"That's what I thought. Does the CIA have accountants?"

"Somebody has to do their books, I guess. Kats?"

"Yeah, Dad?"

"Remember that summer when you were growing the beans? I think they were beans." My mind was wandering, doing surprising things. "That science project for school."

"Peas, Dad. Sure, I remember. What about it?"

"No reason, I guess. I was just thinking about it. You sure were all fired up about it. How old were you, thirteen?"

"Well, it was eighth-grade science, with Mr. Weld. So I guess that would be about right. We used to call him Fartface Weld."

"That's right, Phil Weld." I was thinking of my thirteen-year-old Kats, dressed in shorts and a bathing suit top and her mother's straw hat, working away in the Maine dirt. The memory was so vivid I could practically smell it. "You know, I think I thought it right then—that girl is going to be a scientist."

"You sure this isn't one of those calls, Daddy? You don't have, like, a brain tumor or anything?"

"Positive, Kats. Your mother's at home. Give her a call so she can tell you herself."

"Nah. What do they say on that show? *Fuggetaboutit.* A girl can talk to her dad about peas if she wants to."

"And vice versa." While we'd talked, evening had come on, the sky above and all around purpling with the day's last light. "You get back to your studying, okay? We'll see you in a month."

"You too. And Daddy? Please don't forget this time."

"Forget?"

Another sigh, and too late I remembered. "Daddy, the *tickets.* God, you're *hopeless.* Don't make me go over your head and call Mom."

"Roger wilco," I said. "Two airline tickets for one hopeless Dad."

It is not necessarily the best thing in the world to be friends with a man like Harry Wainwright. There's his money, for starters, which is so much more than the kind of money most people have that there's simply no comparison—a pile so enormous it's like a force of nature, and not a little dangerous to be near, like a mountain that could fall on you at any minute. In a business like mine, you deal with wealthy people constantly—odd, in a way, because fishing isn't what you would call a naturally upscale activity, what with all the blood and bad smells—and one thing you learn is that people with serious money didn't get that way by always being nice. Someone threatens to sue me just about every year; usually it's all just bluster, some trivial complaint that boils down to I-didn't-have-enough-fun, and I tell myself it's a small price to pay for a life that's arguably better than anybody else's. Even so, a man like Harry Wainwright is one to take seriously; right or wrong, he can do you some major damage. I don't mean they'd find you in the trunk of your car somewhere in the eelgrass (though I have dealt with some guys like that—my friend from Providence being exhibit A, I suppose). What I mean is a man like Harry Wainwright can buy whatever he wishes, and if he wanted to buy me, he had the dough to make this happen.

I flew to New York on the last Wednesday in April, just me and the pilot and, thanks to Hal, an industrial-size box of individually wrapped packages of honey peanuts. Attached was a note: "Enjoy the flight; best taken with Scotch." I didn't know how many of them I had to eat to look thankful, so I worked my way through two packets with the help of a glass of thirty-year-old single malt from the plane's well-stocked bar, then flushed a bunch more down the toilet before we landed—not at one of the big New York airports but a smaller field in New Jersey. Hal had sent a limo—another first for me, though after the Learjet, the limo felt like nothing at all—and I put on my necktie as we crossed the Lincoln Tunnel into Manhattan and headed downtown.

In all the years I had known Harry Wainwright, I had never once set foot into anything you might call his world. I'd been to New York, of course, though not for years—my parents had brought me for some kind of hospitality trade show—and my memory of the city was a child's: feeling small and scared on the busy streets, the carnival thrill of a taxi ride, the fussy stiffness of wearing my best clothes and the raw wonderment of watching my lunch, a peanut butter sandwich, pop out of a machine at an Automat in Times Square. Harry's offices were located on Wall Street, fourteen floors of a gleaming tower overlooking Battery Park and, if you craned your neck just so, the New York Stock Exchange. The lobby was a citadel of polished granite and marble; it was close to lunchtime, and men and women with nice haircuts and good suits, many of them with a cell phone pasted to an ear, were hurrying to and fro. I felt a little embarrassed by my rumpled necktie and threadbare blazer, like a kid dressed for his first job interview; the tie, the only one I owned, was twenty years old, an anonymously inde-structible navy blue knit I kept around for weddings and funerals.

At the security desk I was given a visitor's pass and directed to the express elevator, which I rode up to the fortieth floor. The doors slid open, revealing a second lobby of polished stone, and on the far wall, the words H P WAINWRIGHT HOLDINGS, INC. Below this was a wide counter where the receptionist sat, a young black woman with corn-rows and a telephone headset. One minute you're in sunny Florida, poling the flats for bonefish and thinking about a cold beer with your name on it waiting back in the fridge; the next thing you know some body sends a plane and there you are, landing on Mars.

The receptionist took my name and directed me to take a seat, but before I had a chance to, the wall beside the receptionist's desk opened—a door I hadn't noticed, that no one was supposed to notice, I figured—and Hal stepped out, not in a suit as I had expected but in a black T-shirt and jeans and cowboy boots that probably weren't made of ordinary cowhide but something more exotic—elk, or maybe os-trich. I had to remind myself that this was the same Hal I had known since we were kids; Hal's just eight years younger than me, and had been coming to the camp with his dad off and on for years.

"Joe, welcome. Glad you could make it." He offered me his hand to shake. "The flight okay?"

"A little bumpy at the end. Your pilots always drink like that?"

"Only when their paychecks don't clear." He glanced over my shoulder and furrowed his brow. "Okay, where's that lawyer we talked about you having? We did discuss this, didn't we?"

"We did. I decided against it."

Hal shook his head disapprovingly. We were going through the mo-tions, of course, but it had to be done. "Joe, Joe. You Mainers can be so goddamned stubborn. Take my advice on this, will you please? Let me get somebody on the phone for you. I can have them over here for you in a jiff."

"Seriously, Hal," I said. "I don't want one."

"Sally is nobody you want to tangle with without counsel."

"You're only saying that because she's your wife. As far as I can tell she likes me fine."

Hal sighed. "Well, it's your funeral. You might as well come on back. We're all ready for you."

"Harry too?"

"It'll be just me and Sally, I'm afraid. It hasn't been a good week for him. He's pretty much holed up in Bedford these days, Joe."

He led me into a maze of offices and cubicles, all clean and white and nondescript, then up a second elevator and down another long hallway to his office, where his assistant was waiting.

"Zoe, this is Mr. Crosby." He turned briskly to me. "Joe, you need anything, this is the person to ask. She's the real brains of the outfit."

Zoe rose to greet me, and I was hit by a bolt of recognition—we had talked dozens of times on the phone, when she had called to make reservations, or else just to say "Please hold for Mr. Wainwright," meaning Hal. I had made a picture in my mind of an older woman with bifocals, which was, of course, completely incorrect: the woman whose hand I shook was no older than thirty-five, with a mane of black hair and a miniskirt figure. At least I had been right about the glasses, though hers were shaped like eggs and made of a material that was either gold or silver, depending on which way she turned her head under the fluorescent lights.

"He's being nice," she said. "I don't know a thing. Except where the bodies are buried. Can I get you coffee or water, Mr. Crosby?"

Hal frowned. "You still do that?"

"Only for people I like. How about it, Mr. Crosby?"

"It's Joe, please. And no, thank you."

"That must be some place you have up there in Maine. Hal and Sally just rave about it."

I shrugged. "I'm a lucky man."

"Luckier than you may know," Hal said. He poked a thumb across the hall. "Okay, enough love. Let's get this thing rolling. We're actually set up in the conference room."

"The conference room," I said. I looked at Zoe. "Sounds pretty fancy."

"Just how we do things around here," Hal said. "Haven't you figured it out yet, Joe? We're trying to impress you."

Sally was waiting for us, wearing a lawyerish blue suit and seated on the far side of a long table. A handshake seemed wrong, so I gave her a hug and stepped back to look at her. Hal was a good-looking fellow by any estimation, but his marriage was a fair fight: even dressed for court, Sally was about the prettiest woman who crossed my path with any regularity.

"Looks like motherhood suits you, Sally. How about a picture?"

She smiled at my request. "Well, as it so happens . . ."

Out came her wallet, and the snapshot everyone has: a fat, happy baby, so plump she had creases in the middle of her forearms. They'd put one of those frilly little headbands on her so people would know she was a girl, a nervous touch I liked.

"She's just beautiful," I said. "Good for you."

Sally took the photo from me and returned it to her wallet. "That's already way out of date. She's walking now, gets into everything. Hal spent the weekend baby-proofing the apartment."

"You did that, Hal?"

He grinned self-consciously, though I could tell he was proud of himself. "Bet you didn't know I was so handy."

"Come up this August, there's plenty of work for you if you want it."

"Don't laugh, Joe," Hal said. "I just might take you up on that."

We took our places, Hal and Sally on one side of the wide table, myself on the other. The room was all business—just the table, a huge gleaming slab of a thing, and behind Hal, a second, smaller table with a computer and a telephone. On the table between us sat a water pitcher and glasses, and a single manila folder, which Hal opened.

"Okay, the first thing to say here, for the record, is that Sally is present in her capacity as my father's personal attorney. The offer my father wants to make to you is a personal one, not one connected to the company. All right with that?"

I nodded. "Sure. Seems clear."

"Just so long as it's understood." Hal poured himself a glass of water. "Anyway, I might as well cut straight to it. Here's the deal. My father wants to make an offer for the camp, Joe. He wants to buy it, I mean. And he wants to do it right away, or as soon as possible."

This was, of course, exactly what I'd figured on. The plane, the peanuts, the limo ride: a hundred other things besides, and at the end of the day, a man who scouts the water for his living knows things in his gut, as I'd known this.

"What's he offering?"

Hal raised an eyebrow. "Don't look so surprised, Joe."

"I'm not. It's all right."

He sipped the water. "What's all right?"

"All right, I'm listening." I nodded at Hal and Sally in turn. "If the offer's a good one, we can talk about it."

Hal took out the papers and slid them across the desk. "The figure is more than generous, I think. Anyway," he said, and wagged a finger, "it's right there."

I looked the agreement over. Lock, stock, and barrel, Harry Wainwright was offering me $2.3 million for the camp—the buildings, the land, the right-of-way along the river, the leases on the parcels across the lake, everything right down to the leaky canoes and the kitchen pots and pans. In the days before I'd left Big Pine, I'd done a few computations. It was a lot of land, but not especially valuable, and as a business, the camp had never turned more than the thinnest profit. Harry's figure was, as best as I could tell, about twice what it was worth, maybe a little more.

"I'll be honest with you, Joe," Hal was saying. "I'm not in love with this, as a business deal. But I think everybody here knows that's not what this is."

"Jeez, Hal." I flipped back through the agreement, if only to keep my eyes and hands occupied, skimming past pages of information I should have cared about or at least read. "Two million bucks is a lot of money. For that kind of bread, I would have been happy to fly coach."

Hal nodded smartly; the chummy banter was over for the moment. "That's the general idea, Joe. My father wants to get this thing done. What do you think?"

And I paused to wonder: what *did* I think? Every man has his price, and Harry had found mine—more than found it, actually, as a million five would have produced in me more or less the same set of emotions: a heady rush of pure greed, followed by the unsettling awareness that all the problems of my life had been solved in one painless instant. But that, of course, was just the problem. Somebody offers you something you suddenly can't live without, but five minutes ago never knew you needed—well, there's a catch somewhere, the most obvious being that what feels like luck is actually somebody else's wand being waved over your life.

"Just one question, Hal. What does he want to do with it?"

"The camp?" Hal leaned back in his chair. "Keep it in the family, I suppose. There's not much else he *could* do with it. That's really his to decide, Joe."

"No." I shook my head. "I have to know this."

Hal shot a look at Sally, who nodded a lawyerish nod, then turned his eyes back toward me. "He's rewriting his will, taking this into account. That's as far as I can go. And don't ask Sally, because she can't tell you. You've heard of a little thing called attorney-client privilege? She can't even tell *me*."

"You said yourself this wasn't just a business deal."

Hal sighed. "Look, here's the bottom line. He wants to be *helpful,* Joe. Forgive me, but we did a little digging, and we know your situation. You've borrowed pretty heavily in the last few years—"

"College," I interrupted. "For Kate."

"Fair enough. But there's also the place in Florida, and the new boats. You're stretched pretty thin. I know you want to make a go of it down there, and you should. You're entitled. You and Lucy are entitled. With the right seed money, the two of you could really set yourselves up nicely. I know you've made some inquiries about selling one of your leases back to Maine Paper. That's exactly the kind of thing that Harry wants to avoid."

I felt my face grow warm. "Is this the part where you turn on the salesman's charm, Hal? Because where I come from, talking about another man's debts is not a way to make friends. And if you really want to know, they approached *me*. They have for years. I can set my fucking—excuse me, Sally—my fucking watch by it. The answer is always no."

"But how long can it stay no?" Hal took a deep breath and rubbed his eyes. "Look, Joe, I'm not going to try to tell you how to run your business. You're absolutely right, and I apologize. It's been a hell of a week, a hell of a month, really. You don't know the half of it. So if I've spoken too bluntly, I'm sorry. But I also won't insult your intelligence. We've known each other too long. This is a good deal. Hell, it's a *great* deal. We both know that. You're never going to find another buyer with this kind of dough to spend. And with Harry, you don't have to watch the thing broken up and sold back to the loggers. That's the real point, Joe. You can have my word on it, if you like."

I looked at Sally, who so far had said nothing. She was sitting with her hands folded on the table, her face unreadable as the sphinx. "Sally? What do you think of all this?"

She gave a smile I read as cautious. "It's your decision, Joe. I can't tell you what to do."

"You look a little worn-out, Sally. That little girl of yours letting you get any sleep?"

"Not much." She laughed wearily. "But I'm sure you remember what it's like."

"Do I ever. You want real ulcers, wait till she's off at college. You know what's back in style for kids these days? Tattoos. Half of Kate's friends look like merchant seamen, or else gypsies, with all the piercings. Though it'll be something else by the time yours reaches that point."

"I'm sure Kate's more sensible than that."

"Sure," I said. "Sensible. Probably a lot more sensible than her dad." I paused a moment to listen to those words: "her dad." *Roger wilco. Two-million-three for one hopeless Dad.*

"Listen, Joe," Hal was saying, "nobody wants to pressure you. Think about it. Take all this with you, and for god's sake show it to a lawyer. Talk to Lucy, talk to Kate. We've booked a room for you at the St. Regis. Stay as long as you like. See the Empire State Building, take in a show, whatever. It's all on us. The plane can take you back whenever you're ready."

"Lucy told me I should see *Cats*."

Hal grinned encouragingly. "That's the spirit. Sure, see *Cats*. Hang on a second." He swiveled in his chair and picked up the phone. "Zoe? Can we get a ticket for *Cats* for Mr. Crosby for"—he looked at me and raised an eyebrow—"tonight's performance? A good seat, orchestra, somewhere in the middle. No, just have them hold it at the theater." He hung up the phone like a man who was used to getting things done easily. "Alakazoo," he said, and rubbed his hands together. "All set."

"Thanks, Hal. That's nice of you."

He rose from his chair to signal that the meeting was over. "Well, they say you have to see it once. You want anything else while you're in town, you give a ring. I can even get you tickets for the Knicks."

I shook his hand and gave Sally a final hug. "Give our best to Lucy, won't you, Joe?" she said. "And Kate too."

"Sure thing."

"Don't forget these," Hal said, and handed the papers to me. "I mean it, Joe. Have somebody look over that with you. Harry wants everybody to be happy." He rapped his knuckles on the table—mahogany, I guessed, from the deep, clean sound of it. He was probably just as relieved as I was to leave things as they stood. "So, the lake ice out yet?"

I was holding the papers a little awkwardly; they didn't seem like the kind of thing a person should fold and shove into a pocket, and I hadn't thought to bring a briefcase. I settled for putting them back in the manila folder and tucking it under my arm. "It should be. Always happens about this time. I haven't talked to Jordan in a couple of weeks, though."

"Don't know how he stands it up there, all by himself. Young guy like that. I'd go nuts."

"He says he gets a lot of reading done."

"I'll bet he does. If you speak to him, tell him my dad hopes maybe to get up there for some fishing. I doubt it'll happen, but there's nothing he'd like more. Talks about it all the time."

Sally left us, and Hal led me to the elevator, where he shook my hand again. "We really appreciate you coming like this, Joe."

"I was glad to do it."

"Well, just so you know." The elevator bell sounded; the doors slid open on an empty car. "One last thing, Joe."

I had seen this coming too. Where was Hal in all of this? Now that Sally was gone, I was pretty certain I would hear it.

"I'm listening."

He looked quickly over his shoulder to make sure we were alone. "I didn't want to say anything in front of Sally, because she's sort of a fan. But you might want to reconsider *Cats*."

In the years before my mother died, before my father's spirit hardened like a skin of ice and he became the sort of man that people respect without actually getting along with, he liked to tell the story of how he had come to the camp. This took place right after the war, *his* war, a war in which he gave half his face and one emerald-green eye to the Thousand Year Reich on the point of a German sniper's bullet, and though you'd think that such an experience might be a lifetime's singular event, the one that splits it into this "before" and that "after," such was not the case with my father. (That came later, when my mother died of ovarian cancer, three months before her thirty-eighth birthday.) If anything, that sniper did my father a favor; I have no doubt that had he missed, I would have grown up the son of a Boston whiteshoe lawyer who would have spent his years on earth, as many people do, wondering who he was truly supposed to be.

They came to the camp on a winter day in '47, an event I don't remember though I am told I was there, a baby seven months old. Though in later years my father's injury softened—as he aged, the fleshiness that came into his face padded his scars and fractured jawline so that his face appeared not so much collapsed as something merely lived-in—in those first years it was a stark and surprising thing to look at, the sort of face that quiets a room and parents shush their children over, and I think he took my mother and moved up to Maine simply to get away from people. My father had been a handsome man, not movie-star handsome but good-looking in an earnest way that women liked and men took to, and although he was not vain about his appearance, it would have been a hard thing for him to see in people's eyes not the pleasant curiosity he was accustomed to but pity or even fear. More than this, though, a face like my father's is a story—a public story—and I believe he tired of telling it. As long as he wore the face of war he was somebody both smaller and larger than who he imagined himself to be: not Joe Crosby, but Joe Crosby, War Hero. It took me years to understand the importance of this fact, but my father's injury was unusual in that it was nothing he himself could see; if he had lost a leg or arm or taken a bullet to the spine, as happened to many men he knew, the situation might have felt different to him. His was an injury he did not see but saw *out of,* and the fact that the world he saw was for the most part the same place it had always been, save for the pitying looks it gave him in return, made him wish for a life in which his was the only gaze. He spent the better part of two years in the hospital; when he was finally discharged, in March of '46, he returned to law, but only halfheartedly. A few years earlier, an uncle had left him a small inheritance; my father had set this aside, planning to use it to buy his partnership when the time came, but when he heard that the camp had come up for sale—the previous owners had all but abandoned the place and were about to lose it to the county for unpaid taxes—he couldn't write the check fast enough.

He had visited the camp in the late thirties, a Harvard grad slumming away the summer months washing dishes and flirting with the waitresses before entering law school, and at a party in Blue Hill he met my mother; though he never said as much, I am certain that these two events merged in his mind, so that the camp and my mother were, in a way, one and the same, and the chance to buy it must have seemed like the hand of destiny at work. The story he told me was a simple one, perhaps a little strange: all he said was that the first morning after they'd arrived, he climbed to the roof of the lodge and looked at the lake, and knew that he had found his life. I was a child when he told me this, so his words made no sense. Finding your life. How could you find something that was all around you, something that had never been lost to begin with? He might have said he had found the sun at midday and the moon at night. And the thought, too, of my father standing on the roof for the sheer hell of it—a place he warned me never to go, as I would surely fall and break my fool neck—excited and perplexed me. Even back then, in the years before my mother died, my father was a measured man. He distrusted displays of emotion, was not a big talker, and conducted his domestic affairs with the same level-headed punctuality that he used to run his business. He was not an unfeeling man: he had friends, liked a joke, and loved my mother deeply. But as far as I could see, he was hardly the sort to climb a roof and feel some cosmic rightness pouring through him. That was my generation, not his, and though I would eventually spend many hours on the roof myself, I could never reproduce the feeling. How could this be the same man?

I was eight years old when my mother got sick, and though it took her over a year to die, I remember very little of this period. For many years my parents had tried to have another child—I was miles away from any potential playmates, and to let me go through life without the company of a brother or sister seemed simply cruel. But after a series of miscarriages they abandoned the idea. Whether or not this failure was related to the cancer that finally took her life is anybody's guess; the timing tells me it probably was. When my father finally spoke of this, in the last months of his life, he claimed not to remember how many miscarriages she'd had—three or four, he said, though who really knew?—but the last was memorable enough, bloody and awful. My mother was almost six months pregnant when it happened, a sudden hemorrhage that began as she was hanging laundry on the line for the autumn sun to dry, and by the time she got back to the house, a distance of a hundred feet, her skirt and apron were soaked with blood. I was off playing in the woods somewhere, so I saw nothing of what happened next. Before my father could even put a call in to the hospital, a solid hour away in Farmington, my mother began to deliver, right there in the kitchen: a two-pound baby boy who had, in all likelihood, died sometime the day before, when the placenta had separated from the uterine wall. My father had seen enough in the war to know, or at least guess, what to do next: he tied off the cord with twine, and did his best to staunch the bleeding, though it was coming from inside, at the site of the abruption, far beyond his reach. Then he wrapped my baby brother in a towel, called the nearest neighbor, the Rawlings—a couple who lived nine miles away—to tell them to track me down, and drove my mother to the hospital in the truck.

By the time he got there my mother had lost so much blood that it appeared very likely she would die, that it would be a day of two deaths and not just one. This didn't happen, but it is also true that she never fully recovered. She came home from the hospital three weeks later, pale and weak, a woman I hardly recognized. I had been staying at the Rawlings', eating the huge batches of oatmeal cookies that Mrs. Rawling seemed to pull from the oven by the hour and generally feeling left out, because nobody had told me anything. I had even gotten it into my head that she would be bringing home the baby brother or sister I had been promised. In my heart it was a brother, and not even a baby but a boy my own age, so innocent was I of the facts of life. But all hope evaporated at the sight of my father helping my mother from the truck and into our house. There would be no baby, not then, not ever. She could hardly walk, and her skin was so colorless it seemed transparent, as I believed a ghost might look. She hugged me weakly and went up to bed, and all through the winter this weakness did not abate but seemed to widen around her like rings, so that the household fell into a kind of trance, as if we were all lost in a forest, though not together. She could not bring herself to read her novels or play the piano or do any of the things she loved, and when, in August, she began to cough and then to bleed again, this seemed not so much a new development as a continuation of the same decline.

She died the next January, in my parents' bedroom, on an afternoon of brilliant sunshine and breathtaking cold—a day that I imagine was not all that different from the day eight years earlier when my father had climbed the roof of the lodge and found his life. I had been sent to the Rawlings' for the afternoon—by this time I spent so much time at their house that I had a bedroom of my own—and when my father came to fetch me at five o'clock, the appointed hour, and instead of simply honking the horn of the truck from the Rawlings' driveway as he always did, he came into the kitchen and sat at the old oak table and removed his hat and gloves without saying a word, the cold of the outside air clinging to his coat like the smell of cigarettes that followed him everywhere, I knew what had happened without exactly knowing it—I felt it in my bones. I was working on a model kit, a B-17 Flying Fortress. I showed it to him, the landing gear that dropped from the plane's belly to snap into place, the swiveling gun turrets and ailerons, the opening bomb-bay doors. I had taken up the toys of war initially to please him, thinking it was something the two of us might share. But in the year of my mother's illness, I had found myself alone with this interest, just as I had found myself alone with everything else.

My father examined the plane indifferently, saying nothing, then returned it to its place on the table. I realized then that Mrs. Rawling had stepped from the room; she had left us alone.

"Something has happened, Joey."

I had taken out a tiny brush and begun to stroke paint on the plane's fuselage.

"Joey, are you listening to me?"

"I want to fight in a war," I said, still painting.

He gave a startled laugh. "Believe me, you don't. That's the last thing you want."

"You did."

"That's how I know. Joey, put that goddamn thing down, *please*."

I began to, or thought I had, but before I could do this he grabbed the plane from my hand and slammed it onto the newspaper so hard that the wheels snapped off and shot in opposite directions across the kitchen.

"You broke it!"

"Joey, forget the plane. Sweet Jesus Christ. It's a fucking toy."

I had never heard him talk this way—not just the words themselves, but the measured anger of their delivery, like the sound of an axe blade grinding on a stone. I thought he might actually hit me, something else he had never done before.

"I have something to tell you. Your mother has died. Do you understand what this means? She was very sick, and she has passed away."

"You broke my plane, you asshole!"

And then he did hit me, once, with the back of his hand. He was a strong man, and if he had allowed his anger to do as it liked, he probably would have broken my nose. But even as his hand caught me across the cheek—a solid snap that unscrewed my eyes and sent me tumbling backward from my chair—I felt beneath this blow not only his anger but also his restraint, a force even more terrifying, for it was something he commanded. *This is exactly the kind of blow you deserve,* it said.

"Get up," he said.

I lifted my face to see Mrs. Rawling in the kitchen doorway. The funny thing is, I always thought of her as older—an old woman. But when I think about her now, she probably wasn't even forty. Her husband worked as a lineman for the telephone company, a cheerful, rail-thin man who always wore suspenders and liked to do magic tricks with quarters and napkins, and the fact that they had no children of their own—an anomalous condition I have never considered until this moment—probably made my visits as bittersweet as hearing a song from the past and knowing every note without being able to recall its name. I detected in their generosity to me a love that was equal parts sadness, and one time, when I was sleeping at their house and had come down with a fever, I awakened in the middle of the night to find the two of them sitting by my bed, fast asleep.

"What's going on in here?" Sarah Rawling's eyes were white saucers of alarm. She looked at me where I lay on the floor, then at my father, still sitting at the kitchen table with my airplane model spread out on the newspaper. "Joe, have you been drinking?"

"He's fine, Sarah. You can see that. Leave the boy be."

She came to where I was sitting, holding my cheek, and knelt to face me. I was too astonished even to cry. "Joey, did your father strike you?"

"I'll decide what's right for him, Sarah. Go on now, son. Get up."

I somehow made it to my feet. I wanted at that moment only to throw myself into Sarah Rawling's arms, to have her be my mother from that day forward. But I was too ashamed even to look at her and turned my face away.

My father stood and cleared his throat. "Your mother has died today, Joey. You'll need to be a man from now on. That means that if you speak to me as you just did, you'll get what's coming to you. I'm sorry to say that, but it's so. Now get your coat."

I never set foot in the Rawlings' house again, and I got the war I wanted. From that day forward my father and I lived a new kind of life, one in which the two of us, like opposing armies locked in a bitter struggle the cause of which neither one remembers, lobbed listless shells at one another from distant bunkers. I went to school and played with my friends and did my chores around the lodge, but in my heart I might have been a thousand miles away, so little did I care about any of it. I became a good guide—as good as he was, even better—and for that I won a measure of my father's respect. But it wasn't respect I wanted. I wanted, like him, to find my life.

This is exactly what happened, of course, and that is the part of the story in which Harry Wainwright played his part, and why I now found myself in New York, ready to sign over my worldly goods to him, albeit for more money than most people see in a lifetime. Hal was right: I should have skipped *Cats*. I sat through the first act, bored and baffled—it reminded me of some kiddie show on TV, the sort of thing dreamed up by well-meaning adults who've spent no time around actual children—though a couple of the songs weren't so bad, and it wasn't on the whole unpleasant to sit in a darkened theater for a couple of hours without one serious thought in my head, especially given the alternative, which was lying around my hotel room, getting fat on snacks from the minibar and fidgeting with the gold-plated bath fixtures. I'd decided to hang around New York a day or two; with two million bucks on the line, the last thing I wanted was to appear ungrateful. But I was also hoping that something would come along to tell me what to do next.

At intermission I left the theater and walked eight blocks down-town, into Times Square. This was back before the big cleanup, when you couldn't take three steps in Manhattan without tripping over some poor soul sleeping on a greasy blanket and every other business was a peep show or adult "emporium" with some junior lieutenant from the porno brigade sitting on a stool outside to hustle in the crowds—a pretty depressing sight for any dad, and one that made me all the hap-pier to pop for the twenty-two thousand bucks a year it cost to send Kate to a college that boasted about its "high acreage-to-student ratio" and kept her about as sheltered as a pet rabbit. My plan was to see where the New Year's ball dropped; Lucy and I, and Kate when she was old enough, always stayed up to watch this on our grainy black-and-white with aluminum foil crimped to the antenna, a bottle of cold duck for the grown-ups and a glass of ginger ale for Kate. But it was April, and I quickly figured out that I was looking for a landmark that didn't exist but for one day a year. By then it had started to rain; I hailed a cab, told the driver "St. Regis, please"—I had already figured out I didn't need to give the address—and returned to the hotel.

The desk clerk gave me my messages, one from Lucy, one from Hal. I decided these could keep until morning and headed off to the bar for a nightcap, thinking this might clear my head of the show tunes that had seemed cheerfully catchy before but were now merely annoy-ing. As he set me up with peanuts and a cocktail napkin, the bartender asked me if I wanted a Bloody Mary; I gathered from a little placard on the bar that it had been invented there. I took a Dewar's and water in-stead, and spun on my stool in time to see a woman I recognized as Hal's assistant, Zoe, enter the room.

She caught my eye, gave a little wave, and came over to where I was sitting. "Mr. Crosby." She put down her briefcase to offer her hand. Her hair and glasses were damp from the rain.

"It's Joe, remember? Just Joe."

What I was thinking was what anyone would be thinking: no ac-cident, interesting development, good-looking woman, disoriented married man, many miles from home. But this seemed like something from a story I wouldn't even like to read, and the desk clerk's note to call Lucy was, after all, still in my pocket.

"They're pushing the Bloody Marys."

"At this hour?"

"Famous for them, looks like."

She shook a bit of rain from her hair and caught the bartender's eye. "A Jack Daniel's and water, please."

The bartender brought her drink over, and she gave it a couple of quick stirs. "Hal thought I'd find you here. His bet was that you'd make it as far as intermission."

"Does Hal ever get tired of being right?"

She laughed, a little uneasily I thought, tipping her face to turn the frames of her eyeglasses from gold to silver and back again. "That's the one thing our boy Hal will never get tired of."

"Sounds like a story."

"Oh, it is, just not a very interesting one." She jostled the ice in her drink and sipped. "Hal and I used to . . . well, I guess the phrase would be 'go together.' Long before he ever met Sally, who's a totally great gal, incidentally, a good friend, and thinks the world of you."

"That's nice to hear."

She laughed again. "Which part?"

"About you and Sally." My mind caught on something, an idea I hadn't even realized I was having. "You know, in the office today, looking at you and Hal, I sort of thought for a second there—"

"And you wouldn't be the first to think it. But no. All over and done, everybody apprised of the facts." She brought her briefcase up from the floor and removed a plain white envelope, fat with folded paper. "A present from Hal."

I took it from her. On the outside was my name, written in a hand I knew to be Hal's. "Do I open it here?"

"Hal would prefer that you did not. He also told me to tell you that when you're done looking it over, please throw it away."

I tucked it in my jacket pocket. *Daddy, you don't do top secret. Top secret is not your thing.* I said, "If that's how Hal wants it."

"His other advice to me was to get you talking. Those were his exact words, in fact. Get him talking, see what's on his mind."

"I thought Hal was apprised of the facts."

"Apparently not in this case." She shrugged. "I heard what happened today. And personally, I'm glad. You shouldn't make it easy for them."

"I really was ready to sell. I kind of knew that's what they wanted. There wasn't really anything else they *could* want."

I lifted my eyes to the painting over the bar. I hadn't paid it any mind before, but I saw now that it was something quite special: an original Maxfield Parrish, or so the little plaque read, entitled *Old King Cole*. The painting was actually a mural, practically as broad as the bar itself, and done in several panels: Old King Cole on his throne, looking not merry at all but generally bored by life and half in the bag to boot, three men holding violins and doing a sort of jig at his feet. Three men, I thought: three men to serve the king. Roger wilco.

"I don't know why I didn't." I looked back at Zoe. "They're offering me a lot of money. Far more than it's worth, really, though I probably shouldn't say that to you."

"What it's worth is what they'll pay, Joe. And I'm thinking, maybe it's worth a little more to you than that?"

And that, in the end, was the real question; though, strangely, I had yet to put it that way to myself. Was it worth $2.3 million to me, yes or no?

Zoe drained the last of her bourbon and rose to go. "One thing I will tell you, Joe. Hal wants to put this thing together. That means you can do whatever you want. I'm telling you because I like you, and most people seem to think a guy like Hal holds all the cards. In this case, he doesn't. The cards are yours." She looked up at the mural then; a glimmer of recognition crossed her face. "Oh, I get it. Old King Cole. Like the rhyme." She shook her head. "Hal's a regular laugh riot."

"Fiddlers three," I said. "Okay. One and two—that's me and Hal. The king's obvious. What I can't figure out is, who's the third fiddler?"

Smiling, she moved her face toward mine. For a moment I actually thought I was about to be kissed, and was deciding what to do about that—as if the cards were mine. But then she stopped—I could have sworn she was about to wink—and tipped her head at my breast pocket.

"Read that and you'll know."

I kept my bargain with myself and let another twenty-four hours go by before looking at the papers Hal had sent me. You can't make your living as a fishing guide without the patience to let things unfold in due course, and I passed the day as a tourist: window-shopping on Fifth Avenue, taking in the ceiling at Grand Central, riding the subway down to the bottom of the island to see the Statue of Liberty. It was nice to think of Hal's envelope, sitting on the Louis XIV writing desk in my overpriced room at the St. Regis, waiting for me. I returned to the hotel for dinner, ate a steak at the bar under King Cole's bleary gaze, and killed a couple of hours shooting the breeze with a pair of agribusiness executives in from Minneapolis for a trade show (their company manufactured a little gizmo that, from what I could tell, made it possible to control a tractor from outer space), rode the elevator to my room, showered and put on my pajamas, then lay on the big bed before finally opening the envelope. The document it contained was a photocopied addendum to Harry's will, marked "draft," with a little yellow Post-it note affixed: *You never saw this.* I read what it had to say, called Lucy to tell her what I had learned and what I thought our options were, then ripped the thing into pieces and flushed them down the toilet.

In the morning I awoke early, fisherman's hours, and took a walk through Central Park just as the sun was punching through the skyline. I had the place practically to myself for the first half hour, but soon the paths filled up with people: joggers wearing headphones and dog-walkers with their dutiful pooper-scoopers, Rollerbladers who whizzed past me in a burst of musty air, a few nannies pushing strollers and talking together in Spanish. I walked around the reservoir and remembered my life, the days when my mother died and Kate was born and all the rest, and by the time I returned to the St. Regis, a little after nine o'clock, I knew what I would do. I took coffee and a sweet roll from a buffet in the bar and returned to my room to phone Hal.

"Two million five," I said.

"Can you hang on a second, Joe? I have to go outside and fire Zoe." A moment of silence followed, while he put the phone down and did whatever a man like Hal does when he's about to drop a lot of money on what, he knew, was a sentimental whim, and not even his own.

"Okay, my friend. Two point five it is. And if you ever tell anyone what a pushover I am, I will have you *vaporized*. Believe me. I know people who know people. Are we done?"

"Mostly. Draw up the revised agreement but date it for September, after we close down for the season. I'll sell him the camp, but I won't be his employee. It's nothing personal, I've just never worked for anyone and I don't want to start now."

I heard Hal sigh. "Of course it's personal, Joe. It's all *personal*. And September is too late, for reasons that are so obvious I'll assume you're bluffing. How's this: Mid-July, but we'll work something into the paperwork that leaves you in charge for the time being. Management to transfer to his estate at the time of his death, something like that. Sally can figure out the details. Will that satisfy you?"

I understood that it would have to. "All right. That's good of you."

For a moment neither of us spoke.

"Joe, it's not everybody who gets to grant a dying man's last wish. I don't want to get too deep here, but that's what you're doing, and it matters. To all of us. I really mean that."

"I know you do." The receiver was heavy in my hand, and I realized if I stayed on the phone another second, I would probably change my mind. "Just send the plane, will you, Hal? I want to go home."

Harry

When I was diagnosed with what I have come to call "the cancer," and I told my new wife, Frances, that I would surely die
of it, she said something that would surprise anyone but me. She told
me the doctors were wrong.

"You're not going to die of cancer, Harry," she said, and took me
tenderly by the hand, "because, my sweet darling, I'm going to fuck
you to death."

It is true that men of my age (seventy going on Methuselah), mari-
tal status (widowed since the Nixon years), and general station in life
(rich as greedy Midas) have a number of options before them, and
need not spend a single lonely hour if loneliness does not suit them.
There are more than enough perfume-counter clerks, Croatian hand
models, and former-ski-instructors-turned-massage-therapists to go
around, and I have seen more than a few fellow travelers take this
happy road.

But my Frances is no trophy wife. She is, to begin with, fifty-two
years old: young for me, but not by the standards of the role. Nor is she
what might be called attractive, or even, euphemistically, "handsome";
my Frances is a muscular girl, solid and big-boned with a wide face and
strong jaw best suited for public oratory or, perhaps, the boxing ring.
Her hair, which she does not dye, is gray as dishwater; her hands and
feet are large. She is, in sum, constructed more or less as a suburban office building is constructed, low-slung and unobtrusive, built to take
the wind and rain and sun and encourage useful work, her whole physical person communicating nothing more or less than a state of pure

Midwestern practicality. Think: Kansas City. Think: Detroit. Think: Cleveland (where she's from). If God were a real estate developer from Ohio, Eve would have looked exactly like my Frances.

And yet beneath this cunning camouflage of plainness lurks an altogether different sort of woman, a sensual companion of such responsiveness and enthusiasm that she can be likened only to the most celebrated generosities of nature. She says the things she likes to say, grinds her hips into mine with joyful abandon, understands the virtue of interesting underclothes and has never disappointed me in this department; once, during my first stay at the hospital, she arrived at my bedside wearing nothing but a trench coat, a merry-widow, and a pair of shoes I won't describe but will leave to your imagination, as they reside in mine. In the darkness of our room or even the sour, desexualized precincts of the hospital, she moves her sturdy body back and forth above me in a sweetly undulating motion that recalls the great parabolas—the moon and tides and all the ships at sea—and when at last she achieves her final transport, she calls out my name and buries her face and breath in my withered old neck, taking me with her.

I'm no fool. It can't be such a lark to fuck an old man, especially a dying old man. She's had three husbands before me, including, I kid you not, a professional deep-sea diver and the man who invented industrial bubble wrap, and who could blame her if, behind her closed eyes, she is actually reliving some carnal adventure from her past? Nor is it fair to say that we love each other, precisely. Of all the concessions one must make to age, I have discovered this is actually the easiest to face, because its theme is not scarcity but abundance: we have simply loved too many others—spouses, lovers, children, dogs, and all the golden days and hours in our lives—to add one more to the pile. Love there is between us, but it's an impersonal sort of love, more like a recollection of love than the thing itself, and what we have to offer one another is the chance to sip together from the cup of memory.

And where do my own thoughts go? To what precinct of remembered love does my mind take me?

Before my Frances there was my Meredith: the mother of my sons, one living, one not. I loved her enough to help her die, when her affliction, far crueler than my own, had stolen all but breath and speech from her body. This I have come to understand as lovemaking of another kind, a final journey one takes together, as much a part of the weave of human life as the feel of damp linens and paling light on an afternoon when you have conceived a child. And though this is the one thing I know that maybe not everyone else does, I have never told the story.

It begins with a cigarette. A Lucky Strike, filterless, the kind that could burn all the way down to the end. What everyone smoked in those hard-smoking days—as harmless, we thought, as a piece of candy. Though it was not the cigarette that caused anything.

Summer, 1951: We had been out for the evening with friends; Sam was six months old, Hal was not yet born. We were living in Philadelphia, a pair of newlyweds in our first house, an attached brick rowhome on a street of identical brick rowhomes where all day long women and children flowed in and out of one another's houses in a constant, unyielding river: toys and bikes and strollers all over the sidewalks, always in the background the abundant sounds of family life, everyone young and getting started at last. I was working then for wages, a junior supervisor in a factory that made electric switch-gears. It didn't matter what it was: aspirin, hubcaps, tomato soup. It could have been anything. I was little more than a clerk, though at the time I felt lucky, even important. We had no money at all; I had never been so happy.

We returned late that night to the house, nearly midnight; the babysitter, an older woman from around the corner whose husband was a greenskeeper at the town-owned golf course, was fast asleep on the sofa, the radio softly playing on the table beside her. A night out, even at the home of friends, was a splurge for us. I awoke her gently and paid her and walked her to the door.

When I returned to the kitchen I found Meredith smoking at the table.

"Sam all right?"

"Sound asleep." She put her fist to her mouth to yawn and shook her head. "The room was a little warm. I opened a window."

"We should go to bed, you know. He'll be up later."

"I know." She nodded sleepily. "It's just nice to sit awhile when everything's quiet."

I turned my back to take a bottle of milk from the fridge and pour myself a glass. Things had not been easy with Sam; he got a lot of colds, and ear infections that kept him up all night, and could run a fever so high his little body felt like a burning log. Even when he was healthy, there was always around his nose and upper lip a hardened crust of phlegm. But these were minor complaints; it was polio we feared in those days, especially in summer. The previous August, a little girl two blocks away had come down with it: the fever and backache and then the sudden paralysis, and the nighttime dash to the hospital to learn the news that everybody already knew. She had gotten it, it was said, on a family outing to the Jersey Shore. The little girl, whose name was Marie, had survived, but spent three months on an iron lung. Not a parent on the block had drawn an easy breath until all the leaves were down.

These were my last thoughts before I smelled it: a sour, acrid odor that seemed to come from everywhere in the room. My body clenched with a sudden alertness: something was burning. An aroma faintly electrical, but not quite. I turned from the counter and was about to say something, ask Meredith if she smelled it too, when I saw her eyes were closed; she had fallen asleep in her chair, her cigarette still tucked between her first and second fingers where her hand lay on the table-top, smoke curling upward from it like a question mark. I heard a little pop, and at that instant a stronger tang was exhaled into the air around me. I realized then what the odor was. I had smelled it before, in the war.

"Christ, M. Wake up, you've burned yourself."

I seized her hand and shook the cigarette from between her fingers. Bits of paper and tobacco had fused with her melted flesh. I took what was left of the cigarette and crushed it out in the ashtray.

"Get up, quickly."

I pulled her to the sink, where I turned on the tap to run cold water over her hand. But the water that came out of the spigot was tepid. *Ice,* I thought; ice, to quickly cool the burn. I left her at the sink and rummaged frantically through the refrigerator, broke open a tray, and brought a cube out to hold against her hand. Blisters had formed where the cigarette had rested, tumescent bubbles of skin, filling with dark blood.

"Here, hold this."

Wedging the ice between her fingers, I wrapped her hand with my own. Through all of this Meredith had spoken not a single word. Around us, the rank odor hung like a veil. A burn bad enough to smell, I thought.

"Good God, M, didn't you feel it?"

"I guess I didn't." Her voice was quiet, almost apologetic. "I must have had too much to drink."

"You don't seem that drunk. You don't seem drunk at all."

I held the ice against her fingers another minute, then led her upstairs to the bathroom and seated her on the toilet lid. She seemed dazed, more exhausted than alarmed, and yet the pain must have been searing, enough to flood her system with adrenaline. How had she failed to feel it? I carefully washed the wound with a damp cloth, then coated her fingers with thick ointment—diaper cream, though the label said it could be used for burns as well—and wrapped them carefully with gauze.

"A doctor should probably look at this."

I had turned my back to her, to wash my hands at the sink. In the mirror I watched her examining her wrapped hand with an expression of pure bewilderment.

"I just can't explain it," she said finally. "It doesn't hurt in the least."

"Just the shock, probably. The body's defenses." I turned from the sink and did my best to smile. Down the hall, Sam gave a sharp cry, fighting his way out of sleep; in another moment he would be all open eyes and flailing arms, and my attention would have to turn to him. I dried my hands on a towel and kissed Meredith's forehead. Her skin was warm and a little damp; perhaps she'd felt it more than she'd realized.

But this made no sense either. I think at that moment I had actually convinced myself there was nothing to fear.

"You're lucky, you know," I said. "It should have hurt like hell. It's my fault. I shouldn't have let you fall asleep like that."

I was not a soldier in the war. Accounts of my life often err optimistically on this point, the operative assumption being that a man of a certain age and station must have done his duty. Nor can I say that I was a brave boy who wanted to serve but was prevented from doing so by some small defect or painful personal circumstance: heart murmur, fallen arches, a widowed mother with a farm to run. I was hale, alert, and conventionally, if not passionately, patriotic: a solidly useful boy who could carry a pack and fire a rifle and die for his country if it came to that.

I was sixteen when the United States entered the war. We were living then, my parents and I—for I was an only child—in a working-class enclave of Scranton, Pennsylvania. We had moved from Des Moines when I was twelve, when my father, a history and civics teacher, had taken a job as vice principal of the local high school. All of my mother's family was from Scranton (her maiden name was Chernesky), a vast clan of Lithuanian Catholics who, with the exception of my mother, had never moved beyond a five-block radius, and so our relocation had not been so much a step into something new as the inevitable closing of a circle: every summer I'd visited my grandparents and aunts and uncles and cousins, and thought of Pennsylvania, with its downhearted landscape of trashy tangled forests and abandoned pit mines flooded with inky water, as something like a second home—altogether different, and promisingly so, from the open ground and oppressive exposure of the Middle West.

When war was declared, I did what any sixteen-year-old in a provincial city, the son of a respected educator, would do: I waited for my eighteenth birthday—the same day, I believed, that I would enlist. My greatest fear was that the war would end before I had a chance to enter it. But then, in May of '42, a boy I knew slightly—we had wrestled together at the high school—was killed when his plane, a P-51 Mustang, was shot down in a raid over Berck-sur-Mer on the French coast. More followed, one every couple of months, until the following winter, when three boys from our neighborhood died in quick succession, two at the Battle of the Kasserine Pass in the Tunisian Dorsal Mountains, a third in the naval engagement at Guadalcanal.

The last of these was my second cousin—a shy, skinny kid with bad skin who bagged groceries at the corner store and liked to work on an old Ford in the driveway of his parents' house, which was around the block from my own. Charlie had been two years ahead of me in school; like me, he was an only child. The summer before he'd shipped out, he'd come home on a week's leave, and in his starched white uniform and jaunty hat had looked to me utterly transformed, confident and cool, a boy who had stepped into the circle of manhood. Even his skin had cleared up. He was an engineer's mate—all that fooling around with the Ford had taught him a thing or two. I decided on the spot that the navy was what I wanted.

The news of his death reached us on a Saturday afternoon and traveled through the living rooms and kitchens of our neighborhood within hours. His ship had taken a Japanese torpedo broadside, cracked like an egg with the force of the blast and gone down in less than two minutes. No one could say for sure, but it seemed likely that Charlie, like many of his shipmates, had been trapped belowdecks. I thought of the way he had died, what those two minutes must have been like, the chaos and the cold darkness of the rising seawater, and men screaming all around. When the water flooded his compartment, had he tried to swim for it? Had he filled his lungs with all the air he could carry, ducked his head below the surface, and tried to make his way out somehow? Or had he been near the explosion itself and died quickly, all those unlived years of his life blasted away in an instant? I hoped, for Charlie's sake, that it had happened that way, and then felt guilty for hoping anything at all.

Perhaps my courage failed me because of Charlie; maybe it was the thought of his ruined and sorrowful parents, now childless, as mine would be if I were killed, that made me choose as I did. I had no claim on a deferment and didn't want one, and with everyone talking by then—this was the spring of '43—of a European invasion, the infantry was out of the question. The Pacific had become a horror, one blood-spattered island at a time, lunatic Japanese dressed in twigs and leaves carrying knives in their teeth, holed up in caves and fighting till the death. I still wanted the sea, but I also did not wish to die in it like my cousin Charlie, so in June of that year, a week after my high school graduation, my father packed up the car and drove me north to Castine, Maine, where I enrolled in the Maritime Academy. They called us "hurry-ups," and we were: six months of cramming my head with every kind of fact, and then I was at sea, a junior navigational officer on a tanker hauling one hundred thousand barrels of diesel fuel between the refinery in Port Arthur, Texas, and naval bases up and down the East Coast.

Oddly, after so much frantic maneuvering and worry, the war itself turned out to be one of the most peaceful periods of my life. The work was arduous, punctuated by bursts of frenzied activity whenever we made port; but a ship at sea, especially a large cargo vessel, is one of the dreamiest places on earth, a kind of floating nowhere. I passed those two years in a tranquil haze of unraveled time, my days and nights folded into one another by the rhythms of the watch and the hypnotic thrum of our engines, a basal throbbing that seemed to travel upward from the deck's steel plates into my very bones. Though we never made it more than five hundred miles from shore—well inside the safety zone—I felt very much as if I had left the wider world behind. My favorite run was a straight shot across the gulf from the depot in Port Arthur to the naval installation at Key West; on those nights when I wasn't on watch in the wheelhouse, I would stand and smoke on the foredeck, watching the sea and smelling the warm gulf air—always, even so far from land, kissed with a floral sweetness—and feel so alone I didn't feel alone at all, as if I needed no one and nothing in my life. It was a sensation I loved instinctively; it seemed, like the throb of our engines, to have moved inside me; and although I did not know it at the time, I would spend the rest of my life searching to find it again.

I might have remained in the merchant service were it not for

Meredith, whom I met on a night just after the end of the war, when we were docked at the naval yard in Philadelphia and I went ashore with friends, to a restaurant where, at the next table, she was eating with two girls from her office. (She worked as a clerk at the same General Electric plant where I would later work three years.) But that is another story—not a war story, as I mean now to tell. My one true war story is this:

April 30, 1945: We had just made port at the Brooklyn Navy Yard and spent the morning off-loading our tanks into the vast holding pens of diesel fuel that lined the docks. We would lie two days in New York and then set sail again, empty and riding high as we made a long arc south to Port Arthur to start it all again. The war already seemed over, like a long, bad party in its final hour. A few days before, we had learned that a U.S. patrol had converged with a Soviet unit on the Elbe, and rumors were circulating that Hitler was already dead, or gone mad, or both. All that remained was Berlin itself, though Japan was still a question. Roosevelt had been dead three weeks, and nobody trusted Truman yet, this Missouri haberdasher turned president, but these things seemed not to matter; the war would end of its own accord, whoever made the final decisions.

As a navigational officer, even the most junior of one, little was required of me during the off-loading; I spent the afternoon on deck, watching the ships come and go from the harbor, beneath a sky of unseasonable blueness and thick, doughy clouds pushed along by a bracing April wind. A new aircraft carrier, the *Coral Sea,* had just been launched from its locks, and now she lay at anchor, a huge city of floating gray steel almost a thousand feet long, rising twenty stories above the fouled waters of the harbor. I was enough of a patriot to experience an almost visceral stirring at the sight of her, though something else too: that small, unassailable tweak of shame that I had spent the war so far removed from any actual danger. Whenever we were in port, especially the large naval yards at Norfolk and New York, I often found myself among groups of uniformed men, the sailors on shore leave and infantrymen preparing to ship out. They pressed into the waterfront bars and restaurants and movie houses, making every space seem small with their loud voices and the rich haze of their cigarettes. The feeling that passed among them was positively electrical, like some binding, subatomic force. As merchant mariners, we were widely thought of as members of a kind of ancillary navy—technically, we were classified 2B, worker in an essential industry—and never once did anyone confront me directly with an accusation of cowardice. But I knew the truth; I could *feel* the truth. In those same waterfront bars, a sailor might bump into me by accident, or I might find myself standing at the rail beside a group of freshly minted PFCs on the town for one last night of fun before they shipped out; and though at such moments we might exchange a courteous word or two, always their eyes would slide past me quickly, as if I weren't completely visible.

I was watching the *Coral Sea* from the fantail, feeling these things and despite it all a kind of warm happiness to pass a few empty hours in the spring sun, when I was joined by a shipmate, a man named Mauritz. Mauritz was nobody I knew very well or liked all that much; he was an old mariner, thirty years at sea and brown as the whiskey he drank fiercely, and like all the other lifers, he regarded the hurry-ups as a kind of necessary wartime burden, like gas rationing or bad coffee. The one thing I liked about him was that he played jazz guitar, not just well but expertly—in another life he might have been a professional musician. Sometimes at night he would bring his guitar into the mess or out on deck and play for us, his fingers drawing melodies of such tenderness from his instrument that the very air around him seemed different, lighter. I wondered if he had a family—surely the depth of feeling I heard in his music came from some meaningful human attachment—but I never asked, thinking also that he might be alone. I was wondering about this one night when I asked instead what the names of the songs were.

He scowled as if my question were the stupidest thing he had ever heard, and did something with his fingers to tune the strings. "No names." I thought the conversation had ended, but then he winked at me and laughed. "You think of some, you tell me."

Mauritz had been dockside all morning, one of a dozen hands supervising the transfer of diesel from our tanks into the holding pens.

His face and arms were so dirty with oil that the cigarette tucked behind his ear was as startlingly white as a human scalp.

"How's it going down there?"

He wiped his nose with the back of his hand. "A fucking mess.
Man's work, buddy boy. Goddamn gaskets leaked all over." His eyes,
squinting, followed my gaze over the water. "The *Coral Sea?*"

I nodded. "Yeah, that's her."

He settled in against the rail and whistled through his long dark
teeth. "Eighteen five-inch guns on that son of a bitch. Like a destroyer
welded to an airport. They're renaming her the *Roosevelt,* what I hear."
He took the cigarette from behind his ear and tapped it on a thumb-
nail. "You see the papers?"

I told him I hadn't.

"Hitler got married." He barked a pitiless laugh. "Him and that
Kraut cunt are holed up somewhere. Some fucking honeymoon!"

We stood another moment at the rail. Mauritz tapped his cigarette
again, placed it to his lips, and fished in the pocket of his shirt for his
lighter. The air around us was tangy with diesel fuel. It was a smell we
lived with day in, day out, omnipresent as oxygen or the constant
swaying of the ship's deck. Usually I thought nothing of it, but standing beside him, the smell was unusually vivid, much stronger than it
should have been. I was about to say something sarcastic about the
leaking gaskets he had mentioned, when he flicked his Zippo across his
pants leg and lit his cigarette.

"Mother . . . fucker."

Mauritz was looking at his leg; a blue flame had enveloped his right
thigh. Time seemed to slow as we both watched the delicately dancing
blue flame on his body, a vision of wonder and strangeness—as hypnotic, in a way, as the songs from his guitar.

"Maur—"

And then the rest of him went up—up and out and away, the diesel
that had soaked his pants and shirt and even his hair igniting all at
once so that he seemed not so much *on* fire as replaced *by* fire, a man-
size waterfall of flames. The heat and concussion shoved me back
across the deck, and when I looked again all I could see were his eyes,

white disks of pure amazement, and the incongruous image of his cigarette still clamped, somehow, between his blackening lips. I tried to yell but no sound came; my throat was suddenly closed, sealed tight against the heat and smoke of Mauritz as he burned, and in the instant when I should have done something—taken off my jacket to cover him with it, or pushed him to the deck to roll my body over his—he did something instead: he took one step closer to the rail, bent over it from the waist—a maestro taking his bow—and sent himself pitching into the harbor.

He died, of course, after they had plucked him from the harbor and taken him away; what the flames themselves did not accomplish, the septic harbor waters did. But what I remember most of all from that day is the smell—of oil and diesel fuel and dirty harbor water, and the foul sweetness of a human being on fire. As Mauritz fell he pulled the smoke down with him like a rocket's contrail, and when I looked over the rail to find his body, yelling my alarm at last, a rank cloud rose to meet me, overwhelming my senses with such nauseating totality that I had to turn my face away and retch. It was the same smell I smelled again, years later in my kitchen, when Meredith, sick already but not yet knowing it, dozed as her cigarette burned away the flesh from her fingers; the same look I saw in her eyes, as she sat on the toilet of our upstairs bathroom and considered her miraculously painless injury: an expression of the purest wonder, as if, even then, she had somehow grasped its meaning.

It is summer now, the days long, indistinguishable. Visitors come and go in the buttery light. I entered the hospital for the last time in April—a touch of pneumonia, the old man's friend—and now nobody talks as if I will ever leave here. Hal has seen to everything; my room is like something in a hotel. And yet it is the reductions, the final clarities, one takes to heart. I have oxygen to breathe, strong analgesics for comfort, antibiotics to hold infection at bay; I have a nurse to bathe and attend me, orderlies to bring my meals, such as they are, on their rolling metal carts. Chopped beef and leathery breasts of chicken;

browning salads and limp green beans paled from the steam; small, tasteless desserts: a wedge of cake or brownie, a bowl of wobbling gelatin, oatmeal cookies hard as poker chips. They arrive compressed under stretched cellophane, or hidden beneath hatlike silver lids that seem to come from an era long past. The orderlies, usually black men but not always—I confess I think of them as one person, a single being—raise these coverings with an encouraging if manufactured pleasure, like a magician lifting a curtain to reveal, behind it, a single cooing dove. "Well now, what have we got for you today, Mr. Wainwright? Salisbury steak, I see. And cherry pie. Not bad, not bad at all." There was a time when I could not keep even the slightest morsel in my stomach—the months of drugs and radiation and other well-meaning but useless therapies—but now I eat it all, every bite. I am already nostalgic for food.

And Franny did not, after all, fuck me to death. It was the pneumonia that drove her glorious plans into the ditch. We gave it a try or two after that, but in the end held hands, and slept. Like teenagers, I thought, and was glad.

My doctor is named Grosscup. At the onset of my illness I had many—surgeons, oncologists, pulmonary specialists, even a dietician. Now he is all that remains, like a last party guest who cannot find his keys. Under the chairs? On the patio? In the kitchen, put carelessly aside when he went to flirt with one of the caterer's girls? When he finds them, he, too, will depart. Dick is an internist of the old school, loyal as a Labrador, a man who wears brogans and a suit even in summer and carries his tools in a black leather bag that opens like a mouth. He has a kind, wide face, and eyebrows heavy as wool. Every night he stores his stethoscope in the freezer.

"Not true, Harry. I stir my martini with it."

It is afternoon, an afternoon in July. Here and there he moves the end of his frigid instrument across my back.

"That goddamn thing's an ice cube."

"Never mind that. Now breathe. That's it."

A moment passes. He pulls my pajama top back down, instructs me to sit up, and takes gentle hold of my wrist. His thumb where it rests on my skin is rough as sandpaper. A deeper quiet settles over the room; not even the birds are singing. When he is satisfied, he takes my chart from the table and scribbles something in his awful handwriting.

"How's the pain?"

We do this on a scale of one to ten: standard stuff. "Five."

"I know you, so I'll write down seven." He frowns optimistically as he reads the chart. "It says here you're eating. Don't know how, with the goop they serve. Makes airplane food look like the '21.'" Dick furrows his ample brow at me. "How's the breathing?"

"About the same." I don't know why I always lie to him. "Maybe a little worse."

Again he writes. Finally, he puts the chart aside and takes a chair by my bed. Always the problem: the bed is elevated, like an altar. The angle makes talking awkward.

"Here's the question, Harry. Do you want to go home? Because if you do, there are things that can be done." He nods me along. "To make you comfortable."

He is asking me where I want to die, of course. It is not a question one longs to hear. And yet I am glad he has asked it.

"What things?"

He reaches to the floor where his bag, openmouthed, rests. From the interior he produces a pamphlet, tri-folded and glossy, which he stands to give me. *Good Shepherd Hospice* it reads, and beneath that, *Information for the Family.* The illustration is a simple line drawing of a tree.

"There are others. But this is the one I recommend."

I am too tired to read it. A good idea, well-meaning to a fault, but the details, I know, will depress me. "Have you talked to Meredith about this?"

He realizes what I have said before I do. "Meredith, Harry?" Dick shifts in his chair.

"Don't look at me like that." I close my eyes and breathe. "Franny, I meant. Have you talked to Franny?"

"We've spoken about it. She says it's up to you. A nurse will come to the house every day, to monitor your comfort. More, as things progress."

I am suddenly exhausted. More than exhausted—I feel like a cup that somebody has spilled. My eyes refuse to open; the air seems to wander aimlessly in my chest, finding no purchase. To breathe at all seems hardly worth the bother. This is what is meant, I suppose, by things progressing, all of a sudden.

"Harry?"

At a distance I hear Dick's voice, asking me if I want to sleep—am I sleeping, is that it? But it is not just sleeping—and then the sound of his brogans creaking on the floor as he lets himself out. A murmured conversation in the hall: Hal's voice, and a woman's—Sally? Frances? The voices swirl into one another like vapor; I sense a continuous flow of activity around me, and yet I am apart from these events, filled with an inexpressible calm. Time is passing, has passed. My mind goes here and there, telling its usual stories—strange things, like Sam's dying, and Meredith, and Mauritz on fire, and Joe and Lucy and the thing that passed between us—but ordinary things as well: pouring milk onto oatmeal in my parents' kitchen on a winter morning my father planned to take me ice-skating; running alongside Hal as he pedaled his bicycle up our street for the first time, his elbows wobbling on the handlebars, his face filled with all his pleasure and alarm; standing at the counter at the Wanamaker's on Market Street in Philadelphia at Christmastime to select a scarf for Meredith; the lake and mountains, and a perfect hour years ago, casting a flyline over water as still as God's held breath. I move through these memories like a ghost, until they no longer seem to be separate stories at all; they are one and the same, indistinguishable and without pause, and the realization of this fact comes upon me in a burst of sweetness the likes of which I have never felt before.

When I open my eyes, the sky beyond the windows is dark as ink. How much time has passed I do not know. A woman is sitting in the chair by my bed; a nurse, I see, though she is new to me. She is young, with a round face and dark hair; she wears a bit of makeup, both darkening and drawing attention to the delicacy of her features. Beneath her smock I see the gently swollen belly of her pregnancy. The clock on the bedside says it is after one: one A.M. The middle of the night, but what night? I feel as if I have been away for days.

She looks up at me and smiles pleasantly. "Look who's awake." Something is in her hands; knitting needles, I see, and a ball of white yarn. She brings these to rest in her lap. "Well. How do you feel?"

"I'm—" My tongue is heavy as wood in my mouth. "Thirsty."

She puts her needles aside and rises to fill a cup from the pitcher on the bedside table. She leans over me and pours small sips of water into my mouth. All around her is the smell of summer leaves.

"There now. Enough?" I manage a nod, and she returns to her chair, and her knitting. "That was quite a nap you took," she says, not looking at me.

I watch the tatting motions of her needles. The sight is enveloping in a way I cannot express: it seems to cross the boundaries of my senses, as if I am watching a symphony, or listening to roses. Do people know about this? Why have I never watched anyone knit before? I feel this new awareness with my entire body, just as I feel, strangely, that we are the only two people in the building. More than feel: I know this absolutely. It is a fact of nature. We are alone.

"That would be the morphine," she says.

"What?"

She is rolling up her yarn. The sight is so beautiful I want to weep.

"Where is everybody?"

"Here and there." She raises one of her needles and twirls it about. "Around, around."

"What . . . day is it?"

But she does not answer. Her needles click and pause and click again. She pulls a sleeve of yarn along one needle and I see what she is making: baby booties.

"It's all right to sleep if you want. I'll watch over you. Just sleep. It's all you need to do."

"Those are for your baby?"

She smiles. "Oh, I'm not pregnant."

And I see that she is not. Why did I think that she was? She is far too old to be pregnant; she is sixty, or even seventy. She is old as I.

"I have a boy."

Her hands pause. "I know your boy. Sam? He's a fine boy."

"You know him?"

"You must be tired, Harry. It's all right. You sleep. I'll be right here if you need me."

My eyes have closed again. Her words seem to have traveled a great distance to reach me, like a voice across the waters. In the seat by my bed, her needles work away.

"Franny will be along soon. You can be sure of that. And Hal. Everybody."

"Everybody." The word is a sweet morsel in my mouth.

"That's right. Everybody. Meredith, and Sam. All of them. That's how it is, Harry. But you knew that, didn't you?"

"I did." I cannot be sure I have even said these words aloud. "I think I did know it."

"Because that's the secret, Harry," she tells me. "That there are no secrets. Not about this."

Jordan

Why Harry's weird insistence on a dry fly? The fact is, there's a great deal of hair-splitting fussiness when it comes to fly-fishing, most of it as silly as a top hat. We've had folks up here who would fish only for salmon, and then only in the rivers; folks who wouldn't spit on a smallmouth but would marry a trout if they could. There's the old bamboo vs. graphite argument, of course, the high-tech crowd and the low-tech crowd; for every well-heeled investment banker who shows up with a custom-made graphite cannon and enough hand-tied flies to make a down payment on a condo in Vail, there's always another (we call him "the professor," whether or not that's what he does, though it usually is) who fishes for "historical accuracy" (I kid you not), marching around the woods with a twelve-foot twig and a copy of Walton's *The Compleat Angler*, which, if you haven't read it and don't mind the bad spelling, should come in pretty handy if you're ever in seventeenth-century England with some free time to fish.

But if you've been around the sport awhile, and learned it from someone who mostly understood it as an interesting way to catch fish—in my case, my stepfather Vince, an agent for the Maine Department of Conservation—then you understand the nonsense for what it is: one more way for difficult people to be difficult. This is half the fun for them, and since my job is, more or less, to keep everybody happy, far be it from me to object. If you want to fish in period costume, I'll be the first one to fetch your knickers at the cleaners.

Still, Harry's insistence on fishing only dry fly had me stumped. To be sure, the dry fly/wet fly debate is the oldest aesthetic fistfight in the sport, and nearly every year some joker writes an article in one of the trades defending the "purity" of dry fly and generally insinuating that fishing with a nymph or streamer is just one step above putting a chunk of Velveeta on a diaper pin. But Harry was never one to care about such things. It's possible to like both well enough, as Harry always had, letting the fish, the water, the weather, and the time of year make his choice for him—allowing circumstances to give shape to his pleasure, always the best way to go in my view, and probably the closest thing I have to a philosophy of life. That Harry wanted to go trout fishing one last time, but do it all wrong, amounted to a kind of dare. Maybe all he wanted, away from the drugs and the doctors and even the cancer itself, was one last, nifty stroke of luck before the curtain came down.

Harry and his family weren't the only guests at the camp; we were pretty close to full up, and taking a whole day off to guide him would require a little planning. After we'd gotten their gear to the cabin, Kate and I went to the office in the main lodge to sort through the list of duties for the next day. It was going to be a squeeze; we had two parties checking out and three new ones coming in, and half a dozen folks from the Lakeland Inn, the only hotel in town, arriving in the early A.M. for breakfast and a moose-watching canoe-float down the river, picnic lunch included. This was a regular Saturday staple for us, and a money loser at thirty-five bucks a head, but with a healthy payoff at the back end, since half the folks who took the trip fell in love with the place and returned the next year for a week at full price.

A word or two about Kate. I had known Kate for eight years, since she was thirteen and I first came to the camp, and apart from one awkward, early summer, there'd been no nonsense between us. You could say there was a certain logic to the idea that we might eventually take a personal interest in one another, but there were also lots of reasons not to. I got along just great with Joe and Lucy, who treated me like family, and I knew that they'd borrowed up to their necks to send her to tony old Bowdoin and had hopes for her life that probably included a bright young anesthesiologist or management consultant in Boston, not some up-country hermit like me.

But the truth was, and despite my better judgment, I'd begun to think about her differently—think about her all the time. What I mean is, I'd begun to see her not just as Joe and Lucy's daughter but as a person in her own right, and I missed being near her, the sound of her voice and the way she tucked her hair behind her ears and the feeling these things gave me, like the world wasn't such a big place after all, and I was someone in it. The last winter away from her was like a kind of cold storage, and for a couple of snowbound weeks in February, I'd even gotten it into my head to drive the Jeep down to Bowdoin, surprise her at her dorm, maybe whisk her off for a weekend down the coast or holed up in Boston, totally rearranging my life and, if I were lucky, hers. This, of course, was the loneliness talking, and naturally I didn't do it; I knew she had boyfriends at Bowdoin, and I sensed I belonged to one compartment of her life and could not easily pass into the other. What could I do? I put the idea aside like a book I knew wouldn't end well and stayed put.

All of which guaranteed that by the time Kate returned to the camp in June, I had it something awful for her. I was so worried that she would detect my feelings (or worse, that her parents would) that I barely set foot from my cabin until the Fourth of July, leaving only to do my chores and then running like a rabbit straight back to lie on my cot and brood away the hours. I could tell Lucy was on to me; she kept asking me if I were coming down with something, and once or twice hinted that Kate was worried too. The only thing I could think to say was that maybe the winters had started to get to me. The truth was, I had decided the only proper thing to do—a funny word, but the right one—was quit at the end of the summer. But where I'd go and what I'd do, I hadn't the faintest idea.

In the meantime, we had a day's chores to plan, and in the cluttered office, Kate and I went over the schedule. We were pinning our hopes on a staggered arrival for the moose-canoers; if push came to shove, we could delay a group or two in the dining hall so that Kate would have time to drive back from the put-in point, five miles upstream and a forty-minute round-trip, going like a comet. We had just about put everything together when Joe came in, with Hal in tow. I wasn't surprised; clearly there was a pow-wow brewing, and I had a few questions myself about Harry, since I had figured out by then that any fishing we might do would be a total fabrication. Hal gave my upper arm a solid pat and asked how I was doing, but his face was creased with worry. He said hello to Kate, asked her in a chummy way how things were going down at Bowdoin (Hal was a Williams grad himself, and to look at him, probably a letterman who had banged Bowdoin heads aplenty), then let Joe show him to the old plaid sofa.

"Let's all sit," Joe said. "Kate, why don't you stay too. This concerns you as much as anyone."

We arranged our chairs in a circle, while Joe did the next, obvious thing, which was to produce a half-full bottle of very old single malt from the rolltop. He took four coffee mugs from the shelf above the desk, gave each one a hard blow to clean the dust out before pouring the Scotch, then passed the cups around. I swirled the Scotch under my nose, and it smelled just like its color: the luminous brown of old, old wood.

"Am I to take it," Kate said, looking into her mug, "that this means something is up?"

Joe shushed her with a frown, sipped from his drink, and nodded in my direction. "Jordan, Hal here has something to tell you."

Hal set his drink down on the table to his right and gave his knees a little slap. "Well. I guess the upshot is, my father is dying. The particulars aren't important, Jordan, but the doctors say he's very close to the end. It makes no sense at all for him to be here, and I tried to talk him out of it, but he's fished here thirty years and that's what he wants to do. He was actually in the hospital until yesterday morning, when the doctor called and told us he was checking himself out. He'd pretty much decided what he wanted to do, and there's no law saying you have to stay in the hospital if you don't want to. Sally's out of town, so it was all I could do to get January at the day care and hightail it up here." Hal paused and rubbed his face, dusted with a day-old growth of silvering beard. "Frances is in a state, and I can't blame her. But I can hardly blame my father either. It's an awful place to die."

"I'd feel the same," I said, thinking: Attaboy, Harry. Hang a sign on the hospital room door, a silly picture of some old geezer bagging carp, and the words *Gone fishing.* "If it were up to me, I'd say let him do it."

Hal took his Scotch from the table, seemed about to sip, then stopped. "I'm not sure, Jordan, that you know how important you are to my father. But a lot of this actually has to do with you. He needs something from you, something I can't quite put my finger on. Maybe I don't have to, and in any case, it amounts to this: tomorrow, you need to take him out, and do what you need to do to make sure he has a good time, the last good time. If that means he catches anything, great. If not, I wouldn't worry about it too much. Make sure he's comfortable, and if there are any problems, come straight back here. He's very sick, so don't tackle anything you can't handle."

"It's okay, Hal," I said. "I'm happy to do it. You don't need to worry."

"Like I said, just understand how sick he is. And, in case you were wondering, I don't know what to make of this dry fly business any more than you do. I suspect it doesn't much matter. Just getting something in the water would be a pretty neat trick for him."

I looked across the room at Kate, sitting on a folding chair by the cold woodstove, but she was watching Hal, and I couldn't catch her eye.

"Maybe he just wants to make a few of the rules," I said.

"Maybe that's it," Hal said, though I could tell he didn't think so. "Like I said, he's relying on you to understand some things I don't." Here he looked at Joe, who seemed to nod.

"I'll do my best, Hal," I said. "Is that it?"

"Actually, no," Joe said. He silenced me with a raised hand. "Hang on, Jordan. There's more. Go ahead, Hal."

Hal leaned forward on the sofa. He looked at the tips of his fingers, then back up at me. "The other thing I have to tell you, Jordan, and this may come as some surprise, is that my father bought the camp four weeks ago. Bought it outright. And he plans to leave it to you."

So there it was, and the first thing I thought was: mystery solved.

Then: Buying the camp. Leaving it to me. In his will? Yes, in his will, in the last will and testament of one Harrison Wainwright, he of *Business Week* and *Fortune* and the Forbes 500 and all the rest, inventor of the deep-discount pharmaceutical superstore: *that* Harrison Wainwright. A chain of ideas so completely unlikely, so crazy, in fact, that I couldn't, just then, open my mouth and say a blessed word. And—a sudden intuition—I glanced up at the clock to note the time: 9:03 P.M. Sunday, August 19, 1994, at a little after nine on a fine, cold evening in the North Woods of Maine.

"So?" Joe tapped my knee with the back of his hand. "Jordan? What do you say?"

"Jesus, Joe." I looked back at Hal. "He's leaving it to me?"

"That's right, Jordan. When he dies, it's yours, free and clear. There's a provision to protect it from inheritance taxes, which the rest of the estate will absorb. Sally drew it up, so I'd guess it's pretty airtight, knowing Sally. And you should understand that Frances and I are okay with this. I'd be lying if I said we didn't try to talk my father out of it, and probably we could make a case that he was pretty sick when he made this decision, not in his right mind, yada-yada-yada, and maybe make it stick. But in the end it wouldn't be a fair fight, and it wouldn't be the truth, either. My father may have cancer, he may even be a little eccentric, but he's not crazy. So the way this breaks down, there's plenty to go around, and some of it is going around to you, a nice little chunk actually, but nothing that's worth an ugly and expensive scuffle. Understood?"

I nodded. I was actually barely following any of it. "I guess I do."

"Incidentally, he doesn't want you to know about this. My thinking is—and Sally and Frances both agree—it's crazy for you not to. There are no strings attached, and you can do whatever you want with the place. But what he's hoping is that the camp will always be here, that you can stay up here the rest of your life. He wants to take *care* of you, Jordan."

I turned to Joe. "You really sold it?"

Joe shrugged, turning his mouth down in a pained half-frown. I thought he might be about to cry, and who could blame him? Even if

Harry had given him one zillion dollars for the place, the camp had been in Joe's family for almost fifty years. My eyes moved upward to the wall behind his head, covered with old photos, including a faded black-and-white of Joe himself, just a kid of six or seven with one front tooth missing and a haircut that looked like it had been done with pinking shears, holding up an Atlantic salmon just about as big as he was and beaming like a maniac. Joe Sr., the old man himself, stood beside his boy, one hand over his brow, the other, big as a catcher's mitt, tousling little Joe's hair. The photo was taken on the dock below the lodge; I guessed it was Joe's mother, Amy, who had taken it. Looking at the picture, I knew without being told that it was one of the happiest moments of Joe's life, as this was one of the saddest.

"He gave me a fair price. More than fair. You know that Lucy and I have been thinking about selling for a while, anyway." The corner of his mouth gave a tiny twitch, his eyes glazed over with a thin film of tears, and I would have moved heaven and earth at that moment to let him know that, basically, I loved him. He put his cup to his lips and drained the Scotch in one hard swallow. "I'm just glad we didn't have to sell it to the loggers. Or someone who would carve it up."

"I won't, Joe. Jesus. I absolutely won't."

"We know you won't," Hal said. "That is," he said, *the point.*"

I looked at Kate, sitting cross-legged in her chair and watching us. In her hand, her cup was tipped at an angle that told me it was empty, but I couldn't read her face. "You knew?"

"Some of it." She nodded. "That the camp had been sold."

I thought about what she was saying. "But not the rest."

"That it's yours?" Her eyebrows rose. "I'd have to say no. That I didn't know."

"And is it okay?"

"Hell, Jordan." I would have liked a smile right then but didn't get one. "Of course it's okay. Why wouldn't it be?"

"I don't rightly know." And I didn't. As far as I could tell, everybody had gotten just what they wanted, without even asking. "This is going to take a while to sink in," I said.

Hal rose from the couch, and I noticed for the first time how tall he was, nearly a full head taller than Joe, or his own father. He fixed his eyes on me, squinting a little in the weak, yellow light of the office. "It's a lot to think about. But it's all right to be happy, too, Jordan. It's a great gift."

Which was, of course, precisely true. That's exactly what it was.

I said, "Thank you."

He gave me a weary grin. I thought he was about to shake my hand, sealing the bargain, but instead he fixed one hand on my shoulder and gave it a squeeze.

"You're welcome, Jordan."

Lucy

He was a beautiful man, Harry Wainwright. I thought this even before I knew who he was, before he made the fortune that made him famous, or famous to some. I was a waitress, seventeen years old, so sheltered you would have thought I was twelve anywhere else: a girl from an inbred town in northwest Maine where, as we said, half the people spoke French and the other half yelled. The summer began in May, when Joe kissed me behind the metal shop at school. My parents, who owned the sawmill in Norbeck Pond, were friends with Joe's dad; when Joe told me they were hiring a waitress at the camp, I knew they'd let me do it. So, a summer of firsts: my first real job, my first kiss from Joe, my first vision of Harry, for that's what it was: a vision.

I had also become pretty, and knew it. I had started my junior year just another gangly girl from nowhere, big-boned and big-nosed, so plain and unpromising with my drab skin and oily hair that you might have missed me standing against a freshly painted wall. But between the last of the leaves and the first of the blackflies, somebody some-where had said the magic word, and this new thing about me, this prettiness, was something I could suddenly see everywhere I went: in puddles and windows, in the slow smiling eyes of boys at school and the men who worked at my parents' mill—a different look, more re-spectful but also more afraid, like I was a bomb that might go off any second. I saw it in the way my friends treated me, like I was somebody they wouldn't mind becoming, and planned to, someday soon. I saw it in Harry that day.

So in walked Harry for breakfast on a June morning in 1964; he stood a moment in the open doorway, his eyes roaming the room, letting me have a look at him. Not an especially tall man, but he made me think so; slender and strong, his skin flushed pink with fresh air, deep sleep, and a good morning on the water, his eyes so blue that these days I would assume he was wearing contacts, but not back then. I followed those eyes as they scanned the dining room like two blue searchlights, taking everything in; there was the first sprinkling of silver in his hair, which he wore just a little longer than the respectable men I knew but not as long as the drunks at Wiley's, our one bad bar, or the trappers who came into town twice a year, stinking of themselves, to stock up on jerky and rifle shells before beating it back to the woods they'd come from.

The word I might have thought as I looked at him was *handsome,* or even *cute,* what we said of boys we liked, a shorthand for all the new feelings of desire that danced inside us like sparklers on the Fourth of July. Joe was cute; Joe was, with that little bit of a beard he was growing and the way he strutted around the place, knowing everything, even a little bit handsome.

Harry was: beautiful.

"Screen door, hon," I said. I was calling everybody "hon" and "sweetie" that summer, a habit I'd cribbed from the real waitresses at the Pine Tree Café downtown. He met my eyes, and in his face I saw it: that look.

"I'm sorry?"

"Blackflies." I waved a finger at the open door. "You're letting them in."

"Oh, right." A laugh that crinkled the skin around his eyes. "Stupid of me. Hang on." He backed out the door and I heard him call out from the pathway, "Hal? Hal, where'd you go?" I thought he might be calling a dog, which would have been fine; lots of folks brought dogs with them, and they were more than welcome in the dining hall if they didn't smell too bad and knew how to mind. But then the door swung open again and in marched a boy somewhere between eight and eleven, wearing jeans and a sweatshirt and bright red Keds, his hair all whichway, Harry bringing up the rear. They took a table by the big windows and I busied myself with menus and a coffeepot and took them over.

"Cream on the table there," I said, pouring. I raised the pot over the boy's cup, having fun. "What do you say, hon, coffee for you too?"

"How 'bout it, Hal?" The boy blushed and mumbled something; Harry lifted his face to me and shrugged. "Just milk for him, I guess."

"I want chocolate."

Harry shot him a fatherly frown—pure theater, done for me. "Listen to you, with the *I wants*." He tapped his son's elbow with the back of his hand. "Would it kill you to be polite to the young lady?"

Hal sighed and rolled his eyes. "May I have chocolate milk, please?"

"Better." Harry lifted his face to me once more. "You'll have to excuse him. The truth is, he's just some kid I found in the woods." He leaned over the table in my direction and lowered his voice. "Raised by wolves, I think."

"Dad!"

"What?" He widened his eyes in mock alarm. "It's some kind of secret? Better we come clean, Hal."

Now I was the one laughing. "It's perfectly all right, we're pretty informal around here." I pointed at the menu with the back of my pen. "Don't know how hungry you are, but the raspberry pancakes are everybody's favorite. Fresh berries from the farm down the road."

"How about you?" Still with those blue, blue eyes on me.

"How about me?"

He cleared his throat: had I embarrassed him? "Do you like the raspberry pancakes?"

Thirty seconds of chitchat, and I felt like I was riding a swing with my shoes off. I cocked one hip and shrugged. "More of a blueberry fan myself. But they don't come in till August."

He looked at Hal, who gave another of his silent nods.

"The raspberry pancakes, then," Harry said.

I took their menus and tucked them under my arm. "You won't be sorry, because no one is. Have a good morning on the lake, gentlemen?"

He paused and smiled at me and there it was again. Even I could tell he was deciding how far to take this.

"Terrific," he said.

In the kitchen I gave their order to Mrs. Markham, the cook. My brain was buzzing a little, the way a cigarette made me feel, minus the nausea. Joe was sitting at the big kitchen worktable, pulling apart a cinnamon bear claw, and a tang of guilt shot through me: things were moving along with us, we had entered the first, tentative weeks of boyfriend-girlfriend, and here I was, half breathless from flirting with a man as old as my father.

"What's gotten into you?" Joe said, looking at me.

"What are you talking about?"

He pointed at me and whirled his finger around. "You're all pink." He munched the roll and took a drink from his mug of coffee. The air in the room was heavy as the inside of a hive, thick with the smell of airborne grease and dough baking in the oven. "You got that thing that's going around?"

"Never mind me. I'm fine."

I peeked through the door and saw two more parties arriving. For the next hour or so, as the late sleepers straggled in on top of the early risers who'd already been out since dawn, I'd be running without a moment to spare. Mrs. Markham disappeared into the pantry, leaving everything popping and steaming on the stove, and Joe came up behind me and put his hands on my waist.

"I've got some time off after lunch," he said quietly. "What say I put together a little picnic for us? We can take one of the canoes for an hour or two."

I leaned back a little and gave him a noncommittal "Hmm." When things had started to change for me that winter, my mother sat me down one night after dinner over a plate of Toll House cookies for what she called "the boy talk," and the one thing she said that stuck was not to jump at offers like Joe's too quickly; a little hesitancy, she explained, was part of the game. It was sensible advice, and though I'd heard it a thousand times in other ways, I liked the way she said it— "the game," as if the whole history of men and women, garden to grave, was as unserious as a game of Parcheesi on a rainy afternoon. This was the kind of thing my mother was good at, putting your fears at ease with a turn of phrase and a well-timed plate of cookies, though in this case I also knew she was speaking from the kind of second-guess work that all of us eventually do: game or no, she'd married my father right out of high school and had my older brother Lucius (Lucy and Lucius; I still shake my head at that one) about nine months and ten minutes later.

I was thinking about this and looking across the dining room to where Harry was hunched over the table, talking earnestly to Hal, who, after all the surliness, was finally smiling. A first big trip with Dad, I figured. Fish stories over breakfast.

"Say, who is that guy?" I was pleased at how casual I managed to sound. "Over by the windows."

Joe followed my look. "Who, Harry?"

"Yes, Harry." I gave him a little bump with my shoulder. "If that's his name. And get that beard out of my neck. It itches."

Joe stepped back, embarrassed but not very, and rubbed a hand over his cheeks. "Jeez, you're in a mood today. I thought you liked it."

At that moment Mrs. Markham returned from the pantry. During the year, Daphne Markham was a librarian at the elementary school— a woman with a thick waist and glasses on a chain who could shut you up with one steely-eyed glance that went through you like a spear. We were all terrified of her and assumed she'd never married because she was just too mean, but I later learned that this was not the case: she had been married, long ago, in Africa, where she and her husband were missionaries. What became of her husband I never learned, but earlier that summer she had shown me a photograph of herself, much younger, thin as a whip, standing in front of a small timber-framed church and wearing, of all things, a pith helmet.

For a large woman she was surprisingly fast, and she could handle a breakfast rush with the coolheaded precision of a bomber pilot; in one continuous motion she stepped to the stove, flipped a line of pancakes, dropped two slices of bread into the toaster, pulled a plate of rolls from the warmer, and cracked two eggs into a bowl for beating.

"Lucy, order's almost up. Let's get a move on, please."

I looked at Joe, who had returned to the table and his bear claw.

They were a specialty of Daphne's, dripping with honey and completely irresistible. "Well? I promise to like your beard if you answer the question."

Joe shrugged, not interested but willing to play along. "He's just some friend of my dad's. A regular, been up the last few summers. I guided him a few times. I guess that's his kid."

I peeked out the door again. Harry was gesturing toward the window, pointing something out to Hal. At one of the other tables, a man lifted his head and moved his eyes around the room, scowling: Where the hell's my waitress?

"Okay, so he's good-looking," Joe said, and laughed. "Quit your mooning."

I felt my face flush again and backed away from the door. "I am not mooning."

"Sure you're not. He's as old as your dad. He's also some kind of big shot, what my dad tells me. A good tipper too. Usually gives me at least ten bucks. Kinda folds the bill and slips it to me, like I might be embarrassed to take it."

I could somehow see this. "How about his wife? Is she a good tipper, too?"

Joe frowned impatiently, and I felt my stomach tighten. Why was I asking this? And why was I asking Joe, of all people? "How should I know? He always comes by himself, until now." He gave a thoughtful look and wiped his hands on a napkin. "Actually, I heard his wife's sick or something. Don't know why I'd think that, unless maybe he mentioned it." He lifted his eyes to me then and smiled, ready to change the subject. "So, how about it?"

"How about what?"

Joe glanced over at the stove. He pointed at me, then himself, and mouthed the words: *the picnic.*

Behind him, Daphne sighed irritably and banged her spatula against a pan. "Lucy, for heaven's sake, order's up *now.*"

Two new tables seated, orders backing up, and I had forgotten Hal's chocolate milk. "Oh, shit."

Daphne spun and nailed me, hard, with one of her librarian glares.

"Lucy, I won't have that kind of talk in my kitchen. I expect it from the men, but not from you. And Joe," she continued, pointing her spatula, "don't you have anything better to do? Go help your father. Go on now, scoot."

I fetched milk and chocolate from the fridge, made Hal a glass with an extra squirt of syrup—what the heck, maybe I could make him like me after all—and set up the trays, with menus for the new tables tucked under my arm. I was wondering how I'd get it all outside when Joe stepped up and held the door for me. He raised his eyebrows as I passed.

"Okay," I said, and stifled a flirty laugh. There was something about him at that moment, a gentle sweetness, that always worked on me, and I would have kissed him right then if I could have, scratchy beard and all—though for a moment it also struck me that maybe I was thinking of Harry, that I had confused myself that much.

"Okay what?" he said, grinning.

"Just okay," I said, and bumped my hip into his to let him know my meaning, and took my trays outside.

And there they stayed, the two of them mixed together in my mind: Joe and Harry, my handsome boy and this beautiful man who'd blown in from nowhere. I went on the picnic with Joe, giving myself a good case of razor-face as we passed a lazy hour under the birches, and all that week I served Harry his breakfast and lunch and dinner, tucking bright little bits of conversation about absolutely nothing into my trips to his table. Even Hal got the hang of things, trying to woo me with his fish stories and reformed good manners, like a boy trying to impress a friend's older sister. And when my shifts were over I went off to find Joe, my thoughts still full of Harry: a recipe for permanent confusion, if ever there was one. By the end of the week Joe's beard had softened, or else my face had gotten used to it; and then on Saturday I came into the dining room at 6:00 A.M. and found an envelope by the hostess station, with my name on it, and this note: *Off at 5:00 A.M.*

Thanks for the conversation. See you next year. Yours, Harry Wainwright.
I folded it like money, put it in the pocket of my apron, and let it ride
around there for the rest of the summer. Say what you like, but I was
just a girl; I felt like I'd been secretly kissed.

I knew about Meredith, of course, just as Harry knew about Joe.
Bit by bit over the next few summers we let our stories come out—because we wanted to, and because we had no reason to hide them.
Harry was Harry, and I was who I was, the most pertinent detail being
a single mathematical reality: there were twenty-two years between us.
Joe had been right. Harry was, in fact, *exactly* as old as my father, give
or take a month. There was a point in my life when age wouldn't have
mattered, and I'm not sure it ever *should* have mattered, though I say
this as a woman of forty-seven, so consider the source; but it seemed to
matter back then, a great deal in fact, when I was seventeen and Harry
was thirty-nine, a man with a son not much younger than I was and a
slowly dying wife, a man I saw exactly seven days out of every three
hundred sixty-five. There was a way in which we loved each other from
the start, I think, a cosmic symmetry that could not be refused, but it
was a love that was always folded into other loves, and that is the real
story of me and Harry Wainwright.

Which is why I didn't want to see him that way, that August
evening when he arrived; didn't want to see his bones so brittle, his
muscles wasted away, his hair gone thin, or just plain gone, from
chemo; I did not want to see the light dimmed in those blue eyes. I did
not want to see him helped from the car, or strapped to a walker and
oxygen, or see the spittle fall from his chin as he spoke. I also knew he
wouldn't want me there, to see these things, so when Joe told me that
Hal had called from the pay phone in town, putting them thirty minutes away at the most, I went upstairs under some pretense—sheets
and towels to be folded, rooms to be dusted and cleaned—and
watched it all from the window.

As Harry knew, and as I believed he would. When he lifted his head
by the parked Suburban, everyone all clustered around and breathless
for his sake, it was me he was really looking for, and found at once:

those blue eyes hit me where I stood in the window, hit and passed right through; eyes the same ice blue despite the cancer, like lights in the windows of a ruined house.

Who are you here for? I asked him with my own. *For me?* And, *I'm glad you're here, Harry.*

And I heard him answer: *Yes, for you. But I'm dying, Lucy. So not just you: everyone.*

Still I could not make myself go see him; I did my made-up chores and a few extra tasks besides, finished up the books for the night, ate a turkey sandwich and drank a glass of milk in the kitchen with Joe, our custom. Most evenings during the summer months everyone was too busy for a proper meal, so when we ate together our suppers were like this, small and late, both of us too weary to talk. All our long winters together had taught us to do this well, a skill that, I think, many married people never really get the hang of. There were whole weeks of snow when neither of us could recall having spoken one full sentence to the other. And yet of course a lot was said.

We finished our sandwiches and rinsed the plates, and I put a kettle on for tea. It was late, nearly ten o'clock—practically the middle of the night in a place where everybody gets up before five. While the water thrummed on the heat, I stood at the stove, looking out the window at the dark lake. All that summer, since we'd agreed to sell, I'd been looking for ways to say good-bye to it, trying them on like hats. I'd found that the best way was simply not to: instead of thinking anything in particular, I'd just let my mind float over its surface whenever I had a free minute, and by the time my attention turned to something else, I always felt that a little bit more of it had gone somewhere inside me, a morsel I would get to keep.

"You're doing it," Joe said from the table, startling me.

"What do you mean?"

"That thing. You know," he said. "Where you look at it and sort of disappear." He was leaning forward over the table on his elbows. "It's all right. I get it."

The kettle whistled; I made the tea and brought it back to the table with the sugar bowl for Joe, who liked his extra sweet.

"How did Jordan take the news?" I asked.

Joe bobbed his bag in the steaming water. I could still smell the Scotch on him. When he was satisfied with the color of his tea, he spooned in three tablespoons of sugar, squeezed out the bag, and placed it neatly on his spoon. How he slept with all that sugar in him I never could figure out.

"To tell you the truth, I'm not sure he really knew how. How would anyone feel? It's going to be a big change for him. Guide to owner, in two minutes flat."

"Think he can handle it?"

Joe blew the steam over his tea. "If anyone could, it's Jordan."

For a while we sat without talking, letting the tea warm us. I wondered what Joe was thinking. I knew he didn't regret selling the camp, not really—we had been over the deal carefully, considering every angle, and knew it was the right move. All that money in the bank was persuasive: you see those extra zeros on your statement, lined up like eggs in a carton, and it knocks the breath right out of any worries you had about being sorry. Now there would be money for Kate, for her college loans and medical school—Dartmouth Hitchcock was the current fave; her trip out West had more or less convinced her of that, too congested and nothing you could honestly call weather and nobody serious about *anything,* she said—and money for Florida, Joe's new gangster boat and his plans for the business; as well as money for things we hadn't really figured out yet, having never had enough money to begin with: pleasures, like travel and good restaurants, and sensible items like furniture or a new truck when the old one died and maybe a car besides, a nice sedan or one of those big things with four-wheel everyone was driving. So I knew he wasn't sorry, not exactly, but I also knew that the most obvious course is not always an easy one; and Joe was feeling some of that. It was a chilly night, and the kitchen windows were open, filling the room with the coppery smell of the lake and the small noises it made at night: the dark water bulging against the shoreline; the sighing air currents that swished like smoke over its face; the random splashes here and there that I should have expected but somehow always startled me, the way that Kate, when she was a baby, could yank me from the deepest sleep with a single cry from her crib. We listened together, Joe and I, and eventually we heard voices, too: a man's voice, Jordan's or Hal's or maybe one of the other guest's, and then the sounds of footsteps on one of the cabins' old porches and screen doors squeaking open and slamming closed on their springs.

And then we heard something else, the sound muffled a bit by windows and walls, but there it was: somebody was coughing. Not just coughing—think of a dark room without doors and a person trapped inside, trying to fight his way out. It went on and on, a full minute at least, and when it finally ended, the silence felt permanently shattered, like the eerie quiet after somebody breaks a glass.

"Jesus Christ almighty." Joe shuddered, his face gone a little gray. He rose to place his empty mug in the sink. "If I ever sound like that . . ." He rubbed the back of his head. "He shouldn't even be here. What was Hal thinking?"

"Where else should he be?"

Joe braced his back against the sink. "The hospital, for instance? Someplace *near* a hospital?" The coughing started up again, and once again we held fast; there wasn't anything else you *could* do but ride it out, which only made me feel worse—sorry for Harry, sorry for myself, sorry for Joe, and guilty as hell besides.

"God, listen to that. He may actually die here, you know. Right in that cabin, tonight."

"Maybe that's what he wants."

Joe folded his arms over his chest. "Probably it is. Actually, no. I have no idea what he wants. The great Harry Wainwright. How should I know what a guy like that wants?"

"He's dying, Joe. He's sick and he's dying. What does it matter?"

The question caught him off guard; I wished I hadn't asked it, or at least asked it the way I had, so impatiently, as if everything were simple. Joe turned his back to me and began to wash out the mugs.

"Joe, I'm sorry. Let me do that."

He put the mugs in the drying rack and pointed his eyes out the window. Was he doing it too, sending his mind out there to say good-bye?

"Forget it," he said finally. "It's all done." He turned then and dried his hands on a towel. "You know, it's actually a good thing he owns the place. At least that way we're not responsible if anything does happen."

"I know you, and that's not what you're thinking." I stood and went to him. "Know something else? You're a good man, for doing this. You were before, you always have been, and you are now." He wasn't looking at me, so I made him do this, with a kiss that tasted of tea and Scotch. "Now off to bed with you. It'll be a big day tomorrow."

"You coming?"

"In a bit. I thought I'd fix a basket and take it over to their cabin."

His eyes tightened on my face. "Luce—".

"A basket, Joe. What's the harm?"

"That's not what I was talking about." His voice was soft. He gingerly brushed my cheek with his thumb and showed me: it came away wet. I couldn't have said how long I'd been crying or even why.

"Mystery tears," I said. "For this place. For Harry. For all of us, really. Not bad tears." I tried to smile and found I could. "Just the tears of a tired wife."

He brushed some strands of hair from my face. "Hal knows where the kitchen is. Let them fend for themselves. Come to bed."

I leaned my head into his chest. His shirt smelled like fish, and smoke, and the antiperspirant he'd always used, lime and something cinnamony—what Joe smelled like, after a day.

"You know, I think Jordan and Kate . . ." I said, and didn't finish.

I felt his back and shoulders tense a little: a bear keeping watch on his cub, I thought, and loved this about him, as I always had. "Did Kats say something to you?"

"No." I breathed into his shirt. Maybe this was what I'd really been thinking about, all along. "It's just a feeling, really. Mother's intuition. Kind of a vibe she's giving off, you know?"

"A vibe, huh."

I poked a finger into his chest. "Don't laugh."

"Who's laughing?" He nodded above me. "Jordan and Kate. I guess I'll have to think awhile on that. Or not. Their business, I guess."

"She's still our Kats. It's okay to take an interest." I leaned in a little more. "Does the age thing bother you?"

"We don't even know if there's anything going on, Luce."

"Supposing there was. He's thirty. I checked."

"You checked."

I heard myself sigh. "The employment files, Joe."

"You're kidding. We actually *pay* him?"

"Yes, and frankly I can't believe how little. That boy is long overdue for a raise. Though I guess that's a moot point now. Quit fooling around."

"Okay." He gave my shoulders a bit of a squeeze. "No, it doesn't bother me."

"Good. It shouldn't. It's *Jordan* we're talking about here. And we love Jordan, do we not?"

He thought another moment. "I have to say I'm a bit surprised, though. I never really saw her with someone like that. You know, somebody from up here."

It was my turn to laugh. "God, Joe." I pulled away and looked into his puzzled face. "You can still be the thickest man alive."

He frowned good-naturedly, his eyes wide and dark, still uncomprehending. "What are you talking about?"

Twenty years. How could he not know?

"I chose you, didn't I?"

From the sound of Harry's coughing I knew that somebody, Hal probably, would be up most of the night to tend to him, so I made a thermos of strong coffee and assembled some fried chicken and rhubarb pie left over from dinner, put it in a basket with plates and cups and napkins, and stepped outside.

The moon was down, and the air was cool and still. I found my way along the trace between the two rows of cabins, nearly all of them dark by now, their occupants snoring away. The only exception was cabin twelve, which had been booked by a bunch of lawyers on some kind of retreat; approaching, I heard the low, rough voices of men talking and drinking on the porch, and smelled the dry sweetness of cigar smoke. It was an aroma I secretly liked, even as I knew I would hear about it the next day from the other guests. "Was somebody smoking a *cigar* last night?" someone would ask in the dining room, loud enough that the offender, if he was in the room, would have the opportunity to publicly repent. As far as I knew, though, it was still perfectly legal to smoke a cigar in the Maine woods—Joe had smoked his share until I'd finally gotten him to quit—and none of my business. I thought I might stop in to tell them they might want to keep their voices down, but as I passed, the talking ceased; three of them waved from the porch and gave me a polite and nearly simultaneous "good evening," like a group of tipsy teenagers trying to sound sober. A bunch of good boys, these lawyers, and so I waved back and continued on my way.

Cabin ten, where I'd put Hal and his little girl, was dark, January long since tucked in, but the porch light was on at number nine, where Harry and Frances were staying. As I came around the corner I saw Hal, sitting in an Adirondack chair in a cone of light and swirling insects, reading a magazine with his boots up on the railing. A cigar would have done something about those bugs, and I thought of asking the lawyers if they could spare one. But then Hal looked up with an expression of sudden alertness and put one hand over his brow to peer into the darkness beyond the lighted porch.

"Franny?"

I stepped up to the rail with my basket. "Evening, Hal."

Hal unfolded his long limbs from the chair and came over to meet me, bending at the waist to kiss me quickly on the cheek. "Where you been keeping yourself, Luce?"

"Oh, you know." I tried to smile. "Things to do. Sorry I couldn't meet you when you arrived." The cabin behind him was dark and silent, and I kept my voice low. "How's your father doing?"

Hal took a breath and scratched his head. "Asleep, finally. Though to tell you the truth, I'm not even sure it's really sleeping, what he's doing. He just kind of goes away for a while. I'm taking the first shift while Franny gets a little shut-eye."

I held up the basket for him to see. "I brought you something to tide you over."

"That's not the fried chicken, is it?"

I nodded. "Some pie, too."

He leaned forward, smiling. "Good God, Lucy, you're my hero. Pass that over here."

He held out his hands to take it, and I lifted the basket over the rail. Hal raised the top and surveyed the contents before selecting a drumstick and a napkin, and poured himself a cup of coffee from the thermos. A wick of steam rose off it in the chilly air.

"You're a regular mind reader, Luce. I was just sitting here wondering when Franny would relieve me so I could sneak over and raid the kitchen."

"My pleasure." I waited a moment and watched him eat. "I saw your little girl, Hal. She's really something."

He grinned proudly around a mouthful of chicken and took the napkin to his face. "Poor kid, got her mother's looks. I told Sally, the day she turns sixteen is the day I start digging a moat."

"I don't know about that, Hal. I think I can see a little bit of you in there. Remember, I knew you when you were just a kid."

He gave a little laugh. "Just a kid, my fanny." He fished out another drumstick and held it up for emphasis as he talked. "Eleven is not just a kid, Luce. Eleven is a burning pyre of adolescent lust. You and the other waitresses had me so worked up, I could barely think straight."

I felt a charge of pleasure; assuming he didn't mean Daphne Markham—and I surely didn't think he did—or one of the two older women who had tended the dining room with me, women my mother's age if not a little older, I was the only waitress he could have been remembering.

"Those were good days," I said.

"Better than this afternoon, anyway," Hal said. He finished his second drumstick, wrapped up the bones in the napkin, and closed the basket. "Best I should save this for later. Franny might be hungry too. Who knows? Maybe my dad will surprise us all and actually eat something."

"There's enough there for an army. But if you need anything else, you know where the key to the kitchen is."

"Back door, one step to the right, reach up, on the nail." He nodded. "Piece of cake." He raised his gaze past me then, casting his eyes over the lake, and gave a little nod to tell me to look where he was looking. I turned and saw, out on the dock a hundred yards distant, two figures sitting on the edge, their feet dangling over the water. It took me a moment for my eyes to discern what my brain had already guessed: Jordan and, sitting beside him in her gray sweatshirt, Kate.

"Those two getting along?"

"I think they've always liked each other." I was surprised how guarded I sounded. "They've known each other for years."

For a moment we said nothing. The silence of the lake and the late hour seemed to encircle us.

"The truth is," Hal said, "I think my father just wanted to give it to somebody it already belonged to." He looked at his hands a moment. "It's the best kind of present. I'm only telling you in case you were, you know, wondering."

"We all adore Jordan. Everybody's happy for him. Joe too."

Hal stood and lifted the basket from the floor. "Well, I guess I should look in on the patient. Scares me when he's this quiet." He moved around his chair, then stopped, suddenly gone into deeper thought.

"He loves this place, Lucy. That's what it's really all about. When my mother died, I know it saved him, somehow. He told me that once. The summer after she died, he came up here, and that's what got him through it. I'll never forget it. 'It has the pure beauty of having been forgotten.' That's what he said about this place. He said it again this morning."

My eyes were suddenly swimming again. I didn't want Hal to see, so I stepped back from the railing, away from the light.

"Luce?"

"I'm all right," I said. My voice caught a little, and I breathed to settle it, letting the air in my lungs push the tears away. But I knew I was only buying a moment, if that. In another minute I would be crying for real, the kind of tears you've kept inside so long you don't know what they mean anymore, whether they're happy or sad or both, only that they have to come out; as long as they're coming, they own you, body and soul, these tears, and I didn't want this to happen in front of Hal, or Joe, or anybody. I wanted to cry in a dark room somewhere, nobody around for miles to hear me, and cry until I was all cried out.

"It's late," I managed. "I should go. Good night, Hal."

Twenty steps from porch to path, a hundred more down the shore toward the lodge, through the tangled shadows of the trees, the veil of laughter and cigar smoke. *The pure beauty of having been forgotten,* I thought, and that was the end for me.

At least I made it past the lawyers before the tears came.

Jordan

You might think that the news your name had just appeared in a rich man's will would blow you clean over like a March wind, but that wasn't what happened to me. I was surprised, sure, dumbfounded really, and happy as hell, but I didn't spend a second mooning over my good fortune, or wondering what I'd done to deserve it. (Since I'd done nothing.) What I did instead was this: After Hal had gone off to check on his family, and Joe and Kate had left to close down the kitchen for the night with Lucy, I headed down to the lake, sat myself on the dock with my back against the rail, opened a can of beer I'd filched from the fridge—I hadn't touched the Scotch—and set my gear turning. I had run the books with Lucy long enough to know what the cash flow situation was. Kate had won a scholarship, but Bowdoin wasn't cheap; her parents were forty grand in hock for it, and the meter was still running. Without anybody's college degree to pay for, or a condo in the Keys, I figured I could turn a profit pretty quickly. A year from now I'd be running solidly in the black—not printing money, but doing well enough to buy a few ads in the Sunday travel sections of the *Times* and the *Globe,* and maybe a couple of well-timed notices in one of the glossy outdoor travel mags, to get in on the so-called adventure travel boom. The staff, of course, would have to grow. I'd need a couple of extra guides at least and maybe a full-time instructor, and then of course there were the cabins to consider, some modest renovation being the next, obvious step; I was thinking maybe something a bit upscale, with skylights over the bedrooms, good Danish woodwork and jets in the tub, just the sort of thing to attract the cross-country ski crowd, and while I was at it, why not keep the place running all year? (Never mind that I didn't know anything about running a ski resort.) My thinking was all purely hypothetical, the way people will talk about what they'd buy if they won the pick-six, but the more I spun ideas around, the more the whole thing made a kind of sense, as if the camp had always been mine.

And of course, I was really waiting on the dock for Kate, though it was even money whether it would be she or Joe who came to find me. It was Kate I wanted to see that night, there by the lake on the first really chilly night of summer, all my plans hatching. But an hour passed, the beer can grew warm and light in my fist, and I was still alone. Across the lake, the loons, quiet since sunset, piped up again. The lights of Harry's cabin were still on; shapes moved by the window, and I saw Hal come out to the porch, holding January in his arms. It would be a difficult night for all of them, I knew. And when I think of that night, as I like to do, my memory begins here, with Hal on the porch with his daughter in his arms and the sound of the loons, their ghostly, echoing music filling the starry air.

I was just about to give up and head in when I heard footsteps coming down the gravel path to the catwalk behind me. A light step that I knew: Kate.

"Howdy, stranger." She plopped down beside me, and I saw that she had changed into blue jeans and an oversize sweatshirt (PROPERTY OF BOWDOIN ATHLETIC DEPARTMENT). She pulled her knees up to her chest and drew the sweatshirt down over them, bundling herself all the way to her ankles.

"Great loons," she said. "Aren't you cold?"

"Some." I held up my empty can and rattled the dregs. "I'd offer you a beer, but I drank it."

"I should have thought to bring some. Or maybe champagne?"

"Is the news that good?"

Kate sighed and looked out over the lake. "Well, I wish my parents had let me in on the whole story. And I'm a little pissed off at my father for that stunt with the Scotch. But yes, on the whole, yes. It's what they want. That it's you who gets the place is . . . well, something nice. A bonus."

"What about you?"

"Well, that's a question, Jordan." Her voice was serious. "What about me?"

I followed her eyes across the water. The land on the other side wasn't actually part of Harry's estate, though it might just as well have been, since the camp held a ninety-nine-year lease from Maine Paper for two hundred acres rimming the lake to the north and west. I would be a very old man when it ran out. I didn't know exactly where the lines fell, but I didn't have to. It was so much land it didn't matter.

"I guess I was thinking maybe you'd stay. You know, guide in the summers."

"Maybe nothing, Jordan." She hugged herself in the cold. "Say what's on your mind. You want me as a *guide?*"

"That's not what I meant." I didn't know what to say. I thought about the winter just passed, the long months of thinking about her and the hard emptiness it had carved inside me. Until that night—until just a couple of hours ago, in fact—I'd been ready to give up everything: the camp, the life I had here, who I was. "I'd miss you."

She bumped my shoulder with hers. "Better. Now, how bad exactly?"

"Well. A lot. I'd say I'd miss you plenty."

"It wouldn't be the same without me, something like that? I'm not leading the witness here, am I?"

I nodded. It was too dark to see her face clearly, but I thought she was smiling. She enjoyed being smart in just this way, her mind moving a little faster than everybody else's.

"No, it wouldn't be the same. Not at all."

Kate undid her legs from under the sweatshirt and let them fall over the edge of the dock, shifting her weight to balance on her palms. "I don't mean to put words in your mouth, Jordan, but sometimes you work this north-country Mainer thing a little too hard. Maybe it's the winters up here, I don't know, but waiting to hear from Jordan can be pretty trying sometimes."

"It gets pretty quiet," I said. "You spend a lot of time not even really thinking."

"Jordan," she said a little crossly, "I know you. I've had eight years to figure this out. I'll admit there are still some things I don't get. But not *thinking?*" She shook her head. "I don't believe that for a second."

A moment went by, and from Harry's cabin, breaking the stillness, came the sound of muffled coughing. I thought of the plastic mask, the shiny tank with wheels. His long night had only just begun. Kate was perfectly right about me, of course. I wondered why I hadn't thought anyone would notice. But now I knew they had.

"You know, last winter I almost came down to see you at school. I practically had the truck packed before I decided not to."

"Well, you should have, Jordan." She gave a measured nod. "If you'd called, I would have told you to come."

"I wish I had."

"Now we're getting somewhere. Let me ask you something. What else do you wish? That maybe you could kiss me?"

I started to speak but couldn't, and Kate gave a little laugh. "I'm sorry to rattle you, Jordan, but someone's got to."

I began to take a sip of my beer before I remembered it was empty. "I've thought about it," I said.

"Me too, Jordan. Me too. But it hasn't happened. You know, most of the men who want to kiss me at least go ahead and try."

"How do they do?"

"Oh, about average. Some get kissed back. The ones that don't . . . well, I'm sure they'll be all right. Nothing really terrible ever happens, though. Nothing terrible would happen to *you.*"

"It's not that simple," I said. "I don't think your folks would be too crazy about it."

I heard her sigh. "Oh, Jordan, probably they'd like nothing better. You know that as well as I do."

Did I? But I couldn't remember; couldn't say if, sometime between the knock-kneed thirteen-year-old-tomboy Kate I'd first met and the Kate who sat beside me now—the Kate that was, in every way, a free

agent and grown woman, smart and sensible and basically *interesting*—
I'd detected any signals from Joe and Lucy, one way or the other.

"Besides, Jordan. I don't need their permission. You think you do, but
that's because you're a gentleman. All the more reason, if you ask me."

Out on the black lake, the loons went to work again—not the long,
mournful cries of first darkness, but a crazy babbling that seemed to
ricochet to the far shore and back, and the tussling splash of wings on
water. It took a minute for everything to quiet down once more.

"So, it's agreed, then?" Kate said. "You'll kiss me sometime? It's just
an idea I have."

We were holding hands, though I couldn't say exactly how this had
happened. "It seems like a good one."

"And kids, lots of kids. I was an only child, and that wasn't the best
deal around."

"God almighty, Kate."

She laughed again, enjoying herself. "A little fast? Okay, I see your
point. In fact, I can't even kiss you now, much as I'd like to. You might
think it was only because you're rich."

"I'm not rich."

"Oh, yes you are, Jordan. You might be too nice to know it, but you
are." She paused and straightened her back. "So I'm not going to. I
wish somebody had kissed somebody around here a long time ago, but
now we'll have to wait."

I was barely following any of it; I felt like I was being dragged from
a horse, though I was happy too—more than happy. "If you think
that's best."

"And I'm not the prize, you know. I don't necessarily come with
Harry's deal."

"I never thought you did."

She leveled her gaze at me. "Just so that's clear. And I have med
school to think about. It may not seem like it, but that's mostly what's
on my mind right now."

I nodded. "That makes sense to me."

"Good."

We heard Harry's door swing open. A dark form stepped out on the porch: Hal again. With his hands on his hips he arched out his back in a long stretch; catching sight of us, he gave a little wave to tell us everything was all right. He sat down in one of the chairs with his feet up on the railing, and then I saw someone else coming up the path to meet him. It was the right size and shape to be Frances, but when she stepped into the light of the porch lamp I saw it was Lucy. She was carrying a picnic basket—a late supper, I figured—and passed it to Hal over the rail. The two of them spoke quietly for a few minutes before Lucy hurried back the way she'd come. Hal stood a minute before taking the basket inside. At last the light by the door went out.

"I'm worried about her," Kate said finally. "She's taking this hard."

"Your mother you mean?"

Kate nodded. "She's always been fond of him. It wasn't always easy for her up here, but Harry was one of the good things."

For a second we just sat there, looking at one another. I felt her thumb brush over the top of my hand—the smallest gesture, light as air.

"Goddamnit, Jordan."

"What? What's wrong?"

"Am I all alone out here? Are you really that rusty?" She signed impatiently at my blank look. "That was when you were supposed to *try* something."

"Just then? I thought we were supposed to wait."

"We were, Jordan. I never said how long." She shook her head, though I thought she was about to laugh. "Another moment lost," she groaned.

"This is complicated," I said.

"Yes and no." Kate rose, releasing my hand to come around behind me, where she knelt on her haunches and put her arms around my chest, her chin resting in the hollow of my shoulder. It hurt a little, and I think that's what she had in mind. "You lovely, lonely man," she said, close to my ear. "You really *are* this place. Harry knows it, I know it, my folks know it. Everyone knows it but you." Then she pressed her cheek to mine—a bright quick burst of Kate—and was gone.

The Part of Me
That's Missing

Joe

I awoke knowing it would be a last morning: not *the* last morning, but a morning of final things.

I have always been a deep sleeper. My nights are long and restful, dependable as a hammer. The usual gripes of men my age—the acid reflux, pinched plumbing, and insomniac dread that send us prowling the halls to mull over every missed field goal, botched kiss, and embarrassing pratfall of our lives—have yet to affect me, and though I know the day can't be far off, that one of these nights the boom will fall, for now I sleep the sleep of the dreamless dead. According to Lucy I don't even snore. I just kind of snuffle every once in a while into the pillow, like a good golden retriever.

So I awoke that morning as always, 5:10 on the dot without an alarm to tell me so, just the feel of the turning world doing its work and my mind as empty as a bucket, and the first thought that came to me as I lay under the blankets in the chilly room was the fact that Harry had not died, because somebody would have come to tell me if he had; and then this other notion, a strange one: this idea of final things.

Lucy was already up and about; I heard the shower running, then the groan of the old pipes as she turned the water off. Lucy wasn't one to dawdle in the bathroom, and it wouldn't do for her to find me still in bed. I rose and dressed quickly for the day. Khakis and an old denim shirt frayed at the collar and wrists, a Synchilla vest that Kate had given me for Christmas, wool socks and Birkenstocks, which I'd trade for boots when things got rolling; on my belt, a Buck knife and one of those all-in-one tools in a leather holster, the only gizmos I carried. Once we were closed down for the season, I'd planned to do something about those groaning pipes, maybe even rip down the bathroom once and for all and make it nice, with some new fixtures and tile. I'm a man, a hole in the ground is pretty much all I need, but redoing the john was just the sort of project I enjoyed, and it would have made a nice present for Lucy. But those plans were now moot—a relief, in a way, and also strangely depressing. Outside the sky was paling, not black to gray but easing into a kind of mellow tan color, meaning a clear day ahead, and hot: the last real day of summer.

I was standing at the window when Lucy entered the room, wearing a bathrobe and squeezing the water from her hair into a towel.

"So," she said, and looked at me expectantly. "A quiet night?"

"Looks like Harry may get his wish. I think we would have heard if anything had happened."

"I thought so too." She sat down heavily on the bed and looked at her feet. "God, I hardly slept at all."

From the look in her eyes I knew that she was thinking about her own father, who had passed four years before. By then my in-laws, Phil and Maris, had sold the sawmill and moved down to Orchard Beach, into an apartment complex that pretended it wasn't an old folks' home but of course was: no kids allowed, not a single resident under sixty, ramps on all the stairways and handholds in the johns. Phil's arthritis had gotten pretty bad by this point—all that standing around on the hard ground through too many Maine winters—and he was deaf as a fence besides, from listening to the saws; like those old-time hockey players who skate without a helmet, Phil never once used earplugs, though he made everyone else wear them. He and Maris had talked about Arizona or even Las Vegas, someplace warmer and drier for Phil's knees, though this was just talk; they'd never been to either place that I knew of, even to visit. Phil Hansen and I had been through our rough patches over the years. I think we had far too much in common to be completely comfortable with one another, and I sometimes held it against him, the poor care he took of himself.

But in the end we'd let bygones be bygones, and when he'd died of a stroke—actually three strokes spread over as many weeks, bringing him down slowly, like a chopping axe blade—I had served as one of the pallbearers, weeping the whole way from church to gravesite. The funny thing was, it had taken Maris all of six months to pull up stakes and settle in Scottsdale, where she was now keeping company with a widowed dermatologist and had a golf handicap in the low teens. I was pretty sure Phil wouldn't have minded all that much, though Lucy fumed for days whenever we got a postcard from her mother, always with the picture of some golf course on it and three blandly cheerful sentences saying, more or less, why the hell didn't I do this before?

I sat beside Lucy on the bed. She was wriggling into a pair of jeans, and when she stood to pull them over her hips, I stayed where I was. My head felt oddly heavy, and for a second I even considered going back to sleep.

Lucy drew a sweater on over her head and looked at her watch. "Five thirty, Joe. You have a party, don't you?"

I nodded. "The lawyers, cabin five."

"No rush, then." Lucy rolled her eyes a little. "I think you'll find they won't mind a little extra shut-eye."

I'd heard them, too, as I was going to bed. They'd arrived the afternoon before, up from Springfield or Worcester or some other midsize New England city down on its luck, and spent most of the day in town ogling the scenery and laying in enough snacks, beer, and ice to feed a frat house. They asked me after dinner if I could take them out the next morning, "someplace special." A pleasant enough bunch of fellows, I thought, though lately it had seemed to be raining lawyers. They'd said they wanted to get an early start, though everybody does.

"They want to get drunk, it's their problem." I heard the grumpiness in my voice and let it ride. "They said early, early's what they'll get. I thought I'd take them up to the old Zisko Dam. Not much action anywhere else."

At the mirror, Lucy pulled her hair back into a ponytail. "The show must go on, I guess. I'll put together some box lunches for them. Bring the radio with you, too, all right?"

I was watching her face in the mirror. "The radio? Why do I need the radio?"

She turned back to me with a correcting look and slid into her shoes. "For Harry, Joe," she said. "For Harry."

By the time the pickup was loaded it was just six, the sky already lit from end to end though dawn was still a few minutes off. I thought I'd give the lawyers a few extra minutes of sleep, so I drank a quick cup of coffee with Lucy in the kitchen; we had two girls from the high school helping out that summer, but they wouldn't come in till six thirty when their shifts started. I helped Lucy with the sandwiches and snacks and pop—if the lawyers wanted anything harder, it was on their nickel—put these in the truck with the rest of the gear, and drove down the trace to their cabin.

By my reckoning, the lawyers were going to be feeling a lot less chipper this morning than they had the night before: I counted twenty-six empty beer cans on the porch, and enough cigar and ciga-rette butts to send the surgeon general into orbit. An empty fifth of Jack Daniel's Green Label was sitting on the floor, and beside it, a cap-sized pint bottle of what I guessed was schnapps or something worse. This bothered me not one bit—we're hardly the Ritz, or, for that mat-ter, the St. Regis; get drunk as a monkey on Sterno if that's what you like, just try to keep it down—and in fact, the mess they'd made was just the sort of opener I needed: cleaning it up would take a few min-utes and make enough noise to get my lawyers out of bed while also letting them know that perhaps a little better citizenship was the order of the day. I fetched a garbage bag from the truck, tied it to one of the porch posts, and was launching the last of the empties into it when the door swung open and one of them stepped out, a heavyset guy with a tonsure of gray hair, smacking his lips and blinking at the sunlight. I'm good with names, and I remembered his: Bill Owens. The reservation had been in his name, though the American Express he'd given me at check-in was a corporate card, billed to the chemical company they all worked for, an outfit called Sentocor Industrial Lubricants. If anyone needed a little time away in the woods, I figured, it'd be these guys.

"Morning, Joe." He surveyed the wreckage and quickly grabbed a beer can off the floor. "Sorry about the mess. I guess we were all in pretty high spirits last night."

Somebody had left a burning cigar on one of the porch rails, searing a brown rut into the wood. I picked up what was left of it with thumb and forefinger and dropped it in the bag. "Not a problem. You're here to have a good time. I'll have somebody get you guys a bucket of sand for the butts."

He smiled sheepishly. "Right-o. Got it."

"Like I said, it's not a problem." I tied off the bag and took it down to the truck. Lucy had made me a thermos of coffee, but Bill looked like he needed it more than I did. I brought it up to the porch and poured him a cup.

"Here, this should set you straight. Hope you don't mind the cream and sugar, that's how I take it. We better get a move on, though. We can grab you guys a little breakfast on the way."

He took the coffee like a shot of whiskey and gave his head a horsey shake. I could tell he was feeling pretty bad, though part of him was enjoying this fact; the pain was ironclad proof that he was having the time of his life.

"That goddamn bourbon," he said cheerfully. "Whose fucking idea was that?" He raised the cup in a little toast. "Though a shot of it in the coffee would be pretty good about now."

In the cabin I heard footsteps, water running, the low murmurs of men complaining about their hangovers and laughing about it. Bill took another long sip of the coffee, leaned his head back, and actually gargled. You can take the boy out of the frat house, I thought, but thirty years later he'll still gargle his coffee and chew his aspirins dry.

"Okeydokey." He shook the last drops over the edge of the porch and deposited the empty cup on the rail with a purposeful thump. "We are locked and loaded, first sergeant. Give me a minute to round up the troops?"

"Take what you need. It's your day."

"By god, you're right. One hundred *percent* right." He stepped to the rail with his hands in his pockets and gave a long, hungry-eyed look at the lake, like a Roman general looking over the green fields of Gaul. The air had already begun to thicken with the day's building heat, and I felt the first beads of perspiration popping in a damp line along my forehead. The wool socks and vest would have to go.

"This goddamn place," he declared. "Just unbelievable. Like Switzerland or something. Why don't people know about it?"

"A few do. Not many, though."

He stood another moment with his back to me, jangling something in his pockets, keys or loose change, then turned from the rail and squinted his eyes in a way that made me wonder what he thought he'd discovered about me.

"Well, mum's the word, my man," he said, and gave me a chummy wink. It was just the sort of practiced gesture that had probably worked magic on any number of juries trying to decide if his bosses had poisoned the playground or not. "You got kids, Joe?"

"Just the one. Kate's a junior at Bowdoin. She was at the front desk when you checked in."

He nodded. "Sure, Kate. Right. How about that?" I waited to hear about his own—the son in law school following in the old man's foot-steps, the grown daughter married to an architect and pregnant with twins—but all he did was cross his arms over his chest and shake his head with an expression of something like wonder.

"Well." He clapped his palms together. "As you said, time marches on." Never mind that I had said the opposite; it was what he needed to hear. "I'll get these guys moving."

I waited by the truck for five minutes until they emerged. Fresh handshakes and first names all around: besides Bill there was Mike, fifty and change, a wiry, loose-limbed guy with a cropped beard who looked like one of those old-time marathon runners; Pete, a puffy youngster in his mid-thirties—probably the baby of the outfit—who seemed to be suffering the most, if his moist handshake was any indication; and Carl, fat and happy as a hamster, whom they all called Carl Jr. Bill, Mike, Pete, and Carl: four bleary-eyed middle-aged corporate counsels from the poison factory, nursing sour guts and ice-pick whiskey headaches, a little slow out of the gate but on the whole willing to re-up for a second tour and give the day their best manly try.

"Weren't there five of you?" I had counted five the day before.

They all looked at each other and burst into laughter. "Right you are," Bill said, and slapped me on the back. "But I don't think you'll be seeing him for a while. Poor slob looked like he *died.*"

At the deli in town we picked up egg sandwiches, powdered doughnuts, and more coffee all around, then headed south on county 21. It wasn't a particularly pretty drive, the highway hemmed on both sides by mucky lowland swamps, but I took it at a crawl; those wet little shoots were like moose catnip, and hardly a summer went by that some unlucky soul (nobody local; we know better) totaled his car, and sometimes himself, on this very stretch of road. A mature bull with a full antler spread is a sight to behold even when it's nothing new to you, but it's not the size of the thing that does the damage: it's the geometry. Nearly all that weight is suspended four feet in the air on legs as skinny as pipe cleaners, so you catch one broadside, driving, let's say, a late-model Ford Taurus, and before you can say "what the goddamn," seven hundred pounds of permanently startled moose flops right over the hood and through your windshield—what the EMTs up here call "a Maine lap dance." It doesn't take a bull, either; even a yearling can do serious damage.

Bill was riding in the truck with me, his buddies following in Pete's BMW. A good rule of thumb is thirty-five at dusk or dawn, and in the rearview mirror I could see pasty-faced Pete, sighing with exasperation and banging his hands on the wheel. He mouthed a sentence I heard as "Will you fucking *go?*" I was already thinking I maybe didn't like him, and that I wasn't the only one.

Beside me, Bill polished off a second doughnut and cracked the lid on a fresh cup of coffee. He lifted his eyes to the mirror and frowned.

"Oh, don't mind him, that prissy little fuck. Doesn't know when he's having a good time." He slurped his coffee and opened his window to smoke. "You mind?" I shook my head no, and he pulled out a Pall Mall from the pack in his shirt pocket and lit it off the dashboard lighter.

"Oh, Pete's all right. Just got some growing up to do. Going through a nasty divorce, too, not that that's any excuse." He waved his cigarette toward the roadside. "Pull off here a second, willya?"

I let the pickup glide to a halt and waited in the cab while Bill saw to his business. In the rearview, Pete and Carl Jr. shook their heads and shared a laugh at the boss's tiny bladder. What with the smoking and the whiskey, I had Bill pegged for prostate problems for sure, not that any of us can avoid that forever.

"One more good thing about this place," Bill growled, climbing back into the cab with his cigarette still clamped in his teeth. "Man can haul it out anywhere he has a mind."

We drove the last ten miles without talking. The land we were passing through was typical northwest Maine scrub, pretty heavily logged though you wouldn't know this from the highway, and laced with old logging roads that you wouldn't find on any maps. Just past the town of Pine Stump Junction—three blocks of run-down houses, a post office hardly anybody used, and a general store that hadn't been open for a decade—I pulled the truck off the road into a dirt parking area. A few other cars were parked at random angles: a couple of rust-streaked pickups and 4x4s I recognized, but also the usual smattering of wagons and sedans with out-of-state plates, most with expensive Swedish cargo racks pinched to their roofs and the familiar assortment of bumper stickers and window decals favored by the L.L. Bean set: PHILLIPS ACADEMY ANDOVER, ARMS ARE FOR HUGGING, MIDDLEBURY COLLEGE, and my favorite, VISUALIZE WHIRLED PEAS. At the far corner of the lot, beside a rusty Dumpster where the locals went to watch the bears make their evening raids (Kate loved this when she was little; she called it "bear TV"), the undergrowth opened like a garden door onto a dirt trail you might not have noticed unless you were looking.

"Okay," Bill said, "what now?"

I turned off the engine and tossed the keys under the seat. "We hoof it. The dam's about two miles in from here."

"The dam?"

"Old WPA thing connecting the upper and lower Ziskos. Been abandoned for years, since Maine Power built a bigger one upstream and pulled out the turbines. The gate's stuck open, so there's fish by the ton, even when it's hot like this. The big Atlantics come up to feed below the spillway. You'll see."

I walked back to the BMW as Pete's window glided down to meet me. Carl Jr. was smacking on a last doughnut; Marathon Mike, stretched out in back, was fast asleep, his head propped on a sweater against the door.

"This is the place," I told him. "Just park anywhere."

Pete looked around and scowled. "This is a brand-new forty-thousand-dollar BMW. You want me to leave it *here?*"

"That's the idea." There was no use getting mad; it was going to be a long day with these guys. "Just be sure to leave the keys in it for the valet."

In the passenger seat, Carl Jr. slapped the dashboard and burst into laughter. I felt an instant rush of love for him, balancing my already intense dislike of crybaby Pete—though I was also suddenly sure that Mrs. Pete had made off with the whole kit and caboodle, save for one very expensive BMW.

"Very fucking funny, you asshole," Pete said to him. He looked back up at me from the window. Whatever I was going to get, I figured, would have to do for an apology. "Okay, that didn't come out right, I guess."

"No, it didn't."

"Oh, for Christ's sake, just park the thing," Carl Jr. said. "Nobody wants to steal your fucking car."

. . . . .

As far as I know, Kate never minded having a convicted felon for a
father. After all, it wasn't as if I'd hurt anybody, or robbed a bank, or
even cheated on my taxes. (To the contrary: my brief and rather cushy
trip through the federal justice system was enough to turn me into a
model citizen forever. I don't so much as double-park, and you could
eat off my taxes.) Though my crime was in every way a failure of
proper obedience to the proper authority, it's also true that the backward glance of history has been kind to those of us who, for whatever
reason, hit the road when duty called. Some people even call us heroes.

"Congress never declared war. Against Vietnam, I mean."

Kate said this to me on a day of snow in deep midwinter—a school
morning, though with the drifts already a foot deep, nobody was going
anywhere. We were sitting at the kitchen table, drinking cocoa after a
trip outside to fill the bird feeders and taste the snow on our tongues.
The room was warm and close-smelling from the wet clothes we'd
propped by the open stove door to dry.

"Okay," I said, and put down my mug. "What brought this on?"

"They *didn't*. Mrs. Wister said so. We're learning about it in social
studies. She said a lot of people believed Vietnam was wrong."

Shellie Wister was Kate's fourth-grade teacher, something of a local
character who kept a menagerie of rabbits and other small animals in
her classroom and puttered through town in an old lemon-yellow VW
Squareback with a faded peace sign in the window and teardrop crys-
tals swaying from the rearview. She had moved up to the North Woods
to live on a commune sometime in '68 or '69, about the same time I
skipped town. The story went that she had been a society wife down in
Boston who simply woke up one morning to realize her entire life was
built on the murderous lie of warmongering capitalism. Though the
commune was long since defunct, a rocket that had blown up on the
pad, she still lived alone out in the country in a wood-heated cabin,
raising goats and chickens and composing fierce letters to the local
paper on everything from nuclear disarmament to the Nicaraguan
Contras—letters that, despite their argumentative ferocity, always

seemed to me unfailingly polite. Every few years she got herself arrested for chaining herself to a tree or some other good-natured nonsense meant to irritate the loggers, but the school board let her continue teaching despite these outbursts of Thoreauvian civil disobedience (required reading for draft dodgers, by the way), good teachers being about as rare in these parts as plastic surgeons. It was also pretty well accepted that Shellie was a lesbian, though in my opinion this was pure sour grapes: Shellie was a good-looking woman who simply didn't need or want a man, and the ones who tried quickly found this out.

Though she never said as much, I think Shellie thought the two of us shared a bond as criminals of conscience. I didn't have the heart to tell her this wasn't at all the case with me, and that Thoreau would have called me a coward to my face. And in any event, Kate absolutely adored her.

"Well, that's true," I said. "Many people did."

"Your father. My grandfather."

"He was one, that's right."

"Did you?"

I sipped my cocoa and thought. I had been waiting to have this conversation for years. But now that it had finally come, I felt completely unprepared, like a kid taking an exam he'd studied too hard for. Everything I'd planned to say was suddenly forgotten.

"I didn't like it. Nobody likes war, except maybe generals. But on the whole I'd have to say no, I didn't think it was wrong. If there hadn't been a good reason to fight, they wouldn't have asked me to go. That was how I thought of it."

"They didn't ask you. They *drafted* you."

"That's their way of asking, Kats. Like, when me or mom says, Kats, please pick up your room. It's a request, but we mean business. It's sort of the same thing."

"Quakers didn't go. Mrs. Wister told us about them. She said they were . . ." Her brow wrinkled with the effort of a new word. "Conscious objectors."

"The word is *conscientious*. And you're right. But if Mrs. Wister told you about them, then she probably also told you that Quakers are pacifists. You know that word, *pacifists?*"

Across the table, she nodded. "They don't believe in war."

"That's right. Any war. Or any kind of fighting at all. I don't feel that way, and if they'd asked me, that's what I would have said."

She frowned the way she had since she was small, her thoughts turned inward as she prowled the hallways of her argument, looking for an unlocked door.

"You could have been killed."

"True, I might have. But probably not. And in any case, that makes no difference. It was complicated, Kats. Those were crazy days. The truth is, I wanted to go to Vietnam. Well, not wanted. I thought it was my duty to go. But my father asked me not to."

Her eyes flashed—a hunter with the quarry in her sights. "Asked asked, or pick-up-your-room asked?"

"Well, I was a grown man by then, Kats. But yeah, that's pretty much how it happened."

"So, the government told you to do one thing, and your father told you to do another."

"That's right."

"And you had to choose."

"Smart kid. You've got it exactly."

That frown again. She looked into her mug a moment like a diviner reading tea leaves. "Then you *were* one," she said finally.

"One what, Kats?"

"Con . . . scientious objector."

Kate was nine when she said this to me. Nine years old, and she actually said this!

"Mrs. Wister asked me something after class. To give you a message."

I had seen this coming too. "Okay, shoot."

"She wanted to know if you'd come to school someday. To talk about the draft. About being a draft invader."

The mistake was such a treat I decided to let it go by. Draft invader—why hadn't anybody thought of this before?

"I don't really have much to say about it, Kats. Do you want me to?"

"I don't know."

"Four years cleaning fish and feeling homesick. It's not really a very good story. It was pretty smelly, actually."

"And you came back because I was going to be born."

I nodded. "Yup. I missed your mom, and your grandpa was getting sick and needed me to look after things here, and the whole thing had begun to look pretty stupid. But it was mostly for you."

"Tell me again about sleeping on the floor."

This was the part of the story she knew and loved the best—the part in which she was the main character.

"Well, let's see. You were born a bit early. About a month. And after you were born, Mom was pretty weak, and had to stay in bed for a while. So I slept on the floor by your crib to watch over you."

She got out of her chair and climbed onto my lap. "How small was I?"

She knew all of this already, of course, had heard it a hundred times. "The smallest person I'd ever seen, Kats. Five pounds and some-thing." I showed her with my hands. "But not too small. Just the right size for a girl baby."

"Tell me about the snow."

"Who said anything about snow?"

"Daddy!"

"Okay, okay, the snow. A couple of days after you were born there was a big snowstorm—"

"How big?"

"Well, pretty big. Huge, in fact. Four, five feet at least. Snow like you've never seen in your life. And then it got cold, as cold as I've ever felt. Ten, fifteen below zero. It was so cold that if you sneezed it would turn to ice as it came out your nose."

"Daddy, gross!"

"I'm just saying it was cold. And with all that snow and cold the power went out, and there was too much snow even for the plow, so there was no way anybody was going anywhere for a while, it was just the bunch of us all holed up together, me and your granddad, and your mom still weak and you so tiny."

"And you kept me warm."

"That's right. When it got really cold at night I wrapped a blanket around the two of us and held you tight by the fire, and that was how I did it. It was when I knew how glad I was to be home. It was like you were saying to me, Daddy, you're back now, and this is your job, keeping me warm. Just like now. Kats?"

"What?"

"You want me to tell this story to your class?"

She considered this a moment, then shook her head against my chest. "I guess not."

"That's what I was thinking too. But you don't have to tell Mrs. Wister. I'll tell her myself."

Which I did: when school resumed the next day, I instructed Kate not to take the bus home and drove into town to get her instead. Waiting by my truck in the pickup line I told Shellie Wister that Kats and I had talked things over and decided that four years gutting mackerel in New Brunswick and two more pushing a broom and boiling bedsheets in a VA psychiatric hospital weren't anything anybody else's children would actually be interested in. Our family story would stay just that: something for us, and not for the public record.

"I'm sorry to hear it, Joe. Anything I can say to change your mind?"

We were standing by the open door of the truck, our conversation blanketed by the roar of buses and yelling kids and general end-of-the-school-day chaos. Kate had wandered up the salted sidewalk to spend a last minute with her friends; though the air was still cold, the sun was bright as a heat lamp, a shining gift after two solid days under a dome of falling snow. Kate had removed her parka and tied it around herself, the empty arms dangling at her waist. Like most of her friends she was wearing an enormous purple backpack with the name of some singing group on it—New Kids off the Tracks or whatever it was—a Christmas present I had driven nearly two hours down to a Bradlees in Waterville to find. What in blazes did she keep in that thing? When she glanced in my direction I lifted my eyebrows to tell her to move it along.

"It's not that I don't appreciate the offer, Shellie. I just don't have anything interesting to say about it. You'd probably be bored."

"Don't sell yourself short, Joe. The kids could really learn something from you."

"All they'd learn from me is how to pack fish. I'm really not the best person to ask about this stuff."

She let her eyes hold mine another moment. She was wearing a bunchy sweater of raw gray wool, the kind that looks homemade and in Shellie's case almost certainly was. (No doubt she'd woven the wool, too.) A bright purple scarf circled her throat; she smelled a little of wood smoke, and beneath that, almost imperceptibly, a wispy hint of lilacs. I knew what she was doing with her eyes—she was a teacher, teaching—and bless her heart, I thought, thank God above for the Shellie Wisters of the world; though I also wanted very badly to shoehorn Kate from her friends and hit the road without having to explain any more than I already had. Shellie was clutching a clipboard across her chest, and as she stood before me, her dark eyes narrowed thoughtfully, letting the silence do what talk could not, I felt the conversation slip from its course and snap into a fresh line like a tacking sail.

"A lot of us think your father was a great man, you know. He helped a lot of people."

I had to laugh. "Pissed a few off too."

"True, he did. But what's the saying? Real courage is doing the right thing when nobody's looking. Doing the unpopular thing because it's what you believe, and the heck with everybody. It's a hard message to teach, especially these days, with that actor in the White House. All of a sudden it's like Vietnam never happened, like we never learned a thing. It's worse than disgraceful. It's a crime. That's what I'm trying to teach these kids, Joe. To think for themselves. That's what you could tell them about."

Somewhere in this Shellie had placed her hand on my sleeve—not quite holding it, but not just touching it, either. The gesture was unknowable, nothing I could break her gaze to consider, a sensation that would remain at the periphery as long as her hand remained in its mysterious contact with my sleeve. Somehow, it made me feel just as I did whenever I read one of her letters in the paper: like I was in the presence of an actual *grown-up*. The outhouse, the chickens and goats, the clacking loom in her smoky cabin: in the touch of her hand I felt the firm existence of these things, their patient purposefulness and calm utility, the way they expressed a solid life that was far more real, in its way, than the hodgepodge or random impulses that generally pass for adulthood. And here she was, this woman who might have been the second truly charismatic person I had ever met—my father being the first—suggesting I might have something to teach anyone. She had no idea how wrong she was about me, but for a second, just one, I knew what I would have told the class. *Most of us spend our entire lives trying to learn what it means to be brave. What we hope is that simply trying will count for something.*

"Well, I don't want to take too much of your time, Joe. I'm sure you have places to be." She released my sleeve, and just like that, the spell was broken. "Tell Lucy I said hi, won't you? And thank her again for her help with the bake sale. Those cinnamon buns of hers are always the first to sell out."

I couldn't have said how long the two of us had been standing there. Kate was nowhere to be seen. Then the crowds parted and I found her by the bus line, talking to a boy I didn't recognize, a sandy-haired kid in jeans and a flannel shirt holding a hockey stick he kept flicking on the pavement, the two of them standing together on the path in a nervous, happy way that could only mean one thing. *Boys,* I thought, and felt the word drop like a bomb to my stomach. Just a day ago she had crawled into my lap to hear a story of her babyhood. She might have actually put her thumb in her mouth. It wouldn't be long now until her life was full of boys.

"Joe?"

"Right. Sorry." I shook my head and returned my eyes to Shellie, suddenly embarrassed. "Took a bit of a trip there, I guess. Cinnamon rolls. Thanks to Lucy. Got it."

"It's okay, Joe."

"No, no, I'll tell her, first thing."

Her face lifted in a reassuring smile. "I meant about Nicky Pryor. The boy talking to Kate? Forgive me, but I saw you look. You probably know his parents, Cash and Suzie."

I looked again. "Jesus. That's Cash's kid, with the hockey stick? He looks so . . ."

She allowed herself a gentle laugh. "*Mature* is the word you're looking for. But he's a nice boy."

"I was going to say menacing."

"Maybe a little of that too."

Her eyes found mine again. What a pity, I thought, that Shellie had no children of her own. Though of course that wasn't right. She did have them; my Kate was one.

"I know it seems to happen fast, Joe. But believe me, they're still just children. Just barely, but they are. Maybe *trying* to be a little more. Certainly they'd like to be a little more. But it's still . . . oh, I don't know. Just a game. Like dress-ups, when they were small."

"What you're saying is, I've got time yet."

"Hell's bells, Joe." She laughed again, this time with pleasure. "I'd say it just to cheer you up."

In rubber waders, boots, and fly vests, a two-mile walk over even pretty flat terrain can feel like ten, and by the time I got my lawyers to the dam, the bunch of them were a sorry sight, breathing hard as horses and drenched with yeasty-smelling sweat. On the way, Bill had stopped twice more to pee—the poor guy couldn't go half an hour without muttering an apology and taking a trip to the weeds—and though the rest of them were decent about it, waiting by the side of the trail in what passed for respectful silence, I could tell this generosity was motivated less by friendship or goodwill than their own sympathetic pangs of worry. Prostate, I'd figured, though now I was also thinking type 2 diabetes, which my father had toward the end. Either way, I thought Bill would tell me which it was before the day was through. The sun was blasting through the trees when we reached the gate, and as I fumbled with the padlock, I gave them the lay of the land.

"The dam's about a hundred yards down this incline. Maybe another two hundred yards across, and there's a catwalk but no handrails, so be careful. The Army Corps of Engineers keeps a watch station, but nobody's been in it for years. On the other side of the catwalk a trail loops down to the old turbine outlet at the base of the dam. The water's rough and tricky to wade, but you can fish from the rocks if you like."

Bill nodded. "Okay, I'll bite. How rough is rough?"

We could all hear it plainly now, a sound you might mistake as wind in the trees as you hiked up the path, but not this close: the muscular pounding of a thousand gallons of ice-cold water pouring out the vacant turbine channel each and every second. Where we stood you could smell it, too, all that cold water mixing with the air of the valley, like icy breath falling out a freezer.

"It sounds worse than it is. If you're careful and stay clear of the outlet, you should be fine."

We made our way down the last of the path. Where it cleared the trees the ground and sky opened like jaws, giving us a broad view of the two lakes and the dam between them, a wall of white concrete you couldn't look straight into when the sun hit it. The drop on the downstream side was eighty feet; below it, water roiled in a frigid roar of boiling whitecaps, then fanned out in a broadening spillway before emptying, another thousand yards below, into the Lower Zisko. You could fish any part of it, and on any given day it could all be good, but the upper end, where the water was trickiest, was generally best; all that moving cold water churned up the small feeding fish that the landlocks loved, drawing them closer to the surface. The control station stood on our side of the dam, empty as always. A second gate, also unlocked, guarded the entrance to the catwalk, with a large sign of warning: NO TRESPASSING. DANGEROUS WATERS. NO SWIMMING. DO NOT CROSS THE DAM.

Pete stopped at the gate. "I don't know about this. Is it safe? This doesn't look legal. The sign says no trespassing."

They all paused, lawyers thinking about the law and maybe that eighty-foot drop to boot, but then Bill stepped forward and swung the gate wide. "Joe, anybody ever drown out here?"

It had happened, I knew, but not for years. I saw where he was going and thought I'd play along. "All the time," I said.

"Good." He winked at me, then smirked in Pete's direction. "See? We'll make a man of you yet, youngster."

Pete folded his arms across his chest. "I've got an idea. Why don't you go fuck yourself?"

Bill snorted and stepped through the gate. "What is this, fourth grade? Don't be such a pussy, son."

It all seemed like a jolly joke, but by the time we got to the other side, I could tell something was wrong with Pete. His face had gone the white of chalk, and he was breathing in shallow little puffs. I sent the other three ahead to wait while he sat on a big piece of limestone, his rod across his knees.

"It's the heights. I can't stand heights." He looked back the way we'd come and grimaced like he'd seen his death. "Jesus. Is there another way back?"

"Afraid not, unless you call a helicopter."

Pete put his head in his hands, letting himself take a moment just to breathe; his hands were shaking, and for a second, I actually felt sorry for him. Bill, Mike, and Carl Jr. had already made their way down the embankment to the base of the dam and were looking the water over. In a large party, there was always one, and Pete was the one.

"Mother . . . fucker." He gave his head a sharp shake and looked up, squinting into the light. "Did you mean it, about people drowning?"

"Nah. I was just kidding around."

"Well, very fucking funny. What was that thing where the water went in? Christ, it was sucking like a toilet bowl."

He was referring to the wide concrete tube that stuck ten feet or so above the surface of the lake on the upstream side. A series of gates, like the open spaces between rungs on a ladder, pulled water down to the bottom of the dam. Only the top gate was open, but with the water so low, it sat right at the surface, water swirling around it in a whirlpool.

"That's the inlet tower. It used to draw water down to the turbines, though they pulled those out thirty years ago."

"Listen," Pete said, "I probably should tell you I don't know how to do any of this. The only thing I know how to fish for is a can of tuna at Stop and Shop."

"I kind of guessed."

"It gets worse. I can't even swim."

"Not at all?"

He shook his head hopelessly. "Something about my body mass. I can do the strokes okay, but I sink like a rock."

I nodded silently. What was there to say?

"I'll tell you a story," Pete went on. "At Harvard there's this idiotic swim test you have to pass to graduate. The family that built the library lost their son on the *Titanic,* so everybody has to make it across the pool and back just to get their diploma. Like being able to swim would have helped the poor bastard in the middle of the North Atlantic. Know what I did?"

Never mind that this little story was his way of letting me know he'd gone to Harvard. "You cheated?"

"Swimming the thing was out of the question. I actually had a scheme cooked up to have one of my roommates take it for me. But when the last day for the test came, he said he couldn't do it. Guy's all lined up with a big Wall Street job, no way he was taking any chances for me. I went down to the pool, and there was this long line, mostly Asian kids shivering in their skimpy little suits, I have no fucking idea why, but all of them waited like me until the last day. When my turn came, I jumped in and just let myself go under. I just sat on the bottom of the pool and waited for somebody to pull me out. Who fucking knows how long I was down there, but it felt like forever. But then, the lifeguard yanked me out. 'You can't swim?' he asks me. 'Not a stroke,' I say. For a long time the guy just looked at me. Sixty thousand dollars' worth of education, and it all comes down to this one guy, what he's going to do. 'Okay,' he says. 'Get out of here.' I couldn't believe it."

"Lucky break," I said.

"Lucky? I should have killed the guy. Want to know what I did next?"

In truth, I could have done without the rest of the story, but I knew there was no stopping it.

"Marched straight down to the law school and signed up for the LSATs. Right on the spot I decided completely out of the blue to be a lawyer. My girlfriend and I had been planning to join the Peace Corps after graduation, thought maybe we'd go teach in Africa or someplace. I wanted to be a writer, too. I'd actually published some short stories in the campus rag." He laughed miserably. "Can you believe it? Fucking short stories!"

Pete seemed a little young to mourn his life this way, and part of me, the generous part, would have liked to talk him out of this feeling, which was the worst kind of rabbit hole a man could go down on an otherwise promising afternoon. But I saw no chance of this. Streamside speeches on life's disappointments were a staple of the trade, and I had heard enough of them over the years to learn my limits. It also seemed likely to me that it was the girlfriend he regretted losing most of all. He would misremember her completely, of course; she was the muse of his unlived, better life, and in the nostalgic fantasy he was laying out, she would appear as a figure of pure lost opportunity, as soulfully splendid as the *Mona Lisa* in a G-string.

"Looks to me like you're doing okay," I said, trying to move the day along. "Seems to me it was probably a good decision in the long haul."

The lie was obvious, and he met it with a quick, correcting frown. "No offense, hombre, but that's easy for you to say." He gestured downhill, where the other three men were stringing up their rods. Bill was already wading out into the current. "You don't work with these assholes."

I decided not to point out that, technically, I did, at least for today;

it was what I was supposed to be doing that very minute, instead of trying to talk Pete out of believing he'd wasted his life by not going to Africa to screw his girlfriend in a grass hut and write his fucking short stories.

"Oh, the hell with it," Pete said finally. He slapped his knees and rose. "Let's get this over with."

EIGHT

Jordan

But in the morning, Harry Wainwright couldn't fish. He couldn't even get out of bed.

Hal found me in the dining room. His father had gone through a bad night, he told me, up for most of it, with Hal and Frances taking shifts. Hal hadn't actually gone to bed at all, just grabbed a few winks tucked in a chair. We sat together by the big windows overlooking the lake and drank coffee while folks clomped in for breakfast. It was a little before seven; I was already keeping an eye cocked for the moose-canoers, though they usually didn't come along till at least eight o'clock—way past the time they were likely to see any moose, though the canoers as a group were cheerful vacationers out on a lark, ready to have a good time, moose or no.

"Maybe it was the drive up," Hal said, buttering a muffin. "Or not eating anything last night at dinner. Hell, maybe it's just that he's got *cancer*, for god's sake. He doesn't want to call a doctor, and he doesn't want to leave." He paused to chew, using the moment to take a fresh muffin from the basket on the table and pull it into moist halves. "This puts you in something of a bind, I guess."

I drained my coffee and told him no, that under the circumstances I was happy to wait all day; when Harry was ready to go, I'd be the one to take him. But what we were both thinking was plain enough: that maybe Harry had something else up his sleeve, that a bad night passing into an even worse day was what he'd had in mind all along. My heart went out to Hal. He was a nice guy, every bit as bright as his father, I'm sure, but he'd spent most of his adult life in the shadows, doing more or less what he was doing now: protecting the old man, and reassuring ordinary folks like me that the elephant in the dining room wasn't going to sit on them anytime soon. I'd have bet big that morning that Hal would have traded any number of silver spoons just to sit and think awhile about what it meant to be the grown son of a dying father.

Hal tipped back in his chair and looked past me through the windows to the lake, where the mist was lifting in loose swirls the color of ice. Lucy came out of the kitchen, brushing her hands on her red apron, and when Hal saw her, he caught her eye and smiled, raising a single finger from the edge of his cup. Somehow, his eyes looked even more tired when he did this. When people die it is sometimes said to be a blessing, and in Hal's face I saw what this meant. Lucy ducked back through the swinging doors—a sudden wash of kitchen noise, of pots and pans and spattering grease, all of it making me hungry—and Hal turned back to me. He took one last sip of his coffee and fit the empty cup back into its saucer.

"Well. Time to get the kid. If you can believe it, she slept through all of that last night. Now she wants to know why she can't watch Bert and Ernie. I've promised a boat ride instead." He gave one last look out the window and rose to go. "At least we'll have a good day for this, anyway," he said.

After Hal had left, I sat by the window a little longer—the day was shaping up to be a hot one—then got some more coffee and a muffin and took it outside into the damp morning air to get things under way. While Hal and I were talking, one of the moose-canoe parties had come in and sat down to breakfast, a couple with their teenage son (Lucy had shown them to a table, telling them in a voice loud enough for me to hear to take their time, the pancakes were especially good as long as you were *real* hungry, their guide would be along when they were done), and as I exited the lodge I saw two more drifting in my direction from the boat launch: a man about my age with a thin blond woman, pretty enough for me to pay attention. Her hair was still wet from the shower, and her face had the scrubbed look of someone in a soap commercial. The pair of them were dressed head-to-toe in high-tech outdoorsy synthetics, like a pair of models in a catalog, and they were looking around at the place with big smiles on their faces, all keyed up for a hearty meal and a long float down the river. I had them pegged as newlyweds, connecting them to the late-model Toyota with Pennsylvania plates parked by the dining room. Its rear window and one door panel were still smeared with fading congratulations and off-color honeymoon jokes they would probably be just as happy to be rid of, if only they could find a car wash.

"Dining room's right through here," I said, poking a thumb toward the door. They looked like they needed a little nudge to bring them back to earth, though I was as happy to let them ogle the place. They were just the sort of customers who would be back the next year for a week at full-rate with all the goodies. "You folks must be here for the moose run."

They stopped on the path. "That's right. We called yesterday? From the Lakeland Inn?"

"Sure thing." I didn't know a thing about it, not having taken the call. We shook hands all around. "I'm Jordan. Lucy's got a table for breakfast all set for you. She says the pancakes are good."

"Sorry we're so late," the man said. "We just couldn't get our act together this morning."

"Moose aren't going anywhere." They had, of course, already gone. "Take your time. We'll get you upriver whenever you're ready."

"We're staying in town," the woman told me, a little guiltily, and for the second time. A good number of the moose-canoers felt the need to apologize like this, as if staying somewhere else was somehow disloyal. "We tried to get in here, but everything was booked."

"It's a popular place," I agreed. "Lots of folks come back every year. We've got one guest right now who's been coming here thirty summers."

"Thirty summers," the man repeated. "Listen to that." He rocked his head upward, bunched up his lips, and gave a short, sharp whistle of amazement. He turned to his wife. "See what I'm saying?"

"I know, I know."

"Next year, we call *well* ahead," the man said.

She rolled her pale blue eyes. "I'll believe that when I see it," she said, laughing.

"I'll tell you what." I liked these two, and wouldn't have minded being the one to guide them. By the time we reached the put-in point, five bouncy miles upriver, we'd be like old friends, and they'd hardly remember what it was they came to see—guaranteeing that on the off chance a moose actually did cross their path, they'd remember the sight their entire lives. I was glad to see the man had a camera strapped to his belt, since moose as a rule are dumb as buckets and happy to pose.

"We've got some groups checking out this afternoon," I said. "After the run, come back to the lodge and we can show you some of the cabins. You can see if they suit you. You can book right now for next summer if you want. We might even have an opening later in the week. I can look into it for you."

"I bet they're great," the man said. "Right on the lake like that?" He ran a hand through his hair. "Man."

The woman leaned a little closer to me; her cheeks were pale, and I had the sense that, if I put my hands against them, they would be cool to the touch, like bed linens. For a moment I felt the urge, and also felt, strangely, that no one would mind if I actually did this. "We drove up from Philadelphia," she told me. "You could say it's a total hellhole."

"That's a shame," I said. "I bet it's nice to get away. Maybe when you get back, things will seem different for you."

She let her gaze drift past me. Beyond the lodge, the lake was shiny and solid as a ballroom floor under a full morning sun. If they hung around till nightfall, they'd see the same scene in reverse—the surface of the lake so still they'd want to walk across it, a perfect mirror image of the mountains under their feet.

"Pretty nice, isn't it?" I said.

"Nice? Holy mackerel." The man puffed up his cheeks and shook his head. "This must be the prettiest place in God's whole universe."

I watched them head off to the dining room and then went to check on Kate. I found her down by the storage shed, loading up the bed of the pickup with paddles and life preservers and the old Clorox bottles we used as bailers.

"I think we can time this okay," she said. "Don't you have some-place to be?"

"I think I'm stuck here awhile. This thing with Harry might not work after all." I helped Kate hoist the first canoe up onto the rack over the truckbed. "Hal thinks he may be dying. This isn't the leaky one, is it?"

"They *all* leak, Jordan. That's half the fun." She jumped down from the bed and pulled her hair back from her face. She was wearing san-dals, jeans, a gray T-shirt; over the truck's fender I saw the sweatshirt she'd worn the night before. I felt like none of us had gone to bed at all.

"Relax, Jordan. I'll get these folks upstream. Everyone's going to have a great day."

"Two groups are in, I think. I talked to one couple. They seemed nice."

"So, fine. I'll take care of them. We're on schedule." She tilted her head and searched my face. "Jordan?"

"Aw, I'm okay. It was hard to talk to Hal." I found myself digging a toe into the gravel and stopped myself. "I think he made me think of my own father, a little."

"Well, we haven't really talked about him," Kate said, nodding. "Maybe we should start?"

"I wish there was something to tell. The problem is, there isn't."

She sat down on the open tailgate, snuck a peek at her watch, and squinted up at me. "We've got a minute. Tell me anything. What do you remember?"

"He played the guitar. He liked lifting me in the air. His hair felt like touching a broom." I stopped. I had never said any of these things before. They were ordinary, and all that I had, but I had never said them. "I was three."

"What else?"

I closed my eyes and thought. "Wind."

"Wind. You mean what it sounds like?"

"No, not exactly." I opened my eyes. "I think he felt like wind."

"Well, he was a pilot, so maybe that's why. Maybe it was just something that happened one time, something you remember. It doesn't matter which." Her eyes, as she spoke, had never left me. Her gaze felt like a warm room I had stepped into. She stood and took my arm. "I'm glad you're telling me this. Something else, Jordan."

She leaned her face into mine. And I was thinking, for those moments, only of her; as if for the first time in my life I was having a single thought. Then we parted and the thought of Kate was suddenly woven like a thread through everything, all that had ever happened to me, the clean smell of the pines and the lake and the memory of my long lonely winters; the very turning world we stood on. They say that the moment your life appears before your eyes will be your last, but I'm here to say that it's not so very different when you kiss a woman like Kate, whoever your Kate may be.

"So, a big day in more ways than one." She peeked over my left shoulder and then my right, and dropped her voice to a whisper. "You think anyone saw?"

"We'll know soon enough, I guess."

"And you didn't mind?" She peered into my face as if she were reading tiny print. "I didn't ask, which was sort of rude."

"God, no." I would have given it all back, every cent, to kiss her again. "I'm glad you did."

She let her eyes fall. Her lashes, I saw, were thick with moisture. In all the time I'd known her, I didn't think I'd seen so much as a tear from her, and I wondered why she was crying now, what I'd done to deserve it. Then she put her hands to my chest and gently pushed me away.

"Okay," she said, and wiped her eyes quickly with the back of her wrist. "Show's over, folks. Now go help Harry catch his fish."

NINE

Harry

I never saw her again, my nurse with her knitting needles. I had dreamt her, of course, or the morphine had; I knew this without being told, as I also knew not to ask. Still, I thought she might visit me again, or I hoped she would, that night by the lake when I slept but did not sleep, dreamed but did not dream, was awake every minute and also not. The final unmaking of time, all its solid, familiar order undone, so that even the rhythm of day and night has lost its meaning and one is everywhere in one's life at once; all that night I drowned in time. And when dawn came—when the blackness of the shades began to pale, and the sky began the slow unlocking of its captured light—I was so surprised to find I was alive I assumed I actually wasn't. I was dead, but Meredith and Sam were not; while I had slept and died the earth and its heavens had flipped like a cake from a pan, and it was they who were alive, and missing me.

"Pop?" The creak of the cabin door, and behind it, a sweeping arc of day. Morning fills the room; in the chair by my bed, my grown son, Hal. I feel these things without looking. Just lifting my eyelids seems to require an impossible effort, like lifting a piano or reciting the phone book.

"Pop, it's Hal."

I thought I said something. I thought I said, *I dreamed I was dead, Hal. I saw your mother and brother. She was giving him his bottle in the armchair by the window, the one with the maple tree outside. The leaves were fat and green, and it was long ago.*

"How're you feeling, Pop?"

The baby began to cry; his diaper was wet. She changed him on the dresser, softly humming a song through the pins she held in her mouth. That sweet time of bottles and diapers, the smell of talcum and steam from the stove and the quiet house, and days folded into days. The taste of pins. It was a good dream, Hal.

"That's okay, Pop." His hand takes my wrist; he is watching me breathe, I know. I do my best to give him good breaths. But all the air I possess seems to sit at the top of my lungs, the slenderest inch of oxygen, like an ankle-deep puddle marooned by an evaporated sea.

"Well, you rest more." He pats my arm to tell me I've done well. "Okay? Just rest. I'll be back in a little while."

Footsteps, voices, all about me the rising tide of day. I hear the sound of Joe's pickup driving down the trace, the hollow clap of aluminum canoes coming on and off their racks, the bee-like, dopplered buzz of an outboard as it rounds the farthest point—the sounds of departure, of everything streaming away. Franny enters, full of her big-heartedness and the well-intentioned pretense that with a little more shut-eye I will be as right as rain and ready to run the hurdles. She kisses me on the forehead while she smooths my hair with her fingers, tells me about the weather in her loud, husky voice, holds my head to help me take small sips of water from a plastic cup. Harry, she says, are you being good? No fooling around now; rest is what you need. The lake isn't going anywhere, she says. When she is gone, Hal, my good lieutenant, returns with January, and a breakfast of muffins and juice I can smell but not bring myself to look at. From the little girl's lips bubble pleasant bits of wordlike sound: "baboo," "mawmish," "ticknuck." Gibberish, and yet as I watch her from my bed, her thoughts are as clear to me as the voice of an orator at a podium: *Where is Mommy? Why is everyone acting this way, the way they do when I can't sleep because my ears hurt and they take me to the doctor?* Her eyes inspect my useless form with calm appraisal. *I like the ducks, the ducks are interesting. There are ducks in New York, at the park where we go on Sunday and Daddy reads his paper, ducks and a carousel and a zoo with white bears like the ones in my snow globe. I like the bears best of all. If you'd*

asked, I could have told you. Grandpa, is that why we came, because you're
sick, and to see the ducks in Maine?

Is that what it means to be old?

Meredith's hand healed and was soon forgotten. Even the doctor who examined it the next day—complimenting my handiwork, and the choice of diaper ointment—seemed wholly unalarmed. We'd been to a party? How many drinks had she had? She looked tired; was the baby letting her sleep? He waved a flashlight beam over her damp eyes, asked her to hold out her hands and press her palms against his own, to stand on one foot and hop. The last made her laugh with embarrassment; hopping, like some kind of pogo stick! Was that all modern medicine could come up with? Twelve hours since the smell of burning skin had filled the kitchen, and now she was joking. The doctor was nobody we'd seen before: a slim man, olive-complexioned, who exuded a faint aroma of oranges. The lenses of his eyeglasses were thick as paperweights. When he was finished with his questions, he pulled a stool to the examining table and sat. Atop his head floated a disk of pink skin that I watched while he re-dressed her hand and smoked, squinting over the cigarette that bobbed in the corner of his mouth. He had read something lately, he remarked, about cigarettes and their deleterious effect on circulation at the extremities. He tipped one shoulder and frowned. He was no example, he admitted, rising and plucking a speck of tobacco from his tongue, but perhaps she might consider quitting smoking.

"He had the worst halitosis," Meredith said on the ride home. Her hand, wrapped in heavy gauze, lay palm-up on her lap—not part of her, but an object in its own right, like a package she was bringing to a party.

"I thought he smelled like oranges. Isn't that strange? Who smells like oranges?"

The doctor had given her a painkiller of some kind, a large white pill he said would make her drowsy. For a while we drove in silence.

"Maybe I will," she said finally.

"Will what?"

She turned toward me in her seat. Her left hand floated upward, a levitating cloud, and made a little wave. "Quit smoking."

Which she did; she stopped that very day, sweeping through the house to collect the cigarettes and matches and toss them in a bag and out the door, and soon enough the bandages came off, and what happened that summer night in the kitchen on Marvine Road faded from memory—a small and curious episode, but in the end an isolated occurrence, or so we thought, and certainly nothing to fret over. *How did you get that scar?* a friend might ask, passing her a drink at a party. *That scar there on your hand?* And for a moment Meredith would pause to examine it, to hold her hand before her face and turn it in the light like an old letter she'd found in the bottom of a drawer. *Oh, this?* she'd say, her voice brightening with recognition *This scar? You know, it was the funniest thing, what happened, the strangest thing really; we'd just gotten home from a party—Harry, do you remember? That doctor with the awful breath. You always tell it better than I do.*

Then Sam was sick, and what happened that night in the kitchen was mislaid, along with everything else. We were the parents of a sick child, a baby who would not grow, who still, as he passed his first birthday, wore the same clothing, the little T-shirts and fuzzy bags with arms, that we'd bought the week when he was born. It fell upon us swiftly, that awful year, beginning with an autumn cold that became bronchitis, which became pneumonia, and on and on—a period of time that seemed not to pass but to spread like spilled ink into a single, everlasting night of panic. No one understood what was happening; even the doctors could not explain it, not completely. His lungs were weak; there was something wrong with his liver; his heart, for no apparent reason, skipped every sixteenth beat. His body was a magnet for every kind of illness and infection. For a while we thought CF—cystic fibrosis. But the tests said no. Through the winter and spring he worsened: measles, strep throat, roseola with a blast of fever and convulsions; no childhood illness failed to touch him in those months. But when I remember that time, it's not the frantic nighttime dashes to the hospital I think of, or even the long, white hours of the hospital, but odd, unrelated moments when I found myself alone. Dusting off the car in the driveway after a sudden snowfall, in case Sam needed to go to the doctor; standing by the electric doors of the emergency room to wait for news and watching a haze of spring rain floating through the lighted cones of the street lamps; sitting in the kitchen of my quiet house on a morning in July—a morning when our baby was actually home and well—and feeling, for the first time, that Sam would truly die. Other children Sam's age would have been walking, saying their first words, learning to eat from a spoon. Our little boy was learning only how to leave us behind.

He would be forty-five now, a grown man, if he had not died that fall. His final pneumonia took him quickly: a fever that rocketed skyward, the tiny, bottlelike lungs filling, coma, death within hours. After all he'd been through, it seemed a mercy, though of course that was an illusion, something to say to fill the silence of his missing life: the bicycle he would not ride, the books he would not read, the friends he would not have and the girl he would not kiss. The thousand pains and pleasures of his life, shelved in a tomb that the door of early death had sealed. No, there was no mercy in what happened to my boy at all. When he died, he weighed just eleven pounds.

It's said that many marriages do not survive the loss of a child, that such grief is a room parents enter together but depart alone. I have no cause to argue the point, having sat in just that room. From that day forward we loved each other, Meredith and I, but we loved with broken hearts. And when, on a morning not long after we had buried Sam, I came into the kitchen to find Meredith standing at the window, cupping the curve of her stomach in a secret way that I alone understood, I knew we would go on.

Why Sam but not Hal? There is no knowing. I might as well ask, why Meredith and not me? I had a dog once—what a dog he was! A retriever with something else mixed in, a breed that liked to work and herd: Australian shepherd, maybe, or collie. I named him Mauritz, though Hal called him Ritzy, and it stuck. Ritzy the dog. A steadfast member of the team, as relentless as a metronome: Meredith joked that he would have taken a job bagging groceries at the corner market if only he'd had hands. I loved him, as one can only love such a dog; but I also knew what he was. Behind his eyes, twin chestnuts of the most tender soulfulness, lay, encased in its suitcase of bone, a brain that knew nothing at all of time or sorrow or even the true joy that sorrow makes possible—only its own desire to please, an aching, needful love that could achieve its fullest contentment with the most meager offering: a stale biscuit, a walk around the block to do his business, a pat on his golden head. His own existence, its nature and finitude, was a mystery to him; he might have thought he was a person, or else I was a dog. The day I took him to the vet to have him put down—he was thirteen, his hips so bad he could barely walk to his bowl—I could think of only this to say: "You have been a good dog, and a great comfort to me, and I thank you." It was all he wanted to hear. I'd never wished so badly to be the dog he thought I was.

We waited for Hal to grow sick, as his brother had, and to this day I think that because of this fear we never quite loved him well enough: we braced ourselves against his departure with the timid fantasy that he was not our son but a kind of visitor, a nephew or refugee, a child misplaced by unfortunate circumstances and temporarily given to our care. No photo albums or memento books or birthday parties (not until he was twelve and simply insisted; by then we had moved to Chappaqua and Hal couldn't be stopped from showing his friends he had a house with a pool). His entire early childhood went unrecorded and then, as his mother became ill, was subsumed by her struggle. I made my money, grew my business; it's not important how. Two stores became four, four became eight, a phone call from a withering competitor, offering to sell, and then the floodgates opened. My touch was golden; everywhere it was said that Harry Wainwright could do no wrong. And yet the money was nothing, the long hours pure distraction; Sam's death had turned me from a father into a provider, and into this task I poured myself like water from a pitcher. All of which is not to say that Hal is not a fine man, only that I can take no credit for this.

And, giving the loudest laugh to our fears, Hal was not just healthy, but robust. I realized this all at once, on an evening when Hal was fourteen. I was moving the garbage cans to the corner, a pair of large cans on wheels, when, over my shoulder, I felt his presence. The sun was behind us; his shadow, thrown on the driveway, stretched ten feet into the road. The effect was an illusion, a ten-foot-tall boy on eight-foot legs, like a giant from a fairy tale, but when I turned, the image I had just seen conflated in my mind with the actual boy before me, and what I saw wasn't a boy at all, but a man, or nearly. The broad chest, the tight waist, the legs and arms roped with muscle: all of these were a man's. He wore gym shorts, red high-top sneakers, and T-shirt despite the autumn chill—it was October, close to Halloween—and in the crook of one arm he was cradling a basketball. The way he held it, with such casual ease, seemed to transform the object completely, to inject it with vivid life: not a toy but a tool, like a carpenter's hammer or a writer's pen, it had become an extension of all the coiled energy inside him.

"What are you staring at?"

"Nothing. Just taking out the cans."

"You were staring."

I shrugged, still taken aback by the sight of him. I felt a little foolish. I loosened my tie. "How you holding up there? You want to shoot some baskets?"

He frowned. "You never shoot baskets."

"I can try. I used to be pretty good, you know."

He said nothing about this, but released the ball and gave it one firm bounce on the blacktop, catching it cleanly with a single, outstretched palm.

"Back in *Scranton*."

I heard the derision in his voice: Scranton, my boyhood Eden. I hadn't been back for years and years; my father was long dead, my mother living now in Florida. Every quarter I sent a huge check to the

nursing home, and three or four times a year I flew down to visit, usually alone, since Meredith could no longer travel. But Scranton: I'd not
really been back for more than a quick visit since '43, and the day my
father drove me north to the Maritime.

"Sure."

"I'm thinking of trying out for the varsity."

"Hey. That's great. You should."

He bounced the ball again. "I could have done that," he said flatly,
and pointed with his eyes to the cans.

"It's no bother. I've got it." I rolled the last can into its spot by the
curb. "The varsity. That's really terrific, Hal. What does your coach
think?" I tried to remember his name but couldn't. A heavyset man
with a back wide as a tortoise, wearing a whistle on a string. Myers?

"The cans are my job, Pop. That's all I came out here to say."

By this time—the day I saw my son's shadow in the driveway and
knew how much I'd missed—Meredith's hand was no longer a mystery. Another shadow falling across those years of work and worry: as
Hal grew, the inkling that something was seriously wrong with Meredith grew beside him, like a dark flower in an adjacent pot. Small, inexplicable injuries, the kind of mishaps that happen to everyone from
time to time but in Meredith began to accumulate with the force of a
mortal argument. For a while it was a joke: clumsy Meredith, accident-
prone Meredith, Meredith who could trip over her own feet on a bare
floor in broad daylight. She dropped things, knocked things off tables,
sliced her fingers open on knives and can openers, banged into other
cars in parking lots; her arms and legs and hands accumulated scars
like a Russian general's medals. Headaches, and a permanent sheen of
sweat, and she was always, always cold: *For goodness' sake,* she would
grouse, *why is it always so freezing in here? Did somebody forget to pay the
gas bill? What's wrong with this thermostat? What's the point of finally
having a little money if we can't heat the house?* Never mind that it was
summer, the windows wide open, the leaves fat and full of chirping

birds. Once, on a trip to Florida, on a day of ninety-degree heat and humidity heavy as goulash, she wore a wool coat to the beach.

It was when her speech began to flatten and slur—not the way a drunk speaks, the words collapsing under their own weight, but more as a kind of snuffing out, certain syllables inexplicably melting as she spoke: peesh for peach, shuz for shoes, tawble for table—that a diagnosis was achieved. I use the passive deliberately; it was an event without agency, as when one says "It's Tuesday" or "It rained." Syringomyelia: nothing we had ever heard of, and for just a moment, sitting in the doctor's office on Fifth Avenue on a pleasant winter afternoon after a train ride into the city and a good lunch downtown, the newness of the word itself made us fail to feel its weight. Seated on the far side of his desk, we shared a funny look. We had a boy in school, a business to run, ideas about the future: of a house in Maine or Florida, or selling the business and retiring early, of seeing London and Paris and Rome. If we had never heard of it, how bad could it be? Though of course the opposite was true: we'd never heard of it because it was rare, infinitesimally rare, and nothing you would want to know about if you didn't have to, like a brutal little war fought far away among people whose names you couldn't pronounce.

The doctor removed a fountain pen from his shirt pocket and, on a yellow legal pad, quickly sketched a pair of lines with a series of flattened circles between them. A cutaway view of Meredith's spine, we understood; really, it ought to curve a little bit, he said, like so, but we got the idea. He pointed with the tip of his pen to the flattened circles. See these? They were cysts, he explained, fluid-filled spaces where none should be; it was possible Meredith had been born with them, or at least had had them many years. It was hard to say, though in her case he believed the condition had been present for some time. She might have a single cyst, or several. The precise mechanisms were not well understood, he continued, though it was known that over time these cysts elongated, pushing nerve tissue against the bones of her spine. Imagine a balloon, he said, slowly expanding in a tube. Patients usually felt the effects first at the extremities—she said she'd first noticed this some years ago, yes, an incident with a cigarette, when she'd burned herself and not felt it? And, as the condition progressed, other things, the complaints she knew so well: the sweating and the constant coldness, the headaches and stumbling, the cuts and scrapes and difficulties of speech and the lack of sexual responsiveness. (For we had conceded this, too, when pressed, though also saying, well, wasn't such a thing more or less natural, didn't that just generally fade over time in any marriage?) All of this happening as the cysts filled and stretched and did their damage.

We listened like students, feeling somehow chastened; I had the absurd thought that we had fallen into a dream in which we were kids together at school and had been held back after class. The doctor's office door was closed; hung on the wall behind his desk were diplomas, certificates, assorted testaments to his credentials, all in heavy, gilt-edged frames. I tried to read them but failed, realizing only then, and with a mild alarm, that they were written in Latin. Time flattened under their gaze; all our life, it seemed, we had been sitting in offices like these. All right, I said, rousing myself, but about these cysts. When would they stop growing? Or could they be removed somehow? A pained and startled look bloomed across the doctor's face. He was sorry, he said, that he had not been clear. The thing was, they didn't stop growing. And inside the spinal column was far beyond reach. Perhaps someday such a thing would be possible, but that was years away. The nerves, we understood, were slowly being crushed. There was nothing to be done. He was truly, truly sorry. He knew we had a boy, still young. It was not good news, he knew.

How does anyone begin such a new era in their lives? We thanked him and left and took a taxi to the station. The strangest thing of all, how ordinary life goes on: even the condemned man needs to fill the hours. Beneath the smudged heavens of Grand Central, we ate littlenecks at the Oyster Bar, then went to catch our train. Before boarding, Meredith bought a magazine from a vendor on the platform, and a bag of roasted cashews. As the train carried us north, I watched her flipping through the pages, pausing here and there to read an article of interest, chewing on the roasted cashews that she removed, one at a time, from the waxed paper bag. The pages were printed with a cheap ink, and I saw that her fingers were smudged. Neither of us had said a word about the doctor's pronouncement; we had entered a kind of trance, the bubble of first-knowing. Her condition could take ten years to run its course, he'd said, and watching Meredith read her magazine, I felt for the first time in my life the shortness of a decade. Ten years, a hundred years, a thousand—once passed, I thought, time was all the same, all over. When the train stopped at Hartsdale, I saw, under the lights of the platform, that it had begun to snow. The air was as still as held breath, absolutely without motion, and the snow descended through it in loose, unhurried swirls, following barely detectable currents. A moment of churchlike silence: the car was so quiet I could hear the snow falling. I watched it a moment, then closed my eyes and tried to hold this image in my mind, to make it last, but then I felt the yank of the car as the force of the engine was relayed down the line and we were pulled out of the station, away. A surge of cold air behind us, and the conductor marched through the car, grabbing ticket stubs from seat backs, singing the names of the towns that lay ahead: White Plains, Valhalla, Mt. Pleasant, Hawthorne.

Meredith took my hand. "It will be all right," she said.

I wanted to tell her this was so, but couldn't. It would not be all right. I looked at her hand in mine, then back out the window, where the darkness of a winter night hid everything from view.

"You'll see," she said.

Our car was waiting in the station lot, the windshield and fenders dusted with snow. Hal was still at a friend's; we would have the house to ourselves. As we stepped into the front hall I felt a sudden rush of panic. The stairs, the narrow doorways, the bathrooms with their sleek tile floors: everything would have to be changed. Meredith would need a bedroom on the first floor; we would have to add on, or move. What a heavy task, to plan for these things, to sit at the kitchen table over cups of coffee and describe to a carpenter the ramps and handholds we would need to install before they actually became necessary.

The house was cold, even for me. I let Ritzy out into the yard, adjusted the thermostat, and got myself a whiskey; Meredith moved through the house, turning on lights and setting things to rights. I heard her dial the kitchen phone, then her voice, tired but somehow bright, speaking to the mother of the boy Hal had passed the day with: oh yes, absolutely, everything was fine, it was a nice day to be in the city, especially with the holidays over and all that craziness done for the year, and would it be all right, we were wondering, for Hal to spend the night? We so rarely got an evening to ourselves. One of us would come by in the morning, to pick him up for school. Wonderful, she said, loud enough for me to hear. We couldn't thank her enough.

She came to me where I was sitting on the sofa, a glass of whiskey in my hand, though I had yet to take a sip.

"Do you want one?" I raised my glass. "I could make tea too."

She shook her head: no. After all that had happened, after this long day of all long days, she still looked fresh: her gray suit still pressed, her makeup in order, her brown hair framing her face. Around her neck she wore the pearls I had given her for our fifth anniversary; somewhere between the front door and the kitchen she had removed her shoes.

"I always knew, Harry," she said finally. "Not exactly, not the name for it, but the kind of thing it was. In a way I'm relieved to hear it."

"How did you . . . ? " But of course I knew how. It was her body; she'd felt it moving away.

"That's not important. And I don't want to talk about it," she said. "Not now. Not tonight. Maybe not ever." Her eyes were unyielding; she had decided something. "I'm tired, Harry. I need you to warm me up."

"I set the thermostat. I can build a fire too."

"Never mind that." She extended a hand to me. Beneath the skin her bones were rods of ice. "What I mean is, you're my husband, and I want you to come upstairs with me, now."

She led me up the stairs, slowly, each step cautiously planted, as she had learned to do. In our room she turned on a bedside lamp, a blaze of light that neither of us wanted, and she quickly doused it again. The house had never felt so quiet. It seemed as if the whole world had forgotten about us, that the lights had dimmed everywhere, all across the planet. In New York and Chicago, Paris and Peking, in all the towns and villages of the world, humanity had lapsed into a sleep that did not include us, even in dreams. In the dark we undressed and got under the covers of our bed. For months, a year even, making love had been impossible; she was simply not able. We held each other a long while without speaking, both of us crying a little; I thought how we would have to be content with this from now on, holding and crying, but then she left my side. I felt myself sink into the warmth and softness of her, then the familiar pulsing that seemed to come from everywhere at once: from what she was doing and the air of the room and deeper still, through all the walls of the house, into the foundation, straight down through miles of rock to the center of the turning earth, and I closed my eyes and followed it. I understood what she was telling me; this was how we would make love from now on. She would love me with her body, however she could, until this could happen no more.

I want to tell this story truly, so here it must be said that I also loved another, and how that came to pass: the story in which the married man with the sick wife and the son he does not love enough, or *well* enough, because he is simply afraid to, permits himself the one, small present he is forbidden. The story in which he is not a hero, not at all.

And yet to say I loved Lucy would be a lie, or at least a kind of self-flattering half-truth. Those weeks in summer: I took them like medicine, a balm against my life, and Meredith's slow dying. All year long I didn't think of the place at all; I saw to my business and took Meredith to the doctor and learned to dress and bathe her, and hired the nurses that would help me do these things; I learned, in due course, about the drugs she needed for pain and infection, and how to keep her skin healthy and dry, and about the pans and bags, when that time came. When she could no longer hold a book or magazine or even a newspaper, I read them aloud, or sat in our bed beside her, turning the pages as she asked. I did all these things, and then each July, I packed the car, leaving Meredith in the care of her nurse, and drove north, and the camp would be there waiting, as if I'd never left. Nothing was ever stated or planned; and yet Lucy would find me at the check-in desk,

timing some minor chore to coincide with my arrival, or else leave a
basket waiting for me in the cabin, always number nine, and tucked in
with the sandwich and fruit and sweating bottle of beer still cold from
the icebox, a sarcastic, flirty note: *Back for more raspberry pancakes,
huh?* or *Warning, this basket will self-destruct in ten seconds, so eat fast.*
Innocent enough, though they were nothing I could bring myself to
throw away or allow myself to keep.

Hal accompanied me only a handful of times in those years; it was
boring, he said, by which he meant quiet and always the same, and he
missed being at home with his friends. He was an athletic kid who
liked and did well at sports, rough games where boys collided into
other boys: basketball for most of the year but also football in the fall
and lacrosse when he was old enough. Standing in a cold stream or sitting stock-still in the bottom of a canoe for hours at a time, not even
daring to speak so as not to scare the fish—these were as anathema to
his nature as needlepoint. By the summer he was twelve he had had his
fill, and it wasn't for years and years, not until long after his mother
had died, that he joined me again; for now I went alone.

"Tell me about Meredith."

It was the summer of 1968, our fifth July, when Lucy asked me this.
A year of tribulations: King was dead, Bobby Kennedy was dead, there
were riots in the slums and in the prisons, that great liar Johnson had
all but locked himself away, a mad king in his tower; on television
every night we watched the prosecution of a war that seemed to test
not one's patriotism but the human appetite for gore. In March,
Meredith had broken her hip in a fall in the bathroom; two surgeries,
and it was still unclear if she would be able to walk again. The worst
possible year. And yet here I was, drinking a beer on the dock after a
day so idyllic I hadn't wanted even to cast a flyline into it, lest even this
small fingerprint of my presence disturb its perfection. I had spent the
morning walking the long trail that ran beside the river, and then
taken a canoe out for an aimless paddle around the lake. I hadn't spoken a word since breakfast, not until Lucy had seen me on the dock
and taken the Adirondack chair next to mine. That summer she had
taken over the kitchen from Daphne Markham, who, it was said, had

met a man through a Methodist missionary pen-pal service and gone off with him to Ecuador.

We were sitting side by side, watching the lake soak up the last of the light. A scene of such preternatural calm, the effect was distorting, like a spell: two miles away, the pine-clad mountains that rose from the far side had the softened look of Iowa hills in a Grant Wood painting. It seemed possible to reach out and hold one in the hand.

"Fair enough. What do you want to know?"

"Is she pretty, is she smart, does she like hats, what's her favorite color?" Lucy laughed and folded her legs under herself, as limber as a gymnast. "You know, Harry, the *details.*"

I sipped my beer. "Yes to the first, very much, and I've always thought so. Yes again, but not in the same way as you. Absolutely no to hats. As for the last, I don't know. Blue, I think. She used to wear a lot of blue." She let the compliment pass, unremarked: just as well.

"Used to. What happened to blue?"

I took a moment to think. "Well, now that you mention it, she does have a kind of blue dressing gown she likes. My turn?"

"Not so fast. And you know Joe, anyway. Where did you meet her?"

"Why do you want to know that?"

"People meet." She shrugged. "It's always a story."

"In a restaurant, near the end of the war. Where did you meet Joe?"

"High school. I was a dorky little freshman when he was a sopho-more. It was kind of a May-December thing. We didn't get together until later, though. What restaurant?"

"I don't remember the name. It might have been more of a tap-room. It had a separate ladies' entrance, I remember, though you don't see those anymore."

"Thank God for small favors. Was she pregnant when you married her?"

The question caught me so short I laughed. "What gave you that idea?"

"Don't be offended. A bar sounds . . . I don't know, a little ques-tionable. Even one with a, what did you call it"—she deepened her voice mockingly—"a *ladies' entrance.*"

"I'm not offended. But it wasn't that kind of place."

"Okay, it wasn't."

I could have let the matter go. And yet to do so seemed foolish. Why not answer the question? "Well, technically—"

She stopped me with a laugh. "Technically, Harry? Oh, being pregnant is very technical, I've heard. Happened to a girl I knew at school. She was very technically pregnant."

"Point taken." I was not angry at all; far from it. "I don't know why I'm telling you this, but the truth is, yes, she was. Barely, a matter of weeks. We didn't even know ourselves. Or at least I didn't. We just told everybody that Sam was born a little early."

At the mention of his name, a silence fell over us, deeper than the simple absence of sound. She knew about Sam, of course. But I almost never spoke of him, not even with Meredith.

"Oh God, Harry," she said after a moment. "Me and my mouth. I'm sorry."

"No, it's all right." I smiled to reassure her this was so. "It's not bad to talk about him. In a way it's easier up here. I didn't realize it before, but I think he was on my mind all day."

"What were you thinking?"

For a moment, I let my mind drift: where had my thoughts gone, through all the quiet hours?

"It's hard to say, exactly. You don't have specific thoughts, like I bet he'd enjoy this walk in the woods I'm taking, or he'd be this tall by now if he were still alive. It's more a feeling, like he's not so far away." I shrugged, a little embarrassed. "I know that doesn't make a lot of sense."

"I think it does. Maybe it's why you come here like you do."

"Maybe that's it." I paused. "You know, it's not the only reason, Lucy."

Another silence, even of held breath. The mystery of the feeling between us, whatever it was, was suddenly out in the open, like a deer that had stepped without warning from the underbrush. Even the slightest movement would scare it away.

"Harry—"

"You have to go, I know. Feed the masses." I made some nervous business of looking at my watch. "You'd better hurry, actually. I think I'll stay here awhile, finish my beer."

"That wasn't what I was going to say, but you're right." There was sadness in her face, though I somehow felt I wasn't the cause; it was for something I didn't know about. It seemed to spread from her in ripples, like a disturbance on water.

"Harry?"

"Yeah?"

She unwound her legs and rose to go, touching me quickly on the shoulder. "Thanks for saying I'm smart."

The next summer, Joe was gone. The story I heard through the grapevine was that his father had driven him north to Canada just before he was supposed to be inducted; Joe Sr. had a special way up there, involving old logging roads that nobody used or checked. He had arranged a job in New Brunswick for his son, as he had for so many others. A warrant had been issued for Joe's arrest, on the charge of desertion.

The sadness I had seen in Lucy's face that afternoon on the dock seemed to have settled over her like a change of season; it was the first summer that she neither greeted me at check-in nor left a basket in my cabin, and in fact I didn't see her at all until the following morning, when I came into the dining room for breakfast. The place was packed; I lingered at the entrance, pretending to scan the room for a table. Then the kitchen door swung open, exhaling a sweet breath of cinnamon and bacon fat, and there she was, wiping her hands on a dish towel, speaking over her shoulder to somebody at the stove; turning, she caught my eye and smiled. She looked tired, older somehow, as if far more than a year had passed. The skin at her temples was stretched by worry. Her brow was damp, her hair uncombed and tied back in a careless bun. She hugged me quickly and told me I looked well, and that she was sorry she hadn't been able to see me sooner. "I guess you heard" was all she said of Joe.

Later that afternoon everyone gathered in the main lodge, where Joe Sr. had rigged up a television. The room was crowded with guests, some regulars, old friends I knew; someone had brought wine and was passing it around in little paper cups. A man I hadn't seen before said he'd brought a better television, a color Trinitron. A murmur of interest went up—well, why not, if he had brought a better set? But then someone else pointed out that the broadcast would be black-and-white anyway, the images beamed from a quarter million miles away, and the momentum behind the idea was lost.

Lucy appeared and took a place beside me on the sofa. Like some of the other women, she had dressed up a little and put on a bit of makeup, as if for a party.

"I wonder if Joe's watching this," she said. "Do they care in Canada? Do they even have TV?"

"Look," a woman behind us said. "He's coming out."

The opening door, the slow progress down the ladder, the bouncing, marionettelike steps: images at once familiar and completely new, their strangeness magnified by their very ordinariness. As Armstrong's foot touched the surface, a hurrah went up from the room. I suddenly wished I was back in New York, watching this with Meredith and Hal. I resolved to phone home as soon as the broadcast ended. *Did you see it!* I would say. *The moon!*

"I've heard it's all faked," someone said. It was the man with the color set. He looked around the room, grinning like a pumpkin. "This is all being televised from a TV studio in Texas."

When no one laughed, the woman beside him, his wife I guessed, swatted him on the shoulder with a magazine.

"How would you know?" She spoke loudly to friends. "Believe me, he wouldn't know if something was faked if his life depended on it."

That evening after dinner we all went out to the dock and drank champagne, under a wedge of gray moon that seemed somehow closer, as if the world had risen to meet it. It followed a descending arc along the tips of the trees and, just past eleven, disappeared for the night. The champagne had taken hold: some people were swimming, despite the cold. The night had opened like a book. When the swimming ended a call went up for music; somebody ran a long extension cord up the dock to connect a radio to an outlet by the lodge. A wall of static, and then the air was filled with the sound of an orchestra, Basie or Ellington, the first bars of a song I didn't recognize, and scampering up and over the wall-like barricade of strings, the unmistakable voice of Ella Fitzgerald. Bar by bar, the song came into focus, like a picture: "How High the Moon." The sound seemed to reach us not through the airwaves but across a sea of time.

"Hey, everybody," the man with the radio said, "I guess they heard!"

Couples found one another and danced on the dock. Lucy had left the party when the swimming began; sitting by myself, I felt a little relieved that she was gone. Had she stayed, I would have asked her to dance—it was inevitable, a fact ordained by the evening's currents—but I felt this would have been awkward, not only because of what had passed between us the summer before, but also because Joe was gone.

"Come on, Harry." It was the wife of the man with the color television who pulled me to my feet. I could tell she'd had a lot to drink, though we all had. We'd introduced ourselves earlier in the evening; they were Ken and Leonie. She was a trim woman with reddish hair cut short and large, damp eyes—pretty, though in the slightly anxious way of fading beauties after forty. Her husband, a barrel-chested Irishman, was dancing with another woman from their group.

"I'm not much of a dancer," I confessed.

"That's good, because I'm too loaded to care. This is the first *interesting* thing that's happened since we got here."

She placed her head against my shoulder and pulled me in close. Her breath smelled of alcohol and lipstick. I thought of Lucy, wondering where she had gone off to.

"Hey, you're good," Leonie said after a few steps. "I don't know what you were talking about." She pulled her face away and directed her voice to her husband. "That's right, honey," she said cheerfully, "you go on and dance all you want, I've found somebody new."

"Maybe you should dance with him," I offered.

Her hand slid up my back until I felt her fingers lightly moving on the skin of my neck. The gesture was impersonal; I could have been anyone. Her body had turned to liquid, melding against my own.

"He doesn't care, you know," she said quietly. "It's how we do things."

"Really, I have to go after this one song."

"Listen to you," she moaned disapprovingly. "So uptight."

We finished our dance and I made my escape. I hadn't lied; it really was late, nearly one A.M. But it was also true that I'd felt myself on the verge of doing something foolish. Meredith's illness had frozen that part of my life, made such urges seem trivial. But they could not be banished entirely. I'd pulled myself away from the music and dancing the way one says no to a fourth drink. But returning to my cabin down the dark path, I felt lonely, even a little ridiculous. I was forty-four years old; I might have been thirteen, or a hundred.

I undressed and lay in the dark, sleepless with the sugary champagne. Through the windows I could still hear the music of the radio, floating across the lake, and now and again a loud voice or laughter. More splashing: the swimming had resumed. I wondered if Leonie had found someone else to amuse her.

Then I was brightly, urgently awake, and wondering where I was. Someone was knocking on the door, or else I had dreamt this. I picked up my watch from the bedside table and squinted at it in the dark: 3:20. I had slept almost two hours. I lay back on the pillow and had almost forgotten the knocking when it came again: not a vigorous banging, but a quiet, almost uncertain tapping, like a code. I rose and opened the door.

"Harry?"

It was Joe. I flicked on the porch light and opened the screen to step out. His face was bearded and dirty; he was carrying a pack. The look on his face was one of embarrassment, almost fear. He held up his hands against the sudden light.

"Turn it off, please."

"What are you doing here?"

He looked around nervously. "Please, just turn it off. I don't want anyone to see me."

I reached back into the cabin and doused the light. A moment of absolute confusion: I realized he hadn't been looking for me at all.

"Shit, I'm sorry, Harry. Pretend you never saw me, okay?"

"Does your father know you're here?"

"No, and he'd better not. I mean it." He shuddered and shook his head. "Jesus, what the fuck."

Another voice reached us from around the corner. "Joe? Joe, is that you?"

Joe stepped off the porch as Lucy appeared and flew into his arms. He picked her up and gave a happy growl. The months away had released something in him, a kind of animal power. He put her down and looked at her, hugged her again.

"God, you smell," she said. "Where have you been?"

"Long story. Just never ride with chickens, is all I'll say. What the hell, Luce? Didn't you tell me cabin nine? I think I permanently scared the shit out of old Harry here."

She lifted her face and saw me then, standing on the porch; I think she'd forgotten I was there. Old Harry. I understood that she'd been waiting for him, in one of the adjacent cabins, for hours—ever since she'd left the party.

"It's all right," I said.

Joe set himself free and stepped up on the porch again. "Sorry again, Harry. Didn't mean to freak you out like that." He held out his hand, and we shook. His fingers were rough as pumice. "I guess you know I'm a wanted man, so if it's all right with you, mum's the word, okay? If my father knew I was here, he could get in trouble too."

"You can count on me," I said. "I won't breathe a word."

He descended the porch again and joined Lucy on the path. For a moment, we all three just stood there. A part of me was honestly glad for them, and glad for myself, being there to see it, though I felt a strange ache, too. It was as if I could step forward into the darkness and be utterly consumed by it, obliterated without a trace, remembered by no one. Even to set foot off the porch would set this in motion.

"Don't worry about me," I said. "I mean it. You two should get going."

"Harry?" Lucy's voice was a whisper.

I put a finger to my lips. "It's okay," I said quietly. "Go on."

They slipped into the shadows. Their absence was total, as if I'd never seen them at all. How long I stood there I can't recall. I would pack my bags in the morning, I decided. I would leave and not come back. I stood another moment at the rail, saying good-bye. Then I opened the screen door and went inside to bed.

Lucy

I knew Joe would forget all about the radio.

It's easy to say that now, of course, hindsight being what it is; but even as I watched him drive away that August morning, I *knew*. He had either forgotten to put it in the truck, or would leave it there when he arrived at the trailhead, miles out of reach; half on purpose, and half not. As he liked to say, "On accident."

Call it ESP, or marriage, or what you like: I *knew*.

For the time being, though, I had to set my mind to other things: the end of breakfast, and box lunches for groups going out for the day, and sit-down for the rest; dinner, of course, which was never far off. There were sandwiches to assemble and pies to bake, apples and carrots and cookies to bag, vegetables to be washed and sliced and boiled; there was a standing rib roast to thaw for Monday, and, as I stood in the driveway, a delivery of three dozen lobsters, eight dozen littlenecks, and a small fortune in Glouster swordfish bouncing my direction in the back of a delivery truck from Portland. Never mind that we're almost 150 miles inland, as far from the ocean as Albany, New York. It's still Maine; people want their lobsters.

By the time I got back to the kitchen the full breakfast rush was on, tying me up till a little after nine. Jordan and Kate were still off somewhere, shuttling the moose-canoers to the put-in point; Joe was with his lawyers; nearly everyone else was on the lake or river, making good use of the morning. Our summer kitchen staff, Claire and Patty, were cleaning the last of the breakfast dishes and setting up for lunch. Both were rising seniors at Regional, just a few years behind Kate: Patty was one of those local girls you can't help but worry about, late half the time and totally boy crazy—her current beau, a sullen, slack-eyed specimen who picked her up each afternoon in a rusty old Impala before roaring down the drive in a laughing cloud of dust and Marlboro smoke, seemed like nothing but bad news waiting to break—though Claire was totally the opposite, almost a little too angelic, with her golden curls and high, wispy voice, a girl who liked to read fat Russian novels on her breaks and actually sang when she washed the dishes.

A wedge of calm in the storm of morning: I used it to sit down for the first time that day to drink a cup of coffee and finally eat something myself, taking a spot at a clean table by the windows. The lake was calm under a strong sun, its surface uninterrupted except for a few boats here and there, small specks of human activity marked now and again by the glinting arc of a flyline. I wished one of them could be Harry, but after last night, I doubted this would happen.

"Lucy, fish truck's here."

"Thanks, Claire." I rose, already weary; it was going to be a long day. The van was parked by the kitchen entrance. I signed for the delivery, and the girls and I got it all inside, eight bags of squirming lobsters and the littlenecks and swordfish besides, and wedged it into the big storage fridge.

By eleven everything was in order and humming along—I'd even managed to get a couple of pies, blueberry and apple, into the oven—and I left Patty and Claire in the kitchen and went to the office. For a moment I thought to call Joe on the radio, just in case I wasn't wrong, but then decided against it: what would I tell him? There was no word from Hal or Harry, the kitchen was in order, nobody needed him for anything as far as I could tell. There was, of course, the simple urge to hear his voice, an impulse that was never far below the surface. But that's all it was. I gave the transmitter a look or two, as if it might tell me something, then went to the desk to go over a pile of invoices. Even in the best summer, it was always a scrape, moving the money around like poker chips from one pile to another and hoping that I came out square by the end of the season. But not this August. My whole life I had catered to the wealthy: cooked their meals, washed their linens, cleaned their lodgings. Always between us was the understanding that they lived on one side of a line, I on the other. Now I was one of them.

The door swung open as I was writing the last of the checks. Kate's face was flushed with exertion; her eyes widened with surprise, as if she hadn't expected to find me there. In her hand was a freshly skinned orange. She took a seat on the sofa and looked around.

"Isn't it lunchtime? Don't I smell pies burning?"

"Don't be funny." I capped my pen. "Well?"

"Let's see." She was pulling the orange into wedges and popped one into her mouth. "All the moose-canoers are in place and floating downstream. The people from Connecticut are spending the morning in town, stocking up on bug repellent and wondering why they didn't go to Disneyland this year. Cabin two needs towels. Jordan's around here somewhere, making himself useful, no doubt. Patty's crying in the kitchen."

"God, again? What is it this time?"

She shrugged; this had been going on all summer. "The usual boyfriend troubles, I guess. She sure is a raw nerve. Was I ever like that?"

"You were *never* like that."

"Well, that's a relief." She looked at me a moment and grinned mischievously. "Okay, what's missing? Give up? You didn't ask me about Harry."

I felt myself squirm. "Okay. How's Harry?"

"You should go see for yourself. Down the path, four cabins, take a right. You can't miss it."

"I'm a little tied up here, honey."

"I have a friend at school who has an expression for these things." She raised a finger for emphasis. "She says, Kate, that's the denial talking."

I felt myself smile. "What a clever friend."

"Well, her parents are both shrinks, so you have to consider the source. She's also completely bulimic. She thinks nobody knows, but of course we all do." Kate polished off the last of her orange and wiped her hands on her jeans. "God, I'm starving. Isn't there anything to eat around this place?"

"We could feed an army. Boil yourself a lobster if you like."

She shook her head. "Tourist food. I was thinking something more along the lines of a peanut butter and bacon sandwich."

"You know where the kitchen is." I paused, then said something I hadn't planned on. "Kate, are you . . . *involved* with Jordan?"

I could tell I had embarrassed her. Her eyes traveled the room, then found me again. "Speaking of denial." She gave a little laugh. "No, really, Mom, I think you should be more direct."

"Sorry. It's just a strange day. Mothers blurt things out like that. I saw you two on the dock last night."

"I forgive you for spying. What did you think you saw?"

"Just . . . something. Boy-girl stuff. I really wasn't spying. I was just taking some food to Harry's cabin. You can tell me if you want. It's okay if you are."

"Too soon to tell." A kind of happy light was in her face. "He is a good kisser, I will say that. The boy's been saving up."

Now I was the one who was embarrassed. "Maybe I shouldn't be asking."

"Too much information? Okay, something is. A little something. Will Daddy mind?"

"Only if you do."

She wrinkled her brow. "It doesn't seem a little . . . incestuous?"

"God, Kate, where do you get these ideas?"

"Just considering the angles." She made quotation marks with her fingers in the air. "Jordan-the-son-he-never-had, that sort of thing."

"No, I don't think it seems that way."

"Good. Because it doesn't to me at all." She unwound her lanky limbs from the sofa. "One last thing before I go stuff myself. Could we, like, not talk about this anymore? Girl to mother? At least for the time being?"

"If that's what you want."

"Because I'm trying not to jinx it, if something is. Or count my chickens, if it isn't. Because the truth is, I really sort of really, really like him, if you know what I mean."

"Me too." I smiled to tell her this was so. "Just, you know. Be careful? That's what the moms say."

She gave me a little two-fingered salute. "World's careful-est girl, reporting, ma'am. Asking for permission to stop talking about her love life and go eat lunch."

"Granted."

She stepped to the door but paused before opening it. "I said one last thing, but there's another."

"Okay."

She came around behind me and, leaning over my shoulder, kissed me quickly on the cheek. "Go see Harry, Mom. Okay? Just go see him."

If I had my life to do over again, if it were possible to go back and reenter a moment of time and do it differently, and yet have nothing else change, all outcomes the same, I would have done one thing: I would have stayed at the party and danced with Harry Wainwright.

A single dance, nothing more: a dance to tell him I wanted to. I would dance with Harry Wainwright, the two of us laughing at everyone lurching around with too much champagne, our bodies close but not too close for talking. A dance to that first song, whatever it was—I heard it from cabin number six, where I was waiting for Joe—slow and sort of loopy, with a woman's voice, Ella or Sarah, skimming over and around the music like a single bee in flight; the kind of song you can spin a little to or just kind of move your feet in the current. I would dance with him, say thank you when the music ended; I might yawn, putting my hand to my mouth, then say something like, well, it's late. Thank you, Harry. I really have to go. And he would say, you're right, me, too, though I think I might just hang around a few more minutes. It's a nice night to be out. Right, right, of course, well, see you tomorrow, we'd say, each of us speaking over the other, and off I'd go, feeling his eyes still on me as I made my way up the dock to the lodge and then stepped into the shadows, thinking: well, look at you, Lucy-girl. You've danced with Harry Wainwright.

Why Joe thought cabin nine I'll never know; part of me still thinks he simply turned the number upside down in his head. He'd called early that evening from a pay phone in Machias; he'd already crossed the border. A lot of people think Vietnam draft evaders never came home, but the truth is a lot did, and Joe was one. He'd either hitch a ride in the trunk of a friend's car, as he had that night, or else work his passage on a coastal trawler and jump ship at Portland or Grand Manan and thumb the rest of the way. No one in town could see him, of course, and after that night on the porch when Harry caught us, we agreed it was far too risky for him to set foot anywhere near the place. We'd meet at a friend's house, or else rendezvous at the motel in Twining, thirty miles away. Three or four days, though it always felt like less: we'd barely set foot from the room, eating take-out food from the diner up the street and playing cards in our underwear, like a pair of criminals.

Once we even spent a week together in Boston. It was December, close to Christmas, all the stores dressed with lights, though the weather was mild and most days it rained. That is how I remember that week, the constant rain, and the two of us eating in restaurants and going to movies, like regular people. We were staying in somebody's apartment in Central Square: I was never exactly clear on the arrangement. It belonged to a friend of a friend who knew somebody, who knew somebody else—somehow it had made its way into our possession. I took a bus down from Augusta and met Joe at the depot. A single room in an old frame house webbed with fire escapes, with books in towering piles and a mattress on the dusty floor. The books pleased me: I thought we might pass some time reading to one another. But when I looked closer, I saw they were all in German.

The work had made him strong; he became a grown man in those years, my Joe. I could feel this strength in him just by holding his arm as we walked, the two of us close under an umbrella, or waiting for the T, or standing in line for tickets in the never-ending rain. More than the firmness of muscle and bone: the strength in him held a deeper hardness, geological, like cooled steel. His beard was full, with flecks of red. We sat on the bed in our coats and exchanged Christmas presents. I had knitted him a scarf, dark blue, with snowflakes; in his letters he always complained of the cold.

"When did you learn to knit?" He had barely paused to examine it, but wrapped it at once around his neck.

"Don't look too closely, there are lots of mistakes."

"I'm never taking it off." He kissed me quickly and removed a small cardboard box from his rucksack. "Sorry, I didn't have time to wrap it."

It was a charm bracelet, braided silver strands strung with multi-colored chips of polished sea glass.

"Do you like it?"

I held it up to the window so the glass could catch the light. Little bits of refracted color fell on the floor at our feet. "It's beautiful, Joe. I've never seen anything like it."

He looked relieved. "Well, I wasn't sure. You're a hard girl to shop for, Luce. There's a woman in town who does these."

I undid the tiny clasp and slipped it on my wrist. Had my face given me away? Just for a second, as he'd taken the box from his bag, I'd thought it was a ring. Though that was impossible: we'd agreed to do nothing until, somehow, Joe was able to come home—when the war ended, or else some kind of amnesty was declared. It was 1971; that fall, Joe's father had testified before a Congressional committee on behalf of a group called WWII Veterans Against the War. I'd read about it in the *Portland Press Herald*. "Look at my face," he'd said. "I know what it means to sacrifice for my country. Gentlemen, this war isn't worth a hangnail." An editorial in the local paper had described him as "our very own Benedict Arnold," and "a known abettor to deserters, hippies, and other undesirables, whose own son is a wanted criminal." But there were others in town who felt differently. Nobody believed that things could go on as they had much longer.

"It really is beautiful," I said again. I shook my wrist to feel it move against my skin. "Thank you."

We had the apartment for six nights. Joe had arranged passage back to New Brunswick on a commercial groundfisher out of Portland, the day before Christmas. I would see him off and take the bus back home, where I was working in the office at the sawmill and waiting tables at the Pine Tree at night. The deadline hung over our heads like a count-down. Everything we did, the meals we ate and walks we took and movies we saw, even making love, felt like items being ticked off a list. For me, the effect was always the same: the awkwardness of first re-union would yield within hours to a feeling of comfort that I knew was false, ripening over the days into a desperate, melancholy longing punctuated by moments of unfocused anger. Often we quarreled as the time of Joe's departure neared, but the final moments were the same: I would always cry.

Our last night, we ate dinner at a hamburger restaurant near Har-vard Square, a single large room, as harshly lit as a bus station, with an open grill behind the counter and sawdust on the floor. A rowing shell was suspended upside down from the rafters; the room was packed with students, stuffed into booths and wedged shoulder to shoulder at the counter. Joe ordered a T-bone, thick as a Bible; he was always hun-gry. I watched him eat, already missing him, but something else too: I felt like I was missing my life.

He finished his meal and lit a cigarette. "Aren't you going to eat?"

I had barely touched my cheeseburger. I tried to smile. "It's just the heat. And the onions." Everybody in the room was wiping their eyes.

"My father used to come here in the thirties," Joe said. "Everybody complained about the onions then too."

We were seated in a booth at the rear of the restaurant; my back was to the wall. For a moment I let my gaze wander the bright, busy room. Didn't college students go home for Christmas? But I had no idea, really, how such people lived their lives. At a large round table in the center of the room, six of them, five men and a woman, all in bulky sweaters and jeans, were engaged in a fierce conversation, the subject of which I could glean only from single phrases that punched through the din of voices in the room: "diminished capacity," "elements of neg-ligence," something I heard as "actual and proximate cause and dam-age." I realized they were talking in turns; one would stop, close up his notes, and then the discussion would resume as another began to

speak. A pitcher of beer sat on the table; when it was the woman's turn
to lead, the man to her left offered to fill her glass, but she held her
hand over it and shook her head: no. She took a sip of water instead.
Then she opened her notes.

Joe glanced over his shoulder, following my look. "Somebody you
know?"

"Very funny." I shook my head. "Do you ever wish you'd, I don't
know, gone to Harvard?"

Joe laughed a cloud of smoke. "Me? I don't think so."

"College, then. Somewhere."

"The subject never came up. Really, Luce. Be serious."

"Your father did. Why not you?"

"A thousand reasons." He was looking at me incredulously. "What's
gotten into you?"

At the center table, the woman was still speaking from her notes.
Though she was sitting I could tell she was tall and athletically built;
she played a sport, I guessed, or had, something interesting and maybe
a little fancy, like fencing or squash. Perhaps before law school she had
rowed for the college crew team, and liked to come here with her
friends because of the shell that hung from the rafters and the happy
memories it gave her. She had fine features and auburn hair pulled into
a thick ponytail; as she read to the men at her table, one hand or the
other would lift from time to time and move in small circles in the air,
following her thoughts.

"You could have," I said.

Joe's face darkened. "I *could* have done a lot of things." He crushed
out his cigarette and waved for the waitress. "Come on."

We paid the bill and left. Outside the rain had yielded to an easy
snow; already an inch had fallen, clinging fast to every surface, like
cake frosting. In the windshield of a Karman Gia parked at the curb
somebody had written, in letters carved by a thick, gloved finger:
"Make love, not exams." We did not head back to the apartment but
instead walked south, searching for the river. A maze of dormitories
and classroom buildings, their courtyards sealed by iron gates, and
then we emerged on Memorial Drive, a busy four-lane road separating

the campus from the Charles. Cars thrummed by, their hoods and fenders washed by the damp, pushing cones of snowy light; across the river, a ribbon of darkness uncoiling through the city, the Prudential Building stood over all like a great, glowing monolith. My feet were soaked, the snow was falling all around. A feeling almost beyond words: I was suddenly touched by a vivid reality, as if I were seeing everything, the world itself, for the first time. There was nothing for me in Maine; I didn't even have to go back. Just by saying so, I could leave my bubble of waiting and disappear into these streets, join this bright, pulsing world of people and buildings and cars. I could find a job, rent a small apartment. I felt as if I were standing at the edge of a great river of life, an endless current of possibilities as to who I might become. All that remained was for me to step into it.

We returned to the apartment and undressed for bed. The room was freezing; the third night, something had gone wrong with the heating, but of course we were in no position to complain. Whom would we call? How would we even explain who we were? We were anonymous, unseen, we barely even existed. Something as simple as a functioning radiator was beyond our reach. We piled our coats on top of the blankets and got into bed. In the dark I turned to Joe.

"I want to come with you."

"On a dragger? Luce, it's winter."

"Of course not. I could just take the bus like a normal person."

He sighed into the frigid air. "We've been through this," he said. "I wish we could be together, but we have to be patient. You wouldn't like it up there, Luce. I'm broke, I live in a filthy dump with six other guys. We've got mice, it smells to high heaven, nobody ever flushes the god-damned john. It makes this place look like the Taj Mahal. I'm not even working legally. What kind of life is that?"

"You said it yourself. There's going to have to be some kind of pardon."

"Fine, maybe so, but what if there isn't? You want to spend your life as a fugitive? And what if they deport me? Then where would you be?"

"I'd be with you," I said. "That's the important thing." But in his voice I felt him slipping away.

"Not if I'm in jail."

We took a bus the next afternoon to Portland, slept the night in a motel near the water; at five the next morning, still in darkness, I walked him to the dock, where his boat was berthed. A wedge of white steel, eighty feet long: on the side was her name, the *Jenny-Smith,* dripping with rust. The last gear was being hauled aboard: great coils of rope, huge orange barrels, blocks of ice the size of kitchen stoves. They would work the Jordan Basin for ten days, straddling the Hague Line, then let Joe off at Grand Manan, the southernmost island of the Canadian Maritimes. From there he could take a ferry to Blacks Harbour and hitch the rest of the way to LeMaitre.

A man in a bright yellow slicker stood by the gangway, holding a clipboard.

"You Crosby?" He spoke through the cigarette perched in the corner of his mouth.

"That's right."

He made a snorting sound. "Thought we were going to have to leave without you." He looked me over, like a man in a bar. "She coming?"

"No."

With thick, dirty fingers he plucked the cigarette from his lips and flicked the ash away. "Too bad."

Joe

The first one showed up in the fall of '67: a pale, skinny kid, traveling alone, carrying nothing but a bedroll and a canvas rucksack. We were just closing down for the season. He arrived on foot, hiking in from the county road at night, and slept on the porch. I found him that morning in the kitchen; my father was cooking him breakfast.

"This is David," my father announced. "Your cousin."

"I didn't know I had a cousin David."

"He's new."

We nodded warily to one another. He had a phony little mustache—a kid's mustache. My father served him eggs from a cast iron skillet, rinsed the dirty pan in the sink, and wiped his hands on a dish towel. "You, in the office," he said to me.

It was no surprise what he told me. By this time my father was well-known, a kind of public riddle, at least in our town: the war hero who had become an antiwar activist, the man who had given half the visible world to fight Hitler but would not, in his words, "see one American son die to line the pockets of the plutocrats and fatten the résumés of the Joint Chiefs." The vagaries of the Communist threat, and the way it had been used to ratchet up the war, repelled him. "These talking heads. I knew who I was fighting," he used to say, "and he knew me. Kids in pajamas, running through some jungle. I have no quarrel with them, and neither do you. You shoot somebody, you better have a reason to hate him. The fact that he doesn't drink Coca-Cola or drive an Oldsmobile doesn't cut it."

David stayed a day; he seemed nervous, spoke little, and spent most of his time on the porch, reading a well-thumbed paperback. I asked him what it was, and he showed me: *On the Road.* We exchanged no other words. The next morning, my father left with him in the truck before I was awake, returning six hours later, the fenders spattered with mud: long enough, I figured, to reach an unregulated stretch of border on the logging roads that ran north from the highway. I never saw him again, nor learned what became of him, even when, a little over a year later, I followed the same path.

There were other cousin Davids: boys and young men traveling alone, dirty and long-haired, some couples, even a family or two, seeing their son off as if they were sending him to summer camp. A few were deserters, wanted men; others had simply seen what was coming. The logging roads gave them safe passage. At the other end lay jobs, a place to live, friends waiting.

I despised them all. It wasn't that I supported the war; I didn't understand the war. In many ways it was as remote from me as my father's was, separated from my quiet, compact world not by time but by so many thousands of miles it was beyond imagining. Kids in pajamas, fighting other kids who should have *been* in pajamas.

It wasn't long after this that we also got our first visit from the sheriff, Darryl Tanner. I think up until the moment I saw his cruiser coming down the drive I'd somehow never construed what my father was doing as actually illegal. Tanner and I had a little history: my sophomore year in high school, a bunch of us had gotten ourselves arrested on Halloween night for blowing up mailboxes with little quarter-sticks of dynamite. There was beer in the truck, too—not a lot, we'd mostly drunk it by then—but Tanner had made a big show of booking us, fingerprints and all, and waiting till morning to release us to our parents. The charges were dropped, none of us was even close to being of age, but we were all suspended from school for a week.

I was chopping wood by the shed when Tanner's cruiser rolled up. I instantly felt nervous, though I wasn't sure why—it was simply the effect he had on me. For a minute he sat in his car, writing something on a pad. At last he got out and looked over at me.

"Your father around, Joey?"

"Inside," I said.

"He alone?"

"I guess. Why wouldn't he be?"

"No reason." Tanner hitched up his pants. It was a surprisingly warm day for mid-October, and he was sweating in the heat. "Just wouldn't want to drop in unannounced and see something I didn't want to. This is more of a social call."

I picked up the axe again and tried to look busy. "Well, he's inside, like I said."

My father met him on the porch, and the two men disappeared into the lodge. I tried to continue my chores, but couldn't; I crept around to the back of the house, under the office window. Sure enough, they were talking inside.

"Don't know a thing about it, Darryl," my father was saying. His voice was curt. "You can just go on back where you came from."

"Joe, Joe." I could practically see Tanner shaking his head in that disapproving way of his, fingering the brim of his hat. "What you don't seem to get here is I'm doing you a favor. People are talking, Joe. Making some pretty serious accusations, saying you might not be such a loyal American. Course I told them that's nonsense, you being a veteran and all."

"People can say what they like, Darryl. Last I checked, no law says I can't speak my mind."

"And of course, you being a lawyer, you'd know all about the law. I said that too. A lawyer *and* a war hero. What was it, Harvard, Joe? An Ivy League war hero, no less. Last guy you'd think would be, say, harboring draft evaders out here in the woods. Last guy in the world."

"Go on and have a look for yourself. There's no one here."

"That's what Joey tells me, and I'm happy to hear it. That's what I'm telling you, Joe. I don't *want* to look. But you keep on with what you're doing, the day will come I sure as hell will have to. And not just me. Real guys, army guys, from the stockade down in Portland. These people aren't your friends, Joe."

"I see. But you are?"

"For now." I heard the scrape of Tanner's chair as he rose to go. "Anyway, that's what I drove out here to say. I hope I don't have to come back. It's really up to you. I'll let myself out."

I scrambled back to the woodshed in time to see Tanner stepping off the porch. I put up a log to split and took my time tapping the wedge, then lifted my eyes as if I'd only just noticed him standing there.

"You find him okay?"

Tanner nodded. For a moment we just looked at each other. I wondered if he somehow knew I'd been listening.

"There wouldn't be anything you want to tell me, would there, Joey?"

"About what?"

Tanner sighed and shook his head. I didn't like him one bit, but I also understood that no one had made him come out here like he had. He was giving my father fair warning.

"Christ, the two of you. You're a regular chip off the old block, you know that, Joey? Do your pop a favor and tell him to take my advice. No more visitors. *Comprende?*"

"People come, people go, Darryl. It's none of my business."

Darryl opened the door of the cruiser. The conversation seemed over, but then he paused a second, as if he'd only just remembered something.

"You get your draft notice yet, Joey?"

"Leave him out of it, Darryl." We both turned to see my father standing on the porch with his arms crossed over his chest. "You have no business with him." He wagged a finger down the drive. "Go on now."

Tanner smiled, spinning his hat in his hands. "I'm all done here anyway. Think I made my point." He opened his door and turned one last time to me. "And Joey?"

"Yeah?"

He winked. "Happy Halloween."

. . . . . .

I was twenty-one that fall, classified 1-A. The following May I received orders from my draft board to report to Bangor for my physical exam—a letter, blandly impersonal, like a tax form. I went secretly, telling my father only that I would be gone for the day. From the Federal Building on Harlow Street a schoolbus carted us, about thirty men, to the army processing station, a frigid hangar at the National Guard base at the airport. For six hours we pranced around in the cold, wearing only our underwear, cupping our privates as we stood in line after line. A barrage of questions: Did I wear glasses? (No.) Had I ever been charged or convicted of a felony? (Not technically, unless you counted the mailboxes.) Received psychiatric care? (No again, though living with my father, I probably could stand some.)

Tanner's threats notwithstanding, the simple truth was this: I wanted to fight. I didn't care who, or what for. If I'd had a broken leg I would have danced a fox-trot to make them send me anyway. In my heart I knew it, had known it since the day my mother died and I looked up from the Rawlings' floor to see my father standing over me; I was nothing, a being without courage. All my life I had lived his war. I wanted a war of my own.

I received my induction notice in early October. A virtually identical letter: for a moment I thought some mistake had been made and I was being asked to report for a physical a second time, one of those army screwups my father always carped about. But then I read more closely. Back to Bangor, two days after Christmas. Bring my social security card. Settle my affairs. And, at the bottom, a single sentence: "Failure to report to the place and hour of the day named in this order subjects the violator to fine and imprisonment."

I showed my father the letter that night at dinner. He read it slowly, the one good eye squinting. His glass eye was nothing unusual to me—I had never known him otherwise—but still there were times when its misdirected, jewellike gaze seemed aimed right at me.

When he was done he placed the letter aside. "You passed your physical?"

"Last May."

He regarded me a moment, but said nothing about my deception. Probably he had already guessed it. Then: "What are you going to do?"

I had imagined this moment so many times my answer was ready. "I'm going to do my duty," I said.

"Is that a fact. Tell me what that is, you're so sure of yourself."

"To fight. Like you did."

"I see." He nodded. "Let me ask you this. What if we were Germans, and it was 1939. Your boss Hitler has just invaded Poland and told you to come along and join the fun. Would you fight then?"

"We're not Germans. It's not the same."

"That's where you may be wrong. You better hope you're not."

"I'm not wrong."

"Tanner have anything to do with this?"

I wanted to laugh. "Tanner's an asshole."

"What are you fighting for?"

I thought a moment. There was only one answer. "Myself."

I expected him to argue: all these strangers, shuttling through the camp, riding the rails of some underground of which my father was a part. Tanner's warning was no joke. By this time everyone in town knew what my father was doing, or else suspected. There were people who wouldn't have pushed my father out of the way of a logging truck, who would have watched him choke or drown. He'd given everything away, or nearly: his reputation, his name, most of his friends. And yet, when I told him what I intended to do, to fight the war he loathed, the war that seemed to undo the very meaning of his own sacrifice, he had no words. For a moment we sat without speaking, the only sound in the room the rhythm of our own synchronized breathing. I had never been more aware of his presence, the sheer, unassailable fact of him, his mysterious existence. We had lived alone, just the two of us, for thirteen years. Rarely did I speak of my mother, and never to him. Once a year, each June on her birthday, we would put on our suits and take the pickup to the cemetery; but even on those mornings, the silence was like a cold blade between us. We did not say we missed her, or that we loved her; he did not tell me, your mother would be proud of you, I'm sorry she's not still here, to watch you grow up. We always brought flowers—irises, her favorite. After we had placed them on the ground by her headstone, we would stand a moment longer, and then my father would place his hand on my shoulder and, in his smoke-coarsened voice, say, "Well. It's nice here. A pretty spot. I'm glad to see they take good care of it. We'd better get going." I understand now that what I wanted most was simply to know him, and to do that, I had to be like him. But not back then; I might have said I hated him.

Finally, he pushed back from the table and rose.

"If you'll forgive me, I've lost my appetite." He carried his dish to the sink and turned to face me. "When the time comes, I'll take you," he said. "At least let me do that. You won't have to go alone."

A strange energy surged through me in those weeks, like a current in the blood. Until that time, everything in my life had been handed to me: the camp, the small world I lived in. Even Lucy, in a way, whom it seemed I had always known. And the bad things too, like my mother's dying, the hole it scooped in my father's plans of happiness and the kind of man he had become because of it; the stark loneliness of my need for him, so fierce and unrequited, like standing on a treeless plain, wind-blasted and without a scrap of shade, and the feeling always that I was somehow unworthy, not up to the task of being his son. I would go to Vietnam and do what was required of me: stand up straight, say "yes, sir," clean my weapon, and sleep bareheaded in the rain, all things I knew well how to do, and also things I didn't. Shoot and be shot at. Stake my fate on something larger than myself, on the urgent brotherhood of war. Become somebody else: a man who had earned his life.

I don't remember telling Lucy I was going, only that I did it. Sometimes I think I told her on the porch; she swears it was in the office at the mill. In either case it would have felt the same. A year, I probably said, and then I'd be home. Don't believe everything you hear. I'd probably end up in some supply hut, handing out socks and skivvies, listening to American radio. You? she said. I doubt that. Maybe some

city boy, slept his whole life on silk sheets and taking cabs. A man like
you, handing out underwear? They'll know just what to do with you,
Joe Crosby.

My father said nothing else; my impending departure was one
more wedge of silence hammered down between us. There were times
I even imagined that I felt in him a new respect, albeit begrudging, for
the path I had chosen to follow. We were still boarding up for the season when the first snow fell, a week into November. I awoke that
morning and looked out the window and saw, where just a day ago
there had been channels of open water, a solid disk of ice, a world of
absolute stillness mantled in white. Not since I was a young boy had I
taken any pleasure in the first snowfall. For months my father and I
would be locked away, like a pair of convicts grumbling their way
through meals and chores and freezing their asses off. My junior year
in high school our English teacher had taken us down to Orono to see
a college production of *King Lear*—he was the new guy in town,
hadn't yet learned that anything resembling "culture" was pretty much
wasted on a bunch of hick kids with nothing more serious in mind for
their lives than working at the post office or shoving lumber through a
sawmill—and when it came to the part where the mad king talked
about how great it would be to spend the rest of his life in jail with his
daughter, I started laughing so hard I had to leave the theater. We had
to write a paper about the play, and all I could think to say was that
Shakespeare might have been a great writer, but he had obviously never
spent a hard January freeze at the end of an eight-mile driveway with
my old man.

I dressed and went downstairs. I could smell my father's cigarette
smoke even before I reached the kitchen. He slept at most four hours a
night, and had been up since well before dawn. Probably he had already shoveled the walk and dug out the truck. As I entered the
kitchen he turned from the window.

"First snow, I guess," I said.

He looked at me, his face impossible to read, like a headstone faded
by decades of weather. He ran his cigarette under the tap, then deposited the butt in the trash pail under the sink.

"It's stopped for now, but there's more on the way." He cleared his throat. "A bad one. Supposed to start tonight. They're saying a foot, anyway."

I took a cigarette from the pack on the kitchen table. Before that fall I had almost never smoked in front of him. I lit it and sat, his eyes still on me.

"You should call Lucy," he said.

"Why should I call Lucy?"

"Here," he said, and placed the saucer from his empty cup on the table in front of me. "At least use an ashtray."

For a moment we said nothing. I smoked my cigarette and waited.

"You should call Lucy," he said at last, "to tell her you're going away for a while."

"You know something I don't?"

"We're going for a trip."

"A trip." I paused another moment, for effect. Why hadn't I seen this coming? But then I realized I *had* seen it, all along. "Like my cousin David."

He took a place across from me. "Listen, Joey, there are things you don't understand—"

"This isn't up to you, Dad."

"Goddamnit, I know it's not!" He thumped the table with his fist, and I felt my insides jump. But I had long since stopped being afraid of him. His anger seemed weightless, like a bird banging at a window-pane. "If it were up to me you'd already be gone from here, you never even would have taken the physical. We would have filed an appeal months ago. There are things we could have done."

"But we didn't. Did we, Dad?"

He sighed impatiently. "Joey, I'm going to tell you something. I'm going to tell you something and I want you to listen. The night your mother and I came up here, that first night—"

"You've told me the story."

He shook his head. "Not all of it. Just do me a favor and listen. There was a woman, at the station in Augusta. It was snowing, and we had to change trains. She showed us a picture. Her son."

I saw where this was headed. "He'd been killed in the war."

"Yes. In Italy, where I was. Where this—" His hand drifted upward to his cheek but stopped midair. "Close to where this happened. Not far, anyway. He was killed at Salerno. Some army screwup. His company dropped too far behind the lines. I'd heard something about it, but it wasn't until later that I was certain. They were totally annihilated. Germans shot them out of the sky like skeet pigeons."

"That was twenty years ago, Dad."

"Twenty years." His voice was quiet. "Twenty years is nothing, Joey. The boy was dead, you read me? He probably never even got the chance to fire his weapon." He breathed deeply, steadying himself. "But you see, it wasn't wrong, that he died. You could say it was a tragedy, somebody's stupid mistake, or just bad luck. It was easy to get killed for all kinds of reasons. But it wasn't *wrong*. The woman in the office, his mother, she knew that. She knew her son hadn't died for no reason. That's what made it bearable for her. When I understood that, I didn't mind what had happened to me so much anymore. I don't think a day goes by that I don't think about her. We got on the train and came up here, and it was like a gift, a reward for finally figuring that out."

Is it a trick of memory, or did something happen to me at that moment? It was, after all, just a story he was telling me—a war story. I had never heard this one before, but I had heard dozens, even hundreds. Yet listening to him talk that morning, I suddenly felt all my resolve drain out of me, an almost physical sensation. The flat winter light of the kitchen and the miles of quiet all around, the smell of our cigarettes, the feeling, inexpressible, that we had reached, together, a kind of final moment, the end of a story that had begun the day my mother died: all combined to arouse in me a boy's simple desire to help his father. And all at once I understood. I was the only cousin David. Those other boys were nothing. Everything my father had done, he'd done for me, to prepare us for this day.

"What I'm saying to you, Joey, is you're all I have. I know I haven't been the best father. There are things I should have told you, things I should have done." He looked at his chapped hands. "You were there

in the station, you know, with us. Me and your mother. Just a baby."
He stopped; it was as if he had never said any of these words before,
not even to himself. "It was snowing, like today, and it was as if I'd
found something nobody else knew, a way to understand my life. And
then your mother died, and I kept on anyway. I told her I would keep
you safe. Those were the last words I said to her, and that's what I'm
saying to you now. If something happened to you, I couldn't bear it,
Joey."

He rose and stood before me. My father: it was as if I hadn't really
looked at him in years. Beneath his flannel shirt and jeans, his body
had grown thin; his face was gray and lined. White stubble covered his
cheeks, except for a square of pinkish skin where his jaw had shattered,
a bare patch the color of a burn, where hair could never grow. Of
course I would do as he asked; I had been waiting for him to ask it, all
along.

"You were there at the station, you see, in that room," he said quietly. "That's what I'm telling you. That's why I want you to come with
me now, Joey, before the storm."

He had it all arranged; we would drive north, ahead of the weather,
and reach the border in late afternoon, where a man named Marcel
would be waiting to take me the rest of the way. My father had money
for me, two thousand dollars in American cash, and another thousand
Canadian. Upstairs in my room I stuffed my belongings into a duffel
bag: warm clothing, a few pictures, my high school yearbook, some
old letters Lucy had written me on a trip she had taken with her family
to Yosemite that I didn't want anyone finding, though they contained
nothing shocking or even terribly personal. It seemed meager. Hanging from my shoulder, my bag weighed less than twenty pounds. How
did you pack to become a fugitive? Atop my bureau was a framed
black-and-white photo of my mother: a young woman with high
cheekbones and hair the color of onyx, sitting at a great, gleaming piano, wearing a dark dress and smiling. It had been taken by a professional photographer, some kind of publicity shot, when she was a

student at the conservatory. She couldn't have been nineteen years old. A scoop of pearls gleamed across the white skin of her breastbone; she wore a huge corsage. Her eyes, bright and full of pleasure, seemed to shine with all the hopeful reflection of an entire life waiting to unfold. Though, of course, this was an illusion: she had no idea what lay ahead, how little time she had left. I hadn't really looked at the photo in years, and in fact, my memories of my mother bore almost no resemblance to the girl in the picture. She seemed a different woman entirely. When I remembered her, it wasn't even a picture I saw, but more a feeling my mind seemed to wrap around: the heat and sound and smell of her, like a pillow I had slept on for years; the close air of the bedroom where she was sick so long; her quiet, milky voice. But not even these. If I closed my eyes, as I did that snowy November morning, and asked myself to think about her, what I remembered most was a song she used to play: Debussy, the Children's Corner, an airy thing with notes that floated like fireflies on a summer lawn, a thousand of them winking here and there, but never quite where you looked. I think she used to play it for me when I was small, and fussing; at least that's what I remembered her telling me. She would place me on her lap and play, giving me a song to listen to but also her hands to watch: her long white fingers and the long white piano keys moving together like dancers in a dream, to make the music that would quiet me. Her piano, a Steinway baby grand that her parents had bought her for her eighteenth birthday, was still in the lodge, in a room we called the library, where we kept old books and magazines for guests to read. From time to time someone would open the keys and try to play it but would quickly discover how badly out of tune it was. The felts were all moth-eaten; one of the pedals was permanently jammed in the down position. Once in a while I'd thought about getting it fixed, with the idea that I might learn to play. But it had been silent so long, its music sealed away in its coffinlike bulk, that even to open the cabinet seemed impossible.

The truth was, my mother hadn't lived long enough to ever become a person to me, real and distinct; like all small children, I had absorbed her presence as a force of nature, and the day she died this feeling had frozen in me, a piece of stopped time. Looking at her picture now, I realized it meant nothing; my mother was inside that piano, and inside me. For a moment I considered leaving the photo behind, but this seemed foolish, something I might regret later, so I removed it from the frame and tucked it between the pages of an English-French dictionary I still had from high school, thinking this might come in handy, too, and tucked that into my duffel bag as well.

Outside, my father was warming up the truck. The air was damp and still; the low gray sky seemed to bulge with snow, like a river about to overflow its banks. I heaved my bag into the bed and joined him in the cab.

He gently touched my sleeve. The gesture was so surprising I actually looked at it, his hand on my arm. The realization hit me like a fist: this winter he would be alone.

"Did you call her?"

The answer was I hadn't. Lucy would be in the sawmill office at this hour; they would probably be sending everyone home early, due to the snow. How could I explain something I didn't understand myself? I couldn't have said why I was going, only that I was, and that this made me feel ashamed but also relieved, as if some unseen hand had lifted a burden I didn't even know I was carrying. I wondered if this was how cowards felt, or men lost at sea who had given up their struggles and agreed to let the waves take them. In fact, these were the very words I used when, a week later, I wrote to Lucy to tell her what had happened, how instantly sorry I had felt about leaving.

"That's all right," he said when I failed to answer, and with this, one more burden was taken from me. He put the truck in gear. "Maybe it's better if you don't. They have phones up there. It's not like you're going to the moon."

By the time we reached the border it was past three and snowing hard. Marcel was waiting at the roadside, parked in a rusted Jeep with Quebec plates and a huge rack of lights over the roll bar. He was a slender man, strong across the chest, with a neatly trimmed beard and half-glasses he removed to regard me; I thought of him at once as a kind of skinny Santa Claus. He and my father greeted one another with a grave handshake, which I understood was meant for me. My father had brought many men over, but I was his son, his flesh and blood.

I put my duffel bag in the Jeep. Then, in the falling snow, my father hugged me, hard. "Be good now, Joey." Before I could answer he turned and walked to the truck without looking back, got in, and drove away. I watched him until the image was swallowed in the whirling white and silence. A feeling of cold loneliness doused me like water. I had no idea how or even if we would see each other again. The moment had passed so quickly I hadn't even said good-bye.

I got into the Jeep's cab. On the passenger seat lay the Montreal newspaper that Marcel had been reading, and the remains of his lunch, a bacon sandwich wrapped in waxed paper and a thermos of coffee.

"You think he'll get back okay?" I asked.

"It's not him I'm worried about," Marcel said, but when he saw my face he smiled encouragingly. "I've known your father since the war. We served together in Italy. Not many men could go through what he did. A little snow won't slow him down any."

I was suddenly perplexed. "You're American?"

"Half and half." Marcel turned the key, and the Jeep's engine sprang to life. "My mother was Quebecois. My wife's Canadian too. She's from Toronto originally. You'll meet her tomorrow, this snow doesn't get any worse."

We stopped the night outside Quebec City, then drove north the next day up the St. Lawrence Seaway on a winding two-lane road that hugged the immense, barren coastline. The storm had passed; the day was clear and shockingly bright, though in the Jeep's drafty cab, the cold possessed a scathing intensity that felt like the grip of permanent night. Vast, empty fields lined the road on the inland side: peat farms, Marcel explained. Freighters the size of whole city blocks plied the gray waters of the seaway, which was choked at the shoreline with huge sheets of broken ice. There were no proper towns on the route at all, but every thirty minutes or so we passed an isolated settlement of perhaps a half-dozen houses and a store or two, all staring grimly out to sea and looking so weather-beaten they seemed on the verge of collapse. A terrible emptiness opened inside me, deeper than hunger: with each passing mile, I felt myself moving farther away from everything I knew.

"Cheer up," Marcel said, when I muttered something grim about the scenery. "It's really not so bad, you know. You'll get used to it."

"I'm sorry, I didn't mean to be rude. It's just, it all looks so . . . abandoned."

Twilight fell a little after three; we arrived in LeMaitre in darkness. I felt as if we'd been traveling for weeks. A raw wind raked me as I stepped from the cab in front of Marcel's house, my muscles stiff and heavy as iron from two days in the bouncy Jeep. The air was rich with the funk of fish. LeMaitre was a larger town than any I'd seen for hours, though still small by any measure: about five hundred people, nearly all of whom worked in one way or another for Marcel, who owned a fish-processing plant. As we crested the last rise into town I had seen it, a huge building blazing with light at the mouth of the Foché River.

"Home sweet home," Marcel said. "Let's get you inside."

Marcel's wife, Abby, was in the low-ceilinged kitchen, stirring the contents of a gigantic blackened pot. The room was like something from a fairy tale, a cottage in the woods that a lost little boy might stumble upon. A great stone hearth occupied one wall, and bundles of some kind of fragrant herb hung from the ceiling. Rich waves of heat issued from the fireplace, so intense after hours in the frigid Jeep that I could scarcely breathe.

"Abby, this is Joe Crosby's boy."

She stepped toward me; I offered her my hand, and she took it in both of hers. She was, like her husband, a woman of compact dimensions, with eyes the color of moss and dry gray hair that flowed away from her face as if lifted by an unseen wind. She was wearing an apron, and a long denim skirt; her nose, I saw, was rather small. All the words

I might have spoken seemed to flit up and away from my mind like a flock of birds. I stood dumbly, fixed in place. Her hands felt warm as a muffler heated on the stove.

"I know your father, Joey," she said gently.

And I began, at last—as if I'd been waiting all my life for this moment to come and take me in its grip—to weep.

Harry

I didn't return to the camp for three years, after that night on the porch when Joe appeared. It wasn't jealousy that kept me away. What happened to me when Lucy stepped from the darkness and into Joe's arms—the arms she truly belonged in; anyone could have seen that—was the end of an illusion I had taken shelter in, precisely because it *was* an illusion: this idea of some current that flowed between the two of us, perfect in its way because it was never meant to be expressed. Lucy, the camp, my feelings of escape: none of it was my actual life. To learn this was bearable, but I also knew that if I returned, even for a day, the comfort of its memory would be taken from me too. I packed up early the next morning, offered some vague excuse to Joe Sr. about an emergency at home, and drove down the long drive. As I neared the main road, a car approached from the opposite direction: Ken and Leonie in a big fat Cadillac, returning from an errand in town—aspirin, I figured, or more booze. We slowed to pass one another, splashing through the potholes; Leonie waved gaily from the passenger seat, and I returned the wave, even gave my horn a little toot. A laugh escaped my lips, though it was a bitter sound. I thought of Lucy, speaking Joe's name out of the gloom; and then the moment when the two of them had disappeared, leaving me alone. Well, I thought, you're a little old to be so glum about a crush, Harry Wainwright. You got your wake-up call for sure. Live and learn, and get yourself *home*.

A year passed and then another, and the camp faded from my mind. I thought about Lucy from time to time, wondered what had become of her, but my curiosity was mild, for it had no purpose: I might have been wondering about any other friend who had disappeared into the world's hurrying crowds. Each summer, and then in the week after New Year's, I went with Hal someplace new, just the two of us: river rafting in the Grand Canyon, deep-sea fishing in the Sea of Cortez, on safari to the great game reserves of east Africa—his high school graduation present—where under the snowcapped shadow of Mount Kenya we watched elephants bathing in the Pangani River by the dewy light of an equatorial dawn. He had grown into a fine young man, strong and thoughtful, organized in his affairs, perhaps a little melancholy, though that was understandable: his mother was dying, his father seemed only to have just found him, like a book left carelessly on the patio, or a ring of keys he'd mislaid.

Hal left for Williams in the fall of '71; by then Meredith was confined wholly to her bed. She had only the vaguest sensation in her hands and feet; the cysts had done their work. There was the surprising cruelty of pain, pain without nameable source, pain in places that otherwise could feel nothing at all. Even breathing was an effort. There was no place left for the disease to go.

When I remember that year, marked by Hal's departure at one end and Meredith's death at the other, I feel as if I am watching a movie, but a movie without sound. It was as if someone were turning a dial, and with each passing week the signals of ordinary life became less distinct, finally vanishing altogether and leaving the two of us alone. She might have spent her last months in the hospital, but she didn't want this, and neither did I, though I don't remember the two of us ever discussing it. What I do remember is the gathering quiet of the autumn months, then the brief burst of activity when Hal came home from Williamstown for Christmas—we opened our presents in the library, which we had turned into a bedroom for Meredith, all of us putting on the bravest possible show—and then, when he was gone again, sensing in his wake a deeper, final stillness, like a slowing of the blood. It was a cold winter but without snow, a kind of permanent, frozen autumn, as if the calendar had stopped when the wind had torn the last of the leaves away. I rarely set foot from the house; I left my affairs to others, my trusted lieutenants and their trusted lieutenants, an interlocking system of delegated duties I had created to prepare for this very day. Think of a children's game in which sticks are piled high: the object is to build your tower well, to disperse its structural energies in such a manner that you may, at the crucial moment, snatch a single stick from the bottom and leave the whole thing standing. I had played such a game when I was small, and then later with Hal, when he was just a boy, the two of us sitting on the living room carpet or at the kitchen table. A clever trick, a bit of fun to pass the time, but like all such diversions, embedded within it one finds a meaning: do not build a life you cannot step out of.

April came, and with it, a blast of sudden, heavy warmth. Hal had spent the midsemester holiday in Florida, training with the lacrosse team, and in those early days of spring I drove north to watch him play his first real game with the varsity, leaving Meredith at home with Elizabeth, her nurse. We had dinner together at the Williamstown Inn to celebrate: though he had played just a few minutes, he had done well, getting a pair of shots on goal and making one assist in the final minute, a shot that had sailed past the goalie like a rifle bullet to put the Ephmen over the top. Though I knew almost nothing about the sport, I could see that Hal was an astute and skillful player, aggressive when he needed to be but also smart about when to carry the ball and when to give it away.

"The coach wants me to train to tend goal," he explained. He was eating an enormous steak; his hair was still wet from the shower. "We've got a lot of attackmen coming up, but nobody really to take over in the net next year."

"Goalie." I frowned, thinking of that final shot; it was a job for a sitting duck. "I don't know, Hal. Is that what you want?"

He laughed easily. "At least you can see it coming. On attack, half the time you never know what hit you. Like in the movies, one minute you're fine, next thing you know, little birds are chirping around your head." He made a little circular motion with his finger. "I'm quick enough. It's the most important position, really."

"We better not tell your mother."

"Oh, trust me, I won't."

"I'm sorry she couldn't come up. I know she would have liked seeing you."

Hal said nothing. Over the years, the two of us had often spoken this way, as if Meredith's illness were something less than what it was— not a permanent affliction but a temporary circumstance that would soon be set to rights. It was an old habit, well-intentioned but more suited to a boy than the grown man who now sat across the table from me, and I was afraid I'd angered him with this pretense. But then with great deliberateness he put down his knife and fork and looked at me, his face containing a terrible sadness but somehow smiling too. It was, I thought, the very face of bravery. I had never felt so close to him, so enriched by his presence.

"I know," he said. "Tell her all about it, okay? Tell her I wish she'd been here."

"I will. You bet I will."

I left him at his dormitory, slept the night at the inn, and headed home to Westchester the next morning. It was late afternoon when I returned. As I pulled into the driveway I saw Elizabeth putting a small overnight bag in the trunk of her car.

"Is everything all right?"

She was wrapping her hair in a scarf printed with daisies. The late afternoon sun was strong and warm, and we were both squinting. "Mrs. Wainwright gave me the weekend off. She told me to wait until you came, and then I could go. I wanted to visit my sister up in New Haven. I hope that's all right."

"I don't know why it wouldn't be. Is someone else coming?"

A curious look passed over her face. "Well, I . . . I don't know. I assume someone phoned the service. But no one's here yet. She said I could leave when you got home. Do you want me to call?"

I thought a moment and shook my head. "No, that's all right." Elizabeth had been with us two years; I never knew exactly how old she was, but I assumed she was at least sixty. She had no children of her own, but what seemed like a dozen sisters spread from Philadelphia to Boston, whom she was always visiting. I didn't know her all that well,

really, but her duties placed her in a relationship of such intimacy with
Meredith that the two of them had become the closest of confidantes.
I would sometimes enter the library to find her sitting beside Meredith's bed and know that at just that moment the two of them had
stopped talking.

"You can go if you want," I said. "I'll take care of things here."

Yet as I made my way up the front walk, I felt her eyes following
me. I turned and there she was, standing exactly where she had been,
holding her small suitcase by the open door of her little car.

"Lizzy? Is there something else?"

She seemed about to speak, but then she shrugged and gave me a
wan smile. "It's nothing. How was the game?"

"A squeaker, but they won. Hal got an assist, too."

Her face was pleased, but something more: she looked almost relieved. "That's good. I'm sure Mrs. Wainwright will be glad to hear it."

The house was strangely still. In the little telephone room by the
front door I stopped to check for messages and found a long list, written on a yellow legal pad. I glanced over it, but my heart was nowhere
in this, and I put the list aside. The hour was just past four; I was stiff
from the long day in the car, but felt also a lingering excitement from
my visit with Hal. I stood in the telephone room and listened. Not a
sound could be heard; it was as if the house itself had stopped breathing. Even with Hal away at school, the house always had people in it:
Elizabeth, of course, but also our housekeeper, Mrs. Beryl, or one of
the girls she hired to help out. There were always gardeners mowing or
weeding somewhere. My phone messages had been taken by my secretary, Nancy, a divorced woman with two young children she often
brought with her to the house in the afternoons. It was not unusual for
me to find them, a boy and a girl, having milk and cookies in the
kitchen or watching a television program in the den. The last message
had been taken at three thirty. But even without looking, I knew that
Nancy and her children, like the cook and gardener and all the rest,
were nowhere to be found.

I looked in on Meredith and found her sleeping. In the kitchen a
cold supper was waiting for me, and a note from Mrs. Beryl, taped to

the refrigerator: *Mrs. Wainwright gave me the night off, hope that's all right.* I took my plate to the library and had my dinner of cold cuts and cheese and pickles off my knees, watching Meredith sleep and breathe, as another man might have read the paper or watched television as he ate. When I was done, I took my dishes to the kitchen, washed and dried them and set them on the draining board, and by the time I returned, Meredith's eyes were open.

"It's me," I said quietly. "I'm home."

A barely perceptible nod. I took a rag and moistened her lips, then cranked up her bed and held a glass of water with a straw for her to sip. In her throat, the water moved sluggishly, like some enormous pill she was swallowing.

"Do you feel like eating?"

She shook her head slightly, her eyes drifting closed, but only for a moment. The day had ended. Outside, spring twilight fell like a soft cloth across the lawn and over the limbs of the budding trees. I reached to turn on her bedside lamp, but she shook her head again.

"Leave . . . it," she said. Long pauses for breath split the spaces between her words. "Was it . . . a good day?"

I took a chair by the bed. "Hal got an assist. He didn't play until the last half, but I think he really did well. He's thinking of trying out for goalie too. His coach says it's the most important position."

"Tell me . . . all about . . . it."

I did. I told her everything: the handsome look of the field and players, how there was still a bit of snow in the woods around the town, and Hal in his uniform with the pads bursting beneath it, though one could still see how big he was, how strong; and the bond I could feel among his teammates, like the ball that passed between them as they flew down the field, boys stepping into their lives together; and about our dinner together and the long drive home. Darkness came into the room as I talked, but I did not feel its strangeness or its weight; it was the most natural thing in the world to sit in a dark room and tell my wife the story of my journey.

"What did . . . he eat?" she said when I was done.

"When? At the inn, you mean?"

"You . . . forgot . . . to say."

"Steak," I said. I showed her with my fingers. "A great thick porter-house. With béarnaise. Are you hungry, M?"

"No." Her voice was thin, almost a whisper. "We're . . . alone," she said.

"Yes." And then I said it. "You've sent them all away."

From her arm the slightest movement: she was reaching for my tears. I felt this as if she had actually done it, as if her hand were on my cheek.

"Don't . . . be sad."

"Do we have to, M?"

"I can't . . ." she said, but stopped. Can't go on, can't do this alone, can't can't can't. What would I have wanted, if I were she? And as I thought this, I knew my answer, though I had known it many months, all that year in fact, and my mind seemed to move into a place where what was about to happen already had, a room in which there were only two people, M and I, and this final night forever.

"Harry . . . help me . . . do this."

There were medicines everywhere: on her table, in the bathroom, in drawers and the pockets of coats hanging in the closets. A house of medicine. But I knew which one she wanted. The doctor had given it to us with a warning, a warning I understood was also a promise: more than the prescribed dosage, even a little, and it could compromise her breathing. I was so nervous I could barely crush the pills with the back of the spoon I took from the kitchen drawer. Water would have been easier for her, but I chose milk to cloud the taste. In the blazing light of the kitchen I kept my thoughts trained upon these small, mechanical actions, as an archer holds the target in his sights. I mixed the milk and pills together, rinsed the spoon, placed the glass on a saucer, and, dousing the kitchen light behind me, returned to the library.

"I've made you something."

The faintest smile crossed her lips, as if I'd brought her a present. "That . . . there."

"Yes."

She let a moment pass. "Leave it . . . for now. Harry . . . will you do something . . . for me?"

I placed the glass and saucer on the table. "Anything, M."

"Come . . . to bed."

"Get in with you, you mean?"

"Yes," she said. "Like . . . before."

Standing by the bed, I undressed: shoes and socks and pants and shirt. I folded these items carefully, placed my shoes on top, and rested it all on a chair.

"So . . . handsome," she said. "Now . . . come . . . to bed."

I cranked the bed down and climbed in beside her. The mattress was narrow, and had chrome bars on the sides; beneath the sheet I could feel the squeaking friction of the rubber barrier. I pulled her across me, so that her chest lay against my own, her head resting in the hollow of my neck.

"It's good . . . to think . . . of Hal."

"I wish you could have been there, M."

"I was . . . Harry. You . . . told me . . . and I . . . was there. Don't cry . . . Harry."

"I'm sorry, M. I'll try not to."

"Remember . . . that . . . night? I told you . . . it would be . . . all right." A long inhalation of breath. "It will . . . be."

"I know that, M."

"Tell me . . . another . . . story."

"I don't think I can."

"Yes . . . you . . . can." I felt her nod, though this was, I knew, a memory. Her breath was warm and slow on my neck. "I know . . . you, Harry."

I took a deep breath, then heard myself speaking. My voice was strange and far away, seeming to come at once from inside me and from the air of the dark room all around.

"Once upon a time, there was a man and a woman, and they had two boys. The first one was very little. He was sick, and for a time they thought he might die, but eventually he became well, though he stayed little because of this sickness, and his mother and father loved him very much. The second boy grew and became a man, and they loved him, too, though differently. That is what they learned in their lives together: that the little boy, because he stayed little, would always have a special kind of love, but that the other boy, who grew, would be the one who would take care of them, when they themselves grew old. The first love was sweeter, and a little sad, because when the man and the woman felt it, they were remembering. But the second was stronger, because they knew it would last them all the days of their lives. M?"

"Yes . . . Harry?"

"Was the story what you wanted?"

"It . . . was always . . . what I wanted." Then: "Tell me . . . more. Tell me . . . anything."

I did. I told her everything; I talked for hours, or thought I did. I told her every story I knew. Her breathing grew slow and heavy against my chest, like long waves on a beach. And when I was done, she said, quietly, "I'm . . . thirsty."

"I'll get you some water."

"No . . . Harry." She seemed to shake her head. "The . . . other. Please."

"M. I just can't."

"Shhhh . . . don't cry . . . Harry."

"I can't, I can't."

"I am . . . your wife, Harry. I am . . . your wife . . . and I need you . . . to do this."

Then the glass was in my hand. It was warm, from hours of sitting, and thick with the grains of the crushed pills; the mixture had separated a little, leaving a dark layer of medicine at the bottom, and so I took a spoon from the bedside table to stir it, quietly, so as not to disturb the silence of the room with even the slightest contact of metal on glass. I slid behind her, taking her weight on my chest, and held the straw to her lips. She was forty-five years old.

"That's it . . . Harry."

Her sips were small, like a bird taking water from a garden fountain: delicate, and without hesitation. A dozen times she drank, taking the milk and the pills into her. A stream of the bitter liquid ran down the sides of her mouth, onto her chin and neck, and when she was done I used a washcloth to wipe it all away.

"Let's go . . . to sleep . . . Harry."

"M—"

"It's . . . all right," she said, and I felt her move against me and then stop. Her voice was faraway, a dreamer's voice, and I felt a heaviness gather inside me, taking me with her.

"It's . . . all right. Sleep . . . my love."

And God save us all, I did.

THIRTEEN

Lucy

Joe always said it was bad luck to watch him leave from the dock. He kissed me that day, the eve of Christmas, 1971, bounded up the gangway, and I went back to the motel and slept. I awoke to the sound of someone banging on the door, and a high, loud voice, jabbering in Spanish: the chambermaid. I took my watch from the bedside table; it was just past noon. I had long since missed my bus. Already Joe would be fifty miles out to sea.

I yelled something to the maid about coming back later, pulled the blankets tight around me, and by the time I awoke again the sun was setting. I showered and dressed and stepped outside. A stiff wind was blowing off the water. The sun had set completely; the buildings by the water were all dark, but up the hill I could see lights and feel the presence of the city. In the office, I found the same clerk who'd checked us in the night before, watching a football game on television and paring his nails.

"If it's all right, I'd like to stay another night."

He looked at his watch, then at me. "You already did."

"I'm sorry?"

"You've been here two days."

I stood a moment, taking this in. Had I really slept through a day and a night and all the next day besides? Vague memories gathered in my mind, scattered images I'd thought were dreams: a second visit from the chambermaid, more insistent, and rising in the middle of the afternoon to use the bathroom and hearing, from outside, the rush of midday traffic on Commercial Street.

"Listen," the clerk was saying, "what you do is your own business, young lady, but we don't want any druggies in here. This is a family resort."

"What are you talking about?" I wanted to laugh. "It's a motel. And I was just tired."

"Like I said." He cleared his throat. "We don't want any tired people in here. You owe me thirty more dollars, tonight included. Then you be on your way."

There was no point in arguing. I counted out the money from my purse. Joe had given me an extra fifty to help me get home. All told, I had a little over a hundred dollars left—money I had planned to spend in Boston on Christmas presents for my parents, but had not gotten around to using.

As I was leaving the office, the realization hit me all at once, like a gust of wind. I turned at the door; the clerk had already gone back to watching his game.

"If you don't mind my asking, what day is it?"

"Today?" He looked at me and laughed. "It's Christmas Day. You almost missed it."

I couldn't have said why I did what I did, not exactly. It was as if a hidden door had opened, like a passage in a castle wall. Joe, my parents, the whole kit and kaboodle that I called my life: all I had to do was go through the door, and I could leave everything behind. I thought of the girl I had seen in the restaurant in Cambridge, so confident and smart, holding the attention of the men at her table like a spell. I knew that her life—a life of money and good schools and all the choices such things buy—could never be mine. I wasn't going to be a lawyer, or even go to college. But I wanted to know, even for a moment, what it felt like to be someone like her.

I rented a room the next day at the YWCA on Spring Street. Seven dollars a night, and another five to eat, perhaps three more for incidentals: by these calculations, I needed to find a job in five days. There were fourteen restaurants going four or five blocks in each direction from the Y, everything from greasy-spoon diners to chowder houses with big open tanks of lobsters for the tourists. It was the slow season, I figured, but people still had to eat, and I didn't care what kind of place it was, so long as I had work. By now my parents would be wondering what had happened to me—my lie about visiting high school friends in Boston would have long since fallen apart with just a few phone calls—but I didn't want to tell them where I was until I had gotten myself settled. I was twenty-four years old, and never in my life had I done anything so purely on my own.

By the third day I was beginning to panic. Everyplace the story was the same: not hiring, try back in a few weeks. But I didn't have a few weeks. I was down to just thirty dollars, plus the eleven dollars I had to keep aside for bus fare home in case nothing worked out. I had a tidy nest egg sitting in a passbook savings account back in Sagonick—a little over three thousand dollars I'd managed to put away—but I would have had to go home to get it, or ask my parents to wire me the money. I vowed I wouldn't touch it, unless I got truly desperate.

I had one solid lead: a chowder house down on Commercial, just a few hundred yards from the dock where the *Jenny-Smith* had been berthed. I'd visited it the first day, and the manager told me that he might be needing a waitress; one of his girls was pregnant and likely going to quit. I'd been hoping for a job as a line cook, but waitressing or even busing would be fine, I told him. Check back in a couple of days, he said. Maybe he'd know something by then.

I waited until noon on the fourth day before I returned. The weather was a sullen, dispiriting gray, and a steady ten-knot wind whipped up the waters of the harbor, making me think of Joe, now far out to sea. It wasn't until that moment that I realized how angry I was with him. I was wearing the bracelet he'd given me—I hadn't taken it off since our first night together—and, feeling its jangling presence against my wrist, I remembered his words: *There's a woman in town who makes these.* Even as he'd spoken, I'd felt a little chill of suspicion unsnake inside me. We'd been apart for three years. I'd never asked about other women, and he'd never mentioned any, except for someone named Abby, whom I gathered was his boss's wife and an old friend of his father's—a nurse who had taken care of Joe Sr. when he was injured in the war. Apart from that, Joe's descriptions of life in LeMaitre made it sound like a frontier outpost from some novel of the old West, everyone spitting and pissing where they liked. But of course, even in such a place there would be women.

Feeling suddenly determined, I marched through slushy snow up to the front door of the restaurant and stepped inside. Only a few people were eating—mostly men in suits and ties, no doubt the usual lunch crowd from the law firms and government offices over on State, hunched over bowls of chowder and pints of Bass. At the bar I asked for the manager, and a minute later he came striding out of the kitchen.

"Oh, it's you," he said. He was an older man, maybe fifty-five, with square glasses that made his eyes seem large and a comb-over of wispy hair that flapped a little when he walked. "I'm sorry. Maybe in a few more weeks."

The news hit me like a blow. "I don't have a few weeks," I said, and heard the tears pressing on my voice. "I only have another day."

"Did you try O'Neil's? They sometimes need people." O'Neil's was another seafood place, further down Commercial.

"I've tried everywhere." A fat tear spilled onto my cheek, and when I tried to wipe it away, I found I was still wearing my mittens. I removed them and grabbed a cocktail napkin off the bar and blew my nose. "I'm sorry. I don't have to waitress. Just let me sweep up or something. Please. I'm down to my last thirty dollars."

He regarded me another moment. The restaurant seemed to have fallen suddenly quiet. Beyond the windows, the gray sky over the harbor roiled with cold and snow.

"Aw, hell," he said, and scratched the back of his head. "I really shouldn't be doing this. To tell the truth, I had pretty much decided not to hire anybody, with business being so slow. But maybe we can squeeze you in."

"You mean it?"

He seemed about to laugh. "You want the job or not?"

"Yes, absolutely."

"You won't get rich in here. I know you know that, but I'm just saying. We only pay the minimum, a buck forty an hour. That and tips, of course. And I can't give you the dinner shift until you've been on awhile."

"Anything is fine. Really."

He took a peppermint from a wicker basket on the hostess station and popped it into his mouth. Then he leveled his gaze at me. "Listen," he said quietly, sucking on the candy, "I've got to ask. There isn't anything I should know about you, is there?"

"What do you mean?"

"Don't get me wrong. But not many girls come in and say they're down to their last thirty dollars, or whatever it was. There wouldn't be . . . anyone looking for you, would there? Like, say, a husband or boyfriend, something like that? You can tell me if there is."

"No, sir. I just want to work."

He looked at me another moment, deciding what to believe, and finally ended our negotiation with a crisp nod. "Okay, then. But it's Deck, all right? Like the deck of a boat."

"Deck. Got it."

"Ten thirty sharp, tomorrow. Black pants if you have 'em, or else you can pick up a cheap pair at the army-navy down the street. The white shirt you have on should do fine."

I felt myself smiling. "You won't be sorry."

"I'm guessing not." He turned on his heel to go. "Sorry. Stupid of me, but I forgot to ask your name."

"Alice." I'd said it without thinking. It was my mother's middle name. He was being so nice, I felt a little bad about the lie. But I also liked the sound of it, the new taste of it on my tongue: Alice. Who was Alice?

"Okay, Alice," he said. "See you tomorrow."

As easy as that, I got my wish, stepped through the door from my old life and into another. I was no longer Lucy, but Alice: Alice, the waitress from Portland. I started work the next day, as promised, ten thirty

on the dot with a smile on my face and pants so crisply new they rus-
tled when I walked; a week later I was working the dinner shift and
taking in a solid thirty dollars a night in tips. The Y was fine, if a little
noisy, but they wouldn't let me stay longer than a month anyway; one
of the other waitresses told me about an available apartment in the
triple-decker where she lived, and I went one evening to look at it: a
single room with a toilet and tub but no sink except for in the kitchen.
But the windows were big—I thought on clear days I might even be
able to see the water—and it came furnished, with a bed, a table, and
some plywood-and-milk-crate shelves. The only way in was up three
flights of rickety stairs from the rear of the building, open to the
weather and slick with ice. The rent was $120, utilities included; I
took it on the spot, walked back to the Y to fetch my things—a single
suitcase of clothing, a grocery bag of magazines and knicknacks, and
an asparagus fern I'd bought to keep me company—and slept that
night in my own apartment, a feeling as strange and wondrous to me
as a first kiss.

It wasn't until the next day that I finally wrote my parents a letter. I
didn't want to lie, but the truth was too hard to explain—I didn't even
have words for it myself—so I simply told them that I had decided I
needed to set out on my own for a bit, that I was safe and well, and
where they could reach me if they needed to and that they should not
tell Joe where I was if he called. I tucked a twenty-dollar bill in the envelope, and explained that it was money I had planned to spend on
Christmas presents, and that I hoped they would buy themselves
something nice with it. *Dad,* I wrote, *I know you need gloves, you always
do, and Mom, I was thinking you might like some perfume, or else ear-
rings. I'm sorry I had to do this. It has nothing to do with Joe, or not exactly, so please don't be angry with him, or with me. Don't worry, as I really
am okay, better than I've been in a while in fact, and just need some time
for whatever it is that's going on with me.* Weeping, I signed it *Love, Lucy,*
already feeling like an imposter for using this name.

My new life felt simple, clean, uncluttered, like a child's dollhouse,
or the pages of an empty book. I worked the dinner shift from five
to eleven, slept the mornings away, rose at ten to do small chores—

shopping for food, or else laundry; I had very little clothing, and was constantly washing what I had—ate a small, early dinner at my tiny table, then left in twilight for the restaurant. The Y was just a few blocks away from my apartment, and afternoons on my way to work I would go there to swim, something I had never really done before, at least not in a pool. Twenty-five cents, plus a nickel for a towel; when I recall those months, it's these trips to the pool that return most vividly to mind, each sensory detail forever etched in memory. The feel of the towel in my hand, warm from the dryer and so crisped with bleach it felt deep-fried; the cold against my skin as I undressed hurriedly in the frigid locker room; the feeling of immersion, the world above me wiped away, and the building heat of my muscles as they set to work in a rhythm that was a kind of music. Kick-stroke/ kick-stroke/head turn-*breathe,* kick-stroke/ kick-stroke/head turn-*breathe.* I saw other people doing flip-turns and wanted to try it; the first time, I got so much water up my nose the lifeguard came down from his stand to ask me if I would be all right, but before long I had mastered it, and was swimming a mile a day.

If it's true that I was sometimes homesick—a sudden ache, nearly physical, which always took me by surprise—it was also the case that I was happy, and that this happiness felt sweeter for my loneliness. The world seemed to have forgotten me, forgotten *Lucy,* and when I thought about the people and places of my old life, the love I felt for them was tinged with nostalgia, as if I were recalling them across a span of many years. The sensation was so new to me I wondered if it could possibly last, until one deep, cold night in the first week of March, when I awakened to the feeling that someone was watching me. It was late, after three A.M. Not someone, I thought: some*thing.* I rose quickly in my icy apartment, and when I went to my window I was so startled by what I found that I forgot all about the fear that had pulled me from bed. A great, billowing apparition of blue-green light, like pool water, but shot with flecks of gold, hung over the sleeping city, folded like a drape. It moved back and forth, pushed by an invisible wind—a wind of light and stars. I knew what I was looking at; I had seen the aurora borealis before, of course; yet at that moment, standing by my window, I felt as if I were witnessing something far more: the purest light of angels in their heaven, remembering the world.

The next day, a Saturday, I rose early, did a load of laundry in the basement, swam my usual mile. It was just before five when I arrived at the Lobster Tank. Only a few customers were eating, mostly older folks in for the early bird four-dollar special. I took a clean apron and a tray from the pile by the dishwasher and got to work. By six the place was packed. I was putting up an order on the clips when I turned and saw Deck watching me.

"What? Is there something in my teeth?"

"Somebody's in a good mood."

The bell rang behind me: my order. I dressed the plates up with little custard cups of tartar sauce, a piece of lettuce, and lemon wedges, then hoisted the tray onto my shoulder.

"Deck, what?"

"You. Smiling like that."

I laughed, embarrassed. But it was true. "Okay, I'll cut it out."

"No need. One thing I know, a woman only smiles like that when she's in love. Or so May tells me."

May was Deck's wife. She always picked Deck up at the end of the night, waiting outside in her little orange Pinto while we reset the tables; I'd met her in the parking lot my first week on the job. Twice they'd had me out to their house for dinner, the first time with some of the other girls from the restaurant, the second just me alone. May was a secretary at the high school, a big woman but not soft, and when she hugged me, as she now did whenever I saw her, I felt the wind come out of me a little. Their kids were grown and gone: their daughter, Peg, a girl about my age, lived in Nashua, and was married to a fireman; their son, George, had been through some rough patches but had eventually settled down, played semipro hockey for a while, and now taught high school phys-ed someplace down south—Memphis, or Mobile. Their house was out in the country, a post-and-beam thing that looked big from the road but felt snug inside. The second time I'd gone out for dinner, and the hour had gotten late, I'd slept the night in Peg's old room, using one of her old T-shirts as a nightgown.

"We smile for lots of reasons, Deck. We're a mysterious species."

"Well, whatever it is," he said, nodding, "it's nice to see." I thought the conversation was over but then he reached into his back pocket. "Also, and I don't want to kill your mood, but I'm guessing this might be for you."

I put my tray down on the garnish counter and took the letter from his hand. The envelope was small, and thick with folded notebook paper. It was addressed to me, care of my parents, with a big X across the address and, written beside it, *The Lobster Tank, Commercial Street Wharf, Portland, ME.* The second handwriting was my mother's.

"Lucy, huh?"

It took me a moment to gather myself. I suppose I felt the way all liars did, when they were finally found out: guilty, but a little relieved, too. I also realized, holding Joe's letter, that whatever was inside didn't matter to me anywhere near as much as it might have even a few weeks before.

"I'm sorry, Deck. I don't know what to say."

He frowned in a way that struck me as reassuring, though I could also tell I'd hurt his feelings. I'd eaten at his table and slept in his house, and not even told him who I really was.

"It's all right," Deck said finally. "I don't mean to pry."

"Could we maybe keep this between us for now? Just you and me and May."

"If that's how you want it, sure." He stopped, his face a little flustered. "Lucy. Alice. Listen, I know it's not my business. But if there's anything I can help you with, any sort of problem at all . . ."

I looked him in the eye. "It's okay, Deck. Really, I'm all right."

"Well, the offer's open. You ever need someplace to go, Peg's room is yours for the asking. May says so too."

I could have kissed him right then, that sweet man. Over the counter, the bell rang again; I was now stacked up two orders, and could see, through the little window separating the prep area from the dining room, more folks coming in. I hoisted the first tray to my shoulder. "Trust me," I said. "I've got it all under control."

I planned to open the letter when I got home, but in the end I couldn't make myself wait. When my shift was done, and once we'd broken everything down for the night, I got a glass of water and took a stool at the bar. *Dear Lucy* Joe wrote:

Not knowing where to send this, I'm mailing it to your parents. When I didn't hear from you I phoned the house and they told me that you were in Portland, but wouldn't say where. It's funny to think that you never left, after that morning on the dock. I hope you're all right.

Lucy, I'm sorry. I've said this before and I'll say it now. I know how hard this is for you, my being stuck here, and I know you've probably had it with me, with the whole situation. I wish it were different, but it is what it is. There's more talk of an amnesty, but we've heard this before up here, and I'm not sure I'd qualify anyway. The rumor is it will only go to people with dependents. No one really knows. That asshole Nixon is probably going to be reelected, which would deep-six the whole thing.

Lucy, I know I have nothing to offer you. This sounds a little stupid as I write it, sort of old-fashioned, but the truth is you deserve a real life. Abby and Marcel are nice people, and they're looking after me—all of us, really—but there's only so much they can do. It's taken me a while to admit this, but I see it now. I think I figured it out that night in Harvard Square, when we had dinner. You think I didn't see you watching that girl, but I did. I knew you were thinking it should have been you. I wished it for you, Lucy, I really did, and I was sorrier than I'd ever been in my life. This sounds dumb, but maybe it's not too late. I don't know what you're doing now, but I hope it's what you want, and that it will take you where you want to go.

You know the funniest thing? I still wish I'd gone to Vietnam. I read about the war, I see shit on the news, but I still wish I hadn't let my father talk me into leaving. But there I go, blaming him, when it was really something I did, nobody else. A lot of us feel that way, even the die-hard antiwar types. It's hard to stay political when you're standing in the pens surrounded by forty tons of ice and fish, so cold your hands freeze to the pitchfork, and some jerk yelling at you to hurry the hell up before it all rots and turns to cat food, and it looks pretty much as if your life is just fucking over. If I'd gone, by now it would be done with, at least for me. Whatever was supposed to happen would have happened by now.

The other thing I want to tell you is that my father isn't well. A few days after Christmas he had a small stroke. I don't know all the details, and as usual he's pretending it's nothing, but the truth is it's a bad turn. He was shoveling out the truck when it happened and I guess he was outside for a while in the snow before he managed to get into the house and call someone. He had some pretty bad frostbite too, on his hands and feet, which is probably worse than it would otherwise be, without the diabetes. He's out of the hospital now and staying in town for the winter at the Rogues'. I think you know them—Hank Rogue, Rogue Drillers? They have a daughter who was a couple years ahead of us at Regional. Anyway, Hank and my father have always gotten on, probably because they're the two crankiest men in northwest Maine.

The real upshot is, between the stroke and all the rest of it, it doesn't look as if he can hold on to the camp much longer. My guess is he may try to get through next season, but if somebody showed up tomorrow with the money to buy the place he might not say no. It's been a hard run for him the last couple of years, and I think he may be ready to throw in the towel. When I heard about the stroke, I called him and offered to come home, just take my chances, but he flat-out refused. He actually got pretty pissed off and the whole thing dissolved into one more shouting match. I think knowing that I'm up here is the one thing that keeps him going. And I wouldn't be all that much help to him in jail, either.

It's weird to think of the camp, gone just like that. I think I'd gotten to hate the place. Maybe getting away was the reason I came up here to begin with. Now I've spent the last two years missing it. Remember how we used to talk about someday when we'd take it over? It seems like years since we talked like that, and I guess maybe it really has been years.

I know my father has always thought the world of you, Luce, and from what your parents said I get the feeling you may not be able to do this, but if you get the chance to visit him, even just to say hello, I know it would be some help. Though he'd never say as much, I know he's pretty lonely. He doesn't even have a lot of friends left in town, and seeing you would brighten him up. I know it may not be in the cards, and I understand if it isn't, but I just thought I'd ask you.

Lucy, I hope you're happy wherever you are, and try not to worry about me, as I will try not to worry about you, though I'm sure I always will, every day as long as I live. I guess this is something like good-bye. I can barely write the word. I'm sorry, I'm sorry, I'm sorry.

Love,
Joe

I finished the letter and returned it to its envelope. All along I had thought I'd be the one to end it, not the other way around. I was crying a little, though what I felt was not exactly like sadness. Just this: I was alone. I had fallen half in love with my solitude, and now I'd gotten exactly what I'd asked for, and it wasn't what I'd expected at all.

A shot glass appeared on the bar in front of me.

"Here." Deck pulled a bottle of tequila off the shelf and poured. "Drink up."

The glass was heavy in my hand; I took a tiny sip. My mouth bloomed with the heat and sharpness of it, making me swallow, and I felt the liquor burning all the way down to my stomach.

"Go on now, knock it back. Deck's orders."

"I'm not much of a drinker."

"And tomorrow is another day. But I never met a broken heart yet wasn't made a little better by just the right amount of tequila. Go on."

I did as he said, tipping my face to the ceiling and taking the rest of it in a single gulp. My eyes and nose were running, and I wiped them with the back of my hand. "Oh, shit, Deck. Shit, shit, shit."

"We're assholes, we are. Men are worthless. There's no denying it. You want another?"

"What would May say?"

"This was May's idea, actually." He tipped his head toward the front windows and the parking lot, where the Pinto was waiting, chuffing smoke into the air. "Ask her yourself."

The second week of March 1972. For the first time in my life I had no idea what would happen next. Deck pulled an extra glass from under the bar, set it up next to mine, and filled both of them to the lip. He raised his in a little toast.

"To you, Alice," he said.

FOURTEEN

Jordan

It seems now as if there was no time *before*—before Kate, before the camp, before Harry Wainwright and his last day of fishing—but naturally there was, and that is part of the story too. There was being a child, of course, not all that interesting—the fact that I had no father made me less different from other children than you might suppose—and after we had moved to Maine and my mother remarried, my years in high school and college: again, ordinary in every way, chock-full of minor triumphs and failures and bad experiments that pulled me in no direction in particular. I might have become anyone, chosen any kind of life. Out of college, I floated down to Boston with a couple of friends—hard-drinking jokesters with even less on their minds than I had—waited tables in a ferny restaurant in Back Bay while I looked for something better, and ended up, of all things, as a sales representative for a drug company out on Route 128—a job that entailed crisscrossing the city in a big leased Pontiac with a sample bag crammed with capsules and pills to stop your heart and start it again, thin your blood or thicken it, adjust the body's metronome in a hundred different ways. These were boom times, when everyone was making money quick as could be, and I was too—not getting rich exactly, but certainly making more money than I knew how to spend, and under the spell of my success, I actually began to see myself as someone who might prosper in this world. My job, after all, seemed easy as pie, requiring little more than the ability to read a map and recite memorized data to overtired general practitioners who'd try anything once. (The truth was, I didn't really need to understand what I was saying, though my courses in forestry were more help than you'd think.) I had friends, I had money, I had a closet full of suits. It wasn't a cure for cancer or even the common cold, but it was *something*, and it was mine.

And yet. When I tell people about those two years of my life, and they see how differently I do things now, they assume my decision to walk away was just that: a surrender. And they're absolutely right. I did, in fact, give up. But it didn't have anything to do with the money (which was fine), or the long hours (what else would I be doing?), or the feeling that I was wasting my life on trivia (nothing wrong with prescription drugs; just ask the guy who's crawling across the kitchen floor to get to his stash of nitroglycerin in the breadbox). I didn't get fed up, burn out in increments, find myself in some desperate tailspin drinking away the lunch hour and boring the barroom with some cockamamie philosophy I'd cooked up as to why the world was the way it was—i.e., depraved, ruinous, and totally out of control. (This is *exactly* what happened to a guy I knew, a story that ended badly, though most of the salesmen in my group were happy as hamsters to kill their quotas and skeedaddle on home to drive their daughters to ballet lessons and prowl the classifieds with their wives after dinner for a time-share in Stowe or Fort Meyers.) No. What happened was, one sunny April afternoon, fresh from one successful sale and on to the next, and looking forward to a dinner date with friends at a seafood joint near Faneuil Hall—that is to say, with a song in my heart and my life charging downfield like a running back with the game-winning ball—I turned off Storrow Drive into Beacon Hill, and found myself slowed, then slowed some more, then finally stopped in traffic.

It was just three o'clock, too early for the rush. A line of two dozen cars waited ahead of me, and as I leaned my head out the window to see what the problem was, first one and then another began to honk, the noise piling up with a feverish intensity that was, of course, contagious. I was too far back in line to see anything; my bet was an accident, though there were no lights or sirens yet; and as the minutes ticked off, making me later and later, all for no apparent reason, the

whole thing ballooned into a crisis. What I mean is, I couldn't go anywhere—couldn't fucking *go*—and I found myself pounding the wheel
and then the ceiling of the Pontiac with my fist, pounding and pounding until my knuckles shrieked, my heart hammering in my chest, the
blare of the horns smothering my head like a plastic bag, so that I
thought I might actually burst. People had begun to climb out of their
cars, and I took this as a sign; I threw the door open and marched
ahead, toward the intersection where the problem, literally, lay.

It was a man, an older man, and at first I thought he was dead—
that he had stepped into the intersection and been hit by a car. I bul-
lied my way into the small crowd that had gathered around him. He
lay on his back in the middle of the southbound lane with his arms
draped loosely at his sides, and I saw that he was conscious. His eyes
were open, almost *too* open, giving an unblinking blue-eyed gaze to the
sky above, and a policeman was crouched on one knee, asking him in
a South Boston accent the kind of questions you'd expect: could he
stand (not sure), what was his name (Fred something), did he know
where he was (Boston? Near the Ritz?). His clothing was neat and
clean—khakis, a madras shirt, shiny black loafers: the uniform of a
semiretired accountant or a bank loan officer on vacation. Though
some in the crowd were saying he was drunk, I didn't think he was. He
was just *there,* lying in the street as if he didn't have a care in the world,
apparently comfortable and totally uninterested in anything the cop
was saying to him or where he was and why it was worth a fuss. I
craned my neck upward to see what he was seeing: the crowns of the
buildings, an airy gauze of clouds, a blue dome of April sky. Nothing,
really, to account for his look. A second policeman arrived, and then a
third, barking into the radio clipped to his shoulder; an ambulance appeared in the oncoming lane, shoving itself up onto the curb with a
tart bleep of its siren. Two of the cops helped the man up onto the ambulance's tailgate, and while the EMTs were checking him out, waving
a tiny flashlight over his eyeballs and taking his pulse, the third cop
told us all to get back into our cars, there was nothing to see, and so
on. Which, I guess, there wasn't.

It took me only a month after that to quit, though not why you might think, which is one more reason I don't tell the story all that often. It wasn't my father's body I saw there, as my college shrink would have claimed, or even, in some theoretical way, my own, although the poor sap might have been a drug rep as anyone else. I didn't conclude, as a person might in the face of something so desperately mortal, that life was short, do what you want, make every second count—the easy stuff, all of which I knew in the first place. What I saw instead, in a heartbreaking flash, was the absolute arbitrariness of most things. Before I'd walked back to my car, I approached the first cop and asked him what it was all about. He was scribbling in a notebook and looked up at me with a scowl. "Beats me." He barked a nasty laugh. "The guy said he was tired and wanted to lie down!"

And as he said it, I thought: Well, why not? Why not lie down in the middle of the road? Driving away, I suddenly couldn't think of a single reason, hard as I tried. Traffic would stop, the cops would come; they'd haul you off somewhere for observation, maybe a little "treatment"—reuptake inhibitors by the fistful, bad food on metal trays, serious conversations with some joker in a white coat with a blackjack stashed in his sock—while, meanwhile, the world would turn without a stutter. In a crazy way, it actually made sense to lie down, to drop your guard and let the truth come out. I thought: who cares?

Which, of course, was absolutely no way to live. There's more to the story, but before I knew it I had second-guessed myself into the worst kind of box. I went back to my mother's house in Bangor, loafed the summer away under the charade of "getting some thinking done" and "looking for a new direction," and in September answered a want ad in the *Maine Sunday Telegram* that turned out to be Joe's. I drove up to Sagonick and looked the place over; it seemed, then as now, as far away from everything as I could get without actually hauling myself to some dope-smoking Oregon commune or an ashram in India (both of which I actually considered for at least ten minutes), and when Joe put the ring of keys in my hand, I felt in their solid, singing weight the answer to my problems, and knew that I was cured.

End of story; or the beginning, if you like.

All of which is just to say that these were the things on my mind that morning, as much a part of the feel of the day as Kate's kiss, Joe's drunk lawyers, and Harry Wainwright. For two hours I went out with a party from cabin two—a couple of guys who just wanted somebody to show them a good spot and then beat it—then into town for some screws and other things I needed to repair a set of steps by the dock. Lucy had made it clear that I was supposed to stay close to camp, to keep myself available for whenever Harry wanted to go, but I thought a short errand wouldn't hurt, since Harry, even if he experienced some kind of miraculous recovery, would need a while to get ready. I would have asked Kate to come along for the ride, but she was off somewhere, shuttling the moose-canoers, and probably wouldn't be back till nearly noon.

What happened next I can't explain. I was driving into town, mulling over what size screws I wanted and that maybe I should pick up a case of engine oil while I was at it, when I caught myself thinking about my father, and the day I learned he'd died. This in itself was odd, as right till then, driving the Jeep up the long hill into town, the wind and sun roiling around my face, I would have sworn I had no conscious recollections of that day at all. Standing by the canoes, I'd told Kate all that I remembered of him, or thought I had; so maybe finally talking about these things had cleared a space in my mind for other memories to flow in behind them. In any case, the things I suddenly remembered hit me so hard I actually tapped the brake, then found myself pulling the Jeep to a stop by the side of the road.

We were living on base then, the three of us in a small, prefabricated house built of nothing much better than cardboard. It was summer, the air of the tidewater thick as clam chowder. I don't think we had an air conditioner, because the house was always full of whirling fans—table fans, ceiling fans, fans on tall stands that rocked to and fro like the heads of robots—and that was where my memory began: with the feel of fan-pushed air on my face. I was in the kitchen, which was really just a kind of galley with a small extra space for a table and chairs. The fan, an old-fashioned model with metal blades and a cloth-covered cord, was positioned on a chair so that it pointed toward the stove, where my mother had been cooking dinner for the two of us. She had left me alone there when the doorbell rang—I was playing on the floor, pushing a toy dump truck around—and in her absence the fan had worked a kind of magnetic pull on me: I left my playing and went to stand before it, to watch its blur of blades and soak the skin of my face in the cooling relief of its man-made wind. My father flew jets, aircraft held aloft by forces as invisible to me as magic, but there were plenty of propeller-driven planes around, and one could not be a small boy growing up on the grounds of the Oceana Naval Air Station without grasping at least the basics of aeronautical propulsion. In my mind I connected the action of the whirling fan blades to my father's mysterious and important job—a job that, I knew, scared my mother half out of her wits even as she told me constantly what a great, brave man he was—and the longer I waited alone in the kitchen for her return, the more I experienced both a deepening anxiety at her absence—there was a boiling pot on the stove, which I also dimly understood to be a danger—and a strong, almost mystical pull toward the blur of metal that floated before my face. It seemed to contain a strange and ancient power—the power of my father, of men and their machines—and I longed to touch it, a desire sharp as hunger. I had been warned against this a thousand times, as I had been warned against the stove, the electric outlets, strangers who might want to talk to me, and traffic on the street. The urge to obey such commands was strong, but in my mother's lengthy absence I detected a quality of permission. For a long moment, two seconds or ten, I held my hand up in front of the fan to feel its wind more intimately, weighing my options. And then, from the hallway, the sound traveling unmuffled through the cardboard walls of our house, I heard my mother scream.

Which was exactly when my defenses collapsed and I extended a single, outstretched finger toward the fan, through the metal cage that wrapped it, and into the whirling blades. I did it quickly, furtively—so quickly I didn't realize for a moment what I'd done, though the pain was, I imagine, instantaneous. The sharp metal sliced off the end of my finger so neatly that it seemed to simply vanish, and then a jet of blood

shot out from this open tube of flesh into the blades, splattering everything—my hand and face, my arm and shirt, even the wall and floor,
with its vibrant, Martian-red confetti—and it was this fact, as much as
the pain itself, that made me scream too.

Jesus Christ almighty, I thought, and probably said so too, remembering all this in the parked Jeep on the side of the road. A logging
truck roared past me, a hundred tons of naked trees stacked on its bed
like corpses in a mass grave, detonating the air around me and making
the Jeep rock like a toy in a tub. In the silent wash of its departure I
held up and examined my right index finger, its end stublike and flattened, the nail stunted to the shape and size of a shirt button—a familiar sight, nothing I had ever given a second's thought to, or not for
years and years. I'd always thought I'd sliced it somehow on, or with, a
bicycle; I'd even constructed a mental story as to how this had happened, riding my first two-wheeler and then, for no reason at all,
reaching down and sticking my finger into the grinding gears of the
chain ring. But this made no sense. Maybe it was something my
mother had told me, though I quickly tossed this thought aside. It was,
I understood, a tale my mind had told itself.

I drove on into town. At the hardware store, still feeling a little
dazed, I fished through the little file drawers of screws, filling a sack
with the ones I needed—up here we pay by the pound, like fruit—
slung a case of motor oil onto my shoulder, and took it all to the register in back, where the owner, Porter Dante, was sucking on an unlit
cigar and paging through a hunting magazine.

"How do, Porter."

He gave me a curt nod from the chin, the North Woods equivalent
of a full body hug. "Jordan."

He weighed the screws, then wrote up the price on the bag with a
carpenter's pencil. On the wall above him, clipped to pegboard, was a
new display of power tools: not the retail junk you see in Wal-Mart, but
contractor's grade, high-voltage Makitas, all cordless, with rechargeable
battery packs thick as a grown man's fist stuck on the handles.

"Just got them in last week," Porter said, obviously happy to catch me looking. He poked his pencil over his shoulder at the display. "Figuring a few people around here might appreciate the real stuff and save on the drive down to Farmington."

An assortment of drills and drivers of various sizes, a reciprocating saw, three different circular saws with dust collectors and carbide blades, assorted belt- and palm-sanders, even a gruesome-looking thing I guessed was a rebar cutter, though I couldn't be sure: Porter had sunk some serious money into this little display. Positioning them above the register the way he'd done, where you could have a good long look at them while your wallet was out, was a bona fide bear trap for any man between the ages of sixteen and a hundred and probably a few women besides (Kate, for one). I thought about the hours I would be spending that very day shaken to pieces by Joe's old drill, and the death-defying hassle of running a long extension cord up to the lodge and trying to keep it out of the water.

I waved a finger at the board. "Say, Porter, if it's not too much trouble, let me have a peek at that drill, will you?"

A look of sly pleasure skittered across his face. "Which, now?"

"The big drill, the eighteen volt."

He brought the drill down from its pegs and placed it in my hand. It was heavy as a handgun, the plastic of its grip smooth and a little rubbery. A dangling price tag told me it sold for $168.95—a hell of a lot for a drill. I felt like I was holding an atom-smasher.

"Feel the weight of that baby," Porter said proudly, talking around his cigar. "We're talking all-metal gear transmission, dual ball bearings, a three-stage, thirteen-planetary gear system." He rapped the countertop with his knuckles. "That's a *tool*."

I did my best to look like I didn't care one way or the other. But the fact is, once you hold something like that in your hand, part of you marries it forever. "What's a planetary gear system?"

Porter shrugged. "How in hell should I know? Something good, according to the sales rep. Something you *want*. Nice fellow. Should be back on Tuesday, you want to talk to him about it."

I placed the drill on the counter, my heart breaking. "Thanks. I'll think about it."

"You sure now? I can take off five percent for you."

"That's tempting, Porter. Since when did you dicker on anything?"

He frowned. "Since I got into the tool business." He leaned over the counter and looked at the floor. "The oil's yours?"

He rang me up, recorded the bill on the camp account, and handed me the bag of screws. "I'll tell you something I heard. You know my sister-in-law, works over for the county recorder? She tells me some pretty interesting paperwork came across her desk the other day. *Very* interesting. Wondering if you might know anything about it."

"I'm just the handyman, Porter. Nobody tells me a blessed thing."

"From what she tells me, looks like you have a new boss. Maybe you should ask around."

I did my best to meet his gaze in a way that would seem agreeable, while also putting the matter to rest. "You know bosses, Porter. They're all the same."

"Not according to my sister-in-law. She tells me Harry Wainwright bought the place. The great Harry Wainwright. Liza's so dumb she thinks a taco's something Indians live in, but even *she* knew who that was. Spent a bundle, too."

"Sounds like you know more about it than I do."

He looked at me skeptically. "Don't get me wrong, Jordan. I like Harry fine, and his boy too. Been in here from time to time over the years. Wouldn't know he was such a muckety-muck from the way he acts. But even so, a family like that. Up here. Makes people wonder what he's got up his sleeve. This isn't the Hamptons, some chichi place like that. People would like to keep it that way."

"Like I said, Porter, nobody tells me anything. But for what it's worth, I don't think you have to fret."

"Maybe so, and maybe not." He removed the cigar and frowned, taking a moment to regard the damp stump he held between thumb and forefinger. "I read an article in *Time* about this place in Colorado— what's it, Aspen? Nice town until the movie stars found it. Now regular folks are living in trailers and a hammer costs twenty dollars."

I plastered a grin on my face. "Sounds like you'd make out fine, Porter."

"I'm just saying people around here would have reason to be concerned." Porter closed the register drawer with a cling. "So all this is on my mind this morning and what do I see? Joe Crosby passing through town with a nice-looking Beemer trailing behind. They stopped up the corner for coffee, so I had myself a good look. A more suspicious man than I am would have thought they were developers for sure."

It took me a moment to figure out just what he was talking about. "Hate to disappoint you, Porter, but what you saw were clients. Joe was taking them up to the old Zisko Dam."

I couldn't tell if he believed me or not. For a couple of seconds, neither of us spoke. I felt like a man trying to smuggle something through customs.

"God's honest truth, Porter. Just a bunch of lawyers on vacation. They got so drunk last night Joe will probably have to save half of them from drowning. You can ask him if you like."

Porter considered this a moment more. "Aw, hell, Jordan," he said finally, and looked like he might smile. "I don't mean to be giving you any third degree." He leaned over the counter a little and lowered his voice. "Tell you what. I can go ten percent on that drill for you, you keep it under your hat."

"Throw in an extra battery?"

"Comes with two. What are you building, an ark?"

"You never know. But two should do it. Toss in some bits and you've sold yourself a drill."

I left the store, put it all in the Jeep, and headed home. Porter didn't have the whole story, or even half of it, but in his own way he had a point, and I felt the first inkling of a brand-new worry. For eight years I had lived a life as anonymous and consequence-free as you could ever wish for, a life of one chore strung after another, receding to a far horizon that seemed to recede with every forward move I made. It was a life I truly liked, or thought I had. I was free to do as I wished, to think what I wished, and if you described a day of my life, told me what the weather was and how I'd spent my time, then asked me what year that was, I wouldn't have had the slightest clue. It was entirely possible that this was what death felt like, death being, in the end, not so bad, or all that unfamiliar. I felt, driving home, that for the first time in many years, maybe ever, I was coming truly alive, and here's the thing: the problem of being alive is that it makes you frightened.

I was just on the edge of town when I pulled the Jeep over in front of the post office and our one pay phone—the same one Hal had used the night before to tell us they were coming, though that now felt like it had been years and years ago. It was Sunday, a little before twelve, an hour earlier in Houston. I made the call collect.

"Mama, it's me."

"Jordan?" My mother's voice was bright and pleased; we hadn't talked in at least a month. "Listen, Estella's on the other line. Let me get rid of her and I'll be right back."

"If it's a bad time, we can talk later."

"No, no. I'm glad to hear from you." She paused. "Is everything all right?"

"Fit as a fiddle."

"Good to hear it. It's about a hundred and five degrees here, by the way. Just a minute, okay?"

The line went numb as she put me on hold. Estella was my mother's literary agent. About four years ago—just about the time she and my stepfather had moved to Houston so Vince could take an administrative job with the Harris County Parks Department—my mother, always a reader, had gotten it into her head to write romance novels, a task for which she had demonstrated such remarkable proficiency that she now had a three-year, six-book contract. My mother was the most levelheaded person in the world, really, a churchgoing Southern girl who drank her whiskey neat and read a passage from the Bible every night in bed, and I couldn't quite resolve my image of the woman who had raised me with the woman who now churned out novels with titles like *Summer Love* and *Belle of the Ball* at the superhuman rate of one every six months. She traveled constantly to trade shows and book fairs and got fan mail by the sack-load; on the back of her books was a glossy color author pic, in which she was wearing of all things a double-stranded pearl choker and a mink stole (both of which she had assured me were as phony as a magician's mustache).

The line clicked free. "I'm back, honey."

"How's Estella?"

"Fine. Making me money, like she's supposed to. She's having trouble with her dogs."

Estella, I knew, had lots of dogs. "How are you doing?" I said. "What's Vince up to?"

"Oh, you know Vince. He just went out to the store to buy a new deep-fat fryer. His latest thing is learning to make cannolis."

Though born and raised in Bangor, my stepfather was quite serious about his Italian roots, and was always involved in some new culinary project: canning his own tomatoes for sauce, making his own sausages and ravioli, taking trips down to Boston to the North End to hunt up weird things like squid ink pasta or flayed rabbit haunches. Where he shopped for such things in Houston, I had no idea.

"Sounds like a plan."

"It's a mess is what it is. Flour and grease all over the place. The first fryer just about exploded. I'm worried about his cholesterol too." She paused. "But I'm thinking maybe you didn't call to talk about Vince's cholesterol?"

"What makes you say that?"

"Oh, your voice, I guess. Something about it. I'm your *mother*, Jordan. Tell me what's on your mind."

"There's really nothing." I looked at my finger, its strange blunted tip; its tiny, orphaned nail. "I just bought a new drill."

"You men and your toys. If Vince were here I'm sure he'd love to talk about it. You really called to tell me about your drill?"

I thought a moment. "I might be in love too."

"You see?" I could hear the smile in her voice. "There *was* something. There's a nice surprise. I'm happy to hear it. Is she nice? Does she love you back, this person?"

"I think so. I'm hoping so. I'm a bit out of practice. It's Kate."

"Kate. I'm sorry. I know about Kate, don't I?"

"Joe's daughter."

The phone seemed to go dead a second. "Jordan, isn't she, excuse me, about thirteen? Do I need to fly up there right now?"

"That was years ago, Mama. She's going to medical school. Will go, I mean."

"How about that," I heard my mother say. "Kate with the pigtails? She's really a doctor, all grown up?"

I nodded to myself. "It surprised me too."

"Well, that's the thing about it," my mother said. "It always sneaks up on you that way."

"Was it a surprise with Daddy?"

"Daddy." Her voice seemed to catch and hold on this strange word. "Your daddy, you mean?"

"We don't have to talk about it if you don't want to."

"Well, that was a long time ago, Jordan. But yes, it was. You know the story. Do you want me to tell it?"

How many years since she had done this? It seemed like forever, and no time at all. I said, "A dance."

"That's right. But not really the dance itself. After the dance. It was the summer after high school, so I was, I guess about eighteen, not a thing in my head, and a bunch of us went without dates to this thing, I guess you could call it a dance, though it was more like a party. And after, my friend, the one with the car, left with a boy, and your father gave me a ride home. I had no idea who he was, just some flyer from the base. We talked in the car, and I just knew. Both of us knew. I guess you were . . . thinking about him?"

"I guess I was, a little."

"Well, you're entitled. That's perfectly fine if you were."

"Tell me . . ." I stopped to breathe, embarrassed. But more than that: I was afraid.

Her voice was quiet. "Tell you what, Jordan?"

"Tell me . . . about the day he died."

Silence, and I was sorry, so sorry I'd asked it. And yet I had to know.

"Mama—"

"No, no," she answered firmly. "I said you were entitled, didn't I? It was just one of those things, Jordan. The inquest said something about mechanical trouble. A faulty rotor, I think it was."

I'd heard that, too, or remembered so. A faulty rotor, something that went round and round, and then for some reason stopped, sending my father into the sea.

"How'd they know it was a rotor if they never found the plane?"

"Well, they did find it, Jordan. I thought you knew that. It was a pretty expensive piece of military hardware."

"But not Daddy."

"No, honey," she said. "Not your daddy."

The line went quiet, and I heard my mother take a long, melancholy breath. I pictured her in her bedroom office in this distant city her life had taken her to, looking out her window at the lawn and thinking about these old, sorrowful things.

"Mama?"

"I'm sorry, honey. You're just making me a little sad, is all. I was just a baby myself, really. I wasn't even twenty-two when it happened."

I remembered something else. "Everybody called him Hero, didn't they? Short for Heronimus."

"That's right. They did."

Silence fell once more. I looked at my finger again, rubbing the end of it with my thumb. "The day you found out about Daddy. Did anything else happen?"

"Anything else, honey?"

I shook my head. "I don't even know what I'm thinking about."

"I think that was all, Jordan. It was plenty."

I moved the phone to my right hand. Cars passed on the street, tourists, people I knew. In the close heat of the tiny booth, I'd begun to sweat.

"You're a lot like him, you know," my mother said quietly. "I've always thought so."

I said, "Like Daddy."

"Jordan," she said, and I heard her breathing change, "you're making me sad again. It's not your fault. But I'm going to put the phone down now."

Before I could say anything, there was a dull thud on the line. I waited, the receiver pressed to my ear, listening to the soft sound she made as she wept, two thousand miles away. *Please don't cry, Mama,* I thought, *please don't.* A minute passed.

"There now," she said. "All better."

"I'm sorry, Mama. I shouldn't have said anything."

"Don't be, Jordan. You just blindsided me a little bit. It's funny to go back like that."

"Is it a good life down there?" I said. "Are you happy?"

"Shouldn't I be the one asking you that?"

"Well, let's just say."

"Oh, it's hot as hell, Jordan. And the trees are all wrong. It's funny, but that's the thing that gets me the most, the trees. And missing you, sometimes. All the time. But yes. On the whole, yes. It's a good life. Vince is the sweetest man alive, I write my books, the winters are easy as pie." She stopped. "Your *finger,* Jordan." Her voice was amazed. "You put it in the fan. I remember now. That's what you were asking about, wasn't it?"

"I guess it was."

"Your father was always telling me to put it up on the table, someplace high and out of reach, but it was so hot that day, I guess I just forgot. I was cooking dinner, and you were playing on the floor, and then Colonel Graffam came to tell me, and that awful chaplain, I forget his name, everybody hated him. I guess I left you alone and somehow you got it stuck in the fan."

"I think I did it on purpose, Mama. At least that's what I remember."

"Why would you have done that? No, it was my fault, honey, for leaving the fan where I did. God, it was an awful mess, blood everywhere, and you screaming like you did. It was all so crazy. I'd just found out about your father, and there I was, rushing you off to the doctor, not even a second to think about what just happened. The colonel offered to take you but I wouldn't have it, just wrapped your hand in a towel and charged off to the infirmary. How could I have forgotten a thing like that?"

"Sounds to me like you remember pretty well."

"But the thing is, I *didn't*, not at first. Not until you asked about it. Why should that be?" She was silent a moment, lost in this question. Then: "It's all right, isn't it? There isn't something wrong with it?"

"It's fine," I said, and wiggled it, as if she could somehow see. "Same as always. I'm having a little trouble playing the violin, but otherwise, no worries."

I was glad to hear her laugh. "Well, that's a relief," she said. "You gave me a start there. I was worried something was wrong with it. Jordan?"

"Right here, Mama."

"My turn. Are *you* happy? Is it a good life for you?"

"I think so," I said, nodding as if she were right there with me. "I think it is."

"And you love Kate, and she loves you."

I listened to my breathing in the phone, the sound traveling the miles of wire from Maine to Texas and back again. "Somebody may ask me to do something today. Something I don't want to do."

"What kind of thing is that, Jordan?"

I cleared my mind and thought. But the idea of what I was feeling seemed to arc beyond my mind's reach, like a skater racing past me on a frozen pond.

"I don't know," I said finally. "It's just a sense I have."

"A sense." She paused over the word. "Well, whatever it is, I'm sure you'll know what to do when the time comes, Jordan. That's all you can do."

"I hope I can."

"No, honey. I *know* you can. That's the kind of man your father was. I would have kept him longer if I could have, but even so, I was never one bit sorry. I want you to remember that."

And suddenly, just like that, I wasn't afraid anymore. A new feeling flowed into me, strong and purposeful, and with it, a sudden awareness of my surroundings, the place and hour where I stood. It was just past noon; the sun was high. I think I loved my mother more just then than I had ever done in my life.

"I will, Mama," I said, and realized it was the second promise I'd made in a day. "I will."

ALMOST NOTHING

FIFTEEN

Harry

May, and the drowsy blur of spring: we buried Meredith, Hal and I. The funeral was held at St. Thomas's on Fifth Avenue—gigantic and faintly frenetic, like a huge, grieving carnival, though for most of our friends, Meredith was already a memory, gone for years. When this was done, we traveled together the next morning, just the two of us, to Philadelphia, where we planned to bury her beside Sam.

It was just past noon when we arrived. I hadn't been back to the cemetery for several years, not since the worst of Meredith's illness had consumed me. As the limo pulled up, I saw the funeral director waiting for us at the gravesite. Beside Sam's small headstone was Meredith's casket, suspended on a metal bier with straps to lower it, and next to that, a mound of freshly turned, coffee-colored earth. It was a strange and unsettling experience to see these things, a feeling I had not prepared for—this place that had for so long been the site of one grave, now remade for two, like a hidden symmetry revealed.

But something else was different, wrong. A sky too abundant, and a feeling of exposure; the air itself seemed distorted, hazy with dust and unfiltered heat. As we stepped from the limo, the full magnitude hit me like a fist. Not a hundred yards away, where before had stood a field of headstones, there now was naked earth. A fleet of bulldozers, giant earthmovers with their beetlelike carriages and wide gleaming blades: half the cemetery had been scraped away.

"What the *fuck*," Hal said.

He was wearing sunglasses, his chest and shoulders broad as a bodyguard's inside his dark suit; his anger seemed fierce, a black force uncoiling inside him. Days and days of grim death—the awful phone call he surely knew was coming, then the bleak journey down from Williamstown, and of course the funeral itself—and now this. I actually worried that he might hit someone, or else turn and strike the car. But then he shuddered, reaching a hand out to brace himself against the limo's gleaming fender, and I saw his strength was false; there was nothing at all behind it. The slightest puff of air might have brought him to his knees.

"Jesus." He shook his head despondently. "What the fuck."

"I know." I put a hand on his shoulder. "Wait here."

I left him at the car and approached the funeral director, a man with long gray sideburns who was wearing a slightly too-tight suit of blended navy, a suit he must have had dozens of. Under the warm sun, his brow was glazed with sweat. Without pausing to shake his hand I pointed past him toward the construction site.

"You mind telling me what that's all about?"

He turned, a quick dart of the head to follow my gesture.

"I'm sorry," he said nervously. "I thought you knew."

"Knew what?"

The color had drained from his face. "The new interstate, Mr. Wainwright. The Blue Route. It's going to run from Conshohocken all the way down to Chester. They started work last fall."

The air was so full of grit I could taste it, feel it grinding between my teeth. "No, I sure as goddamn hell did *not* know."

Hal had stepped away from the car to join us where we stood, under the wispy shade of a threadbare hemlock—just a sapling when we had buried Sam, but now thirty feet tall. The plan was that we were going to read a poem: Emily Dickinson, a little thing without a title, not a dozen lines long, about death coming in a carriage. That was all: no priest or other mourners, no long line of cars in the dust, just the two of us and the warm spring wind and these words of good-bye. Now we would have to read it over the roar of heavy machinery and men in hard hats yelling to one another about the baseball scores.

"How can they do that? It's a cemetery, for god's sake."

"Eminent domain, Mr. Wainwright. I'm afraid it means the state can do whatever it wants."

A bolt of raw anger surged through me. "I know what eminent domain is. Who the fuck do you think you're talking to?"

He stiffened his back and swallowed. No doubt he wanted to tell me to go to hell, and he wouldn't have been wrong. But his voice when he spoke was calm, professional. "I'm truly sorry, Mr. Wainwright," he said. "If you wish, I'm sure we can make other arrangements."

"Our son is buried here. He's been here twenty years."

He nodded. "And believe me, I do sympathize. You're not the first to complain. But the state's promised to build a retaining wall to deflect the noise and fumes. If you came back a year from now it would all be different. It's really just a question of the timing."

Timing, I thought. Good God. But it was Hal who spoke next.

"What's to stop them from digging up this end of the cemetery?"

"Well, technically nothing." The director took a handkerchief from his back pocket to mop his forehead. "But as far as I know, the state has no plans to condemn any other parcels. This area should remain just as it is."

"Christ," I said. "They better not."

I felt completely powerless. How had I missed this? What else had escaped my attention? What would Meredith have said, if she'd known we were going to bury her within a hundred yards of the Pennsylvania Turnpike? A canvas tarp was spread on the ground around her casket, dressed with flowers, banks and banks of them piled high, and on the casket too—all of their petals coated with a film of gray dust.

"Mr. Wainwright? Shall we go ahead with the service, then?"

I turned my eyes to Hal. He knew nothing of what had happened that night in the library. No one did, except for Elizabeth, who probably had guessed, and perhaps Mrs. Beryl as well, who would have wondered why Meredith had given her that particular night off. But I knew neither would ever say a word. Nobody official had bothered to examine the situation more closely; as far as the world knew, Meredith had died in her sleep.

"Pop?"

I managed a nod. Hal turned on his heel to the director.

"All right then," he said. "Let's do this."

We decided to stay the night in Philadelphia. I can't recall whose idea this was, but I think we both knew, instinctively, that it was the right one. The long drive home, and the eerie quiet of the house on our arrival, the specter of Meredith's bedroom still waiting to be dismantled; the two of us puttering around the place, trying to figure out how to occupy ourselves, what or even if to eat and whether or not to turn on the television, and when to go to bed. It was a prospect I dreaded almost physically; surely Hal had envisioned these things too, and the idea of a night in a good hotel, and a meal together in a city we hadn't lived in for years, seemed like just the ticket.

We rented a suite at the Rittenhouse and decided to send the car away; it would be a simple enough matter to take a train back to New York the next morning. We'd brought no luggage with us, but even this odd fact seemed unimportant. At the front desk we gave the concierge a list of things we'd need for the night, toiletries and fresh shirts and underclothes for the morning, and rode the elevator up to our two-room suite, so neutrally decorated we could have been just about anywhere: San Francisco, Paris, even Bangkok. I went to the windows and opened the drapes. It was midafternoon, a Friday in spring. Our suite overlooked Rittenhouse Square, a section of town that always reminded me of certain parts of London: polished and old-world, its slope-shouldered brownstones and old churches laid out on a grid of hushed, well-planted streets that radiated from a central park with pathways and green lawns and, at the center, a pool with a sundial and a sculpture of a lion. From where I stood at the wide windows, eleven stories up, a soft haze of pink-and-white dogwood blossoms seemed to float over the square, punctuated by an understory of red azalea bushes in riotous bloom. A scene of mute activity, like the opening shot of a movie: men in shirtsleeves, hurrying to and fro; the usual lovers lazing on the lawn; women in scarves and spring jackets, some pushing strollers or accompanied by young children, bits of birdlike color that seemed to gather and disperse according to some unseen physical principle; a pair of long-haired college boys tossing a Frisbee, and, hunched over a cluster of concrete tables, a group of black men playing chess. Upon everything the sun poured down like a golden liquid. After such a day, it was a handsome sight—a vision of human life that seemed to hold the properties of eternity—but soon the scene would change: between the buildings and above them, a billowing bulk of storm clouds had sailed into view. First the puffy crowns, churning heavenward on waves of heat; and then, as I watched, the dark prow and undersides, dragging a blade of shadow, like a great ship docking over the city. A spring thunderstorm: of course. The heat had been building all day. As I watched, a greenish gloom descended over the park, into a hundred upturned faces, and then the wind arrived. It raked the dogwoods like a claw, swirling the air with petals; the Frisbee, ripped from its trajectory, squirted upward and shot out over Walnut Street, away. I turned from the window as huge, penny-size drops of rain began to thud against it.

"Hal?"

A moment of inexplicable panic: my heart contracted with a fear as biological as breathing, as if he were a little boy again, and I had lost him in a crowd. But when I looked through the door I found him, stretched out on one of the room's two big beds. He was still wearing his tie, though he had taken off his jacket, which hung from the corner of a chair. One foot was bare, the other clad in a sock he hadn't managed to remove before unconsciousness had taken him. A minute passed as I watched him sleep. Outside, the sizzle of lightning, and moments later, the rattling afterthought of thunder. I selfishly wished the noise would rouse him, so we could watch the storm together, but all he did was turn against the pillow. At last I closed the drapes and pulled a blanket over him and sealed the door behind me.

I slept two hours on the sofa, dreaming of rain, and awoke to darkness and the knowledge that the storm had passed. Beyond the window the evening sky was the color of a bruise; a single star glittered in the twilight. Voices reached me from the bedroom, and then the vapid music of a commercial. I checked my watch; it was nearly eight thirty.

Hal was sitting up in bed, watching television. His eyes flicked toward me as I entered the room.

"News flash. You snore, Pop."

I sat beside him on the bed. Time seemed to have slipped its moorings entirely; it seemed like whole days had passed since we'd visited the cemetery. My body was suffused with an unexpected physical contentment, as if I'd received an injection of iron. I gave Hal's knee a shake. "Hungry?"

Hal's eyes had returned to the television: *Star Trek*. He nodded slightly, his mind still lost in the program. "God, will you get a load of this guy." He gestured dismissively toward the screen, where the actor Leonard Nimoy, wearing a Greek robe and laurel wreath, was strumming on a lyre. "Oh," Hal said, as if he'd just thought of something. "The concierge dropped off our stuff a while ago."

"Really? I didn't hear a thing."

"Well, we all heard *you*, like I said." He cheerfully tapped the wall behind his head. "The people next door called to ask if somebody was strangling a walrus."

"Very funny."

I rose and stretched. Atop the bureau I found a shopping bag from Brooks Brothers—the fresh shirts and underclothes we'd requested—and a selection of toiletries on a glass tray: toothbrushes and paste, razors, a tin of old-fashioned beard cream. My desire to leave the hotel room was suddenly acute; even to remain another minute would steal some essential energy from us. Though the shirts were for the morning, I opened the bag, removed the one I knew to be my size—a robin's-egg blue, with some bit of white snaking through the weave—and changed quickly. The room had grown dark, save for the flickering, fish-tank glow of the television.

"What do you say, Hal?" I clapped my hands together. "Turn that thing off and let's get some dinner."

At last he pulled his eyes from the television. A thin smile crossed his lips. "Okay," he said. "You know me. I can always eat."

We set out into streets washed clean as laundry by the rain. The air had cooled and smelled of damp concrete. We walked up the block to a brasserie the concierge had recommended, the sort of restaurant he would probably suggest to two men, but not a man and a woman together: dimly masculine, with a long mahogany bar and just a few tables pushed against the wall. The menu was written on a chalkboard the apron-clad waiter brought around to each table and propped on a folding chair, waiting with a look of boredom while we read. We ordered quickly and each drank a beer while we waited for our meal: a plate of oysters followed by slablike chops of veal and heaps of mashed potatoes in a dark, smoky gravy. We were hungry and spoke little, saying just enough to keep silence at bay, but the truth was, it was not an evening for talk; I was satisfied for the moment just to share Hal's company. All day, since the cemetery, the feeling had grown within me that I was leaving the world, and that it would be Hal's from now on. It was not a feeling I knew or had a name for. But as I sat in the restaurant watching Hal eat, each measured portion finding its way from plate to fork to mouth, the sheer fact of his physical existence seemed as inseparable from my being as my own flesh, my blood and bone. Our time together would be short. In two days, he would be returning to Williamstown, to take his final exams and finish out the semester. I had called the dean, to ask if he could be somehow excused from this obligation, and though I was told that under such circumstances arrangements could be made for him to take makeups at some later date, Hal had refused. The last thing he wanted, he said, was to have a bunch of tests hanging over him. He'd made plans to spend the summer on Martha's Vineyard, where a group of his friends from the lacrosse team had rented a house and planned to get jobs—construction, bartending, whatever they could find. It didn't matter; the point was to be together, I knew. So there was this, too: the emptiness, oddly pleasurable, of missing him.

When the waiter came to clear our plates, Hal settled back in his chair and issued a small, satisfied groan.

"How about some dessert?" He had always loved sweets, could pack them away like a longshoreman.

He shook his head. "I don't think so."

I lifted my face to the waiter. "Just coffee, then."

The waiter marched briskly away, returning moments later with cups and saucers and a small pitcher of cream.

Hal shook his head with a bitter laugh. "A fucking freeway."

"I know."

"Mom hated freeways," he said. "She hated *driving*."

"What could we do?"

He shrugged. The answer was what it was, though I also felt his disappointment: I was his father, I should have done something, carried an entire highway in my hands if that's what the situation required. He took a sip of his coffee and returned it to its place on the table. A shadow fell over his face.

"You know, maybe I shouldn't say this. But when we got to the cemetery, I realized I'd forgotten all about Sam. I mean, I knew he was there. But somehow it hadn't really sunk in that we were burying Mom in the same place."

"That's perfectly understandable. If you want to know the truth, I thought the same thing."

"Yeah, well. Even so. He was my brother." He frowned, disconcerted. "Just that word. *Brother*. Even to say it."

It was almost eleven; the room was nearly empty. At a long table in the rear of the restaurant, a group of busboys were smoking cigarettes while they rolled out clean napkins and silverware for the next day.

"This may sound, I don't know, kind of weird," Hal said, "but did you ever think I *was* him?"

"How do you mean?"

"Not that I believe in reincarnation, any of that. It's probably the stupidest idea I ever heard of, that you come back as a bug or something. But still, it must have seemed strange, the timing of it. His dying, then me born right after." He stopped and shook his head. "I don't even know what I'm saying."

In fact, the idea was not so surprising. Once or twice Meredith and I had even said as much, not really believing it, but trying to take some small comfort in the idea. Over time, though, as we spoke of Sam less and less, the notion had faded away.

"Never," I said, and did my best to smile. "Not once."

"Not at all?"

"I promise. Sam was Sam, you're you. That's the whole story."

Silence fell again. "You know," Hal said, "sometimes Mom, I don't know, she would look at me. Just look at me. And I would feel like she was seeing somebody else."

"Sam you mean."

He shrugged a little nervously, his eyes cast down to the table. "Or maybe me, but also not me. I remember once when it happened, I was doing homework in the kitchen, back before she got so sick. I looked up and she was watching me, you know, that kind of intense look she sometimes had? And I thought, 'I'm Sam. I'm not Hal. I'm Sam, right here.' Like I knew. I almost told her." He lifted a little in his chair. "Crazy, huh?"

In the split second that our eyes met, I saw how painful this memory was for him. It came from a place inside him that I had never seen.

"I don't think it's crazy at all. I wish you'd told me."

He laughed uneasily and looked away. "Now, *that* would have been some conversation."

We paid our bill and left. The sidewalks were empty, like the corridors of an abandoned city. A crisp breeze made me pull my collar around my neck as we walked: a last vestige of the spring chill, sneaking in behind the day's departed heat. When we reached the door of the hotel, Hal stopped and took my elbow.

"Listen," he said, and looked at his watch. "I probably should have said something before. But if it's okay, I'm going to go meet some people."

I was astonished. "What are you talking about? Who do you know in Philadelphia?"

"You remember Dave Rosen, Josh Miner, those guys? They both go to Penn now. I called them when you were asleep just to say hello, and they said they were planning to go out later. They asked if I wanted to come along."

"Where would they be going? It's nearly midnight."

He tipped a shoulder, doing his best to look as if the invitation was inconsequential to him. "Some place on South Street. I don't think it's far. I can grab a cab. I think Josh has a car; he can drive me back to the hotel."

Now that we were standing still, the air was so brisk I shivered. I felt a little ridiculous—because I was so disappointed, but even more, because I'd let Hal see this. I shook my head to clear this thought away. "Never mind. Of course, go ahead. It's probably just what you need."

"You know, you could come if you want, Pop. I'm sure those guys would get a kick out of seeing you."

A kick. I let the word hang in my mind and thought about his friends. Loud voices in the kitchen and car doors slamming in the drive, strange coats and piles of books in the hallway, the tang of animal sweat when I entered a room they had just departed and the feeling that the electricity humming off their bodies still crackled the air. For years they had moved on the periphery of my life like a pack, young men so brimming with life that being in their presence was like standing beside some muscular spectacle of nature, a geyser blowing its top or a hive of swarming bees. Josh was a tall kid, slender with hair the color of a lit match, like his father, a lawyer whose path I had crossed a few times in the city; Josh had played on the basketball team with Hal, all elbows and long limbs crashing under the boards. The other boy I couldn't remember, but didn't need to; he was part of the herd. The invitation was not really meant to be accepted, of course. Still, on another night, I might have called Hal's bluff and gone along.

"I think it's a little late for me. Just don't stay out all night. We have a long day tomorrow."

His face was delighted. "You're really okay with this?"

"Hal, enough," I said, and waved him toward the taxi stand. "I'm fine. Go before I change my mind."

He got into a taxi and sped off. The hotel lobby was empty, except for the desk clerk and a lone porter, a black man in uniform, dozing on a stool by the elevator. Even the bar was dark, closed down for the night. Upstairs, I undressed and got into bed, my mind humming with wakefulness. I didn't have anything to read, not even a newspaper. The television glared at me from across the room, but the thought of turning it on, as tempting as this was, filled me with a kind of nausea. At last, not knowing what else to do, I turned out the light.

When I awoke, it was after three. I'd neglected to close the drapes, and the ambient light of the city pulsed across the ceiling. The bed next to mine was empty. I lay still for a moment, gathering myself. I realized it was Hal's voice, coming from the other room, that had awakened me. Who could he be talking to?

I rose and opened the door. The lights were off, and for a moment I just stood there, uncertain of what I was seeing. Hal was on the couch. Somebody was with him—a girl. The same ghostly light flickered across them. The image and the sounds I was hearing suddenly coalesced in my mind, a feeling like falling, as if I'd placed my foot on a step that wasn't there.

"Hal?"

"Jesus!"

A burst of activity on the sofa, and a flash of light-glazed skin; I turned away quickly and shut the door behind me. I sat on the bed, my heart hammering in my chest.

"Dad?" Hal was standing in the door. His shirt was on but unbuttoned; his belt hung loosely at his waist. If there had been light to see his face I knew it would have been flushed red with desire, embarrassment, a thousand agitations.

"Goddamn it, Hal."

"Dad, I'm sorry. I thought you were asleep."

"I *was* asleep. What were you thinking, bringing a girl here at, what . . . three in the morning? Who the hell *is* that?" I shook my head. "Forget it, I don't even want to know."

"We met at the club. She's a friend of Josh's." He stood another moment. Part of him was deciding, I knew, what right he had to be angry with me, for bursting in.

"Look, I said I was sorry. I didn't mean to upset you. I don't know what else to say. She has a car, she can just go if you want."

"Of course that's what I want. Jesus Christ, Hal. What the hell is on your mind? A girl like that."

"She's nice, Dad. Okay? It's not what you think. She's a fine arts major."

"I don't care if she's the president of the United States. Just get her out of here."

He turned and left the room. I heard the two of them talking, low enough so that I couldn't make out the words, then the sounds of their departure. I lay back in bed, not knowing if I would see him again that night, or even the next morning. But then, just a minute later, Hal returned. Without a word, he undressed and got into bed.

"Dad? I'm sorry. Okay? I wasn't thinking, I admit that."

I took a deep breath and held it. I had no idea what to say. The fog of anger had passed, and I knew I had handled the situation badly; the truth was, if I were Hal, I might have done exactly the same thing. A feeling of desolation burned through me, but something else too. That flash of skin, the soft murmurs my body knew but hadn't heard in years—I realized they had aroused me.

"That's all right," I said. "Just . . . forget about it."

I watched the ceiling, the drifting light. Time seemed to have bent under the weight of the evening's events, so that the morning was both hours, and minutes, away. I closed my eyes to will away the image of what I'd seen, our day in the cemetery, the remembered taste of dust in my mouth—all of it. Even the thing I could not name: the stream of gritty milk on her chin, the feel of the rubber sheet beneath me, M's slow breathing against my chest, those long waves, fading and fading.

"Dad?"

My eyes popped open; amazingly, I had dozed.

"Dad, are you awake?"

From across the gap separating our beds came a soft, damp sound of breathing. It took me another moment to realize Hal was crying.

"I'm sorry, I'm sorry."

"It's all right, son." I rose on my elbows. He was facing away. "Really, it's okay."

"Not about the girl." He shook his head against the pillow. "About before, what I said in the restaurant."

I felt completely at sea. "What are you talking about?"

"I never thought it, about Sam." I heard him sniff, then rub his face on the sheet. "I don't know why I told you I did. I sometimes wished it was true. But it never was."

My heart was pierced with a sadness I'd never known before. The feeling, always, of a shadow over his life: I'd thought it was his mother's illness. But it was Sam.

"What did she say?" Hal asked quietly. "Mom, at the end."

I paused and thought. "She said that she loved you. She said she wished she could have seen your game."

"Did she say she loved Sam?"

"Yes, she did. She loved you both."

The clock said it was just past four A.M.; the night seemed endless, not a thing merely of time but also space, like a vast ocean spreading over the world.

"That's good," Hal said finally. "I'm glad she said that too. Dad?"

"Yes, Hal?"

He rose on his elbows and turned to face me; his cheeks were streaked with tears. "It's okay, about Mom. I don't want to talk about it, but I just wanted to say that."

I don't want to talk about it. My breath caught in my chest; I closed my eyes. The words seemed to swirl inside me, releasing a memory, from years ago: Meredith and that first night, when we'd returned from her doctor in New York. *I don't want to talk about it. Not now. Not tonight. Maybe not ever.*

I opened my eyes: Hal.

"How did you—?"

He shook his head to cut me off. "She told me, that's all. Months ago. She knew what would happen, and she told me. I promised I wouldn't say anything more about it."

Here is grief, I thought, here is grief at last: the full measure and heft of it, the warp and woof. I watched myself enter it as if I were stepping into a pool of the calmest, darkest waters, the surface reaching to my knees, my waist, the point of my chin—a feeling like happiness, everything drifting away, the weight of my body and its parts dissolving into the great sea of time and all the world's sorrows. I paused to breathe. How strange, even to breathe! The tip of my nose, my hair and its roots, my solitary, beating heart: each detail of my physical existence had become both part of me and also not, as vivid as a jewel on felt and just as elsewhere. I had begun to sob, tears pouring forth at last, but even this—the sounds of my weeping and the rough unveiling of each breath sweeping through me—seemed to be happening to another man. My face was in my hands.

"Pop? Pop, what is it?"

I tried to answer but failed, and then Hal was beside me. I missed him, as I missed everyone, and as he put his arms around me, all I could think was, how strange he doesn't know. He doesn't know I've died.

After that night, it took me just a month to dismantle what was left of my life. Hal returned to school, took his exams, stopped at the house to deposit his belongings before driving off to spend a week in the city with friends. We talked a few times on the phone, always in bright, clipped sentences, speaking only of schedules and who could be reached where on which days. There were simply no more words for what had happened, no sentences to add to the recognition that had passed between us. He returned to the house for Memorial Day weekend and then, on Tuesday, packed up his suitcases and headed off again, crammed into the back of a friend's Volkswagen that announced both its arrival and departure with a single beep of its horn. I stood in the driveway and watched him go, then went inside to my office and called a realtor to put the house up for sale. How much was I thinking, the woman asked excitedly, in terms of price? And what were my plans, where would I be looking to move? I had already forgotten the woman's name; though I told her she had come recommended to me by friends, in fact I had taken her right out of the yellow pages, giving the matter less thought than hiring a plumber. Well, I said, I didn't really know. I was going away, I told her, and gave her my lawyer's telephone number; get the contracts over to me right away, I instructed, and I'll sign them and he can take it from there.

When this was done I wrote letters to the housekeeper, the cook, and my secretary, letting them all go; I cut each one a check for five thousand dollars, put them in envelopes wrapped by their individual letters, and left them where they would be easily found on the kitchen table. I was completing this task when the bell rang: the realtor. When I opened the door I was immediately pleased; before me stood a woman about fifty, her face plain as a schoolteacher's. Though she'd done her best to look presentable, putting on lipstick and heels, she possessed none of the high sheen of someone who sold upmarket real estate. Her car sat in the drive, an ancient Volvo with rust on the quarter panels where road salt had gnawed through the paint; one of the tires was missing a hubcap. Up close she smelled a little of liquor, some candy-sweet cordial that probably came in a bottle shaped like a mermaid. A listing like mine must have felt like she'd won the lottery. Her face fell with confusion when I didn't invite her in to have a look around—I could already hear what she would say when she returned to the office: *Harry Wainwright! That huge place on Seminole! And he didn't even ask me in!*—but she brightened when I took the contract from the leather folder she held under her arm and signed it on the spot, giving her an exclusive, with a six-month time frame. We shook hands—hers a little damp in the summer heat, though that could have been my own—and I sent her on her way.

Back at my desk, I wrote a note to my lawyer, explaining my plans to sell the house, and one to my accountant, saying more or less the same; I wrote a check to Williams, Hal's tuition for the coming year, and another to the lawn service, to carry them through till fall. By this time it was early evening; I made myself a sandwich, poured a glass of beer, and took it back to the office, to continue my work. I paid my taxes, made a promised donation to Hal's private school, resigned from the country club and the board of the local hospital, and fired the gardener, for stealing tools. When this was done I washed a load of laundry, reading a magazine while my clothes flip-flopped in the damp heat, then descended the stairs to the basement, to extinguish the pilots and shut off the gas. I thought for a minute about draining the pipes, thinking this customary, but how this was accomplished was a mystery to me, a thing I'd never learned; and in any event, the house would certainly be someone else's before winter. I turned on the sump pump, opened the fuse box—not even certain what I was looking for, though it seemed fine—and checked the bulkhead door.

Upstairs, I emptied the contents of the refrigerator into garbage bags and hauled these to the garage; I filled the cans and dragged them outside where the carting service would see them and sealed the lids tight with rubber cords, so the raccoons could not get in. I stacked the patio chairs and covered them with a tarp. In the backyard, I saw that a large limb had fallen from the big oak that stood beside the garden; it was too heavy to move on my own, so I retrieved an axe from the gardener's shed, whacked it into smaller pieces, and carted them beyond the house's circumference of light, where the lawn met a tangle of woods, and left them in the weeds.

The work had made me sweat, and I thought to take a shower before I remembered that I had already shut off the water heater. No matter; the house was cool and dry. I changed my shirt and poured myself a Scotch and ascended to the attic to fetch a suitcase, brought this down to the bedroom, and packed it quickly. It was a little after nine, later than I'd hoped, but to consider this contingency too closely seemed fraught; one moment of doubt, and my courage would collapse. I carried my case downstairs, out through the breezeway to the garage, where my car, a Jag, was parked; I went back into the kitchen, made a pot of coffee to fill a thermos, retrieved a warm jacket and a pair of boots from the hallway closet, then moved through the house one final time, top to bottom and back to front, dousing the lights as I went. When I reached the door connecting the house to the garage, I removed my key from my ring, placed it on the little table by the door, and set the lock; I stepped through the door and closed it behind me, listening for the little click as the mechanism dropped into place—an irrevocable sound, final as a plunge. I placed the jacket and boots on the backseat with my suitcase. Then I got into the Jag and started the engine.

It took only a minute, what happened next. Sitting at the wheel, the engine roaring under me, I lifted my eyes to the mirror and saw, with mild surprise, that I had neglected to open the garage door. *Ah, my mind said, the door is closed; I never opened the door.* My right foot pressed the gas pedal, pressed it again. The car was fussy as a thoroughbred; half the time, the damn thing wouldn't start at all, or else the choke would stick and flood the carburetor. But not that night. The engine eased onto its idle, pushing more gray exhaust into the air of the sealed room. I pressed the gas again and watched the tachometer leap. A wondrous calm had eclipsed my awareness of events, floating inside me like a bubble. The windows of the car were open; I felt a tickle in my nose, accompanied by a curious lightening of the senses, and heard this as a sentence: *My nose is tickling.* In the rearview mirror, the image of the closed door wavered like a mirage as the garage filled up with smoke.

Another ten seconds, twenty, thirty. It's hard to say how long I sat. Long enough, and then I wasn't sitting anymore: I was outside the car in the smoky garage, hauling the door open to a blast of evening air. Twice I coughed, but only twice, and before the air had cleared— quick as anything, quick as death—I was back at the wheel. I put the Jag into reverse, the smooth engagement of its gears like something snapping into place inside me, and backed away; my head still roaring with the fumes, I turned the wheel and gunned down the drive, lifting my eyes quickly one last time to see the garage door—a message to any who might care to look—standing open behind me.

SIXTEEN

Lucy

I didn't go, not right away; it took me three more months, after I received Joe's letter, to work up the nerve. And even then, I hedged my bets. I didn't want to let go of my apartment, not for good, so I put an ad on the bulletin board at the Y, and two days later sublet it to a couple of Irish girls looking for a place to spend the summer while waitressing on the waterfront. In early April I'd written my parents and asked them to sell my car and send the money on to me; a month later a fat envelope arrived at the restaurant, with a piece of blank paper wrapped around fifteen twenty-dollar bills. It was more than I'd expected—my car was actually an old one of my parents', a rusted Rambler station wagon with nearly 120,000 miles on it—so I decided to hold a hundred back and used the remaining two hundred dollars to buy an ancient VW bug that one of the line cooks had been trying to unload all winter. The car was the color of a rotten pumpkin and stank of stale smoke and old socks, but it ran; with the leftover hundred I bought a pair of retreads for the front, new wiper blades, and a little pine air freshener to hang from the mirror, and parked the car in the street outside my apartment, waiting like a jet on a runway for the day of my departure.

The morning I left, a Monday in the second week of June, Deck and May came to see me off. It didn't feel quite like summer yet, but a sharp, salty wind was blowing off the harbor, and seagulls wheeled promisingly in the air over the house. I stood in the gravel driveway beside my car, and hugged Deck and May, feeling very much as if, sublet or no, I would never see them again. The Irish girls didn't seem like the types to spend the summer worrying about my asparagus fern, but it seemed silly to take it with me, so I'd carted it downstairs with my suitcase, and gave it to May and Deck.

"I'm sorry, this is the only present I could think of."

"We'll take it as a loan." Deck hugged me again, tightly, pressing me into his chest. Since that night at the Lobster Tank, when Deck had poured shot after shot to ease my aching heart—I'd gotten good and drunk, as ordered, and awoke the next morning in Peg's room to see May placing my clothing, freshly washed and folded, at the foot of the bed—the two of them had been like family. Not a week went by that I wasn't at their house for dinner at least once, and I sometimes spent whole weekends there. One funny thing: they never called me Lucy. To them, I was Alice.

They were the kindest people I had ever known, and it suddenly seemed absurd to leave them. But then Deck blinked and looked aside, brushing an eye with his thumb. "Go on with you, then," he said.

I got in the car and drove away. I hadn't actually turned the engine over for almost four weeks, and oily-smelling smoke huffed out the tailpipe in a blue plume that billowed behind me. But after a few miles it settled in and actually drove quite nicely. I cried for a while, but by the time I was out of town I knew I was done with this. *Look at you, Lucy girl,* I thought, and turned north, away from the water, so that I was watching the seasons turning in reverse; where I was headed it was still just spring. *Look at you, going home, where nobody knows you've been Alice.*

I had no idea what I was looking for, only that I would find it, or not, when I got there. My parents were away until July, visiting my father's sister in North Carolina. Only this part of my trip was strategic: I had two weeks before I would see them, and by then I would know what to do.

My immediate destination was the Rogues', where Joe had said his father was staying. Hank Rogue was a crotchety cuss, even by the standards of my town; I had a memory from years ago of standing in the yard behind our house and watching him back his drilling rig right over my mother's flower beds, then step, scowling, from his cab, a cigarette bobbing in the corner of his mouth, spitting once at his feet and then lifting his head to give me a look that said: "Got a problem with this?" His wife was a mousy thing with a permanently sad look stitched on her face who punched a register at the IGA; the story went that the pair of them were actually divorced, but Hank had refused to move out, so they'd stayed that way for years. The only mental image I had of their daughter was taken from a dance my freshman year at Regional: a tall girl in a macramé poncho, sitting on a stone wall outside the gymnasium, loud music throbbing inside—"Smoke on the Water" or "Brown Sugar" or "Takin' Care of Business," the usual cover crap that were the only things the local bands knew how to play—drinking from a widemouthed bottle in a paper sack that one of her friends had handed her, and then her laughing in a way that made me think of a bird flying into a window—something stopped midair. It wasn't a promising picture, the sort that usually ended badly in my town, but then the girl, whose name was Suzanne, astounded everyone by taking first place in the all-state spelling bee and winning a full ride to a college in Texas nobody had ever heard of. As far as I knew, she'd never been back.

The Rogues lived in a little house with pea-green asbestos siding just behind the fire station, hard to miss because of Hank's drilling rig parked in the yard like the wreck of an alien spacecraft. Four hours after leaving Portland I parked behind it and released my cramping hands from the wheel—I hadn't noticed how tightly I'd been holding on. A cold wind was blowing, and some of the trees were only just beginning to bud out. I had a feeling of exposure, as if, at any second, everybody I'd ever known would leap from the bushes and demand to learn where I'd been all these months.

When Hank Rogue answered my knock, I knew at once he had no idea who I was. He was wearing loose denim overalls, same as the day he'd spat at his feet in my parents' yard, and his hands were caked with grime and oil. The skin of his face had the bubbled texture of cooking pancake batter. A sour smell of cigarettes and unwashed skin floated through the open door.

"I'm Lucy," I explained, and heard the nervousness in my voice. "Lucy Hansen. Phil and Maris's girl?"

He gave a slow, indecipherable nod, and tipped his head slightly to flick his eyes over my shoulder, as if my parents might be standing behind me.

"They got problems with their well?"

"No, nothing like that. They're in North Carolina, actually." I felt ridiculous. Why was I explaining this to him? "I'm here to see Joe Crosby. Somebody told me he was staying here."

"He's here, all right," he answered flatly, and crossed his arms over his barrellike chest. "Sleeping."

"His son asked me to look in on him. Would it be all right if I came in?"

His eyebrows lifted in a warning. "I said he was sleeping now, didn't I? That'll have to satisfy you."

This was a wrinkle I hadn't considered: that I might get to the door and simply be turned away. "Please, Mr. Rogue, I've come a long way."

"Thought you said you were Phil Hansen's girl."

"I am, Mr. Rogue," I said. "I've been . . . away. In Portland. I just drove up this afternoon. I used to cook for Joe at the camp."

"He owe you money, then?"

"No, of course not," I said. "I'm just a friend."

He snorted. "Ain't you heard? Joe Crosby ain't got none a' those."

"Well, he does, and I'm one."

He considered me another moment. His eyes flicked up and down my body like a butcher eyeing a carcass.

"You're a persistent one," he said finally, and stepped back from the door. "Suppose you might as well come in. He won't like being woke up, though. You'll see for yourself."

He led me into the kitchen. Dirty plates were piled like poker chips under a dripping tap, and opened cans were strewn everywhere—chili, beef stew, Campbell's soup, their crinkled lids all standing at attention. A half-gallon jug of off-brand bourbon, mostly empty, sat on the counter. The room reeked of wet dog, though I saw no trace of one. Beyond the kitchen was another door.

"Through there," Hank said, and pointed.

The room was dark, its one window covered with a yellowed shade;

what light there was seemed soaked up by the wavy paneling that served for walls. It took a moment for my eyes to adjust. The space was tiny, obviously some kind of makeshift addition hammered onto the back of the house—the sort of extra room where people usually stored tools or skis or muddy shoes. A thin cot was pushed against the far wall, and beside it, an orange crate, covered with pill bottles. Joe's father was sitting beneath the window in an overstuffed chair, his head rocked back and mouth slightly open, hands folded at his waist. His glass eye was slightly open; the other one was closed. A chrome cane with a rubber tip leaned against the wall beside him.

"Joe?" I knelt before him on the plywood floor. His body seemed smaller than I remembered, half swallowed by the immense chair. He needed a haircut, and his fingernails were long as a woman's; a smell rose off him, sharp and a little sweet, like overripe fruit. I took one of his hands and gently shook it.

"Joe, it's Lucy Hansen."

His eye flickered open. He tipped his head and looked at me a moment without recognition.

"It's Lucy Hansen," I said again.

"Lucy." His face brightened slightly; he licked his lips and swallowed. His mouth seemed off-kilter, as if he'd just gotten back from the dentist and the Novocain hadn't quite worn off. It was hard to tell, of course, Joe's face being what it was, but between this and the cane, I wondered if he'd had a second stroke, or if the first one had been more serious than he'd let on. Hank Rogue, the filthy kitchen, this dismal little storage room with its caved-in cot: no one deserved this. It all felt like a terrible punishment for my being gone. It was all I could do not to burst into tears.

His voice when he spoke was thick in his throat. "Lucy, what are you doing here?"

I squeezed his hand. "Joey sent me. I'm here to take you home."

I turned over the orange crate and quickly filled it with his pills and the small pile of folded shirts and pants I found on the floor at the foot of the bed. With my other hand I pulled him upright, surprised by how light he was, and guided the cane into his hand. He was breathing hard, and I heard a phlegmy rattle in his chest that worried me. Then I turned to see Hank Rogue standing in the doorway.

"What the hell you think you're doing?"

"What does it look like?" I said. "We're leaving."

"Is that right? The fuck you are."

I positioned myself in front of him, holding the crate between us. The urge to cry was gone; taking its place was a feeling of pure anger, like a thunderhead climbing inside me.

"Get out of my way," I said.

He reached a hand down to his crotch and rubbed. His eyes went soft, trying to hold my gaze. "Little girl."

Which was when I took two steps forward and rammed the crate, hard as I could, into Hank Rogue. I had no idea what I was doing, but it worked; momentum was on my side, and all that swimming had made me strong. The crate caught him across the loose flesh of his stomach, pushing the wind from his lungs and sending him tumbling out of the room. He crashed backward into the kitchen table, tried to grab the edge for balance as it slid away behind him, then went down hard. He was a big man, and the whole house seemed to shudder under the weight of his fall.

"You fucking cunt!"

I did the only next thing I could think of, which was to grab the half-empty jug of bourbon from the counter. It had a curved handle, perfect for throwing, and glass sides thick as a windshield. Without aiming I flung it, like a center spikes a volleyball, in the general direction of Hank Rogue. A perfect shot: he managed to deflect the bottle with his hand but the corner still caught him over the eye, knocking him down again before it smacked, miraculously unbroken, into the wall behind him. A line of blood surged along his brow.

The blow hadn't knocked him out, but I knew I'd bought the time we needed. I turned to Joe's father, where he stood at the door with his cane. It took me a moment to realize that the look of mute wonder on his face was meant for me.

"I'll be god . . . damned."

"Quick as you can, Joe."

He let me lead him across the kitchen. Hank had risen to a sitting position, a fat palm pressed to his bleeding head. It was possible I'd hurt him badly, but I didn't spend a second fretting over this. All I wanted was to get away. Outside, I helped Joe down the front stoop and across the weedy yard and into the VW, then shoved the orange crate into the back, scattering the bottles of pills everywhere. I'd gotten myself into the driver's seat and was fumbling for the keys—too damn many of them, keys that seemed to multiply and tangle in my hand like scarves pulled from a magician's sleeve—when the clock ran out: I heard a bellow and looked up just as Hank burst out of the house, swinging a baseball bat. For an instant, my brain seized with a vision of Suzanne, sitting on the gymnasium wall, and her high, frightened laugh. Whatever had happened to her, I knew how the story had ended: she'd run for her life.

"You little bitch!"

Joe turned toward me in the passenger seat. "Lucy—"

"Got it!"

The key found the ignition; the engine caught and held, and I shoved the car into reverse and hit the gas just as Hank, realizing he'd never reach us in time, launched the bat straight for us. I didn't have a second to be afraid; I saw it coming, closed my eyes, and ducked. The hard, heavy end of it punched the front hood with a sonorous clang, pinwheeling the thing up and over the car like a majorette's baton. In another instant I heard it strike the pavement behind us and bounce harmlessly away—just a child's toy rattling in the street. A high, wild joy filled me as I swung out into the road and turned and sped away.

We'd reached the corner when Joe finally spoke. "Where'd you learn to do that?"

"Pure instinct. You *lived* with that guy? Tell me you weren't paying him, Joe."

Beside me, Joe said nothing.

"Jesus, Joe. What happened to his wife?"

"Gone. Last winter." He looked at his hands. "It wasn't so bad. Just twenty-five a week. Plus help with the groceries."

I figured it was worse than that but held my tongue. We passed through town; I realized I was speeding and made a conscious effort to slow the car to thirty-five. The streets were empty, just a few cars and pickups parked here and there, their fenders spangled with spring mud. Most of the tourist businesses were still closed for the season. As we passed the police station, a pang of dread quickened my heart: whatever else was true, hitting Hank Rogue in the head with a bourbon bottle was certainly against the law. All he had to do was wander down to the station and file a report, and I would be a wanted woman. But in another moment this fear left me. Who would believe that little Lucy Hansen had laid out the likes of Hank Rogue?

"Well, I wish you'd told me," I said. "Told *somebody*. I never would have let you stay there."

We reached the edge of town and the intersection of Highway 9. To the left, forty-five minutes away, thirty if I gunned it, lay the hospital in Farmington. Right would take us to the camp. It was just six o'clock, barely late afternoon that time of year, but in the half hour since I'd rolled into town, thick, doughy clouds had moved in from the north, sucking the light away. It felt more like deep fall than the June evening it was. I considered both options, and then a third: taking him back to Portland.

"Joe, we have to get you to a doctor."

He shook his head. "No hospitals."

"Don't be stubborn. You're sick. On top of everything else, I think you might have pneumonia."

But the look on his face told me this line of argument would get me nowhere. I'd rescued him from Hank Rogue's clutches; for now, that would have to do. I heard myself sigh.

"Jesus, I really shouldn't be doing this. Promise me you'll let me call someone? At least let Paul Kagan have a look at you."

He nodded grudgingly. "All right."

The spring thaw had done its damage. The road to the camp, a tricky proposition even in the best years, was a minefield of potholes deep enough to make me worry about banging the oil pan; by the old stone bridge, where Forest Creek emptied into the river, a section had been so completely washed away I had to stop and let Joe direct me across it, the VW leaning so precariously I thought I was going into the drink for sure. It took us almost an hour to drive those last eight miles, and by the time we reached the camp, the rattle in Joe's chest had blossomed into a nasty cough.

I took the keys from him. "Let's get you inside."

The building was dark, the shutters closed tight. The only sound was the soft whistle of the wind in the pines. The scene was so desolate to my eyes I might have been gone for years. A misty rain was falling into the lake, so light you might not have noticed except for the fanning shapes that drifted over its surface in the waning light. Holding the box of pills and clothes, I managed to get the door open and Joe inside and find a light switch. In the main room, I got Joe down on the sofa, then went to look at the kitchen. A bowl of something long hardened sat on the table, and beside it, a mug stained brown from evaporated coffee—Joe's breakfast, the morning he'd had his stroke. The big fridge held only a quart of milk long soured, a package of American cheese, a few sticks of moldy butter, and a six-pack of Budweiser. The cheese was probably okay—hell, that stuff could last a year—and the beer was a welcome sight, but everything else was a total loss. I threw the milk and butter in the trash and opened the kitchen tap. A few puffs of air, a groan from somewhere below me, and a blast of brown water gushed from the spigot. I sipped a beer while I let the water clear over Joe's six-month-old dirty breakfast dishes, then filled a saucepan and put it on the stove for tea. I found some not-too-stale crackers in the pantry, and melted the cheese over them in the broiler, then took it all out to the main room.

Joe was sleeping where I'd left him, facing the cold hearth. His face was flushed with fever; I stood and watched him, listening to the wet clutter of his breathing and second-guessing my decision not to take him down to Farmington General. But the hour was late, the road was too bad to try again in darkness, and I figured this was a discussion that would have to wait till morning.

"Joe?" I showed him the tray. "I made you something to eat."

He roused himself and did his best to nibble at the crackers, his crooked mouth sputtering crumbs when the coughing took him, then gingerly sipped the tea. The room was clammy as a ship at sea; I'd have to look into lighting the furnace, too, or at least get a fire going. When he was done I took the tray and put it aside.

"Off to bed with you now."

Upstairs, I stripped his bed and remade it with fresh linens, and waited outside his door while he undressed. I'd brought all his medicines upstairs, and when he was ready, I carried them in and helped him with the bottles: seven of them, each containing a different-colored pill the purpose of which I could only guess at. When he was done he lay back on the pillow, and I drew a heavy blanket over him.

"What happened to you, Lucy?"

I sat on the edge of the bed. All day I had been running on adrenaline, and just the feel of the mattress beneath me left me suddenly exhausted. I could have put my head down and instantly been asleep.

"It's a long story."

"Were you with Joey? It's all right if you were. I know he comes back to see you."

I nodded. "For a while, at Christmas. I told my parents I was visiting a girlfriend in Boston, but it was Joe. After that I was in Portland."

"How did he look?"

For almost four years, we had never spoken of these things. I thought his question strange, but then I didn't. The Joe he remembered was a boy, or nearly. By now his son was somebody else entirely.

"Stronger. A little sad. It's hard for him up there. I think he wants to come home."

"Your parents were worried, Lucy."

I felt a familiar shiver of guilt move through me, the same one that had dogged me for months. "I know they were. I'm sorry about that. But there wasn't any helping it."

"What did you do in Portland?"

The rain was rattling the metal roof outside his window; I let my mind drift through the memories of my time away, listening to the sound the rain made.

"Nothing all that interesting, though I guess it felt like it at the time. I waitressed at a restaurant on Commercial. I swam a lot too. I had a little apartment." I shrugged and made an effort to smile; already I sounded nostalgic. "It's not important. Let's just think about getting you well."

As I'd spoken, a deeper stillness had enclosed him. His breathing was slow and even, and I thought for a moment he had fallen asleep. I rose and tightened the blanket around his chest. I was about to shut out the light when he spoke again, the words seeming to come from deep inside him.

"I didn't know what I would do without you here, Lucy."

I bent down, fingered his hair aside, and kissed him on the forehead, something I had never done before. The heat of his fever lingered on my lips and fingers, like a faint electric charge; it would be a long night, I knew.

"Well, I'm here now," I said quietly, and shut out the light. "Don't worry. I'm not going anywhere."

I spent most of the night in a chair by his bed, finally moving down to the sofa just before dawn. A little after eight, I telephoned the doctor. Paul Kagan had been the town's only physician as long as I could remember, the sort of cradle-to-grave practitioner you think exists only in movies: gruff, wise, and beloved, a man who on any given day might see a toddler with an earache or somebody in their eighties with enough problems to sink a battleship. He kept his office in the back of his small, shingled house by the post office, and as a child the thing I always liked best about it was the big tank of tropical fish in the waiting room.

I told him about what I'd seen at the Rogues', the cough and fever, and my suspicion of pneumonia.

"If he's as you say, you should take him down to Farmington."

"I don't think he'll go."

I heard Paul sigh. Given the general crustiness of his clientele, half of them holed up in trailers and shacks miles from anything you might call a respectable road, this was a conversation he probably had five times a day.

"Well, I'm seeing Sarah Rawling later this afternoon. She's out your way, more or less. I guess I could come then. Woman's got congestive heart failure, and she won't go to the damn hospital either."

"You're an angel."

He chuckled. "Hardly, but spread it around. Where you been keeping yourself, Lucy? Your mother said you'd gotten some great new job someplace. Sort of thought maybe we'd seen the last of you."

"Just needed to get away for a bit, I guess."

"Don't we all. Course, I never will. You should come in and see the fish. I got some new ones just last month, real beauties."

"I'll do that."

"Think three o'clock, maybe a little earlier. He gets any worse, though, no fooling—you get him down to Farmington, don't wait for me. He's not as tough as he thinks he is."

I returned to Joe's bedroom. He was resting quietly—the worst of the coughing had abated for the moment—and I decided not to rouse him. I was wearing the same jeans and blouse I'd put on a day ago in Portland, and would have liked a shower, but even this seemed like work. For a while I dozed in the chair. Sometime in the night the rain had blown through; a weak, unhurried sun, the sun of illness, pulsed in the drapes. For lunch I made the last of the cheese and crackers, though Joe ate just a few bites, and I finished what was left. How would I get into town for groceries? I wondered; what would become of us, stranded out here? And, a dark thought I couldn't push away, much as I wished to: what would I do if he died?

I was in the kitchen, taking stock of the larder—not much, just a few cans of soup and some stale spaghetti I thought I might be able to do something with for dinner—when the phone rang. I hoped it might be Paul, but the voice on the other end was a woman's.

"I know it's probably too late, but do you think we could get a reservation for the last week in July?"

For a second I was lost. "I'm sorry. The camp's closed."

"Oh." The woman seemed not to believe me. "Really? We were there last year, and my husband just *loved* it."

"Like I said, we're closed. You might want to try the Lakeland Inn."

I gave her the number and hung up the phone. Not five minutes later it rang again. The voice this time was a man's.

"Is this Crosby's?" Before I could answer he charged ahead. "I've been trying to get through for days. Listen, Joe said he'd hold the same week in August for us, party of four, name of Gaudio. I was wondering if we could move it up a week. We're taking the boy off to college, and I didn't realize he'd have to be down there before Labor Day."

"I'm sorry, Mr. Gaudio. The camp's closed. It doesn't look like we're going to be open this season."

"Closed." Like the first caller, he paused, taking this in. "Closed, like out of *business?*"

I didn't really know the answer. The question seemed too large. "Why don't I take your number?"

"And do what with it?" he huffed impatiently. "See here. We had an agreement, young lady. Are you people going to live up to it or not?"

"No," I said, and hung up.

It went on like this. Over the next couple of hours I fielded three more phone calls, each replaying more or less the same conversation: a question about a reservation and my news that the camp was closed, followed by incredulity, various forms of bargaining (one man actually asked if we would be selling off any of the furniture), more apologies, expressions of anger and disappointment, and so on, until one of us hung up on the other. It was all perfectly understandable—who wants to hear that the rug's been yanked from under their one week of reliable fun?—and I wondered why I hadn't thought of this before. Usually the camp opened two weeks after Memorial Day. What would happen when people who had booked the year before just started showing up?

I was fretting about this when I heard a car outside, and then, below me, Paul Kagan's heavy steps in the main room.

"Lucy?"

I went to the top of the stairs and called down. "Up here!"

He met me on the landing. Paul Kagan was probably close to re-tirement, but like many fixtures of small town life, he seemed ageless, a permanent fifty-five. He appeared a little flustered at the sight of me, not certain if he should kiss me hello or not, and we settled on an awk-ward hug.

"How's the patient?" He was carrying an instrument bag, old leather so crinkled it looked chewed.

"His temperature's 101. And he won't eat a thing. The cough's got-ten a little better though."

We entered the room together. Joe was sitting up against a pile of pillows, his face white as paper. I realized for the first time that he was afraid, though I didn't know how much of this was caused by his ill-ness, and how much by the prospect of being examined by a doctor.

"How we doing, Joe?" Paul said loudly. He sat on the bed and opened the bag at his feet, removing a thermometer, which he began to shake down.

Joe stifled a cough. "Been better."

"Oh, you don't look so bad to me. Don't know what Lucy's so wor-ried about. Let's see about that temperature."

He nimbly popped the thermometer into Joe's mouth, then took his wrist and counted off his pulse. Paul had unusually large, long-fingered hands, which I knew he kept soft with a bottle of moisturizer stationed on his desk.

"You've been taking your pills?"

"Hm-mm-hmm."

"No need to talk, just nod."

Joe nodded. Paul released his wrist and bent at the waist to take out his stethoscope and blood pressure kit from the bag. He placed the head of his stethoscope in the crook of Joe's elbow and listened as he pumped the little bulb, his eyes turned up to the ceiling, away. The cuff gave a little hiss of gas as he released the pressure. He pulled the thermometer from Joe's mouth and peeked at it quickly, frowning.

"All right, handsome, off with the shirt so we can hear those lungs."

With slow fingers Joe undid his pajama top and leaned forward from the pillows for Paul to reach behind him.

"Deep breath now. That's it." Paul padded the stethoscope up and down his back. "So Lucy tells me you were staying with Hank Rogue."

"For a bit."

Paul paused to listen, then moved the stethoscope again. "Funny thing. I suppose you could call it a coincidence, but guess who came in yesterday afternoon with a nasty cut on his head?"

My whole body clenched with alarm. "God. Was he all right?"

Paul's mouth dipped in a frown. "Light concussion. Took a few stitches, but no permanent damage." He pulled the stethoscope from his ears and gave me a dark, knowing look. "Just between us, couldn't have happened to a nastier son of a bitch. You do what I do, you learn a few things about people."

I thought of Hank's hand groping downward, his eyes gone soft where he stood in the door, and about his daughter, gone to Texas without a trace. *Little girl.* A cold shudder of revulsion snaked through me.

"Okay, all set here. You can button up, Joe." Paul gave Joe's leg a solid pat, rose from the bed, and tipped his head toward the door. "Lucy?"

We stepped into the low-ceilinged hallway, sealing Joe's room behind us with a muffled snap.

"Well, I think you're right," Paul said quietly. "I'm hearing some fluid, mostly on the left side. The temperature has me worried. We really should get films."

"Films?"

"I'm sorry." He circled his hand over his chest. "An X ray, to see what's going on in there." He shrugged. "As for the rest, it's hard to say. He's got a touch of malnutrition. You see this in stroke patients. It's hard to eat, so they just give up on it."

"I really don't think he'll go."

Paul nodded gravely. "I figured that. Okay, let's run a course of antibiotics, just to be on the safe side. It's a question of whether he improves in the next twenty-four hours. He could turn a corner, or this could all gather fast into a real emergency. Keep him warm, give him lots of fluids, and watch his temperature. Any signs of trouble, *any*, and I want you to get him down to Farmington."

Downstairs, he wrote out a prescription for penicillin and gave me a bottle he kept in his bag to get Joe started.

"Like I said, mind that temperature. And try to get him to eat something. I know it won't be easy, but do your best." He cleared his throat. "His boy's still away?"

I took the prescription from his hand and nodded.

"You'll be all right out here by yourself?"

"Have to be, I guess."

He frowned with concern, holding my eyes with his. "Well, you've got the number. Don't be afraid to use it."

I walked him to the door. I hadn't been out of the house all day, and as I stepped onto the porch, a wave of shockingly warm, dense air washed over me, prickling my skin. While Joe and I had been locked away, the weather had turned like a clock with a too-tight spring, leaping straight into midsummer.

Paul trotted down the steps into the ricocheting sunlight and opened the door to his car. "One other thing, Lucy."

I was looking at the prescription in my hand. How I'd get into town to fill it I hadn't a guess, though I kept this worry to myself. There was barely anything left in the house to eat. I looked at him and tried to smile. "What's that?"

"Next time, skip the whiskey bottle and hit that bastard with a hammer."

He reached into the car to put his bag on the floor by the driver's seat, then stopped abruptly, his attention directed out over the lake. He placed a flat hand over his eyes.

"I thought you said the camp was closed."

"It is. The place was all shut up until yesterday."

Paul pointed. "Then who's that?"

Alarmed, I stepped quickly off the porch to investigate, cupping my brow as Paul had done. The lake's face shimmered like pounded tin in the misty heat, a blinding brightness. Someone, a stranger, was standing on the dock, his hands in his pants pockets, facing away.

"What the hell . . ."

The stranger turned then, and I saw. Those blue searchlight eyes hit me where I stood. He turned, and as he turned, his face and form and all that he was opened to me, like the pages of a book, one I'd read years ago and had forgotten. Somebody had come, after all. Somebody was already here.

"Lucy?"

"It's all right, Paul," I said, calling back to him, for I had already begun making my way down the hill. "It's all right. I know him."

It was Harry Wainwright.

SEVENTEEN

Joe

These goddamn lawyers: if I had ten cents for every one I've watched splashing around in the shallows, his fly rod snarling in the trees above, I wouldn't have sold the camp, to Harry Wainwright or anyone else. I'd let the place rot under the pines and retire to Florida on my gangster Chris-Craft like the rich man I'd be, and if anybody asked me what I wanted on my headstone, when that day came, I'd tell them to write: "Here lies a man who earned it, every dime."

None of them, not just Crybaby Pete (I couldn't help it: the name had stuck in my mind like Velcro) was much of a fisherman; the Atlantics were everywhere, piling up below the aqueducts, but a sharp breeze had blown up just past noon, and even Bill, who seemed to know best what he was doing, was having trouble reaching them.

"Punch it!" I called out from the bank. I stood and mimed the motion. "Don't let your backcast drop—shove that sucker out there."

"Goddamn, this wind." He pulled in his line and set to cast again. For a moment the breeze stilled, and he managed a solid cast, straight and clean. The instant his pattern hit the roiling water his rod bent like a twig and I heard the whiz of line running out.

"Holy mother!"

I knew he was about to panic. "Set the hook now," I called to him, scrambling down the bank. "Just a lift."

But the excitement was too much: he yanked his rod upward, and the pattern sprang away, soaring back over his head.

"Fuck! Fuck it to hell!"

He climbed back out to me, splashing all the way. "Okay, you tell me what happened."

I asked to see his rod. As I'd suspected, the drag was clamped down tight as a jar lid. I loosened it a turn and held it up to show him.

"See this? Forget the drag, at least until you're sure you've got one on. Just use a finger to tighten the line when you set the hook. A quick jerk, but no higher than your shoulder." I demonstrated once more, then passed it back to him. "These are heavy fish, they break off real easy."

He fingered the line as I had done, lifting the tip of his rod just so.

"That's it."

"Why'd I give up golf? I still feel like an idiot."

"It's trickier than it sounds." I shrugged. "It just takes practice."

"These fish, like fucking movie stars. Won't come out of their trailers."

A bit downstream, Carl Jr. and Marathon Mike seemed to be having better luck; while I watched, each of them got into a fish, first Carl and then Mike, so that, for a magic minute, both had something on their lines. Just a couple of rainbows, but Mike's was a nice one, over ten inches, and he held it up with a satisfied grin to show me before setting it back down into the riverbed. A bright, splashing flick of its tail, and off it went, none the worse for wear.

I was watching this when Pete stepped up beside me. He'd been gone about an hour, claiming he wanted to try the shallows down where the spillway opened out into the lake. Though, of course, this was a lie; he'd just wanted to go off somewhere to bob his line in the water and be left alone to think about his woe-filled, Ivy-educated life.

"Any luck?"

"Some." He didn't elaborate. I could smell a bit of whiskey rising off him; in one of those bulging vest pockets, I figured, was a flask, now mostly empty. The air was full of the cold water that roared with pulverizing force out of the aqueduct; even standing in bright sunshine, it was impossible not to feel its chill.

"How about these guys?" he asked, not at all interested.

"Nothing much. Couple of rainbows. The Atlantics are being fussy."

"How's Bill doing?"

"Nada so far."

My answer seemed to satisfy him. He walked up the bank and took a beer from the cooler.

"Have one?"

"On duty." I gave him my you-go-ahead-without-me smile. "Maybe later."

"Aw, come on, Joe." Pete patted the rock next to his. "Fuck it. Have a beer."

There was no harm in this, really, though I knew that if I sat to drink with him I'd soon enough be getting an earful: the nitty-gritty of his divorce, the whole unhappy inventory of who-got-what. I could practically hear it already—the final ugly words, and some sour, eleventh-hour scuffle over a dog no one really wanted, the sound of luggage being hauled in anger into the trunk of someone's car and the spray of gravel in the driveway. It was nothing I wanted, but on the other hand, given the way the day was shaping up, I would probably hear about this sooner or later, and four hours of standing in the sun had made me thirsty.

I took a can and sat beside him. It was good beer, something Belgian I'd never had before and wouldn't expect to find in a can.

"I think I had something on for a while there," Pete said.

"There you go."

He ran a hand over his damp hair. The flesh around his jowls and neck had a kind of looseness that made me think he'd been heavy as a kid, not truly fat but big enough that certain things had not come easy, and that this might explain a good deal about him.

"Didn't have a good guess what to do about it, though. I was actually sort of relieved when he got away. Tell me again, why is this fun?"

"Couldn't say. People seem to like it, though."

"So to you, this is all just a day at the office."

"Never had an office, not the way you mean."

Pete sighed good-naturedly and rolled his eyes. "He couldn't say. Christ." He pulled on his beer and looked at me. "You are one mono-syllabic son of a bitch, if you pardon my saying so."

"You think?"

He laughed, getting the joke before I did. "Touché."

For a moment we sat and sipped our beers. Bill, still trying to cast through the wind to the Atlantics below the aqueduct, had closed the gap by wading out another ten feet into chest-high water. I thought about saying something to reel him in a bit, but then figured what the hell, it was his vacation. The worst that could happen was a long, wet walk back to the truck.

"So," Pete said, "I screwed Bill's wife. Did I tell you that?"

This, of course, was exactly the sort of thing I had expected to hear, minus the specifics. "Can't say you did, Pete. That's something I'd re-member."

He rubbed his eyes and squinted out over the water. "You don't have to worry, he doesn't know." He gave his head a little shake. "Christ, you should see her. Beverly, I mean. It's his second wife, you know. The first one—" He waved his beer out over the water, to mean *long gone*. "So, Carol and I had just split up, over all kinds of other crap—you know, stupid stuff that basically added up to we couldn't stand the sight of each other another minute, and I ran into Bev at, get this, the office Christmas party, and she's wearing this thing, showing off her brand-new rack, flirtatious as hell, you know how that is." I had no idea, needless to say, not that it mattered. "I'd heard she liked to horse around a bit. We got to talking, and next thing I know I'm call-ing her up and the two of us are up in Boston riding the linens at the Copley Plaza."

At just this moment Bill's rod bent hard; he swiveled his head quickly to look for me, like a kid showing off to his old man, shouting, "Woo-hoo!"

"See?" Pete said to me, lifting his can toward the water. "Dumb-ass doesn't have a clue."

"You don't mind my asking, where was Bill while all this was going on?"

Pete drained the last of his beer and crunched the can in his fist. "Oh, off in East Jesus someplace, tramping around in the cattails with some douche bag from the EPA. He really loves that stuff." He frowned suddenly and gave me a worried look. "Why do you ask? He say something to you?"

A crazy question; of course he hadn't. That Pete would ask it told me just how tippy the whole situation was. "Just filling in the details."

"So he *didn't* say anything."

"No, but let me toss an idea your way. You guys always take vacations together?"

Pete mulled this over. "I see what you're driving at. I do. But I'm telling you, you're barking up the wrong tree. If he knew, I would have heard about it. Believe me."

We sat another minute, watching Bill fighting what looked to be a pretty-good-size Atlantic. I just hoped he had the good sense to break off before it dragged him into the drink and filled his waders with water the temperature of a thawed Popsicle. I was figuring by this point that Bill didn't just suspect something was going on—he absolutely knew, probably right down to the hour. This little outing was his way of saying, *Up yours, junior, see if I care. I've got you in my sights.*

"She's a lot younger than him," Pete said.

"I had a feeling."

"Guess how old."

I heard myself sigh irritably: guessing games, like junior high. "I don't know, thirty?"

"Close, Joe, very close. Twenty-eight. Twenty-fucking-eight." Pete scratched his cheek and flicked a bit of grunge away. "Probably I'm not the only one, I admit that. Given what everybody says. But I mean—Jesus, if you only knew."

The day had gotten strange under the spell of this conversation; the air seemed full of bad energy, like incoming weather, something about to break open. He was in love with her, of course, or thought he was. This fact was plain as day, just as it was also plain that Beverly Christmas didn't give a sweet goddamn about Crybaby Pete. Whatever had gotten her up to the Copley for a weekend of bouncy fun probably had less to do with love or even Pete himself than the price of peas in Paraguay.

"Christ," Pete moaned, and shook his head again. I could have been miles away, the way he was talking. "I'm a complete mess. She won't even take my calls now."

"That could be for the best, you know."

"Yeah, maybe." He scowled, suddenly angry. "Maybe I'm about to get my ass fired on top of everything else. Ever think of that?"

I held my tongue, though of course this was exactly what he needed, and so richly deserved. A little trip to the woodshed, and a chance, behind closed doors, to come clean. On the other side: blood and pain, a memory of pure hurt, but then the calm, open spaces the mind makes when the worst is over and the body steps out into sunlight again.

Pete climbed to his feet and placed his hands at the small of his back to stretch. "Aw, just look at him, the big dumb shit. He's having the time of his life, I'll bet."

By this point Bill had actually managed to get his fish under control and was thrashing around in the shallows, his rod hand held high over his head to keep the line tight while, with the other, he made unsuccessful, scooping lunges with his net. Done properly, this can be one of the most satisfyingly graceful moments in the sport, but in Bill's case, it was like watching a man trying to hail a taxi while simultaneously chasing a piece of blowing litter down the street. Who was going to tire out first, man or fish, was anybody's guess. For a second I thought he'd done it, but then the fish darted around him in a burst of speed that wrapped the leader hopelessly around Bill's legs. He cursed and waved me over.

"Joe? A little help here?"

I rose from the bank and splashed down to him, letting the icy water fill my shoes. I didn't need the net, because no one really does; bending at the waist, I snatched Bill's fish and rolled it over on its back, calming it as quick as a mallet whack. With my free hand I reached up to release the pliers from my belt and used them to back the hook out of the Atlantic's jaw. I waited another moment, moving the fish gently back and forth to run water over its gills, then rolled it over again, wrapped thumb and forefinger around its tail, and lifted it from the streambed to hand it to Bill. Four pounds easy, though it always feels like more: a heavy fish, thick as a man's forearm and translucently white along the underbelly, like a single clenched muscle.

"God-*damn*." Bill's chest was pulsing with exertion; from under his heavy rubber waders squeaked the sour tang of sweat. He turned toward shore and held out the fish in triumph. "Hey, Pete, get a load of this!"

Pete, standing where I'd left him, had opened another beer. He raised the can in a listless toast. "Nice fish."

"What are you talking about?" Bill snarled happily. "This is a *great* fish. This is Moby goddamn *Dick*. Haven't I taught you anything, junior?"

"What do you want me to say? I think I saw one just like it at the A&P."

Bill shook his head and muttered, "Jesus, that guy." But I could see how incurably happy he was, holding this fish. "What do you think?" he asked me, wagging his eyebrows conspiratorially. "Let's keep this one."

"It's your license. State says you can keep three per day."

He made a face of disbelief. "Don't go soft on me now, Joe. Who cares what the state says? Let's you and me eat this bad boy up."

"I'm not much for salmon, to tell you the truth. But you want me to clean it up for you, I'd be glad to. Lucy can cook it for your supper if you like."

At just this moment, while we watched, the flesh beneath the fish's tail opened like a hatch and a rush of milky fluid roared out, splashing over Bill's hands and down the front of his vest. His whole body jerked like he'd been hit with an electric current as he thrust the fish away from his body.

"Christ! What the fuck is that?"

It took me a moment to realize what we'd seen. "He's a she," I explained. "Those are her eggs."

"No fucking way. That's *disgusting*."

"Hey, Bill!" Pete yelled from shore. I could hear the beer and whiskey boiling in his voice. "Looks like she digs you!"

"Will you shut the hell up?" Bill's face had gone a mild green. Still clutching the fish like a piece of firewood, he gazed down with horror at the front of his vest. The fluid had left behind pinkish clots that stuck like glue to the fabric. "God, this crap's all over me."

"It's no big deal," I said. "It happens sometimes."

He wiped his cheek with the knob of his shoulder. "Jesus."

The fish's mouth was snapping at the air in frantic little puffs, revealing gleaming fencerows of tiny, diamond-bright teeth. Much longer and the question of letting it go would be moot. Without the strength to fight the current, she'd be smashed to atoms against the rocks, or simply float downstream and drown.

"Aw, the hell with it," Bill said finally. He lifted the fish so they were nose to nose, and spoke into its face. "Okay, missy, I guess today's your lucky day." At that he stepped out a few feet into deeper water, wobbling a little on the rocks; with a splash the fish was gone.

I watched him watch it go. It was just past four, a tricky hour: the sun had slid behind us, dipping the stream in shadow, while above us the dam's sloping wall seemed to swell with captured light. The mist from the outlets washed over us in breeze-fed bursts, the air sun-warmed one minute and ice-cold the next, like a drafty old house in winter. All that water, all that stone. Around us, a thousand square miles of empty forest, a whole forgotten world of it and enough silence to let you hear the planet spin, or make you mad, if you thought too long about it. I sniffed my hand where I had touched the fish: clean, and a little salty, like blood. And then I saw I *was* bleeding. The hook or maybe a lucky snap of the fish's jaw I hadn't felt: I made a fist and a bullet of blood bubbled from the ball of flesh between my thumb and forefinger, a perfect little orb that made me think of a time, long ago, when somebody had brought a telescope up to the camp and showed me Mars.

Bill had returned to where I was standing in the moist silt at the edge of the streambed. "You cut yourself, Joe?"

I shrugged and licked it away. Just a drop, but it filled my mouth, all my senses curling around the metallic taste of blood.

"It's nothing," I said. "A scratch."

Dear Joe, Lucy wrote:

I hope you're all right, and don't mind hearing from me like this. I wanted to tell you that your father is well. It's a long story, and I hope that sometime I have the chance to tell you all of it. His situation at the Rogues' was pretty bad, and I'm glad you wrote to tell me where he was. I only wish I'd gotten up there sooner. But he's home now and finally on the mend, after a bout with pneumonia and what turned out to be a kidney infection that gave us all a scare. Please don't worry, as I am looking after him, and Paul Kagan comes out once a week to tell him to do whatever I say and take his pills and do his best to eat.

I've decided to stay on at the camp through the summer, and here's the big news—we actually managed to open! After all that's happened, it seems almost a miracle. I'd like to take the credit, but I can't. A few days after we got here, people just started showing up—turns out your father never canceled any of the advance reservations—and it was either open for the season or turn them away. The truth is, I was all set just to lock the gate and forget the whole thing, but here's surprise number two: the first person to show up was none other than Harry Wainwright! (I still remember that night on the porch by cabin nine—what a shock we gave him! I still swear I told you cabin six. How long ago that all seems now.) It was Harry's idea to open, and now the two of us are more or less running the place, or trying to. It seems a little strange, a man like Harry running around with fresh towels and handing out picnic lunches and hauling out the kitchen trash, but Harry says he doesn't mind, far from it, and he's even taught me a little bit about how to do the books. We're badly in the red, by the way. According to Harry, your father pretty much ran his finances out of an old coffee can, and hasn't paid a cent of tax to the county since about the time you left. Harry has spent most evenings the last two weeks just trying to put it all in some kind of order we can get a handle on. The general word is that with a few more bookings we may be okay by the end of the season, as long as we can get by with only a couple of part-time guides and one girl in the kitchen. Harry also has a scheme to poach a few tourists from the Lakeland Inn with a kind of daylong outing to look for moose. I can't see that this will make much difference, but Harry says it could bring in some nice extra money.

In a way it's a lucky turn for Harry too. I'm sure you remember that his wife was very sick, and she passed away last spring. Harry didn't tell me this right away, but I could tell something had happened—I more or less guessed what it was—and when he finally came out with it, a lot of things suddenly fell into place in my mind. He seems very grateful to have something to do, and for now, the camp is keeping both of us plenty busy.

Well, Joe. Should I say that I miss you? I do, maybe more than ever. It's very strange to be here without you, like I'm still feeling a part of my body that's just not there anymore. I thought I'd gotten used to it, but I guess I really haven't. I'm sorry about everything, especially that I disappeared the way I did. But I think it was the best thing for both of us. My parents are still furious, will barely say a word to me, though when I see my mother she always hugs me very hard, which makes me feel just terrible.

We are all glued to the television over the election, and wondering what it will mean for you. I don't know if you know this, but the other big news down here is that eighteen-year-olds can vote. I hardly remember being eighteen. But I know I would have voted against that asshole Nixon (pardon my French!), so maybe there's hope. Your father says McGovern's a saint, and saints never stand a chance. Oh, well. What he means is, we all want you home. Me, too.

Take care of yourself, Joe.

All my love,
Lucy

There was a woman, of course, as Lucy guessed—not the one who made the bracelets, a widow who kept a little shop next door to one of the town's three bad bars, but her oldest girl, Michelle: a divorced woman in her forties with hair the color of dry tobacco, a seven-year-old daughter, and a sad but warming smile. Jobs outside the plant were scarce but Michelle had a good one, working for LeMaitre's little newspaper, laying type and editing the classifieds, which, in a town where everything was theoretically for sale if a catch was light, took up ninety percent of its pages. For some time, the better part of a year, we took care of one another, doing all the small things and exchanging all the customary comforts, and if I never told her I loved her, this seemed at the time a small thing, a minor lack. About her ex-husband, Naomi's father, Michelle spoke not one single word in all the time I knew her.

The day I received the letter from Lucy began at 5:00 A.M., me and half a dozen other lumpers standing around the wharf in our oilskins and boots in the predawn cold, waiting for the plant crew to show and smoking first cigarettes; once the work started, it would be another three hours before any of us could smoke again. The *High Chaparral* was in, fifty feet of rust and stink, sitting low in the oily water, its belly fat with fish.

When the plant whistle blew, Marcel came down to where we were standing.

"The usual shares, gents," he announced, and lit a smoke of his own. "Three dollars a thousand. Deckman gets a buck. Joe and Lewis in the hold, Larry works the jilson. Let's be quick now, get this done by noon."

We stepped aboard and lifted the hatch, careful not to leave it upside down—bad luck for certain—then descended the rattling aluminum ladder into the hold, a clammy alley running the length of the ship, with four pens on either side and a big one across the stern, all of it lighted only by the fretted glare of a couple of bare bulbs in metal cages. In the pens, behind pieces of plywood nailed in place, lay seventy thousand pounds of cod, blackbacks, and pollock, cocooned in ice.

Larry yelled down through the hatch when the jilson was set: "Flats first!" he said, meaning cod.

We moved to the forward pen, used an ice shaver to jimmy loose the pen boards, and ice and fish poured out. I filled my basket and hooked it to the jilson, gave it a yank.

"Yuuuuup!"

Away it went, snatched from the hold and out over the wharf, where Larry guided it into the hopper; from there it would be wheeled up to the long tables of the plant, gutted and filleted, the meat then packed again in ice and loaded on trucks to carry it to Boston or New York or Montreal. The trick was to keep the baskets coming, so that by the time Larry lowered the jilson again, another was ready to go.

For a year I'd worked the tables for wages, or else manned the loading docks. Lumping the hold was harder work, but it paid better: at three bucks for every thousand pounds of fish, split two ways plus a dollar for Larry, we'd walk away with a hundred and five dollars in our pockets, all before lunch.

"Yuuuuup!"

Lewis was Canadian, a lifer, his face red as a slab of steak. We'd worked together a year and had a rhythm down: one of us would step into a pen with a short-handled pitchfork to shovel it out, while the other loaded the jilson, the two of us trading places with every basket to keep the jilson moving.

"Yuuuuup!"

At nine we stopped to smoke. Five pens were empty, including the big one at the stern. Both of us had stripped down to our oilskins and gloves, the sweat steaming off us in the dark hold, the meaty vapors of our bodies mixing with the gunmetal smell of fish and ice. Lewis nudged me with his elbow.

"Drink?"

Lewis passed me his flask. I wiped off the spout, took a sip, and passed it back. Both of us knew not to stop long enough to light a second cigarette. We were better than half done but the last half was always the largest.

"You going out on the Bodie?" he asked me after a minute.

The *Chase Bodine* had come in a week before; the captain was assembling a crew for a run to the Grand Banks and had offered me a spot.

"Might. Can't say."

"Ford's been hitting." Lewis took a long drag on his cigarette and exhaled, using his pinky to pluck a fleck of tobacco from his tongue.

He examined it a moment, like it might be something he needed, before flicking it away. "Everyone says so. There's at least three thousand in it this time of year. That's good money."

"So why don't you go?"

He laughed out smoke. "Thirty days, a thousand miles out? Gives me the willies just thinking about it. And Ford didn't offer, either." He crushed out the last of his cigarette. "Back to work, Joey."

We sent the last of the fish up to the plant a little after noon, scooped out the rest of the ice and dumped it overboard, and hosed down the hold. It was one o'clock when I walked up to the plant office. Marcel ran his enterprise with a machinelike efficiency, but his office looked like a hurricane had hit it: piles of paper everywhere, file cabinets full to bursting, invoices and shipping orders and punchcards for employees long gone stacked on every surface. One time I'd noticed, held in place between the mounds of paper, a half-full cup of coffee, tipped at a thirty-degree angle and somehow suspended at least six inches above the desktop. It hadn't spilled a drop.

Marcel removed an envelope of cash from the top drawer and handed it to me: a hundred and five, plus ten more. I held up the extra bill.

"What's this for?"

He smiled, pleased I'd noticed. "A little bonus. For finishing by noon."

"We didn't, Marcel. We only just got done five minutes ago."

"I put ten in Lewis's envelope too. I don't hear him complaining."

I deposited the envelope in the chest pocket of my slicker. "That's because Lewis only has nine fingers to count on. You know, this is no way to run a business."

"Maybe not, but I'll do as I like." He leaned back in his chair. "Listen, Joe, I heard Ford Conklin's offered you a spot on the Bodie. You considering it?"

The truth was, I'd barely thought about it. "Might be. The money's good. Everybody says Ford's been doing well."

Marcel gave a measured nod. "He has. Ford's put more than a few dollars in my pocket, I'll say that. But the banks are a haul, Joe. And it's getting late in the season. I'll tell you, if it were up to me, I'd say what the hell, go. But Abby, she's not so hot on the idea." He paused and looked out the window beyond his desk. It was a sunless day, the seaway and the sky above both gray as slabs of granite. Far off to the north, a pair of tankers plied the water at the crook of the horizon. Twenty thousand deadweight tons of oceangoing steel apiece, though at this distance, they looked no bigger than a couple of tin toys moving through the crosshairs in a carnival shooting gallery. "Anyway," Marcel said, and rapped his desk, "I just thought I'd tell you. If it makes a difference, I might be having an opening for a foreman in the next couple of weeks. With you the paperwork's a little funny, of course, but I think we could work something out. And we sure could use you."

I'm sure my face showed my surprise. "Thanks."

"Just keep it in mind. And the person you should thank is Abby, because this is really her idea." He turned to one of the piles, fingering the contents, and produced an envelope. "Before I forget, this came to the house this morning."

He handed me the letter over his desk, and at once I saw it was from Lucy. With anybody else I might have waited to read it, but not Marcel. He and Abby had taken good care of me, and if my time of exile had a bright spot, it was those two. I took a chair before his desk, its great towers of paper, and read.

"Everything all right?" Marcel asked me when I was done.

I folded the letter and tucked it into my slicker with Marcel's envelope of money. "Sure. Why wouldn't it be?"

"No reason. Just, a lot of guys get letters from home, it's not necessarily good news." For a moment neither of us spoke. "Well, think about the other, won't you?"

"I will," I said, and rose to go. "Thanks, Marcel. I really will give it some thought."

I saw Ford that night at the Breakaway. Michelle was with me; she had left her daughter, Naomi, with her mother, our custom on nights when either of us had just been paid. Like all the bars in town, the Break-away was little more than a dirty box to drink in, the scene of so many fistfights of such chaotic brutality that the owners had long since given up replacing the glass in the front windows and just left them boarded up. We decided to spring for a couple of real drinks, good Scotch in tumblers instead of the fifty-cent beers we otherwise drank. We were drinking our second when I saw Ford come in.

In a town like LeMaitre, a fishing boat captain, particularly one who was making money, has an exalted status. As Ford moved through the bar, the crowds parted in his path, all eyes on him and measuring his progress as he approached our table.

"Joe." He removed his cap and raked his fingers back through his pepper-gray hair; around us the crowds returned to their beer and talk. "Shelle."

"Have a seat, Ford?"

His eyes moved over the table. "Not just now, thanks. Heard the *High Chap* brought in seventy thousand."

I shook the ice in my glass. "Felt like more."

He nodded equably. "That's what we like to hear. Everybody making money. I don't like to press, Joe, but I've got a crew to put together. Had a chance to think about my offer?"

Early that morning, talking to Lewis, I'd found myself thinking I'd go; but now I wasn't so sure. It wasn't Lucy's letter, or even Marcel's offer of a better job, that had unsettled me, but something else Marcel had said: that Abby didn't want me to go. It felt like an omen, and I had been around the docks long enough to have picked up more than a trace of superstition. Nonsense, but there it was. On the other hand, three grand was three grand.

"A four percent share, Joe. Can't hold your place much longer."

"Who else is interested?"

"Lots of folks. Lewis O'Day, for one."

"Lewis?"

"Spoke to me this afternoon. Said you could have first crack, but if you didn't want it, he'd sign on. I'd rather have you."

Michelle scoffed and ground out her cigarette in the ashtray we had already half filled. "That old rumhound? He'd probably fall overboard before you left the dock."

Ford rubbed his chin thoughtfully, eyes narrowed. "No secret he drinks. But he's been out to sea plenty in his day. I'm thinking I could rely on him well enough. And he's clear he wants to go."

I finished my drink and returned the empty glass to the table. The Scotch I'd drunk, or the thought of Lewis taking my place: whatever the reason, declining Ford's offer suddenly seemed foolish, all air with nothing to push against. Abby would worry, but that was Abby. Nothing was keeping me here. A month at sea—what did I have to lose?

"Okay," I said, and gave my glass a conclusive thump on the wood. "Count me in."

Michelle sat up abruptly. "Joe—"

I didn't let her finish. I looked at Ford again. "When do we leave?"

"Tuesday next. Back at the end of September."

"All right. I'll be there, Ford."

He left us to go find the pay phone, and I turned my attention to Michelle. She was sitting stock-still, her spine straight against the back of the booth.

"What?"

"Why did you *do* that?"

"What's the matter, Shelle? The money's good, you know that."

She laughed bitterly, looking away. "How can I be so goddamn stupid?"

"What are you talking about?"

As her eyes caught the light I saw a glint of tears. But her face was hard, her jaw set. "You think I don't know what you're doing? I've been down this road before."

"What road, Shelle? Are you listening? It's just a month."

"Foreman, Joe. That's a *good job*. You didn't even ask me."

I reached my hand across the table to touch her arm, but she pulled away.

"Don't," she said, and sat back, her palms raised, her face almost in a panic. "Just . . . forget it, Joe. Will you? Please? Do me a favor and forget it." Her eyes fell to the table and she shook her head again. "What the hell is wrong with me? Why am I such a fucking idiot?"

"I really don't know what the problem is, Shelle. We're going to the banks, that's all."

"Great, the banks. Have fun. Look us up when you get back, okay?"

A moment of silence passed. She lit another cigarette.

"Shelle—"

"That's not the point, Joe." She rose to her feet, not looking at me, and crushed out the cigarette she had only just lit, three hard stubs into the ashtray. "You asshole," she said, and before I could answer— Michelle's last words to me still ringing in my ears—I was sitting alone at the table with my empty glass.

We returned in October, ahead of the weather, making port on a day so bright with autumn sun that the surface of the sea seemed shattered. I'd said good-bye to no one—not Michelle, or Lewis, or even Abby and Marcel—and no one was waiting on the wharf to meet me. I wanted it that way. Michelle had seen it before I had. After that night at the bar, I knew what four years had turned me into: a man without love, on whom any kind of love was wasted. Once the hold was cleaned and tallied, I went to the weighing station with my duffel bag, took my share, and marched straight out to the loading docks behind the plant. A single refrigerated truck was parked there, the driver sitting on the running board, reading a fat paperback.

I held up my duffel bag to show him. "Mind some company?"

He lifted his broad face, squinting into the sun behind me. I hadn't shaved or showered and had lost so much weight my pants were cinched tight at the waist with a lanyard. In my pocket, Ford's wad of folded cash, three thousand and change, felt fat as a bar of soap.

He made no expression at all. "Don't you want to know where I'm going?"

"Okay. Where are you going?"

He folded down a corner of the page to mark his place and closed his book. I glimpsed the title: *The Godfather.* "Toronto."

It didn't seem far. "How about after that?"

"Iowa."

"Iowa? What's in Iowa?"

"Three vowels." He slapped his knees and laughed like he'd been waiting his whole life to tell this joke. "Hell if I know what else."

I thought about the border, and what might happen to me there. But I had already decided I didn't care. "Sounds perfect," I said, and heaved my bag up into the cab, though that was the easy part—I'd carried everything with me, and it still weighed almost nothing.

EIGHTEEN

Lucy

Kate was right: I needed to go see Harry.

Still, I knew I wasn't the reason he had come, not anymore. All that was over and done. For years and years, since the summer after Kate turned four, he'd made his annual trip, fished a little, eaten in the dining hall, even smoked a cigar or two with Joe out on the dock as the years went by. "Harry, good to see you," we'd all say in the driveway when he pulled in, and he'd shake Joe's hand and kiss me quickly on the cheek, and ask about the water or the weather, and although for a week the place would seem different to me, simply because Harry was in it, it was a bargain we'd all learned to live with. More than live with: I can honestly say it made me happy.

Harry made me happy.

I saw him just one other time, at Joe's father's funeral. This was, in fact, the only time in my life that I saw Harry Wainwright in a season not summer. The icy depths of January: Kate was still little enough to sit on my knee, big and squirmy enough that it took all my effort to keep her there. The service was held in a small, wood-framed chapel that usually closed for the winter, though it was a pretty spot, framed like a picture by tall pines with a creek off to one side and a view of Long Ridge, and when somebody in town died in the off-season, it was understood that arrangements could be made.

Joe's father's last couple of years had not been easy. Though he'd rebounded from the stroke, a bad cold the following winter ballooned into pneumonia again, this time landing him in the hospital on oxygen, and while he was there, the doctors diagnosed him with a fast-moving lymphoma that had already spread to the nodes around his stomach. It was supposed to take six months but in the end took three times that, and though all the doctors attributed this delay to a simple case of north-country grit—the phrase, unspoken but always understood, was "too mean to die"—I knew what he was really waiting for. In October '75, Joe finished the last of his sentence at the federal prison camp at Fort Devens, rode the bus home to all of us, and was with his father two months later when he passed away.

It was a small group that gathered that morning, maybe thirty people, though the room was tight and seemed full. The building had no central heating, but one of the chapel's board members had come in early to light the small woodstove, which now gave off a crackling, wooly warmth, enough to make people unzip, but not remove, their coats. My parents were there, and the few friends Joe's dad had managed to keep over the years, and one surprise: Hank Rogue. I hadn't laid eyes on him since the day I'd clocked him with the bourbon bottle, and I honestly couldn't be certain he even remembered who I was. My first impression, seeing him, was pure amazement: he was one of those people who seemed to have vanished completely from my life, to such an extent that I somehow assumed he'd died. He took a pew right up front on the opposite side, holding his cap on his knees and speaking to no one, and when I looked over at him, hoping to catch his eye—a wicked impulse, I confess, to extract some acknowledgment of my victory over him that June day—I was astonished to see that his pockmarked face was streaked with tears.

Joe's father hadn't wanted a religious service; he hadn't been to a church of any kind in twenty years. But to do nothing seemed desolate, and at the last minute I'd talked Joe into letting Father Molyneaux, the priest from the Catholic church over in Twining, say a few words. He was stepping up to the lectern when I felt a whisper of cold air on my neck and swiveled around to see Harry standing at the open chapel door, stamping his feet and dusting blown snow from the sleeves of his overcoat. He caught my eye and gave a little wave.

"How did he know?" I whispered to Joe.

Joe had lost a lot of weight during his time at Fort Devens, but I hadn't really noticed how much until that moment, when I saw how loose his collar was around his neck. Like all the men in the room, he was wearing a tie beneath his parka. He answered without looking at me. "I called him."

"You did that?"

His voice was terse; he was in no mood to talk. "My father wanted him here."

Father Molyneaux said the usual prayers, we all sang a hymn— badly, for we had no accompaniment to help us find the right key— and then Joe stepped to the front of the room.

"Well," he began, and nervously cleared his throat. I thought I saw him glance to the back of the chapel to find Harry. "Thank you all for coming. At least we have a nice day for this, right?" A titter of laughter floated over the room; in my lap, Kate wriggled and looked about, wondering what the joke was.

"I'm no good at this sort of thing," Joe went on, "and it's cold. All I want to say is, my father would have appreciated everyone being here. I've been away awhile, but in the last couple of months he talked a lot about this place, and how much it meant to him. He also talked a lot about the war. We're here to remember him, and I guess the easiest way to sum up my father is to say that he was a soldier. I know that idea may seem strange to some, but I think everybody who's here knows that's true. On the morning he was wounded, he had served 342 days as a battlefield platoon leader, and he hated everything about it. But he loved his men, and when the war was over, he loved this place. He wasn't always the happiest man, or the easiest to get along with, and I'm guessing some of you know that"—Joe paused as a second frisson of knowing laughter moved through the crowd—"but he also was the bravest man I ever knew. It took me a long time, maybe right up until these last couple of months, to really understand this."

Joe stopped again, opened his mouth as if he were going to say something else, but then seemed to change his mind. "Anyway, that's all. Like I said, it's cold. Thank you, everyone, for coming."

A few other people got up to speak, most to tell a story or two about a nice thing Joe Sr. had done for them, and then Father

Molyneaux led us in a closing prayer. When this was done, Joe returned to the front of the room and gave the signal for the pallbearers to come forward. Six men: Joe, of course, my father, Paul Kagan, Porter Dante, a man Joe had introduced me to earlier that day as Marcel Lebeau, and, striding from the back of the church, still in his smoke-gray chesterfield overcoat and cashmere scarf, Harry. They arranged themselves around the casket, three on a side with my father and Joe at the front, and hoisted it onto their shoulders. For an awful moment I think everyone worried they might drop it—a casket is a heavy thing, no matter who's inside—but they gave no sign of strain, and without a word they carried it straight through the church and outside to the waiting hearse. There would be no burial until spring; for now, the casket would go to the funeral home, where it would wait for the ground to thaw.

"What's inna box?" Kate asked, too loudly, as they passed.

I gripped her mittened hands to shush her. "Your grandfather," I whispered.

Outside, the sun was blinding bright, making the air seem somehow colder, and I scanned the lot with a hand over my eyes, Kate wedged to my hip. But I didn't see Harry anywhere, and all the cars were ones I knew and could connect to someone inside—the rusted sedan I knew to be Paul's, Porter's big Ford pickup with the plough in front, my father's old Lincoln Continental, even Hank Rogue's filthy drilling rig, like a big grease stain on the snow. Harry's Jag was nowhere to be seen. Joe was leaning down into the front window of the hearse, speaking with the driver; a moment later he tapped the roof and off it went. Somebody asked me if folks were going for coffee, meaning the Pine Tree Café, since that was the only place in town open in winter, and I said I guessed we were.

It wasn't until we were in bed for the night that I asked Joe about Harry. In the odd, intervening hours, first at the restaurant and then back at the lodge as we made supper and got Kate bathed and down for the night, I had actually begun to wonder if I'd seen him at all, or had somehow imagined this. A little over three years had passed since we'd said our last good-bye, and his sudden, unannounced appearance at the church door, and his equally abrupt disappearance into the bright sun and snow, combined in my mind to give the whole thing a feeling of unreality.

"So that was really Harry," I said.

We were lying close together but not touching, our bodies registering the fact that the two of us were still not quite used to being together again. And in a way, it felt like our first real night under the same roof as married people. I had been able to see him during his two years at the prison camp at Fort Devens, but these visits were awkward and sad, the two of us sitting across from one another at a cafeteria table under a big clock that ticked off each minute we had together, while a pair of bored MPs did their best to look like they're weren't listening. When Joe had finally come home, his father had been there with us all those nights, Joe and I taking shifts to tend to him and barely ever asleep in the same bed together.

Joe nodded against the pillow. "Yeah, that was Harry."

I nestled against him and put my face close to his. "That was good of you, Joe. To call him, I mean."

"It wasn't my idea," he said flatly. "Like I said, Dad asked me to."

"Even so. I'm sure he appreciated it."

I heard him sigh. "What's done is done."

Just then I heard Kate's soft, barefooted trudge; I lifted my head to find her standing by our bed, clutching her ratty old baby blanket. She still wasn't used to seeing anyone else in bed with me, and seemed to view Joe as a perplexing intrusion—nearly every night since Joe had gone away she had spent part or even all of her nights snuggled under the covers with me, just the two of us. My mother had scolded me for this, said it was a bad habit she would never grow out of, but I'd let Kate do it as much for me as for her.

"What is it, honey? Do you need to go?"

She rubbed her eyes and stretched her jaw in a dreamy, loose-jointed yawn that I knew meant she was still asleep, or mostly. "Come up," she said quietly.

I drew back the covers and extended a hand to help her into bed. Without a word she rolled her weight over my chest and wedged herself down between me and Joe, pulling her baby blanket to her face and finding her mouth with her thumb. In another moment came the soft sound of her sucking, a rhythm so closely aligned with my own heart's beating that it seemed to come from inside me. Even before she was born I had felt her as a vivid physical presence, each hiccup and poke like the tapping of a private code, as if to say: I'm here. Once, in my third trimester on a night I couldn't sleep, I swore I heard her singing.

Joe's voice rose into the darkness. "Luce?"

"Uh-huh?" Kate's face was inches from my own, swarming my senses with the damp, doughy scent of her skin and hair.

"It's all right," Joe said, his voice so soft I could barely hear him. He reached over Kate to touch me, his fingers finding the hard bone of my elbow and resting there. "It's all right," he said again. "It's all over now. Let's go to sleep."

August 1972. The camp had been up and running six weeks. A blur of days: I was overseeing the kitchen and taking care of the cabins and even guiding when there was no one else to do it, not that I knew a blessed thing about fishing; I just took my parties where Harry told me to go and pointed at the water. Besides the regular guests we had couples coming in from the Lakeland Inn nearly every morning to take the canoe trip down the river—Harry's idea had turned out right as rain, a solid money maker—and as soon as breakfast was over I would load up the truck and run a group to the put-in point, racing back in time to start lunch, move a load of towels to the dryer, call the party supply company down in Portland to order the old movies we were showing in the lodge every Saturday night on a clicky old projector. I had taken up residence in one of the upstairs bedrooms—though I'd brought a few things over from my parents' house, I was mostly still living out of the suitcase I'd taken with me to Boston, all those months ago. At night I fell into bed so bone-weary that I doubted anything short of an atomic blast would awaken me; but then as the clock inched toward five I'd find myself awake and counting cracks in the ceiling, my body twitching like a teenager's, and before the sun was up I'd rise from bed, put on my bathing suit in the predawn cold, and spend the first thirty minutes of the morning swimming up and down the shoreline, sixty laps from dock to headland, each turn of my head showing me a patch of sky that was one shade lighter than it was before.

And as I swam each morning I thought: Lucy, you are happy. Lucy, you are alive, you are living your actual life. But then I thought of Joe, and knew this wasn't so. I was living *our* life, the one we'd planned and hoped for; but I was doing this without him.

And then I thought of Harry.

To say that what transpired was a simple case of mistaken identity me for Meredith, Harry for Joe—would not be completely wrong, and in hindsight I suppose that's the explanation all parties involved have decided it's easiest to live with, not that anybody's ever said as much. But it's also true that what happened that summer—beginning with the moment I discovered Harry on the dock and threw my arms around him, crying with relief, the hug and my tears embarrassing both of us so badly that another month would pass before we would actually touch each other again, even in passing—was a thing in its own right, a simple fact, as time and tides are facts. I did not fall in love with Harry, nor he with me, but *something* fell, and when it did, what remained was the two of us standing in a moment that felt as if neither past nor future had any place within it, that time was flowing all around it like a stream around a rock, and that this moment would be sealed forever, a secret life the two of us had lived together.

So I swam and cooked and slept and rose each day to start it all again, and all the while I felt my mind moving toward something, though at the time I could not say exactly what: there was pleasure in wondering what it could be, and I didn't want to examine it too closely, so as not to scare it away.

Joe's dad was still weak—the kidney infection had finally landed him down in Farmington for five days, when he confessed to passing blood—and Paul Kagan had instructed us not to let him do very much at all. He took his meals in the kitchen and used the rear stairs to go

back and forth to his room, keeping out of sight except for the odd afternoon when I helped him down to the dock to smoke and read his
paper, or Harry drove him to Paul's office in town for a checkup. On
the busiest days it was possible to forget he was there at all. I thought
he'd want to help Harry with the books, but even this idea seemed not
to interest him: if I hadn't known better, I might have thought he'd
simply given up. But in my heart I believed this couldn't happen, not
until Joe was finally home.

I knew the money situation was tight, but not how bad, until a Friday evening in August when Harry told me what was going on. It was
past ten, everything buttoned down for the night, and the two of us
were drinking a beer in the office while we went over a few invoices
and computed the week's payroll. The end of the season was in view—
the birches had taken on a faded, exhausted look, and that morning I'd
noticed dry leaves underfoot as I walked the trace to the cabins—and I
think both of us felt the speed of its approach. What lay beyond was a
mystery, for both of us. Harry's house in New York had been sold; the
buyers had asked if he'd be interested in selling the furniture, and he'd
let them have that too. He still had his company, but he almost never
spoke of this, and I had the feeling he almost wished he didn't. He was
mulling over a few ideas about what to do next, including reactivating
his merchant mariner's rating and going back to sea; one night he told
me a story about a man he'd known during the war, a lifelong mariner
who played guitar on deck at night, and how he'd heard in the notes
that came from his strings the whole history of his life, a sweet sadness
Harry had carried inside him ever since, and how he had always
wanted to go back to sea again, to learn what was in that music. As for
me, I had decided to stay at least through the winter to take care of
Joe's dad. After that, I didn't know.

We finished up our paperwork and Harry went to the kitchen to
get us each a second beer—probably not the best idea, given the hour,
but it was surprisingly easy to say yes. More and more I'd found myself
reluctant to go to bed no matter how tired I was, especially if Harry
was up and felt like talking. When he returned we went over the week's
bookings for a while, and then I asked him about the taxes.

Harry frowned. "Well, it's not good."

"How much does he owe?"

"Are you ready? A little over forty thousand dollars. Forty-one something."

The figure stopped me flat; I'd had no idea. "Jesus, Harry."

"I know, it's a lot. The good news is that local governments are usually slow about these things, especially in places like this. The records are a mess, a lot of people are in arrears. Sometimes it isn't until somebody dies that the county catches on. Then the heirs have to pay up, or the county takes the property."

"Could he borrow the money somehow?"

"He could. But he won't. And I'm making it sound simpler than it is. The county might have already filed a lien. If so, he can't borrow against the place, which is all he has for collateral. The business itself has a value of basically zero. He could maybe sell off a piece of land and satisfy the tax bill at settlement, assuming we could even find a buyer, but odds are it won't pass a title search. Then the whole thing would blow up in our face."

"How about the leases on the land on the other side?"

Harry sipped his beer. "Thought of that, too, but it won't work. Technically, all Joe has is an easement. The way the contracts are written, he'd actually have to *pay* Maine Paper to break the lease. Or so my lawyers tell me. The upshot is, more money, which Joe doesn't have."

I sat and thought. I still had my savings account, but that came to only a few thousand dollars. My car, my clothes, every possession I had—none of it amounted to more than a couple of hundred more. Forty thousand: it was beyond imagining.

"Can we negotiate with the county?"

"Maybe. But I wouldn't recommend it. They'd probably say no, for starters, and then we've tipped our hand. Once the county gets a serious look at the tax records, they could just seize the property with thirty days' notice."

"So there's nothing to do but keep our mouths shut and pay."

Harry nodded grimly. "Basically, that's it."

It was late; I caught myself yawning into my hand. A long day stretched ahead of us. A big party was coming in—three cabins, including number nine, which Harry had agreed to surrender for the week. Joe had offered him a room upstairs, but Harry had said no, the office couch would do just fine. He was always up so early, he said, it barely mattered where he slept.

"You'll be all right down here?" I asked him.

From time to time that summer, at odd moments when he probably thought no one was watching, a kind of darkness crossed his face—a flitting shadow, like a bird behind a shade. When this happened he suddenly looked much older, as if all the thoughts he toted inside were simply too much to bear, the heaviest load ever carried by a man. I saw it now. But then he gave me a slow, deliberate smile, and the shadow vanished.

"Sure thing." He looked me in the eye. "You know, you should try not to worry, Luce. This will all work out somehow."

"I just can't imagine this place being gone."

"You'll have it." He nodded. "I promise. You and Joe."

I thought for a moment he meant Joe Sr. But of course that wasn't right: he meant Joe, my Joe.

"Harry—"

He cut me off, suddenly embarrassed. "It's okay," he said. "I know . . ." He stopped. "I just know, is all."

The room had gotten very still. We were alone, and also not: Joe was there, my Joe, and also Meredith, the shadow behind Harry's eyes, and the people we had all once been: the Lucy I was at seventeen, and the Harry I had met so long ago, standing by the dining room door he'd forgotten to close. All these people, and not just our memories of them: they hovered like ghosts, like living presences among us. I looked at Harry, wondering if he had felt it too, but he gave no sign.

Finally he cleared his throat. "So—" he began.

"Right. It's late." I stood, and so did Harry. "Thanks for the beer."

"Anytime."

What did I want to tell him? That Joe was never coming back, that I had put him aside in my heart, that whatever was going to happen in my life would happen without him? But I knew that wasn't so, would never be so. Joe was why I'd come home, why I'd stopped being Alice.

And yet here we were, Harry and I, doing just what I'd always thought I'd do with Joe: the beer and talk, the close heat of the office, the feeling, deep in my bones, of days passing into days. He had stepped into the space I had held for Joe, and I suddenly wanted to kiss him, to seal this bargain, a desire so sharp it felt like pain. The thought was so powerfully alive in my mind that for a second I thought I'd actually gone ahead and done it.

"Well, good night, Lucy."

And all I said was good night.

The final Saturday of August: a day that began with a bang of thunder and sheets of soaking rain, though the temperature rose through the morning well into the eighties even as the rain poured down, so that it was both too hot and too wet to do anything but lie around like logs and complain about the weather. Saturday was checkout day: about half the cabins emptied by noon. In two more weeks we'd be closing down for the summer, though the season already felt over. With no one else going out on the water, and all the moose-canoers canceled, Harry took Joe's dad into town to Porter's for supplies, leaving me to keep the remaining guests occupied in the main room with board games and apple cobbler and pots of fresh coffee.

Just before sundown the last of the rain blew through, leaving in its wake a dome of dry air that seemed to settle in place with an audible snap. As dinner was winding down and guests were drifting out to the porch or back to their cabins, I stepped out the kitchen door and walked down to the water to take the air. All those hours cooped up in the lodge had made me antsy, and I eyed the lake hungrily, wishing I had time for a swim.

I heard the screen door slam behind me and turned to see Harry walking down the lawn. The summer had made him tanner than I'd ever seen; he was wearing khakis and an oxford cloth shirt the color of butter, wrinkled and rolled to the elbows, and for just a moment as he came and stood beside me, his hands in his pockets, I caught my mind drifting in the fan of golden hair on his ropy forearms.

"Thank God that's over," he said. "I thought we'd have a mutiny if the rain kept up." He ran a hand over the back of his head and lifted his chin toward the water. "What do you say we show the movie out here? It'd be a nice treat after today."

"On the dock, you mean?"

"Sure, why not? With this breeze the bugs won't be too bad."

I liked the idea, and while Harry went to see about chairs and setting up the screen, I returned to the office to find out what title the rental company had sent us. Usually I was working in the kitchen when it arrived by UPS on Thursday mornings, three dented canisters containing two cartoons and a feature, but not that week, and it had sat for two days on the office desk without my having a free moment even to peek. Most were old black-and-whites you could just as easily see on TV at three in the morning, cornball romances or tough-guy private-eye stuff, but the guests loved them, and when the cartoons were over and the kids whisked off to bed, it usually took less than five minutes for the grown-ups to break out the hard stuff, everybody getting cheerfully soused and yelling out the lines they knew or else bawling their eyes out.

I saw we were in luck: a couple of Road Runners, always a crowd-pleaser, followed by *Casablanca.* I'd seen it a dozen times, of course, but I still vividly remembered the first time, munching on popcorn in a friend's finished basement while her parents slept upstairs, the two of us later sneaking cigarettes in her bedroom and trying to hold them like Bogey while blowing the smoke out an open window. I grabbed a sweater and carried the canisters down to the dock, where the guests were beginning to gather. Some of the men were carrying chairs down from the dining room; Harry was fiddling with the projector, aiming a square of light at the screen and trying to get the angle just so. A hum of anticipation: the dreary day had been rescued. Above us, the first stars were coming out.

Harry looked up from the projector and grinned. "What's playing?"

"You'll see," I said, and handed him the first canister. I felt it, too; the evening was like a marvelous present, waiting to be opened. "It's perfect. People will know every line."

After the cartoons, we broke for thirty minutes so everyone could get the youngest children down for the night, then Harry started up the movie again and the bottles and paper cups came out. The ricocheting click of the projector and Bogey's smoke-cured voice muttering out his sorrows; Ingrid Bergman's enormous eyes, like pools of light floating over the water; Sam's tinkling piano and the elusive letters of transport and the final, mad dash for the airfield and the last plane out, all debts of love and honor served: "Maybe not today, maybe not tomorrow, but soon, and for the rest of your life . . ." As Rick and Louis walked away across the foggy tarmac, everybody shouted the final line and broke into applause.

Afterward the group dispersed, but no one was in the mood to sleep. Islands of conversation drifted all around the lawn and cabins, punctuated by bursts of boozy laughter. This always happened once or twice a summer: out of the blue a spontaneous party would seize the place like a fever, and nobody would make it to bed until three or four in the morning. I'd had a couple of drinks myself, Scotch with something sweet in it that someone had passed me in a paper cup. Once the chairs and projector were put away in the storage closet, I went upstairs and dressed in my suit to clear my head with a swim. Party or no, I would still be up by six to cook breakfast, even if nobody showed.

The water was cold from the rain, but I swam my laps easily, my brain still cloudy from the liquor. When I was done I lay on my back, just floating, my face lifted to a veil of stars so thick I felt I could brush them with my hand. It was almost over, my strange, happy summer, and I would have stayed that way forever if I could have, floating and looking, to freeze the feeling in my mind. Then I heard running footsteps and a splash.

"God, it's freezing!" Harry dove beneath the surface again and reappeared a few feet in front of me, treading water. "Tell me again why you do this."

I righted myself and took a step toward him. "You can stand here, you know."

He bobbed on his toes. "Oh. So I see."

He reached his hand to my face and kissed me then, or I kissed him; who kissed who I couldn't say. We kissed each other, the taste of it mixed up with the metallic flavor of the lake and the sweetened Scotch I'd drunk and all the time in which we'd never kissed each other. When we stopped I said, "What are we doing?" And then, "I'm cold."

"Where will you go, Lucy?"

"I don't know," I said. "I don't know, I don't know."

"You can come with me. We can go anywhere."

"Anywhere is not a good idea, Harry," I said. "If there's one thing I know, I'm not a girl who can just go anywhere."

"You're shivering."

My chin and then my whole body were trembling. I wanted him to kiss me again. "I've been meaning to tell you, Harry. Your eyes. There's something about them, how blue they are. So very, very blue."

"It's all right, then?"

"Yes," I said, and felt it fold around me: the feeling of a secret, and the moment of bottled time. "It's all right. It's all right, Harry."

"They've forgotten us," Harry was saying. "We're like this place. Nobody knows it but us."

We were kissing again, still kissing. "But we'll know. That's the thing, isn't it? We'll know."

"That's right," he said. "We'll always know." Then he took my hand and said, "Come on."

And that was how it happened.

Two weeks later, Harry was gone. He left behind three things. The first two I found in his cabin, meant for me. A check for forty-one thousand dollars, made out to the county. And the pills he'd planned to use to kill himself, the same ones he had used to help Meredith die.

In the two weeks that Harry and I were lovers, he told me about Meredith, and not just what happened at the end. He told me about how they had met, and fallen in love, and what she wore the day they married, and about the day Sam was born and seeing Hal that autumn evening in the driveway, holding his basketball: all of it. He took his time, letting the night pass as he told the story, the two of us curled like cats on the creaky cot in his cabin; when he finished the sun was rising, and together we swam in the lake that now seemed like it was only ours and went to the kitchen to warm ourselves with coffee and wait for the sounds from the dining room, the footsteps and clearing throats, that would mean another twelve hours would pass before we could be alone again. About the pills and his plans for them, he didn't say; but when I was cleaning out his cabin the afternoon after I'd discovered that the Jag was missing from the spot where it had sat, collecting tree sap and pollen, since June, and found them in the medicine cabinet, and then saw what they were and who they were for, I knew. *You saved me,* the pills said to me, and in my head I answered, *No, you saved me, Harry. I think we saved each other.* I opened the bottle and counted them out in my palm: thirteen, shaped like tiny eggs. Thirteen ways to sleep and dream your life away. I was standing next to the open toilet; I opened my fingers and watched them fall into the water, one by one by one, knowing they were another secret I was meant to keep, and would.

Another two weeks passed. On a bright afternoon in mid-September, I took my last swim of the year. The leaves were pouring down; the water was cold as ice under a thinning autumn sun. Around the lake, the woods flamed with a thousand hues of red and orange. I did my laps quickly, my mind on nothing, and when I was done I spread a towel on the dock to give my skin a final taste of summer.

I might have slept awhile, and dreamed, or else my thoughts were simply drifting, pushed by the currents of heat that moved along my body. I thought of my first night in my apartment in Portland, and the aurora borealis I had watched from the window in March, that curtain of shimmering, angelic light; I thought of Joe, disappearing up the gangplank of the *Jenny-Smith,* his footsteps echoing on the cold metal, and the winter sun in the curtains of the motel room where I awoke two days later; and Harry rising from the water to kiss me. A hundred images from my life, and then a hundred more, unspooling like film in the clicky projector, the sound growing louder and louder until I knew it was my heart, clicking in my chest; and beneath it the feeling, almost beyond words, that something new was moving inside me: something was happening, something was coming near. *What in the world?*

I sat bolt upright, too fast. My head felt weightless, made of air. A black wave rose to my throat, and the next thing I knew was the world turned upside down as I hung my head over the edge of the dock to vomit; and what the third thing was.

NINETEEN

Joe

I made it all the way to California before I turned around. Another ocean on another coast: the buildings, the light, the sea itself, everything was strange and wrong, bleached by the light in a way that seemed dirty. I'd arrived in LA the night before on a bus from Nogales; the hour was too late to find a place to stay, so I'd slept on a hard bench in the station, then in the morning found my way on a series of city buses to the pier in Santa Monica. I was twenty pounds underweight, my jeans and T-shirt stiff with grime; my beard, flecked with equal parts red and gray, climbed halfway up my cheeks. I'd traded the duffel bag for a backpack in New Mexico, where I'd briefly worked crating artichokes, a vegetable I'd never eaten. It was March, still winter back home. The air around the Santa Monica pier smelled of flowers and the sea. On the concrete path that edged the shore, grown men and women were roller-skating, something I thought only children did. Other people were walking, so I did too, down the shore to Venice, past the weight-lifting cages and T-shirt stands and head shops, and farther still, until I found myself on a section of beach that looked like nobody ever went there, beneath the airport glide path. I slept that night under an empty lifeguard station, listening to the heavy roar of the planes that flew so low I could feel the air compress around me as they passed; in the morning I walked back north and found a little coffee shop where I ate a buttered roll and washed up in the men's room. My face in the chipped mirror was one I hardly recognized. A feeling of finality washed over me; I'd gone as far as I could, and it wasn't enough. "Go home," I said to my reflection. "It's over. Go home, Joe."

I stepped back into the restaurant and asked the counterman if he knew where the nearest freeway on-ramp was, and he told me, with an impatient wave of his hand, that I was practically standing on it. Go out the back door, he said, walk another two blocks, and that's the 10. Take you all the way to Florida.

I arrived in town on April Fool's Day, in the cab of a logging truck that had brought me up from Portland. The driver let me out on Main Street, near the boarded-up bulk of the Lakeland Inn, before zooming off; clenching the collar of my threadbare jean jacket against the wind, I hiked up to the pay phone to call the lodge.

I had been gone a little over four years—four years, five months, and an odd number of days—and I knew I should have felt *something*, joy or sadness or maybe just relief. But the truth is, all I felt was tired. There was no other place for me to go, no spot on earth for me but the one I was finally in, even if that would be taken from me soon enough. I wondered how long it would take before I was arrested, who would see me first and make the call. But even this question aroused in me little more than a passing curiosity, as if I were thinking of another person entirely, some unlucky soul I had heard about on the television news in Albuquerque or over a pitcher of beer in a taproom in Omaha. As I stood in the booth, breathing on my bare hands for warmth and listening to the phone in the lodge ringing for the twentieth, unanswered time, a VW Squareback coasted by me. The driver, a youngish woman I didn't recognize—Shellie Wister, though I didn't know that then—turned her head to give me a long, appraising look as she passed. For an instant I felt my stomach twist with fear, then thought how stupid this was. For all anybody could tell from the window of a moving car, I was just some vagrant, using the telephone.

The only thing to do was walk. I stepped from the booth and looked at the sky, a churning bulk of gray. The ground was bare, but that meant nothing; I had left in snow, and unless I missed my guess, I would be returning in it too.

I arrived at the camp in darkness, half frozen. For the last five miles I had walked with my fingers in my mouth. Only a single light glowed from the living room. The weather had held off, but you could taste snow in the air. I tried the front door but it was locked, so I went around back to the kitchen, where we had always hidden a key on a nail, and let myself in.

I should have been hungry, but the cold had taken my appetite away; it was all I could do to get a fire going and huddle on the sofa with a blanket around me. Eventually I slept, and awoke to a sweep of headlights across the ceiling. The sound of the front door squeaking open on its hinges, and voices murmuring in the hall: one was my father's, the other I knew but couldn't place. I watched from the sofa as the two men made their way into the darkened room and fumbled for the light switch.

"Joey, Jesus Christ!"

My father, backlighted in the golden glow of the lamp, stood before me. My first impression was that he had become old, an old man. His face had yellowed like newspaper; his hair was nearly gone. He stood oddly, leaning slightly to one side, supporting his weight on a silver cane, which, at the instant I saw it, he dropped with a slap on the hard plank floor. The last of his strength seemed to be leaving him at just that moment.

"Joey, Joey, my God."

I rose and put my arms around him. "It's all right, Dad. I'm home."

"Joey, Joey."

"I tried to call. I got no answer."

"We were at the hospital." The voice was the second man's; I'd almost forgotten he was there. I brought the image into focus: Paul Kagan.

"The hospital." I looked at Paul. "What's wrong? Is he all right?"

My father shook his head. "It's not me. It's Lucy."

"Lucy? What's wrong?"

"When did you come back?" my father said. "You should have told me, Joey."

"Dad, what are you talking about? What's at the hospital?"

"Your daughter, Joey." He looked me firmly in the eye. "Lucy wouldn't tell me, but I knew. Your daughter was born last night."

And so a family story was made: how I had returned the previous summer, unknown, under cover of darkness, to be with Lucy; and how eight months later, knowing the child we had conceived on that visit was about to be born, I had come home to claim her, and face the music of my life. A story in which I was in one way a hero, and another way not; but a story nevertheless, built foursquare on the moment when my father looked me in the eye and told me Kate was mine, and I didn't say a word, my silence saying yes. I never learned if he knew the truth, and even in the final weeks of his life I didn't find the courage to ask him. But my heart tells me he did not; one thing my father never could do was lie. He might have had an easier life if this had been possible, but it simply wasn't.

We brought Lucy and Kate home two days later. Lucy had gone into labor early on the morning of the first day of her thirty-fifth week, and when my father couldn't get Paul Kagan on the phone, he had somehow driven her down to Farmington. By the time they arrived her labor had stopped, but they admitted her anyway, and when her contractions returned the following evening, my father was there. These were the old days, when a man at a birth (except for the doctor— *always* a man) was as rare as a comet in a June sky, so when I say my father was present, I mean sitting just outside the room, probably hankering hard for a cigarette nobody would let him smoke. One Joe Crosby in place of another: he told me he'd been glad to do it and knew I would have been there if I could.

Lucy was very weak, and the day we brought her home the snow, which had held itself at bay, arrived: a heavy spring storm, flakes the size of pennies that fell from an absolutely windless sky, so that the only sound to be heard was just that: the sound of falling snow. The power failed the next evening, a beautiful, sudden dimming that seemed to freeze time, taking the furnace and phones with it, and then the cold slid in behind the snow, a heart-stopping plunge that set a record for the month of April when, on the second day, the temperature hit minus twenty-two. Lucy's early labor had been caused by high blood pressure, and the drugs they'd given her to keep her from seizing left her ill and exhausted, almost unable to talk. I nailed blankets over the windows and filled the hearth with wood, and when Kate wasn't feeding I took her with me to the big room by the fireplace, where I held her against my bare chest under piles of old quilts. I didn't know a thing about babies, but it turned out I didn't need to. It happened like this: She was another man's child, and then she wasn't. I held my little five-pound Kate against my skin, each one of my senses tuned to the little puffs of air that moved from her chest as she breathed and slept, and as the days slid by, taking all my loneliness with them, that's what she became: my Kate.

My story should end there, and in a way it does: lying on the sofa under the blankets, I agreed to be her father, that this would be my life from now on. I married Lucy, as I had always meant to, and when my father died, the camp became ours, Lucy's, Kate's, and mine, and it was a life I was happy to have. But between those days of cold and Kate and everything else, there was one thing left to do.

At the end of the fourth day the power came on, and the next morning I heard the sound of chained tires outside: Porter Dante, pushing his plow. I put on my coat and boots and slogged through waist-deep snow to fetch a shovel from the shed; it was still below freezing, so the snow was dry, but it still took the rest of the morning to dig out the truck and clear a walkway to the door. After so many days inside, my body took gratefully to the work, and by the time I was through I had stripped down to a T-shirt and was still sweating like a prize-fighter. My father always kept a pack of Larks in the glove compartment of his truck; I shook one out and lit it, my first in months, and sat on the porch steps to watch the smoke from my lungs drift away into the snowy limbs. When I was done I smoked another, tossed the butts away, and returned to the house.

Lucy and Kate were sleeping. My father was sitting in the kitchen, nursing a cup of tea.

"We're out of everything," I said. "The roads are probably clear by now. I thought I'd go into town."

"You smell like smoke. Didn't think you did that anymore."

I shrugged. "I don't, not really. I helped myself to a couple of yours, though."

He sighed, rising to rinse his cup. On a shelf above the sink was an old mayonnaise jar where he kept a few bills; balancing on his cane, he reached into it and handed me a twenty.

"Just be careful," he said.

The IGA was open but the shelves were nearly bare, picked clean in the panicked hours before the storm. I took what I could find—milk, eggs, instant coffee, a package of bacon, a big bag of Oreos, some cans of beans and vegetables and a jumbo pack of diapers—and loaded it all in the truck. The sun had finally broken through the clouds, a welcome sight, and the streets were already half flooded with slushy runoff. Despite my father's warning I wasn't worried about being seen, not really; the storm seemed to have wiped everything, all other cares, away.

I was a mile from the county road when Darryl Tanner's police cruiser appeared at the crest of the next hill. Too late: there was nowhere to turn, no way to pull off and let him pass without seeing me. I dropped my speed to the limit, forty-five, and prayed my beard would be enough to throw him off the trail, though of course there was no way to disguise the truck itself, a pea-green '58 Ford with the camp name painted on the driver's door. Tanner would know perfectly well whose truck it was and wonder who in hell was driving it, beard or no. My only hope was that the driving was slick enough that Tanner would be too busy keeping his cruiser on the road to give me a serious look. As we passed each other he lifted a finger off the steering wheel in greeting; I returned the gesture, my breath stuck in my chest. I lifted my eyes to the mirror and counted to three, each second taking Tanner's cruiser farther away from me.

"You didn't even see me!" I cried out, and slapped the wheel with joy. "It's me, you asshole!"

Then I saw it: the flash of Tanner's brake lights in my mirror, like two red eyes flaring. The gesture was pure reflex, the barest tap of the foot; it was over in a heartbeat. But in that instant I knew his body was registering what his mind had told him; that he knew just who he'd seen.

They arrived the morning of the next day, Tanner's cruiser followed by an army jeep. I watched from a window upstairs in Lucy's room, where she was feeding Kate. Tanner and two MPs got out and spoke a moment; from his gestures I could tell he was pointing out where the various exits were, in case I decided to make a run for it. One of the MPs split off, headed for the rear of the house.

My father appeared in the bedroom door. "Joey—"

I turned from the window as Tanner and the other MP vanished from view beneath the snow-covered porch roof below me. "It's okay, Dad. I'll talk to them."

Lucy lifted Kate onto her shoulder to burp her, and looked up at the two of us from bed. "Talk to who? What's going on?"

I kissed the top of Kate's head. From downstairs I heard three hard pounds on the front door. "Don't worry. I'll be back in a minute."

I opened the door just as Tanner had lifted his fist to bang a second time. "There's no cause to make such a racket, Darryl. We can hear you fine."

He looked around me through the screen. "Your father home, Joey?"

"Just me and Lucy." The MP stood behind him, his hand on his holster. He looked like a senior in high school. "You can tell your buddy no use slogging around in the snow. I'm right here. And for god's sake stop fooling with that gun. We've got a baby in the house."

Tanner frowned. "They're just doing it by the numbers, Joey."

The second MP appeared at the base of the porch, clumps of snow stuck to him all the way up to his waist. He was a little out of breath. "Is that the guy?"

"Right here, in the flesh." I pushed open the screen door. "Might as well do this inside so we don't let all the cold air in. Mind your shoes now, everyone."

I led them to the main room, where my father was waiting with Lucy and, swaddled to her chin, Kate.

"Well, look here." He might have been the sheriff, ready to haul me off to jail, but Darryl was a grandfather too. Smiling broadly, he took off his hat and approached Lucy. "May I?"

She turned Kate around to show him, and Darryl bent at the neck to look. He gave a little admiring whistle.

"What do you call her?"

"Kate."

"Well, hello, Miss Kate." He touched her ear and shifted his eyes to me. "This have something to do with you, Joey?"

"You could say that."

"Well, good for you. Though under the circumstances I'm afraid it doesn't change a thing." Darryl looked at my father then. "Joey says you're not here. Good thing, because if you were, that would be aiding and abetting."

My father folded his arms over his chest. "Cut the crap, Darryl. You want to arrest me, too, go right ahead."

"Joe, if I'd wanted to arrest you, I could have done it long ago. Joey, I'm afraid you're a different story. I'm guessing you know why these gentlemen are here."

"Was I speeding?"

Darryl sighed impatiently. "I'll say it to both of you, right now, and excuse me, Lucy, especially with the new baby and all. But you can just knock it the hell off. This isn't a social call, and we're not talking about a few mailboxes, Joey. I've got an outstanding warrant for you on the charge of desertion, and it's my job to arrest you and turn you over to these nice fellows, and that's exactly what I'm going to do. Is that clear to everyone?"

"Nice speech, Darryl," I said. I looked at the two MPs. "How about it, guys, you want some coffee?"

The taller one, whom I guessed was in charge, checked his watch. His face had a bit of acne. "We don't have to be back on base until fifteen hundred."

Darryl frowned. "A little coffee isn't going to solve this, Joey."

"Didn't say it would. Just trying to be hospitable." I turned to Lucy. "You think my father could mind the baby a minute?"

Lucy passed Kate to my father. Tanner cleared his throat and looked at me cautiously. "No funny stuff, all right, Joey? I would hate to see you make a run for it."

I wanted to laugh. "Christ, Darryl, where would I go?" I showed the MPs where the kitchen was. "Coffee right through there, guys, cream in the fridge, sugar over the stove. Help yourself to some cookies too. We'll be back in a minute."

Lucy followed me upstairs to her room and shut the door behind us. "Joe, they're going to arrest you."

"I know." We sat together on the bed. "I'll tell you something. I want them to. Not for any reason other than to have this be over. A couple of years, probably. I've heard of guys who've gotten less."

She began to cry. "I'm sorry, I'm sorry."

I took her hands and made her look at me. I'd never felt so certain of anything in my life. "Don't be, because I'm not. Not anymore. I'm tired of running, Lucy. I need to come home."

"I want you to, Joe. I think that's all I ever wanted."

"Good. Here's the other thing. I'm sorry this is so fast, but it has to be. I'll raise Kate, be her father. You can tell Harry, but not for a while, at least until we know what's going to happen to me. I just want us to be together, a family. Agreed?"

I was prepared to tell her more, but I didn't have to. She put her arms around me, nodding fiercely.

When we came downstairs five minutes later, everyone was waiting in the kitchen. One of the MPs was holding Kate in his lap while the other was doing itsy-bitsy spider for her. When they saw us the one who was holding her stood quickly, his face flustered with embarrassment, and handed her back to Lucy.

"Sorry, ma'am. Your father said it would be all right. She sure is a cutie. I've got a niece not much bigger than that."

Lucy let the error pass. "I don't think I got your name, soldier."

"Samuels, ma'am. Corporal Samuels." He tipped his head toward his companion. "That's Hickock."

"Well, you held her very nicely, Corporal Samuels. You ever want a job babysitting, you come by, all right?"

He nodded nervously, his face pink as a ham. "Yes, ma'am."

Lucy and I sat at the table and told Darryl Tanner what we wanted to do. He listened to what we had to say, helping himself to Oreos from the open bag on the table as we talked.

"That's a new one on me," he said when we were finished, and scratched his head. "Problem is, the state of Maine says a three-day wait once you get the license. But I might be able to pull a string or two, assuming it's all right with these fellows. What do you say, gentlemen? A little detour?"

They exchanged a look and shrugged. "As long as it's on the way," Hickock said. "One guy, we stopped at his mother's house to help him move a sofa."

Tanner went to the office to use the phone. A few minutes later he returned, rubbing his hands together.

"Well, you're in luck. Woman who answered in the county clerk's office knows my sister pretty well. French Catholic, so this is right up her alley. She says she can backdate the license, so long as we all keep it under our hats. The question of officiation is another issue. The county clerk is away in Florida, got stranded by the storm. But she's looking around to see who she can scare up."

Lucy, Kate, and I rode together in the back of Tanner's cruiser, my father and the MPs following in the jeep. By the time we arrived in Farmington it was after two. We stopped in a diner across from the courthouse for hamburgers and Cokes while Lucy changed Kate's diaper and the MPs phoned the stockade to tell them we were running late, and then we walked across the street, where the woman Tanner had spoken to on the phone was waiting for us in the clerk's office. She was a woman in her fifties, round as a beachball and with hair frizzed by too many trips to the beauty parlor. When she saw the MPs she gave a startled look.

"Friends of the family," I said.

Lucy and I filled out the paperwork, each of us holding Kate while the other one signed the license. Then we followed the woman into an empty courtroom.

"You all have a seat," she said. "He'll be along in just a minute."

"Who will?" Lucy asked, bouncing Kate.

"Carl Hinkle, fellow who owns the shoe store around the corner," she said.

A little while later the door opened and in walked a slender man wearing a parka over his brown suit, and shiny new loafers.

"Is this my happy couple?" His eyes found the MPs, then Kate, sitting in Lucy's lap. "I see. I guess we better get a move on."

"Is this legal?" Lucy asked.

He showed us his JP's license, a slip of damp paper he produced from the folds of his wallet. Kate had begun to fuss, so we all waited while Lucy fed her, holding her inside her heavy coat.

"Do you want me to say a few words?" Carl asked me quietly. One of the MPs had brought a deck of cards, and the two of them and Darryl Tanner were playing a round of hearts. "Perhaps," he offered, "given your situation, you'd like something quicker."

"Take your time," I said.

After the ceremony we signed some more papers and walked around the block to the shoe store, where Carl told Lucy and me to pick something out. Lucy selected a pair of black mary-janes, and little pink lace-ups for Kate. I tried on a pair of loafers, like Carl's, but these seemed impractical given where I was headed, and I opted for a pair of steel-toed work boots instead. When we tried to pay, Carl refused.

"Comes with the service," he explained. "Footwear is a living, but it's the weddings that are my real calling."

He kissed Lucy on the cheek, shook my hand and then my father's. Outside by the jeep, Darryl Tanner officially transferred my custody to the MPs, and Hickock took out a pair of handcuffs from a compartment on his belt.

"I'm real sorry about this, Joe."

"That's okay. Could we do it in front?"

He shook his head. "Can't. I'll make 'em real loose, though." He clicked the bracelets closed and regarded my feet. "Those are good boots," he said.

The day was late. I looked toward the snowy sidewalk, where my father and Darryl were standing.

"You make sure my family gets home all right, Darryl. And Dad, look after my girls now. I'm counting on you."

He nodded soberly. "You have my word, Joey."

I kissed Lucy, then Kate, leaning against them. We were all three crying a little. It was me who stopped first, though that was only because somebody had to. Then the MPs helped me into the back of the jeep and took me away.

TWENTY

Jordan

By two I'd seen neither Harry nor Hal (I'd spoken briefly with Frances as she made her way back and forth to the kitchen for sandwiches and sodas; no change, was the gist of what she said); the moose-canoers were still somewhere upstream floating our direction; Joe was still out with the lawyers at the old Zisko Dam; and I found myself with absolutely nothing to do but wait. I killed a couple of hours rebuilding the loose stair-risers to cabin three—whatever a three-stage, thirteen planetary gear system was, it drove a deckscrew like a champ—and when that was done, lubed and cleaned out a couple of the outboards, working down by the dock below Harry's cabin. Once in a while I saw Hal step out with January, or Frances would appear to stretch and wave or head off to the kitchen or phone. Sometime after four, Lucy came down, bringing me a thermos of coffee and a bacon sandwich, and while I ate we sat together on the dock, just as we had done a thousand times before—spinning out the coming week's details, the chores that needed to be done and who was coming in for how many days and which cabins needed to be tidied and stocked. When I'd finished my sandwich and thanked her, she rose, tucking the thermos under her elbow, and looked back at the cabin where Harry and his family were waiting out the afternoon.

"It just breaks my heart to see him like this," she said. "You know, with everything else that's gone on, it's easy to forget that he's just a human being, afraid to die like the rest of us."

"You think he's just trying to take his mind off it?"

"Some. Sure." She pushed her bangs off her forehead, glazed with sweat in the afternoon heat. "He's a proud man. You didn't know him as a young man, but I did. One thing he was, was proud."

The way she said this, an awful sadness stitched to her voice, made me think she'd said more than she wanted to. "Luce—"

She held up a hand. "That's all, Jordan. I'm happy it's you he picked. He could have picked anyone, you know."

"I'm still not sure why me."

"Don't take this the wrong way. But I don't think it's anything you did. I think it probably has more to do with who you are."

"That's what Kate said."

"Did she? Well, I think she's right, Jordan. What you have to understand is that this is a gift he's giving everyone, not just you. There's a lot of history here. That's why we can't refuse."

She paused, let her eyes drift from my face back to the cabin, and then turned to give me a shining, distant smile—a smile that came straight from the past.

"Well. I've said too much as it is. If you don't mind my butting my nose in a little, you should know that I think my daughter has some pretty strong feelings for you. And I approve."

"Thank you, Lucy. That means a lot."

"And Joe does too. I don't think I have to ask you how you feel?"

For a long, long moment we looked at one another. And then—I swear this is true—I knew. Somehow, I knew. Lucy had loved Harry once. It didn't make sense, but it also did; it explained absolutely everything. Lucy had loved him once, maybe loved him still.

Behind us Harry's cabin door creaked open on its hinges; we turned our heads and watched Hal emerge, squinting in the sunlight. He clomped down to the dock and stood beside Lucy, rocking on his handsome old boots.

"Afternoon." He smoothed out his ponytail and then held a hand over his eyes against the glare streaming off the lake. "Day's almost gone."

"There's time yet," I said.

"I almost wish there weren't. The news is, he wants to go."

I looked at Lucy, whose face told me nothing—where had she gone, I wondered, what memory?—then back quickly to Hal.

"You're sure about this?"

"Am I sure?" He gave a tired laugh. "Hell, Jordan, if it were up to me we'd already be in Portland. Or back in New York. Christ, we never would have left in the first place." He shook his head and turned on his heels to go. "Get your stuff, Jordan. My father's coming out."

It was after five by the time we got him ready. After Hal's announcement, I went to get the gear, which I had waiting in the office: an extra fly rod (Harry would have his own), my vest, a knapsack of miscellaneous tack and tools. Earlier in the day Lucy had made a picnic lunch and left it in the big cooler in the kitchen; I didn't know if Harry had eaten or how long we'd be on the water, so I packed this too, tucking it in the wheelbarrow beside the floatable cushions I'd taken from the shed to make a kind of bed for Harry in the bottom of the boat. Other things: a blanket, a couple of heavy sweaters, a flashlight the size of a billy club that I could also use to brain a fish if that's what Harry wanted. I put it all in the wheelbarrow, then had one last thought and returned to the office and opened the desk drawer where Joe kept the Scotch. I looked at the bottle and gave it a shake. Only four fingers were left, and I poured half of that into a thermos, mixed it with some reheated coffee left over from lunch and a couple of spoonfuls of sugar, and topped it off with a swirl of heavy cream. It would get cold, I knew, when the sun went down.

The day had given me the chance to make a plan, and what I had in mind for Harry was simple enough. Harry couldn't stand, which meant we'd have to fish from the boat; because he wanted to fish the surface, the best place to lie would be the shallows on the far side of the lake where the river fed into it. There was a chance we'd get something, but not much of one. All the big insect hatches were over, and anyone who fly-fishes will tell you that casting blind on still waters may be a pleasant way to kill a couple of hours, but is as close as you get to a complete waste of time. Time, of course, was exactly what Harry didn't have.

I trundled all my supplies down to the dock, where everyone was waiting: Hal, holding January on his hip, Lucy, and Kate, who scrambled up the path to help with the gear. Joe was still nowhere to be seen; I heard Hal ask Lucy if she'd heard anything, and she said no, she'd been trying to raise him on the radio all day. Probably he'd left it somewhere out of reach, she said, or had forgotten to turn it on.

Kate had just returned from town with a load of toilet paper and other sundries and was waiting for the newlyweds, to show them some of the cabins.

"Your first customers," she said, nudging me with her elbow as we unloaded the wheelbarrow. "I bet they book for at least a week."

"They seemed to like the place."

"They were sweet. But they liked *you,* is what they liked."

And then the door swung open, and Harry came out. Hal handed his daughter off to Lucy and trotted up the dock to the porch, and with Frances hovering nearby, helped him down onto the lawn. I pulled the skiff around to shore, where Kate and I nosed it up onto the grass. From the wheelbarrow I took the cushions and laid them out between the middle and rear seats and covered the edge of the bench with the blanket, so Harry could lean against it without too much pain. This wouldn't leave much room for me, but that was the idea; sitting on the rear bench with my knees apart, Harry's back and shoulders tucked between them, I could help him with his fly rod and maneuver the boat too.

Harry wasn't using the walker, a good sign, and it seemed to me that he looked a little better than he had the night before. He moved slowly but not hesitantly, lifting and planting his feet with calm precision as he made his way down to us, like a skater testing the ice. In his old jeans and sweater and canvas fishing vest bulging with fly boxes, he might have been one more old guy out to bag himself a trout on a summer evening, if you didn't look too closely—didn't notice the unnatural slowness with which Hal and Frances seemed to move beside him, each of them cupping one of his elbows, or the box that hung from Harry's shoulder: a gleaming cube about half the size of an automobile battery, with the sculpted curves and sterile whiteness of expensive respiratory prosthetics. A tube ran from the box to the back of Harry's neck, reappearing as a necklace under his nose. As he approached, I heard the box making a kind of clicking noise, and beneath that, the tiny whistling of the oxygen, like a breeze through a cracked window. On his other shoulder he carried a wicker creel, a lovely old relic with brass eyelets and soft leather hinges the color of the creamed coffee. He moved down the lawn by inches. A mist of white whiskers frosted his chin and cheeks. When he reached us at the boat he studied it carefully.

"I see we're ready," he said.

"Yes, sir. The cushions should be comfortable, and keep you off the bottom so you'll stay dry."

He gave me a tight, businesslike nod and regarded the boat again. "Now, how I'm going to get in there I don't think I know."

"I thought Hal and I could lift you. If that's all right."

"Fair enough," Harry said. He gave a short, wet cough to clear his throat. "I don't weigh what I used to by a long shot."

Frances took the respirator from his shoulder, and I positioned myself to one side and slightly behind him; he bent his knees, released a sigh, and in an instant all of Harry Wainwright filled my arms again, amazing me a second time with his lightness. He was right; there wasn't much left. Hal and Kate took up positions on the far side of the boat, and together we lowered Harry Wainwright to the cushions.

He looked around cheerfully from his new position. "Like the gondolas of Venice," Harry said. "Have you been there, Jordan?"

"No, sir, I can't say I have." I was pleased to hear him talk this way—to hear him talk about anything at all. "You know how much I have to do around here. I bet it's nice, though."

"You should go," he said. "When all this is over, do yourself a favor and go. The Rialto, the Piazza San Marco, *il Canale Grande.*" He said the last with a startlingly elegant trill to his voice, then crinkled his brow when he saw my face. "Don't look so surprised, Jordan."

I couldn't help but smile. "It means 'big canal,' right?"

He waved a finger in the air. "*Grand* Canal, Jordan."

Hal returned from the porch with Harry's rod and laid it beside him. The respirator, clicking away, was tucked on the floor by his side, and Hal wrapped it in a garbage bag. "Pop, remember, you have to keep this thing dry. Jordan? It's important."

Frances bent her face close to Harry's and brushed his hair into place with her fingers. "You do what Jordan tells you," she said.

"This is what happens when you're old and about to die," Harry said. "Everybody treats you like a child. It's the best part."

Hal pulled me aside, lowering his voice to speak in confidence. "Get him back by sundown, okay? No matter what he says." He glanced over my shoulder at his father, bobbing in the water. "He's not as good as he seems. We've got the car packed and ready to go."

"It's all right, Hal. I'll take good care of him. You have my word."

"I want you to know, Jordan, how grateful we are to you. I don't think I've told you this before. Harry truly thinks of you as one of us. You know that, but I wanted you to hear it from me."

"I appreciate that." I didn't know what else to say, so I put my hand out, and we shook. "I'm glad to do it."

I waded into the lake, where Kate and Lucy were holding the boat in two feet of water, and hoisted myself onto the rear seat, being mindful not to get the respirator wet. With Harry between my knees, it was a tight fit, but I thought we'd be able to manage, as long as Harry could bend forward at the waist to reach his rod. I pivoted to start the outboard—a neat trick, with so little room—when Harry stopped me.

"Jordan, I was hoping we could row."

I don't know why this surprised me; of course that's what he wanted. "It'll take us an hour at least to get to the inlet."

"Even so," Harry said.

I glanced at Hal, who shrugged. I climbed back out of the boat and stepped back in amidships, easing myself onto the second seat. Kate went up to the shed to get a pair of oars and waded out to hand them to me. Harry and I were facing one another now.

"See?" Harry said. "It's better this way. Now we can talk." Kate was still holding the side of the boat, and he took her hand, folding her fingers under his. For a moment all I could hear was the sound of water lapping against the boat and the mechanical ticking of Harry's respirator. His voice was moist and soft and far away. "It's a crazy thing to want, isn't it?"

"Not at all." Kate smiled into his face. "I think it's perfect. You should do what makes you happy, Harry." She leaned over the boat and kissed his forehead. "For luck," she said.

"Thank you." Harry turned his eyes to look at Lucy, holding January at the water's edge: Lucy, with a little girl in her arms. "Thank you, everyone."

And so at last—all eyes upon us, the afternoon sun declining and evening coming on—we went.

TWENTY-ONE

Joe

Hickock was right: they were good boots. I wore them all two years, six months, three weeks, and six days I spent in the care of the United States Federal Bureau of Prisons, the first eight months at the Allenwood Federal Correctional Institute in the mountains of central Pennsylvania, the rest at the prison camp attached to the army psychiatric hospital at Fort Devens, just outside Boston. I was assigned to the laundry, and when a few months had passed and I had proved myself a model prisoner—silent, incurious, interested only in making my way through the small business of each day and on to the next—I got myself reassigned to an orderly detail, pushing carts of soggy food from room to room and cleaning out pans and breaking up fights over the channel changer and Ping-Pong table. It was easy time to do; it was all the time in the world, with a world of nothing in it.

I had been sentenced to thirty-six months. This in itself was a shock, but my lawyer assured me that the chances were small I'd have to do all of it, so long as I kept my nose clean. Draft resisters had become a political hot potato; almost certainly some kind of clemency was going to be granted now that the last troops had pulled out of Southeast Asia, and the fact that I had turned myself in (not quite true, but that was how we spun it, with a little help from Darryl Tanner) would count in my favor. Once this Watergate thing got really cooking, he joked, they'd be needing the cell space for half the Republican National Committee, most of the CIA, and every last asshole in the Nixon White House, right down to the wives. Twenty months max, he assured me. Probably a little less.

Of course, that wasn't what happened, at least not soon enough for me. My lawyer's earnest letters to the review board about my dying father ("a decorated hero of the Second World War"), the infant daughter I had barely held in my arms, my flawless record as a guest of the Federal Bureau of Prisons—all were met with stony silence. As I turned the corner on year two and looked down the long corridor of my remaining federal time, with no sign at all that I was going to get out ahead of schedule, I pulled my mind back from all thoughts of home like a turtle tucking his head into his shell. I figured I was in for the full bite, clemency or no. So when, with just six months to go, the block PO came to find me and announced that the word had come down, the troops were going home for Christmas, that I should pack my things and report to the watch commander's office on the double because the hour of my liberty was at hand, I heard the sound of a string being pulled, and knew whose finger was upon it.

Kate, the camp itself, my final days with my father, good days of talk when at last we spoke of my mother and made our peace—it was Harry Wainwright who gave all these things to me. Many times I've thought I hated him for it, as any man might who feels the power of another over his life. And I've hated myself for this as much as I've hated Harry, who did nothing wrong but love a place and the people in it, so deeply that he would want to die only there. So there's that, too: my envy of him. Not for his money, which I have never cared about; nor Kate, who might have been Harry's the day she was made but became my own on those nights of cold and snow; or even Lucy, who thought I had given her up. None of these. I envied him the fact that it was always his, who loved it, more than it had ever been mine, who would have left it if he could.

Five o'clock, the day ticking away: back at camp, I knew, Harry had either gotten his wish, or not. My goal was to keep the lawyers on the water until six or so—enough time, I calculated, to let things run their course at home and give everybody their money's worth. Bill and Pete had been circling each other all day like a pair of alley cats itching for a scrap, but I doubted they had anything serious in mind: these were lawyers, after all, pure paper tigers who could beat you to death with their diplomas but hadn't thrown an actual punch since seventh grade, and a few hours in the Maine woods wasn't going to change that. Whatever Bill knew or thought he knew—and I'd be lying if I said I didn't feel for the poor son of a bitch, who, beneath all the bluster, seemed as lost as Corduroy the Bear—it would all come out in the wash, no question. But when it did, this would happen over a long table with glasses of water nobody touched and a court stenographer tapping away in a corner, and I would be long gone, not even a memory.

At least the fish were being cooperative. After the morning's struggles, the wind had settled down to an easy breeze, and even Pete seemed to have gotten the hang of things, hauling the Atlantics and brookies in like a pro. I sat on the shore with nothing to do but watch; I even treated myself to a few casts when one or the other of them broke for beer or a sandwich and handed me his rod. Not a bad day, I thought, under the circumstances. Not a bad day at all.

Which only goes to show that you should never tempt fate like this, not when you're miles from the nearest highway with two men who are sleeping with the same woman. It started with a shout, a hundred yards below me; I turned into the sun to see two figures, backlighted in shadow, squaring off in an awkward posture of bent elbows and tucked chins that I recognized at once: men who didn't know how to fight, getting ready to give it a go.

Carl Jr., seated beside me on the rocks, rolled his eyes. "Now what? Those two, they're like a couple of kids in grade school."

But by the time we got there—Marathon Mike joined us, splashing up from the shallows—enough time had passed that the momentum toward an actual fight seemed to have abated, and it looked like we were going to get off easy, not with fists but words. Bill was bent at the waist, taking big gulps of air, his hands riding his hips; I thought for a moment he was about to be sick. Pete didn't look a whole lot better; he was drunker than the rest of them, for starters, was working on a bad sunburn, and hadn't had a bite of lunch, taking it from his flask instead. He was standing in a few inches of water, his rod lying half in the sand, where the reel was sure to gum up good, and his face was twisted up like he was about to cry.

"What the hell is going on?" I asked.

"Go on," Bill said, "tell everybody what you told me. I'm sure they'll think it's just as hilarious as I do."

"Shut up. Shut up, you prick."

"Oh, I'm the prick. Listen to you."

"Christ almighty," Carl groaned. "Like I need this on my vacation."

"Hear that?" Bill said to Pete. "Hear how stupid you sound?"

"I love her."

Bill spat onto the sand and gave a hard laugh. "Sure you love her. You *love* her. Christ. You think I don't know about it? I told her to do it, you little douche bag."

"You're fucking lying."

"Is that right? Ask her yourself. Go fuck him, I said. You'll get a real kick out of that itty-bitty dick of his. Make him fall in love with you while you're at it."

Pete looked like he was about to explode. "Shut up shut up shut up."

"Oh, we had a good laugh about that one. You *love* her. My prick was in her the whole time, buddy boy. What do you say to that?"

Pete flew at him then, right on cue; with an animal growl he hurled himself forward, arms wide, nothing in him able to organize his attack into anything solid and real. I reached for his sleeve but missed, and in another instant he had his arms around Bill, the two of them grappling like prize-fighters in a corner. Only there was no corner: the momentum was Pete's. As Bill absorbed the impact, his legs twisted under him and he went down hard, into the rocky river, all of Pete on top of him.

"Get this fucker off me!"

It took all three of us to unhook Pete and haul him to his feet, his face streaked with helpless tears and his arms uselessly flailing. Then he somehow got away from us and threw himself on Bill again. It was me who got to him this time, yanking him by the collar and hurling him away.

"You, onshore, now!"

His breath jammed in his throat. "He—"

"Now, goddamnit!"

Bill had risen to a sitting position in the water. While Mike and Carl took Pete onshore, I knelt beside him. A bit of blood was in his hair; a small cut, an inch or two, split the skin above his right ear.

"This doesn't look too bad. How do you feel?"

He shook his head, still trying to find his breath. "Little bastard got the jump on me."

"Wasn't like you didn't egg him on."

He fingered the cut and examined the blood on his fingers. "Christ. Look at this. My fucking head is killing me."

"It could be a concussion. We should get you to a doctor."

Bill let his hands fall into the water, cupping his palms and letting the water drain through. "It was all bullshit, you know. About . . . well, all of it."

"I had a feeling," I said. "Looks like he bought it, though."

"I kinda knew, but also kinda didn't." He looked past me then, toward shore, where Pete was still being minded by the other two men. "You smug fuck! You miserable piece of shit! When I get through with you, you'll never work another day in your life!" He returned his eyes to me and lowered his voice again. "That ought to hold him. That's the trick, to make the other guy think you know more than you do. Which in my case is usually zilch."

"I doubt that."

"You'd be surprised." He frowned dispiritedly. "Truth is, he's a better lawyer than I am. Probably a better lay too."

I thought of Pete, lying at the bottom of the Hah-vahd pool; his grass hut and his girlfriend and his fucking short stories. There was no side to take here, nobody even to like when it came right down to it, and mostly I felt sorry for everyone.

"I'm sure he thinks he is."

"Christ. He *loves* her." He shook his head again, looking at nothing. "Help me up?"

I eased him to his feet. He seemed a bit unsteady, favoring one leg, and I kept a hand on his elbow as we stepped from the streambed onto the riverbank. And something else: his right eye was blinking.

"You're a good guy, Joe. For putting up with this."

"All in a day's work."

"I know you don't mean that, but thanks." We had exited the river a short shouting distance from where Pete and the other two still stood. Bill lifted his voice to them. "Hear that? I'm making your apologies to our host, you rude asshole!"

"Let it go," Carl snapped. "For god's sake, Bill, just shut up."

"Oh, the hell with it," Bill said to me.

I released his elbow and looked him over. Blink, blink, blink. "You sure you're all right?"

"Nothing an aspirin and a leak won't cure." He gave me a hollow smile, like somebody pretending to like an awful present; where this all was headed I hadn't a guess. "You like lawyer jokes, Joe?"

I shrugged, playing along. "Sure, why not."

"Here's my favorite. Why's divorce so expensive? Give up?"

I told him I did.

"Because it's worth it!" He laughed and shook his head. "That fucking kills me. Wait here a sec, willya?"

He headed up the path, under the shadow of the dam. I checked my watch; it was a little after six. Suddenly, the only thing I wanted was just to be home, Harry or no. I would have called Lucy to tell her so, if I hadn't left the radio in the truck, two miles away.

"What's he doing?"

Carl had come up beside me, holding a hand over his brow. I craned my neck upward to follow his gaze. For a moment I didn't see a thing, just the dam wall, rising imperiously against the sky. Then I found him: Bill, crossing the narrow catwalk, eighty feet above us. He removed his vest and dropped it on the ground beside him, then drew down his suspenders.

Carl said, "I think he's . . . taking a piss."

He was. At the edge of the catwalk, Bill bunched his waders to his knees, unzipped his fly, and released a stream onto the curved wall below, making a little heart-shaped stain on the stone. Mike and Pete were with me now too, the four of us with our faces angled upward, like stargazers following a comet's path. When Bill was done, he shook it off, redid his pants, tipped his face to the sky with what I took to be a look of satisfaction. Then he stepped backward and disappeared from view.

I turned to Pete. "I think that was for you, buddy boy."

"No, wait a second," Pete said. His eyes were still fixed on the dam. "The catwalk is only, what, five feet wide?"

"About that."

"So we should be able to see him. Where the hell did he go?"

I looked again. Pete was right: Bill was nowhere to be seen. I counted off five seconds, then ten. Still nothing.

Jesus Christ, I thought. Jesus, Jesus Christ.

And then I was running up the dam.

ADRIFT
IN THE HEAVENS

TWENTY-TWO

Harry

My nurse and her needles: all that day I waited for her. But it was noon, it was two, it was three o'clock, and still she did not come. I knew she wasn't real, she was a trick the drugs had played; I knew this to be true, and still I longed for her, as one longs for sunshine after days and days of rain. Through the long hours Franny came and went, my dear friend Franny, and Hal, his strength almost pitiable, for it could accomplish nothing—everyone waiting, like me, for word to go.

Am I hungry? they inquire. Do I need help with the toilet? Is the blanket too warm, too tight? How's the breathing, Harry, do you need the valve adjusted, the little valve right here?

I answer all their questions, complain plausibly of pain though I feel almost nothing, agree reasonably to this and that. The hours open and close. Then:

Harry?

Pure happiness fills me, traveling my body like a beam of light.

It's you, I say. *You're here.*

Seated, she leans forward at the waist; from a canvas bag at her feet she removes her yarn, her diamond-bright needles. She places the yarn in her wide lap: pure white yarn wound in a dense orb, like the insides of a baseball. A quick motion of the hands and she begins her work, pulling and tatting like a pianist at the keys, bringing forth a bolt of tightly woven fabric, white as snow, whiter even than that—a whiteness of absolute perfection. The sight is so beautiful I want to weep.

It's a scarf, she says.

A scarf. The word seems too meager for what she has made.

Did I say that? She laughs, a gentle sound. *I don't know what it is.*

I cannot see her face. Perhaps this is the drugs, or the way the light falls in the room: late afternoon light, cool and still as liquid. Perhaps my eyes are closed.

I feel my chest rise. *How is Sam?*

Sam?

You said you saw him. My tongue is heavy in my mouth. I wonder if I am speaking at all, or am somehow communicating these thoughts by mind alone. *Before. In the hospital.*

He's fine, Harry. Everyone's fine. Just waiting to see what you want to do.

I miss him.

Sam.

He's a good boy. I wish he would cry more. Shouldn't a baby cry more?

A salty wetness on my lips. Still I cannot open my eyes. I feel as if I am half inside a dream, a pleasant dream in which I am shutting all the windows of a house as the rain pours down outside. But the rain is snow, the snow is cloth, a long bolt of perfect white cloth, rolling onto the floor. A shroud, I think. A shroud to wrap my little boy in, who never cried much.

Do you believe you'll see him, Harry?

I am nodding, full of belief. How could I have ever doubted this? *Yes, yes I do. Lucy?*

A pause. Her hand has found my own, resting on the sheet.

I'm going to die, Lucy.

I know, Harry.

I'm sorry.

Why are you sorry?

Because . . . I left you.

It's all right, Harry. You didn't know.

But I think I did. Isn't that strange? I think I did know.

It's not so strange. I'm glad it happened, Harry.

I'm glad too. I try to think of what else to say, but there is only this, this gladness. Then:

Do you remember, Lucy, that night on the porch? That strange night, when Joe came to find you. There was a woman who wanted to dance with me.

A woman?

Just some woman. She was nobody, really. And then I woke up and Joe was there, and you stepped from the bushes and hugged him. He must have had the wrong cabin.

That was quite a night, Harry.

I'm sorry I stayed away after that. It was childish.

But you came back, didn't you. You came back, and everything was all right. Nothing would be here if you hadn't come back.

A moment passes in silence, vaporous time swirling around us.

I planned to kill myself here, Lucy.

A pause. *When was that, Harry?*

With Meredith's pills. Did you find them? I left them where I thought you would.

I think I did, Harry. A bottle of pills?

I tried once before, you know. With the car. After so much time, how wonderful finally to say these things. It is as if I have been carrying a heavy suitcase for years and years, only to discover I can simply put it down. *It was the night before I found you on the dock.*

When was this, Harry? You tried to crash your car?

I want to laugh. Crash the Jag! A thought so absurd, so impossible, I see at once how small, how meager my efforts.

Harry? Are you all right?

I'm sorry. It's just . . . so funny. It was very odd, what happened. Almost an accident. I left it running in the garage. I sat for the longest time. The strangest thing. Lucy?

Again that pause. Is it Lucy next to me? But of course it is; it is my Lucy, come at last.

Yes, Harry?

I'm sorry, for Joe. It must have been hard for him, all these years. I wish I could have said that to him.

But now it's she who's laughing, a laugh that seems to come from everywhere and all around, and from the deepest caves of memory; my mother, still young, on a day we all went on a picnic and the dog got into the basket where she'd put the pie, a hound with a black nose whose name I no longer recall; Meredith, in the bar on the evening we met, laughing at something her friend had said to her, then lifting her eyes to find my own; a young girl tucking a strand of damp hair behind an ear as she tells me about the pancakes, and fresh raspberries from the farm up the road. All of these and more.

Oh, Harry, don't you know? You helped him most of all.

How did I—?

She squeezes my hand, and at once I understand; the knowledge passes into me like a current, and the circle closes at last.

With me, Harry, she says, her voice a whisper, not even there, and I follow it into sleep. *That was the present you gave us all. You brought him home with me.*

The hour is late: I awaken in darkness, alone. A feeling of vivid consciousness courses through me. I can barely move—my body is the same, more wood than flesh—and yet my mind is suddenly, fiercely alive inside it. From the outer room, voices reach me like a drifting scent—Hal and Franny, talking together in low, worried tones of the hospital, the distance to doctors and machines to keep me alive—and beyond them, Lucy and Jordan, speaking to one another on the dock. Each word of their conversations is vivid to me, their voices all overlapping but somehow coherent, and as I listen my mind stretches outward to a far horizon of sound, so that not just these words but every noise for miles around is equal to every other: a girl in the kitchen humming as she scrubs a pot, the sighing expansion of the lake against the shoreline, each cylinder firing in a distant outboard and the swirling hum of its prop. Magnificent: my very atoms seem to trill with sound.

"Hal."

A pause, then his boots on the planking and a blaze of afternoon sunlight through the open door: the day is not as far gone as I'd imagined.

"Look who's up." Hal eyes me appraisingly and takes a seat on the edge of the narrow bed. I lift myself on the pillow as he hands me a cup of water to drink.

"I was wondering when we'd hear from you. How are you feeling?"

The water is so tepid I can barely sense its presence in my mouth. A thin stream dribbles down my chin, which unnerves me; I don't want Hal to know that I am leaving my body behind, that my strength is a force of will alone.

"Better, I think. Much better, actually."

He draws a circle in front of his chest. "How's the breathing?"

Obediently, I draw air into my lungs to show him. The urge to cough is intense, sharp as a lit match, yet somehow I manage to contain it.

"See that?" I clear my throat, my eyes filling. "Fit as a fiddle. Tell Jordan to get ready."

His eyes darken skeptically. "Pop, Franny and I were just talking. After last night, we really think enough's enough. What do you say let's get you down to Farmington."

"I know what you said. I heard every word." I clear my thoughts to let the sounds come. "Listen, Hal. Can you hear that?"

He frowns in confusion. "I don't know what you're talking about, Pop."

"Just listen." I close my eyes as the sounds fill me up. A wash of undifferentiated noise, and then it comes again: not humming, but singing. Her voice rises and falls on the notes, over the rush of water running from the tap.

"A girl, singing in the kitchen. It's something old, the song. Something she shouldn't know but does."

I open my eyes to see Hal staring at me, a new kind of alarm written on his face. I do not want to be difficult, and yet the point must be made. I am not dying in the hospital.

" 'St. Louis Blues'? No, 'Sentimental Journey.' "

"I'm not going to argue with you, Pop. Let's get you to the doctor, okay?"

"No."

A moment passes under his gaze. I am weak, I am dying, there is nothing I can accomplish without his final permission. At the end it must always come to this, this acceptance of one's fate, obedient as a dog. *I have loved you, Hal,* I think. *You are my one boy. Let me do this.*

At last he rises. "Christ, Franny's going to have my head for this. All right, Pop. This is your show now. I'll go tell Jordan to get ready."

And then the day really is late. The hour lurches forward, halts, proceeds again—though almost imperceptibly, as if I am a chip of straw drifting on a vast, celestial tide. My mind opens to a feeling of perfect stillness and, above me, a sky unlocking stars. This thing with sound has left me; only the slow swish of the oars reaches my ears, a music of its own to match the rhythmic breathing of my boatman as he pulls us out from shore. This boy I've chosen: he is strong, good-hearted, he feels the earth in his blood. His face is darkened in shadow, like a hood. He will not fail me.

There is no time, I think. And then: there is only time. Snow from the train window, and the last breaths, and sleep. The needles never unworking. All time is time passed, it is a history of good-byes.

It is all I have left to wish for, the one thing I have ever truly wanted: to slip into that current.

TWENTY-THREE

Joe

We had been floating in the drain for two hours, Bill and I, when I thought it: today was the day I was going to die.

Bill had fallen backward off the dam; the drop was less than twenty feet on the upstream side, but the current took him fast: weighed down by his sodden waders, he was swept into the vortex that swirled around the open gate of the inlet. He would have gone straight through, but at the last second he managed to grab hold of the edge of the open gate and pull his body out of the worst of the current, pinning himself against the concrete wall of the tower.

This was how I found him when I got to the top of the dam, Pete and Mike and Carl Jr. huffing up behind me. Pete ran to the old army corps station to look for a life ring or rope, but of course there was none, nobody had manned the tower for thirty years since they'd pulled out the turbines; and in the next instant, as the four of us stood on the dam shouting useless encouragements like "you just hold on, help's on the way," I realized, with a thump in my gut, that doing the only thing I could think of, dumb as it was, was still better than watching the poor guy drown.

I unclipped the ring of keys from my belt and handed them to Mike. "There's a radio under the passenger seat. You ever use one?"

"Not since the army."

"You know how to find the emergency channel?"

"Channel 9?"

"Attaboy. You don't raise anyone, I want you to take the main highway back to town. The sheriff's office is three blocks on your left, next to the post office. You remember the way back to the truck?"

His face went blank. "Sort of."

"Sort of. Okay, take Carl with you, then."

Mike let his eyes fall over Carl, his big belly hanging over his pants buckle. "I think I'd be quicker on my own, Joe."

Carl stiffened. "What the hell is that supposed to mean?"

"No offense, buddy, but you're not exactly built for speed."

"None taken, you Mick runt. At least I paid attention to the path."

"Enough," I barked, cutting in. Couldn't these guys ever get along? "You're both going because I need this done. Is that understood?" They nodded, chastened like schoolboys; neither one, I could tell, was used to being given orders. "Good. Now, straight over the ridge, stay on the main path. There are a couple of forks, but follow the orange blaze and you'll be fine. If you've walked more than thirty minutes, you've missed a turn, so backtrack until you pick up the orange blaze again. Pete, you stay put, I may need you. Now, the two of you, go."

Away they scampered up the hill, Mike at a brisk jog, Carl bringing up the rear, one hand pulling up his sagging pants from behind. I watched them go, then removed my shoes and vest, took my wallet out of my back pocket and handed it to Pete, moved to the edge of the dam, gave one last look to gauge the drop, and stepped off.

I hit hard but entered cleanly, my knees bent and together, my toes pointed like a ballerina's. The current was fierce, a blast of cold force that wrapped around me like a fist and pushed me under; I sank and sank, waiting to feel the loosening grip of its hold and watching the bubbles rising around my face, and just when I thought that I had somehow miscalculated and was headed straight for the bottom, the current released me and I felt myself rising toward the surface. Three hard pulls and I broke into the light, but then the current whipped me around again. In a flash I saw Pete, standing above me on the dam, then Bill, holding fast to the open gate, the eddying current twisting me like a top, so that it was all I could do to keep my head above water and hope that, like Bill, I could manage to grab hold of something before I was sucked clean through. I hit the tower dead-on, grabbing the edge with both hands, scrabbling the worn concrete below the surface for purchase; something sharp bit into the soft meat of my palm—a piece of old rebar jutting from the side, rusty and sharp as a corkscrew—and I had never been so glad for anything in my life. Gripping the bar, I pulled my body backward against the pounding water rushing in, easing myself free of the opening, then twisted around so that I could wedge myself against the wall of the tower next to Bill.

"I don't want to seem ungrateful," Bill said over the roar. "But what the fuck did you do that for?"

"I'm here to rescue you."

He laughed, choking on the water that was slapping our faces. "Swell. Now we're both cooked."

Pete was waving to us from the top of the dam. "Are you all right!?" I pulled an arm out of the current to give him a thumbs-up.

"Oh, *fuck* him," Bill said.

"How do you feel?"

"Not so hot." His face was dead white, and I saw that his eyes weren't quite moving together. His speech might have been a little off too: with all the noise from all the water, it was hard to tell. I was figuring him for a small stroke, though it could have been a lot of things.

"Don't know what happened. I blacked out, next thing I knew here I was."

"Guess you'll have to be cutting back on the Pall Malls."

"There's a fucking idea. I could go for one right now." He managed a smile. "Okay, pardner, what next?"

Before I'd jumped, I'd hoped that the two of us might manage to pull ourselves around to the other side of the tower, where the current would be milder, and make a swim toward shore. But I realized now how hopeless that was. The whirlpool was too strong, the sides of the tower were slick as a mirror, worn smooth by years and years of pounding, and in any case, Bill wasn't going anywhere. He was barely holding on where he was, and from the color of his face, I seriously wondered how long he'd stay conscious. The cold would help awhile, but then it wouldn't. Fifty-five degrees, tops: general lore said a couple of hours at the most, assuming you could keep yourself moving, which we couldn't: the two of us were pinned to the tower like a couple of donkey tails, icy water pouring over our bones. Already I could feel it eating away at my edges. So, an hour, but maybe not even that: if Bill passed out, or let go of the bar even for a second, that would be the end of it.

"What's next is, we sit tight and enjoy the scenery. I sent Mike and Carl to fetch the cavalry."

"Carl? Mike I understand, but what you send that old lard-ass for?"

I paused to squirt a mouthful of water. "They'll make it fine. All we have to do is stay put. Think we can get you out of those waders?"

Which proved tricky: With Bill's left hand all but useless, he couldn't keep hold of the bar and reach down to his boots at the same time. For a while he tried kicking them off, then scraping his heels against the side of the tower, but he couldn't get any traction in the fast-moving water. And they were far below my reach.

"Just great. This is how they'll find me, pants around my knees."

I could see how exhausted he was. "I've got an idea," I said. "I might be able to pull the boots off if I could use both feet. Pull yourself in and let me try to get behind you."

The trick was reaching one hand around him to grab the bar on the other side. But the instant I let go, the current twisted me back toward the opening. A dozen times the same thing happened, no matter what I did.

"Fuck." I was out of breath from exertion, my teeth chattering like somebody tapping out a code. "It isn't going to work."

"No, it will," Bill said. "I'll let go, so the current pulls me toward you, then you can get your arm around me. Use my weight for leverage."

It was chancy, but I saw how it could work. One thing for certain; the waders had to go. Sooner or later, somebody would come to help, and with his waders bunched around his feet, Bill couldn't maneuver at all, even to grab hold of a towrope.

"We'll have to time it right. Let go on my mark. One . . ."

He nodded tersely. "Two . . ."

"Three—"

Bill released the bar, and I let my left hand drop; as I spun out from the wall, pivoting on my right hand, Bill crashed into me in a backward hug, and for an instant, as we tangled together, I thought I was going to lose my grip and send us down the drain for sure. But then I felt the pressure of his weight twisting us upstream, and I thought: bingo. With a stab of my left hand I found the bar again and I hauled us both, face-first, back against the tower, Bill wedged into the narrow space between me and the wall.

I took a gulp of air. "This should do it, I think. Hang on."

I wrapped my feet around his boots. A couple of hard yanks and off they came, bubbling to the surface a second later, two bodiless legs spinning in the vortex. I watched them go shooting down the drain.

"Better?"

I could no longer see his face, but I felt him nod. His energy was gone. We'd been in the water at least twenty minutes, Bill a little more; I couldn't look at my watch to make sure, but I could tell from the light that it was past seven. I knew my hands were sliced to ribbons on the rebar, though the pain was vague, and I was glad that the cold had spared me at least this. I dipped my face to take a sip of iron-tasting water that made my fillings hum.

"Okay, then," I said, and felt a shadow on my neck that meant the sun had slipped behind the mountains. "Now we wait."

But thirty minutes stretched to sixty, then ninety. I knew that Mike and Carl had gotten lost, either on the trail or driving back to town. Apart from a yell every once in a while from Pete, followed by my terse reply, no one spoke. Held in my arms, Bill seemed to doze, and for a few minutes I did, too, my hands somehow holding fast to the bar; I opened my eyes to see that the first stars were out, pinpricks of light in an otherwise vast and featureless sky, and it suddenly seemed curious to me, curious in a way I cannot express, the simple fact of stars. I knew I was cold, my body temperature was starting to fall, but somehow this understanding seemed to have no importance, no relationship to physical fact. I was so cold it almost felt like being warm.

"Joe?"

"Right here."

"Nobody's coming, are they?"

The right thing to say was, of course they are, just hold on a little longer. But the cold had softened my resolve, and there seemed no reason to lie. "Something must have happened. I thought they'd be back by now."

"Joe, I don't think I can stay awake much longer. I'm all fucked up here."

"That makes two of us. I can't even feel my hands anymore."

"That's not what I mean." Bill's voice had an empty sound, like something was missing inside it. He let a moment go by. "I hope you don't mind," he said then, "but I'm going to let go of the bar."

"Not a good idea. I can't hold on without your help."

"Joe, listen. It's not your fault. I shouldn't have been horsing around up on the dam like that. I'm deadweight, but I know you, you could hold this thing all night if you had to. Just let me go."

I stiffened my hold on the bar to make my point. "It's not going to happen."

"Sure it is, buddy, sure it is. You've got a family to think of. What's your girl's name? Kate? Do the right thing, Joe. Think of Kate and let me go."

The cold or the late hour or just the hopeless mess I'd made of things; think of Kate, he said, and so I did. *Kats,* my mind said, *wherever you are, your old man's in a bit of a jam here. You're one smart cookie. You're my Kats. What the hell do I do now?*

It was a kind of prayer, I suppose, this sending the mind outward, and what came back to me was a memory of our trip together that spring, to California—we'd rented a car after all, to drive up from LA to San Francisco on the coast highway—and a moment, purely happy, when we'd stopped at a turnout near San Clemente to stretch our legs and look at the view. Beside the roadway there was a little picnic area, with weathered tables and rusty trash cans, everything wind-blasted and not a tree in sight, just sea-smoothed rocks and banks of ice plant reclining like steps to the water; we took a table and sat, drinking bottled water and passing back and forth a little baggie of yogurt-covered peanuts that Kate had bought that morning at a health-food shop in Santa Barbara. All of it: the place itself, so beautiful and barren; the ache in my back and eyes from hours on the road; the taste of water and the peanuts, the yogurt sweet as cake icing over the hard saltiness of their interior; and the feeling of the two of us sitting there without speaking, without needing to. It was as if something opened inside me, a kind of boundless love. I hadn't been back to California for twenty years, not since the day I'd stepped from the restaurant in Santa Monica and begun my journey home, and I suddenly thought it would be all right if she knew, that it had always been all right—that the time had come at last to tell her the real story, about that year.

"You know, it's nice here," she said, looking out over the water.

"That's just what I was thinking."

"A little far away, though." A breeze had kicked up, tousling her hair. "I know you went to a lot of trouble to bring me out here. But I've been thinking, maybe it would be better if I stayed closer to home."

"It's your life, Kats. You don't need to worry about your mother and me. Besides, we're gone all winter." By this time, I hadn't actually sold the camp, not technically—agreements made, paperwork still churning through the system—so I had told her nothing about this.

"Yeah, well . . ." She shrugged. "It's not really Mom I'm thinking about."

"Is it a boy?"

"God, Dad." She gave an annoyed laugh. "No, it's not a boy. It's just . . . I don't know, *everything*. Mom, you, all of it. My whole stupid life."

"I just want you to be happy, Kats."

She sighed heavily. "I know you do. But what does that mean, Dad? Sometimes I wish I was like, I don't know, those other kids, Mary Prossert or Susan Jude. I think Mary's, what, cutting hair now? And Susan's probably still with that dork boyfriend of hers, always tearing through the woods on his ATV. They don't have to worry about their organic final, or med school, or California, or any of it."

"You're a smart kid, kiddo. Comes with the territory. You'll figure it out."

She frowned miserably, looking at the table. "Sometimes I don't feel so smart."

"Well, you're doing better than I am. I *never* feel smart."

She laughed a little at that, and I was glad I'd eased her out of the worst of it. "But you're happy."

"Mostly," I agreed. "Not always. Happiness may be overrated, Kats. I do know I'm happy I'm your dad."

She lifted her face to look at me. "Well, that's my point."

"How's that your point?" But as I said it, I understood, and my heart cracked like an egg.

Not a boy: me. She didn't want to leave *me*.

"It's okay," I said, and unwound my legs from the picnic table to stand. Everything was suddenly swimming. I cleared my throat and held out the keys to the rental. "You feel like driving?"

She took the keys and looked at them strangely. "They've gotten lost," she said in a distant voice. "They're like children, lost in the woods."

"Kats? Who's lost?"

"You don't have much time, Daddy," she said. I felt myself rising, lifting away. "You're cold. You should go through the dam."

Go through the dam.

My head snapped back, my eyes flew open: I beheld the night sky and stars, and remembered where I was. A memory that had become a dream, or something else: an answer.

Go through the dam.

"Joe, listen—"

"We'll do it together," I said quickly. "Listen to me, I know this'll work. We can go through the drain to the other side."

"Joe, that's crazy. We'll fucking drown. I don't think I can swim at all."

"You won't have to." It was all coming clear. Sixty feet down, another hundred or so through the empty turbine tube. The tower would be tight, and there was a hard turn somewhere at the bottom, but the pressure would yank us through. If we didn't get stuck somewhere or beaten to death against the sides of the tube, we'd shoot out the other side like rifle bullets, into the deep pool at the dam's base.

"I'll hold on to you. It's just fifty yards. I know what I'm talking about."

I twisted my neck to look for Pete, sitting on the edge of the dam.

"Pete, go down below! We're going through the drain!"

He cupped an ear. "What?"

"The outlet!" I did my best to wave him in the right direction, hoping he could see me in the dark. "Just go! We'll be coming out there!"

Pete rose to his feet, then headed at a trot across the catwalk to the trailhead. I braced the soles of my feet against the wall of the tower to push off. Our best chance to negotiate the turn at the bottom was a clean entry, straight through the gate and down the drain.

"Joe, this is suicide."

"Maybe. But it's the best idea I've got."

He managed a laugh. "You're one brave son of a bitch, you know that?"

I wanted to laugh too. I would have, if I weren't so afraid. A crazy anticipation whirled inside me, half wild desire, half raw terror. It made me feel weirdly alive. I shifted my feet against the tower, tensing the muscles, preparing to spring.

"I'll tell you a story about that later, if you want. Ready?"

I didn't wait for his answer. I released the bar, wrapped my arms tight around his waist, and pushed away hard. We didn't make it a yard before the whirlpool took us, a thousand pressing hands; I had just enough time to fill my lungs with air and think how stupid this was, how truly, truly stupid, we were going to drown for sure, before we hit the gate, rolled headfirst, and plunged into the darkness.

TWENTY-FOUR

Lucy

A night of waiting: after Harry and Jordan had set out, I returned to the lodge; there was still dinner to think of, and guests to feed. I found Patty in the kitchen, crying as usual, and I surprised myself by speaking to her curtly, then softened with guilt, gave her a motherly hug, and sent her home for the night. A little teenage heartbreak wasn't what was bothering me; I still hadn't heard from Joe. Usually he returned by six, making him, by the time we were sending out dessert—the apple pies I'd baked that morning—at least two hours overdue.

The last empty dessert dishes were coming in when Hal entered the kitchen. I knew he hadn't eaten and had kept a plate of swordfish warm for him.

"Any sign of them?" I asked.

He sat at the table and shook his head. "Not a peep. And it's gotten awfully dark out there."

I put the plate in front of him. He picked at it politely, though I could tell he wasn't hungry. I shooed Claire from the room, dried my hands on a dish towel, and sat across from him.

"You should eat."

Hal put his fork aside. "Yeah, I know."

I covered his hand with mine. "They'll be okay, Hal. Jordan knows what he's doing. Probably they just got into some fish. I bet they're having a high old time out there, just like your dad wanted."

Hal said nothing. We both knew how late it was. With no moon up, the lake would be dark as an inkwell.

"Joe back yet?"

I shook my head. "No, and to tell you the truth, I'm a little worried about him, too. It's not like him to be out this late."

"So there we are."

I nodded. "There we are."

I cleared away his plate and excused myself to go check the radio. This was pointless, I knew; I'd long since given up any hope of raising him, but I felt I had to do something. I sat at the console and set the dial.

"Station tango-yankee-juliet-two-zero-one-seven, this is Crosby Camp, looking for Joe Crosby. Over." I released the button and waited. The night was clear and reception should have been good. For a moment I heard nothing but the empty hiss of the open channel. Then:

"Lucy, that you?"

I jolted upright in my chair. But the voice wasn't Joe's. I wanted to cry with disappointment.

"Hey, Porter. Just looking for Joe. He took a party down to Zisko Dam this morning, and I haven't been able to raise him. He's way overdue. Over."

For a moment the line was clogged with static. I adjusted the squelch, recapturing Porter's voice in midreply.

". . . truck about an hour ago. Over."

A truck, I thought hopefully: he was talking about Joe's truck. "Say again, Porter. Over."

"Said a rescue truck went tearing out of here an hour ago. Headed south on County 21, could be toward the dam. Over."

What happened next seemed to happen all at once: I dropped the mike, ran outside to the car, stopped, thought to go back in and call Darryl Tanner, then to go find Kate. A rescue truck, headed toward the dam. It could be anything, I told myself, could have nothing to do with Joe, or if it did, it didn't have to be Joe himself, but someone else in his group—one of the lawyers with their fat cigars and diets of whiskey and butter.

It could be, but it wasn't. It was Joe. All day long I'd been thinking of Harry, and it was Joe.

Kate stepped out of the darkness toward me. "Mom?"

She was looking at the car keys in my hand. I was so flustered I'd completely forgotten where I'd thought to go. The dam? The hospital?

"Honey, your father—"

"I know, where the hell is he? Because I really think we need to put together some kind of search team for Harry and Jordan. Hal's down at the docks getting a boat ready. I thought I'd take one too, so we can cover more area."

I didn't know what to say, how to explain. All I had was a snippet of Porter's voice on the radio.

"Kate, your father . . . on the radio . . ."

"Mom, are you okay? Because I actually wanted to tell you something else." She took a step closer, into the glow of the porch light. "Don't be mad, but I went to talk to Harry this afternoon. I knew you wouldn't go, because of Daddy. I sort of . . . well, I sort of pretended I was you."

I was lost, completely at sea. "You did what?"

"I told you not to be mad. I didn't mean to. It's just kind of how things worked out." She took me by the elbow. "He really loves you, Mom. That's what he told me. I just thought you should know."

"Oh, Kate, what have you done?"

Then the trees were full of light, flashing red and white, so much whirling light we both looked up, amazed. I heard the engine and looked down the drive just as Darryl Tanner's police cruiser made the last turn and his headlights hit us dead-on.

"What's he doing here?" Kate said.

The cruiser rolled to a stop. I stood stock-still, listening to the tick of its engine. I thought, *Joe is dead, drowned in the river. Darryl has come to tell me my husband has died.*

But then the passenger door opened and Joe climbed out. The breath I was holding came out of my chest in a rush. He was barefoot, and as he stepped forward I saw in the glare of the headlights that he was dressed in an ill-fitting sheriff's uniform. A towel lay around his neck.

"Joe, my God, what happened?"

He put his arms around me and held me, hard. His hair was damp and cool between my fingers. Behind us, Darryl climbed out of the cruiser and stood with his hat in his hands.

"Joe, what is it?"

"I'm all right," he said. "I'm all right, I'm all right."

Still he held on. No one moved or spoke. When at last he pulled away, I saw his eyes were different, full of something—not fear or sorrow or even relief, but Joe himself. They were simply full of Joe.

"Tell me," I whispered.

He looked past my shoulder to Kate, standing behind us, and then returned his eyes to me.

"Where's Harry?" he said.

Jordan

For a time I simply rowed. Harry didn't ask me where we were going; I'd mentioned the river mouth and that was enough, and in any event it was the obvious place, as clear to Harry as it was to me. So, in silence, I pulled on the oars; the wind had died, the lake was glassy calm, but the boat was heavy and not meant for rowing, so it was hard, involving work, getting Harry where he needed to go. I thought about Kate, whom I loved, and Joe and Lucy, whom I also loved, and about my father, his spirit soaring in the stars above and his body gone under the sea; I thought about the sounds the trees make in December when there's no one around for miles, and about my mother's voice on the phone when she told me of that sad day when she was just a girl; I thought how time passes, and how love is just another word for time. I thought all these things and rowed, rowed, rowed, feeling the sweat cool on my shoulders and brow as I watched the camp disappear over the stern when we rounded the point; and soon Harry, silent since our departure, tipped his old head forward and slept.

It was dusk by the time we reached the inlet. I pulled the oars in, letting the boat drift, and watched the lake bottom to see where the drop-off was. Above us to the north, the river entered the lake, forming a shallow delta where the current spread like the fingers of a hand; about a hundred feet from shore, the bottom dropped in a sheer wall from five feet to more than twenty. Close in, the water was the color of weak tea, and just as clear; when we reached the edge, I'd know. Trout might hold on either side, and our best chance would come at nightfall or just after, when the air cooled and some fish might rise to feed on the surface.

I positioned the boat just above the drop-off on the shallow side. Harry was still sleeping, his chin resting on his chest. A shock of white hair fell over his forehead; his body was slack and calm. We nosed into the current and I set the anchor. The shadow of the mountains to the west lay long across the lake water, drinking up the last of the light.

Harry lifted his head and blinked at me. "We're there?"

"Yes, sir," I said.

He scootched up a little on the cushions, wiped a bead of moisture from his chin, and gave a squinty look around. "Marvelous," he said.

"It's the best time, isn't it?"

Harry slid a hand into his vest and removed an envelope. I guessed that it contained the deed to the camp, or a letter more or less explaining that fact. He held it out to me.

"This is for you, Jordan."

I took the envelope and examined it. The paper was heavy and felt like cream in my hands. The upper-left-hand corner bore the name of a New York law firm—Sally's, I guessed—etched into the paper in a curvy script, like the writing in a hymnal. I imagined the great office from which it had come: the deep carpeting, the heavy wood furniture, the smell of cigar smoke in its silent boardrooms long after everyone had gone for the night. It was just paper, but it felt like a letter from the very heart of the world. I decided not to open it, and placed it in the picnic basket that Lucy had prepared for us, in with the sandwiches wrapped in waxed paper and the thermos of spiked coffee and the bag of peanut butter cookies.

Harry frowned. "You're not going to look?"

"There's no need," I said. "You've always been very generous. You don't have to give me anything, really. It's a pleasure just to be out here on a night like this."

"Hal told you."

I nodded. "We talked. I guess you could say yes, he told me."

"Well, I thought he might," Harry said. He took two deep breaths, exhaling through his mouth. His lips were dry and cracked, and he licked them with a slow, heavy tongue. "Oh, Hal's all right. I don't think he meant to spoil anything. Do you accept it?"

"The camp?" I said. "Yes. Of course." I stopped. "It's my home."

Harry smiled weakly. "Then that's all I need to hear. We don't have to say anything more about it. It makes me happy that you'll be here, looking after things. I'm very sentimental about this place, Jordan."

A shiver snaked through his body, running the length of him like an electric current from toes to jaw. I took the blanket from the pile of gear in the bow, and without quite standing, I laid it across him, tucking it under his arms.

"My father brought me to a place like this when I was nine," Harry said. "I hate to tell you how long ago that was. He was a great man. Hard, in his way, but there was kindness in him. I remember him whenever I'm here." He paused and shook with a tight, dry cough. "The real problem isn't the dying, so much. It's being sick before you die. I can barely fucking move, Jordan. There's no justice in it."

The light was almost gone; full-on dark was maybe thirty minutes away, but the sun had dipped below the mountain ridge, etching the jagged line of its peaks into the deepening sky. The water around us was fantastically still.

"I've got some dinner packed here," I told him. "You never know when we might have some risers. You should keep your strength up."

Harry eyed the basket, then shook his head. "You know what I'd really like, Jordan?" A smile crept over his face. "A cigarette. I'm dying of lung cancer, and all I want is a cigarette. I haven't smoked for thirty years, not since that surgeon general thing."

"It couldn't hurt now, I guess. I don't have one, though."

"It's just as well. Franny would smell it," he said. "Franny would smell it, and there'd be hell to pay."

"I have some whiskey, if you want. I mixed it in with the coffee."

I removed the thermos from the basket and poured the coffee into two aluminum mugs. I handed one to Harry and guided his finger through the handle. The coffee was bitter and old, but with the Scotch and the cream and sugar it was at least drinkable, and its warmth filled my chest. I wondered how long it would be before someone came to find us.

"It's good," Harry said. He took another sip, struggling to swallow. "But I don't think I can drink. You go ahead, though."

"I brought some nymphs and streamers along. It might be worthwhile, drifting something in the current."

"Not just yet," Harry said. "Something may rise." He gave me a wink. "We may get lucky yet."

"There's always a chance."

"I hope that's true," Harry said. "I *believe* it's true. How many times have we fished together, Jordan?"

I sipped my coffee and tried to count. "A lot. Thirty or forty, anyway."

"Was it your father who taught you?"

"My father died when I was small."

"Of course," Harry said. "Forgive me, Jordan. I knew that. He was a pilot, wasn't he?"

I nodded. "I had a stepfather, though. I learned a lot from him. And from Joe."

"There's no one better," Harry said. "You know, I don't think I can fish, Jordan. I thought I might feel up to it, but I was wrong." A deeper exhaustion suddenly came into his face; it was like nothing I had ever seen, or wanted to. He breathed deeply, holding each gulp of air in his chest as if to keep it there as long as he could; as if it weren't just oxygen, but something marvelous—a beautiful memory of air. He closed his eyes and let his head rock forward. I thought he was going to sleep, but then he looked up, letting his eyes rove across the lake before lighting them on me again.

"Jordan, I have something to ask you. Would you help me into the lake?"

"You want to fish from shore, you mean?"

We looked at one another, and then I understood.

"Dying hurts, Jordan, but that's not the reason. Pain is nothing, really. I'm afraid I won't die here. They'll take me back, and I couldn't stand that."

I sat and thought awhile. I didn't doubt that it was sincerely what he wanted, but in the end, I knew what I was going to say.

"I'm sorry, Mr. Wainwright. I just can't. I more or less told Hal I wouldn't, too."

Harry nodded, considering. "Well. You're perfectly right. I hope you can forgive me for asking."

"It's not something to forgive," I said. "I would if I could. It's just not something I'm capable of. I'm truly sorry." And I was, too. "Hal expects me to bring you back. Franny too."

"I could climb out of the boat on my own," he said. "It wouldn't be easy, but I could manage it somehow."

I nodded. "You could," I said.

"What would you do then?"

I tossed the rest of my coffee over the side. "I'd have to say I'd probably go in after you, Mr. Wainwright. Then we'd both be wet and cold, and the fish would be spooked. No use wrecking our evening like that."

He smiled then, and so did I, and I realized that the moment I had feared was now behind me. The lake had turned a deep black-blue, the same color as the sky, and all around and above us the stars were poking through the twilight, their pinpoints of light doubled in the lake's still surface. Harry's shivering had returned, but I didn't think it was the falling temperature that was doing it. I poured myself another cup of coffee and sipped it slowly. Harry's arms and neck grew loose, and for a while I watched him, his thin chest rising and falling under the blanket. When the coffee was gone I rose from the bench, negotiated my way across the boat, and wedged myself in behind him. Straddling his back, I crept my weight forward until he was leaning against me. It was cold, and I had begun to shiver too; I wished I'd thought to put on my sweater before I'd moved, but there was no way to get it now. I wrapped my arms around him. We are adrift in the heavens, I thought.

Sometime later, Harry awoke. "Franny?"

"It's Jordan," I said. "I came behind you, to keep you warm."

"Oh," he said. "Not Franny?"

"No, sir," I said. "She's back on shore, waiting for you."

"Lucy?"

"Her too. Everyone," I said.

Once again, he slept. Night fell, and fell some more. It was time to head home, I knew. Harry's head lay against my chest, a ghostly halo of white, and I thought, touching his hair, what dreams are these? What last sweet dreams of life on earth?

And then it happened; all around us, suddenly, a great swarm, as if the stars had freed themselves from gravity's pull and ascended from the waters. A hatch. And everywhere, breaking the stillness, the sound of trout rising, the bright splash of their tails as they slapped the water to feed on the insects that spun on the surface. The rods lay on the benches before us, out of reach, forgotten. It didn't matter. We floated among them. I closed my eyes and listened until the splashing faded, feeling only pure happiness that I had been there to witness it.

And then, sometime later, I saw the light, then heard the motor that churned behind it. It blinked around the point, tangled in the trees, rounded the corner again; it raked across us, making me blink against its brightness. Hal and Franny. The light split—a second boat, I realized, Joe and Lucy running beside them—and then peeled off again: Kate. They floated toward us in the darkness.

"Jordan?" I felt Harry stir. "Jordan, should we go to them?"

I watched the lights come on. "Whenever you're ready, Harry."

KATE

The thing is, I knew it, knew it all.

I was thirteen the summer I learned that Harry was my father. This was Jordan's first summer at the camp, and though the timing was pure coincidence, these two events remain twined together in my mind: figuring out, bit by bit, then all at once, that I wasn't who I thought I was, and at the same time feeling every cell in my body come alive at the slightest glance from this charmingly mopey man who called me "miss" for a month before he actually used my name.

Fartface Weld and eighth-grade bio, and the summer I will forever think of as the Summer of Peas: it was the first year we spent the winter in town, leaving the camp to Jordan, and returned to the camp in June, where I busied myself with the kind of project that could only interest a thirteen-year-old with a moody brew of sex and science on her mind. That spring we'd studied genetics in school, and at the end of the semester, Mr. Weld gave us instructions for reproducing—he said the word with a wink—Gregor Mendel's famous experiment with garden peas. Phil Weld's nickname was pure adolescent spite; a gifted teacher, he was the kind of troublesome adult who could make you actually want to do something you knew would be boring, and standing six foot two beneath a curly crown of salt-and-pepper hair, there wasn't the slightest thing fart-facey about him. Whether it was the budding scientist lumbering to life inside me, or the persuasive power of Mr. Weld's twinkling, sex-filled smile, I can't say. But as soon as he handed me the sheet of instructions, still warm and smelling of ink from the ditto machine, along with four little packets of fast-growing seeds, the idea of spending my summer retracing the steps of a nineteenth-century Czechoslovakian monk seemed like just the ticket. The temperature still skimmed the freezing mark at night, so I planted my crop on a trestle table on the back porch with a plug-in heater for warmth: a dozen rows square of dwarf pea plants germinating in egg cartons that I fussed over like pets, waiting for the day when I could extract the seeds, replant the offspring, and see what I'd discovered.

By July my plants were too big for the porch, and my father helped me dig a garden patch under the kitchen window. By this time we'd all gotten used to having Jordan around, though this wasn't hard; he barely said anything more than "pass the butter," though sometimes in the afternoon, if there was a gap in the schedule, he and my father went off together to fish, returning after dark smelling of trout and cigar smoke. This aroused in me a brand-new jealousy, a feeling of sibling rivalry that actually magnified my heart-twisting crush, and as the summer wore on, I did anything I could to interfere with these outings: inventing small but urgent errands I needed done in town, or else parading around from dawn till dusk in a bikini top and skimpy shorts with the hope that Jordan would notice—ridiculous, as I had nearly nothing to show, and Jordan was far too gentlemanly even to glance in my direction.

Forty-five days after germination, I extracted the seeds and replanted. With luck, by the time school resumed and we moved back into town, leaving Jordan to close the place down for the season, I would have a full set of data to present to the handsome, and no doubt flabbergasted, Mr. Weld: how many seeds were wrinkled and how many smooth, how many pods full and how many constricted, how many flowers purple and how many white, my findings all laid out on blue-lined graph paper with hand-drawn illustrations. My immersion was total; even my dreams were full of peas, weeding peas, collecting peas, eating peas. One night, I swear this is true, I even dreamed of a wedding where the guests threw not rice but peas.

Labor Day weeked arrived. My second crop was in, and I spent Sunday afternoon locked away in my bedroom, completing my report. My results for the most part conformed to Mendel's ratios, but then I found a problem. Too many of my second generation had short stems, a recessive trait. The explanation was obvious—some of my peas had pollinated on their own behind my back. But I had devoted so much time to my experiment, an entire summer, that the thought of failure was impossible. Sitting at my desk, close to tears, I made a quick decision: I would fudge my data. I recalculated, rewrote my first page with the new numbers, and closed up my notebook.

Downstairs, I found my mother at the sink. She was paring red delicious apples, taking them from a bushel basket on the kitchen table. The skin curled away under her knife like a skater's figure eight. I took one from the basket and polished it on my sleeve. For a few minutes I sat and watched her.

"So, how did it go?" she asked me finally.

I didn't answer. I was looking at her ears, and remembering something I'd learned in class. Dominant and recessive traits: if both parents had a recessive feature, say, long fingers or a straight hairline, it meant the dominant gene wasn't present, and their child would have to be the same. "Go look at your parents' ears," Mr. Weld had said, and drew our attention to a photo in the textbook: the side of a woman's face, her earlobe a dangling peninsula of flesh below the ear's point of attachment with the jawline. "If your earlobes are unattached, like this, it means you carry a dominant gene. One of your parents would have to have it too."

"Always?" a kid asked. I turned in my chair and saw that it was Bobby Devry. Even in our school, where no one had very much money, there were kids who were known to be flat-out poor, and Bobby was one. He seemed to be sick most of the time, always with a runny nose at the very least, and bore the sallow complexion and bulging eyes of the chronically malnourished. His family lived out in a trailer in the woods east of town; the story I always heard was that his parents were first cousins.

"One hundred percent," Mr. Weld said confidently. "It's a law of nature."

"Maybe you should look at your uncles' ears, Bobby," someone snickered, and got a good, nasty laugh at that.

That same afternoon my father picked me up from school, and in the cab of his truck, remembering what Mr. Weld had said, I looked at his earlobes: attached. One smooth line of skin from the curve of the ear to the jawline. Mine were unattached; I knew this without even looking, because over Christmas break, as a present, my mother had taken me down to the mall in Farmington and let me have them pierced. Sitting in the truck, I let my hand drift up to my right ear, felt the soft fold of skin and the little gold stud that had shot from the jeweler's gun. So, one of my parents had to have ears like mine, but it wasn't my father, so it had to be my mother. I noted this, thinking how nice it was that the two of us girls should be the same, and then I didn't think about it at all, until, sitting in the kitchen on Labor Day weekend, I looked at my mother's ears.

Hers were attached too.

"Kate, you're staring."

I didn't say anything. I was gathering data. Her straight hairline (to my pesky widow's peak), her freckle-free complexion (mine so dotted I sometimes rubbed my face with lemon juice), her brown eyes to my twinkling blue.

"I'm sorry," I managed to say. "How did what go?"

She put her knife down on the counter and rolled her eyes impatiently. "Your report? Your peas? I'm sorry, did I miss something, or isn't this the most important thing in your life these days?"

I felt a stab of shame. Just five minutes ago, it had seemed so easy, so obvious. Just rewrite the numbers; no one would ever check. But that was wrong: somebody would check, somebody would figure it out. *A law of nature.* "All right, I guess."

"Just all right?" Her face was incredulous. "You worked all summer on it."

We looked at each other another moment, and then the guilt and confusion burst open inside me, and I erupted in tears. I was not a crier, and my mother looked at me with alarm.

"Kate, what is it?" She came to where I was sitting and knelt before me. "Tell me, sweetheart."

"I'm adopted," I said.

She smoothed my hair with her fingers. "Of course you're not adopted. What's gotten into you?" Her eyes darkened, searching my face. "Did someone say something to you?"

I tried to explain but couldn't. Ears, peas, hairlines, my hopeless love for Jordan and the shame at having cheated: it was all gibberish, twisted up like tangled line and half drowned by tears. All summer I had been trying to prove something, something about myself, and all I had to show for it was the knowledge that I wasn't who I thought I was at all. I was a liar, and adopted, the adopted liar of parents who were also liars, because they'd never told me.

My mother finally got me calmed down and led me upstairs. Though it was only five o'clock, I cried myself to sleep, and when I awoke the room was rinsed by moonlight. My mother was sitting on the edge of the bed, wearing a thin nightgown that moved in the same breeze that shifted the curtains of the open window.

"Mom?" I sat up on my elbows. "What time is it?"

"It's late," she said softly. Her gaze was pointed not at me but away, out where the moon lay its golden, tremulous path across the lake. "I'm going to tell you something, sweetheart. I'm going to tell you something, and you must promise that you will never tell your daddy that you know."

"My daddy?"

She gave a pale smile—a smile, I understand now, of pure relief, joy even, at finally telling someone, and not just someone: telling me.

"Yes, sweetheart. Your *daddy.*"

Ten years have passed since that night on the lake when Harry, despite his best efforts, did not die. He was still conscious by the time we got to him, but just barely, and I hoped for his sake that he wouldn't make it back to camp, since that was clearly what he wanted. Hal said he wanted to move his father to his boat, but Jordan insisted he remain where he was: he was the guide, and he would bring Harry back in, as promised, though he said he didn't want to drop the outboard and agreed to take a towline instead. We must have made a strange sight:

Hal pulling Jordan, my parents running to starboard, me to port, our four separate boats in close-order formation like a flock of birds gliding home through the dark. Darryl Tanner was waiting on the dock, and once we got Harry into the packed Suburban along with Frances and the sleeping January, Darryl led them away to the hospital under the same whirling red lights that had carried my father home. Harry never woke up completely, or said a word to anyone that I knew of, and I was glad for that. The final leg of his journey must have seemed strange and sorrowful to him—this last, pressing departure from the place he loved—and by the time he got to the hospital, or so I'm told, he had lapsed into the deathlike sleep from which he never awakened.

Bill didn't die either, though by all rights he should have. My father was right: Bill didn't have much time left. Apart from the hypothermia, the fall in the riverbed that had started it all had ruptured the middle meningeal artery—the cavity behind his right eye was slowly filling with blood—and at some point on his trip through the dam, either in the tube or when he and my father popped out into the rocky riverbed below, he suffered a compound fracture of the left tibia, a dislocated shoulder, a ruptured spleen, and a hammer blow to the face that knocked out all his front teeth. Pete and my father managed to pull him out of the river, just about the time that Mike and Carl, who had taken the wrong trail and emerged on the county road two miles from my father's truck, flagged down the passing logger who put in the radio call that sent Darryl Tanner and the EMTs streaming pell-mell out of town. A helicopter airlifted Bill straight from the site to Farmington General, where he spent the night in the first of three surgeries, and in the morning he was wheeled into the same intensive care ward where, just a few yards away—adding one more symmetry to the day's events—Harry Wainwright lay dying. My parents took a room at a motel across the highway from the hospital, my mother keeping watch at Harry's bedside, my father shuttling back and forth between the two men, and when Harry died two days later, my father stayed on another week, until Bill was out of danger.

For a few months, my father's trip through the dam made him famous. A story in the *Portland Press Herald* went out on the wires the next morning, and the first call from the networks came by breakfast the following day. The caller introduced herself as a producer from the *Today* show—was I the daughter of the man everyone was calling the Hero of the Dam? I said I guessed I was, told her how to reach my father at the hospital, and stood with him the next morning in the parking lot as he held the little earpiece against the side of his head and awkwardly answered the questions I couldn't hear. After that, CBS and ABC both jumped on the bandwagon; once Bill was out of the hospital, both he and my father were flown down to New York to do their morning shows, and by the end of the week they had posed for pictures in magazines from *People* to *Sports Illustrated* and inked deals for both a segment on *48 Hours* and a television movie-of-the-week, with Richard Dean Anderson attached to star. The movie was never made, of course, much to my father's relief; he was embarrassed by the whole thing and maintained every step of the way that he'd really done nothing. But well into the following summer and even for a time after that, the buzz in town was all about locations and shooting schedules and whether or not they'd be casting locals as extras, and to this day, rumors of Richard Dean Anderson sightings—like Big Foot, the Loch Ness Monster, and little green men from Mars—will occasionally make the rounds and set the whole thing going again.

Was my father a hero? Absolutely. But in my book, it wasn't his trip through the dam that made him so, no matter how the media played it. What he did was brave, and completely crazy, and if you didn't know the man, it might surprise you plenty. But he'd done far braver things in his life—*all* his life—not the least of which was warming another man's child against his skin while outside the snow poured down, and loving that child so fiercely she became his own. *Your daddy.* I've never thought differently, not for a second, and in a world darkened by secrets, where one true light is still enough to guide you home, that's mine.

Once the hubbub died down and my parents returned to Big Pine, I thought things would return to normal, and for a while they did. My father bought Frank DeMizio's Chris-Craft, just as he'd planned, and in the spring my parents moved into a new two-story house down the road from their condo. They rented out their old place to Bill, who had quit his job in Worcester and was waiting for his divorce to come through; when Bill decided to stay on permanently, my father took him on as a partner. A year later, he got a call from Frank DeMizio, the naked gangster himself, fresh from eighteen months in the federal pen for tax evasion, and the three of them—a lawyer and two federal ex-cons—decided to go into business together, fixing up and selling vintage wooden powerboats, with Hal bankrolling them as a silent partner. Frank, just as my father had always assured me, really was a nice guy underneath all the rough stuff; he also turned out to be something of a genius at restoration. So, while Frank oversaw the shop on Big Pine, Bill and my father scoured the country, the two of them gone for weeks at a time hunting down forgotten classics moldering in barns and boatyards, from tiny lake runabouts to big oceangoing fifty-footers they shipped south on the back of a semi.

I was in medical school by then—Dartmouth Hitchcock, after all—sleeping four hours a night or less, and my father would sometimes telephone me at odd hours, telling me about a boat he and Bill had found in someplace weird, a garage in Goose Bay or a cornfield in Kalamazoo. *You should see this thing, Kats,* he always said, his voice crackly with distance, and always some odd sound in the background, the airy whoosh of traffic on an interstate, or music coming from a roadhouse jukebox. *Christ, Kats, it's like finding the* Mona Lisa *at a garage sale, we couldn't whip out the checkbook fast enough.* Sitting in the kitchen of my tiny third-floor apartment with a pot of black coffee warming on the stove and Netter's *Atlas of Human Anatomy* propped on the table in front of me, or lying in my dark bedroom with the phone pressed to my ear, I would listen to his voice and the sounds around it, trying to send my mind down the miles of wire to where he was. *You studying hard?* he always asked. *You don't mind me calling so late, do you, Kats?* Not at all, I said, you know I don't, and smiled, thinking how strange it was, and nice too, that in the end it was my father, not I, who had flown the nest. We'd talk awhile about the boat he'd found, and about school, and what my mother was up to and when I'd next be coming down to Florida; when the time came to end our call, he'd clear his throat and say, *Well. Better go. I miss you, Kats.* I know you do, Daddy, I always said, and told him I missed him, too, and after a moment of silence the two of us would hang up the phone together, never saying the word *good-bye.*

In the summer of '99, a month after I'd started my residency in internal medicine at Brigham and Women's Hospital in Boston, my father flew with Bill to Salt Lake City to look at a boat he had seen advertised in *WoodenBoat* magazine, and at the last minute they decided to add a side trip to Lake Tahoe. They could have flown but decided to drive instead, eight hours across the dry mountains and sagebrush bowls of northern Nevada on Interstate 80. They were thirty miles east of the town of Elko when my father, in the passenger seat, asked Bill to stop the car.

Here, you mean? Bill asked. What for?

Just stop, please.

Bill pulled to the side of the road, and without another word, my father got out. What Bill told me later was that he thought my father simply wanted to take a leak and was too polite to say so. He stepped away from the car, mounted the metal guardrail, and made his way down the sandy embankment. Except for the highway, there was nothing around for miles; it was noon, not a cloud in the sky, and probably over a hundred degrees. To the north, a line of mountains shifted in the wavy haze. Perplexed, Bill got out of the car and watched my father from the guardrail. About a hundred feet from the road, my father stopped in his tracks, put his hands on his hips, and tipped his face to the empty, sun-bleached sky. Bill said he seemed almost frozen, like a statue. My father stayed that way ten seconds: ten tiny seconds to leave his life. *Kats,* he thought, and two thousand miles away, I heard; I hear him still, in the smallest things, in the shifting wind and jostling leaves, and the sound snow makes when it falls. *Kats, something is happening. Kats, you're my one, remember that.* Then he collapsed, probably already dead, onto the desert floor.

·   ·   ·   ·   ·

I live here now, where I always did and always will, the lake and woods and mountains unchangeable, as much a part of me as my own fingerprints.

I married Jordan, of course. The night after he and Harry returned from their last trip together on the lake, and everybody had gone off to the hospital, we were left alone, and that was all it took. We stayed up most of the night, talking in his cabin—talking and kissing—both of us too wired, too relieved, too happy to sleep, and when dawn came, that was where it found me. Two weeks later when I left for school, it was Jordan who drove me in the truck. It wasn't easy, the months of shuttling back and forth, the weird looks I sometimes got from my friends over this man who was, in every way, completely unlike them. Yet we managed to stay together, through that year and then all through my time in med school. When I moved down to Boston to start my residency, Jordan shut up the camp and came with me; I confess it surprised me, how easily he took to city life, eating in restaurants and going to movies and riding the T to his job managing an Orvis store in Back Bay. For a while I even thought we might stay on after my residency, buy a condo in Brookline or a little house in Needham, shop for food and furniture and preschools when that day came, and generally merge ourselves into the flow of ordinary life. It was an attractive fantasy, the sort of thing a person could easily fall for, but in my heart I knew it was somebody else's, and not where I really belonged. At the start of my third and final year, we returned to Maine and opened up the camp for a week, and were married on the dock; Paul Kagan gave me away, and after the ceremony he asked me if I'd be interested in taking over his practice. He'd been trying to retire for close to twenty years, but no one wanted the job; if I was willing, he could probably rig it so the state of Maine would pick up my loan payments. He'd sell it for a dollar, he said, and my solemn oath to feed the fish. I jumped at it.

And my mother? After my father died, she stayed in Big Pine awhile, almost three years. But I knew she was lonely, and Florida had always been his idea, not hers. Eventually she moved back to Maine, rented an apartment in Portland, and bought a little café near the harbor, which she rechristened Alice's. Deck had died ten years before, but May was still in town, living just where she always had—a woman of over eighty years, still spry in the way that only old women from northern climes can be, though she used a cane to get around and was half blind from glaucoma. My mother began stopping by her house once a week to read her the Sunday paper, and the two became fast friends; they even took a trip to Europe together, a bus-junket tour of twelve cities in fourteen days, and the following winter went on a cruise to South America. Last year, when May's eyesight failed completely, my mother gave up the apartment and moved into her house. I thought this meant no more trips, but I was wrong: last I heard, they were deciding between another cruise, to Alaska this time, or else Australia. They must seem a curious pair—this old, old woman with a cane and a huge plastic shield over eyeglasses thick as cut crystal, and my mother, who is still quite young really, and looks it. I keep waiting for her to invite me along on one of these trips, but so far she hasn't, and I think I know why: for now, and for a little while longer, she gets to be the daughter.

I had delivered over a hundred babies, so when I became pregnant in the fall of '03, Jordan and I decided to go about our lives as usual as long as we could. We both knew the risks: if anything happened, there would be no other doctor around, the hospital was an hour away, and I had a family history of miscarriage, preeclampsia, and premature labor. But I was young and healthy, and taking everything into consideration from both a personal and professional point of view, I saw no reason why we couldn't plan to stay at the camp until I was within a week or so of my due date. I took my blood pressure each morning before I saw my first patient, cleared out an hour in the afternoons so I could rest, filled my office fridge and glove compartment with snacks and bottled water, and in general went about my business as if nothing were out of the ordinary. And for a long time, just about thirty-seven weeks, nothing was.

On a night in late April, Jordan and I were watching television—
we'd sprung for a satellite hookup to watch the Sox—when I began to
feel contractions. Nothing regular or strong, just a quick tightening
across the belly, and because I was eight months along, I thought little
of this; having a few contractions every now and then was completely
normal, the body's way of preparing itself for the big show. The week
before, I'd driven to my OB in Farmington, and as far as either of us
could tell, the baby hadn't even dropped yet. They didn't hurt at all,
nothing more unpleasant than the feeling I might have gotten from
doing a sit-up. I even placed Jordan's hand over my belly so he could
feel them, though he said he couldn't; the sensations were inside. We
watched the rest of the game, cursing ourselves for staying up so late
when the Sox had lost again, and went upstairs to bed.

Sometime around four in the morning I awakened with a start:
something was wrong. I felt it then, a contraction so intense it seemed
to shove all the air from my chest, and in the dark I fumbled for Jordan, unable even to cry out. I told myself to count the seconds, but
somewhere after thirty I gave up—the pain was too strong.

Jordan flicked on the light and sat up beside me. "Kate, what is it?"

I took a deep breath to calm myself. I tried to speak but couldn't,
and when I opened my mouth a wave of nausea seized me; I tore back
the sheets and raced from the room, barely making it to the toilet in
time for dinner and the ice cream we'd eaten during the ball game to
come up.

Jordan was kneeling beside me. "Kate, tell me what's going on."

"I don't know, I don't know." I gripped the sides of the toilet as another contraction surged through me. I felt my water break, a warm
wetness that soaked my nightshirt and the backs of my thighs, and behind this, unmistakably, the urge to push.

"Oh, Jesus, I think the baby's coming."

"*Tonight?* You're only eight months."

"Not just tonight." I heard myself hiccup, the sound ricocheting
inside the porcelain bowl. Strange, but it was the hiccup that made me
understand. "Right now."

Jordan dashed to the phone. In a wink he was back at my side, helping me to stand. "I called the ambulance. They'll be here in thirty minutes."

"Too long," I managed to say. "You'll have to do it."

"Deliver the baby? You're kidding."

"It's your baby, Jordan. Who else is there? Oh, Christ . . ." I braced myself against the bathroom wall; the contractions were barely thirty seconds apart, not even, and hard as a vise. My head swarmed with panic. What was supposed to take twelve hours or more was happening in ten minutes. With my family history, I was going to have a baby an hour from the nearest hospital. How could we have been so dumb?

"Get me to the bed," I said.

He helped me down the hall. The room seemed changed somehow, both the place where I had slept for years and someplace entirely new. Jordan stood at the foot of the bed in his boxers and T-shirt; his face was pale with fear.

"Tell me what to do, Kate. I don't know what to do."

"She'll be little." It was the only thing I could think of. "Get some blankets from the nursery."

"Jesus. What about you?"

"I'll be fine." I folded his hand into mine. I was shaking, though I didn't feel cold. "You'll be fine. My body knows what to do. Just take care of our baby."

I closed my eyes, let the next contraction take me, felt my knees rising to meet my hands like the ends of a circle joining. She is coming, I thought, she is practically here. We would call her Josephine, our little baby Joe. There would be blood, a lot of blood. I'm sorry for the blood, Jordan. I bore down and time stopped.

"Oh, God, Kate. I can see her."

I released my knees, felt the baby creep back up inside me. The pain was so vast it had become something else, a pain too large for one life, one person. It filled me like a kind of love. I'd barely caught a breath before the next contraction came.

Seconds passed, minutes, hours. I pushed and pushed and pushed. *Like love,* I thought, and that's what I was thinking when I heard it: the sound of Jordan's happy weeping, and the sharp music of a child's first cry.

ACKNOWLEDGMENTS

Many individuals offered their expertise in the research and writing of this book. My thanks to: Tom Barbash, James Sullivan, Paul Molyneaux, Annette O'Connor, Craig Pendelton, John Baky, Anthony Kurtz, Tisha Bridge, Andrea McGeary, Anne Marie Risavy, Margo Lipschultz, and Skip Graffam.

The battlefield events described in the prologue are loosely based on the experiences of my wife's grandfather, Herbert William Mauritz (1916–2002), who served as a technical sergeant with Baker Company of the 612th Tank Destroyer Battalion and was wounded by sniper fire at the Battle of Normandy. His eulogy, written by my father-in-law, Gary Kurtzahn, was instrumental.

For financial support during the writing of this manuscript, I am indebted to the College of Arts and Sciences of La Salle University, the Pew Foundation, and the Mrs. Giles Whiting Foundation.

Special thanks, now and always, are owed to the two heroic women of my writing life: my agent, Ellen Levine, a tireless advocate and true friend; and my editor at The Dial Press, Susan Kamil, whose brilliance with the page is matched only by the warmth and generosity of her spirit.

This is a love story, and it's a story about fathers and daughters. This is stuff you can't make up, and I'm the luckiest man alive, because I didn't have to. From the bottom of my heart, I thank my wife, Leslie, for all the nights of talk when we figured out this book together, and Iris, for teaching me what it means to be the father of a daughter. This book is theirs.

ABOUT THE AUTHOR

Born and raised in New England, Justin Cronin is the author of the novel-in-stories *Mary and O'Neil*, which won the PEN/Hemingway Award and the Stephen Crane Prize. Other awards for his fiction include a Whiting Writer's Award, an NEA fellowship, and a Pew Fellowship in the Arts. He is a professor of English at Rice University and lives with his family in Houston, Texas.

Quechee Library
P.O. Box 384
Quechee, VT 05059

3 VSPI 025521624

O/W Libraries

W/D

Quechee Library
P.O. Box 384
Quechee, VT 05059